Praise for The V Girl

"Literally one of the most unique novels I have eve~~r read~~ 't was intense, romantic, dangerous and touch~~ing~~ novel that will knock you sideways."

— Benjami~~n~~ ~~Jo~~nes

"I am both completely heartbroke~~n~~ ~~and overwhelmed~~ by the beauty of this book."

— happytailsandtales.blogspot.com

"This book will make you laugh, make you cry and leave you feeling raw and emotional. I honestly couldn't have loved this book more."

— lunalandbooks

"It was an intense, fast-paced, unique ride. One I'm not going to forget so soon."

— FOABBookBlog

"The V Girl is about changing your own destiny, fighting for your rights, falling in love in such desperate times and what it means to be human. It's dark, unique and addictive. I demand more, Mya!"

— Inthelandofgodsandmonsters.tumblr.com

"The V Girl by Mya Robarts is a riveting debut that explores a unique and at times difficult concept in an entertaining and fast paced read that will tug at your emotions and leave you wanting the next chapter as soon as possible."

— Rachel @ The Rest Is Still Unwritten

"The relationships between Lila and her friends, family and Aleksey are well sketched, and often extremely moving. Her sexual awakening is also very lovingly done, with the choice of when, where and who with, so explicitly hers – despite the rape culture she lives within – that it made me want to cheer."

— wonderlandjen

"I applauded the truth bombs dropped throughout the book about a female's value being more than the condition of her hymen."

— seejennyread.com

MYA ROBARTS

A COMING OF AGE STORY
V Institute Press

Summary: Eighteen-year-old Lila makes attempts to lose her virginity in a country that has legalized rape.

1. Coming of age—Fiction 2. Romance—Fiction 3.Sexual abuse—Fiction 4.War—Fiction

ISBN-13: 978-0997203103

First Paperback Edition: July 2016
First published in e-book June 2015 by KDP

V Institute
Press

For all the

RAINNMakers

www.rainn.org

THE V GIRL

A COMING OF AGE STORY

Preface

" *Copulation without conversation*
does not constitute fraternization. "

Saying among Allied troops during WW2

IN THE BARELY-LIT ROOM, there are only some gym mattresses and a couple of mirrors. I've set the mirrors so that I can watch myself losing the V of my nickname.

My "one-hour stand" climbs onto the mattresses and touches my naked, trembling body. His breathing becomes ragged; his eyes are dark.

I never imagined my first time would be like this. In my imagination, when I had my first time, I would be in love. I always thought that I would allow myself to be with someone in that way only if I really, *really* loved that person. He would also be unconditionally in love with me. He would be someone who would look at me as though I was his sun.

I wanted to lose my virginity to someone who adores me. Preferably someone who would have said the five magic words: "Lila, will you marry me?" I wanted to have sex for the first time with someone I'd consider worthy enough to spend the rest of my life with. If only I had more time. Eighteen is too young in my book to have met the person to whom I'd want to commit my life.

I wish this occasion could have been a romantic, spur-of-the-moment situation. One thing leading to another in a natural manner and then … I wouldn't be a V-girl anymore.

That would have been ideal. But I don't live in an ideal world; I live in a world defined by a civil war. My deflowering can't be romantic or spontaneous. I've been preparing my first sexual encounter since I heard that the troops were on their way to Starville.

I don't love my sexual partner. He doesn't love me, either. But it has to be *him*, or it's going to be a random guy from the troops … through force.

My "lover" hesitates for a moment. I feel his weight pressing me to the mattress. His body tenses. I wait for him to make the next move, but I'm afraid he has changed his mind.

Chapter

1

21st Year of the 2nd Civil War

Involved parties: Patriot Army, Nationalist
Army
**Number of Nationalist States of America
casualties:** 12,954,988
**Number of Patriot States of America
casualties:** 3,859,895

The broody warrior

AS I RIDE THE TRAIN past the abandoned and razed cities, I think about the troops and their history of sexual abuse. A history that includes victims like my mother.

Since I'm untouched, I may end up like her.

My first time can't involve sexual assault. I won't have a gigantic, smelly soldier enjoying every scream of pain and every tear as he shouts obscenities at me during the troops' so-called recruitment ceremony.

Violence

Torture

Humiliation

I can't bear the thought. I need to lose my innocence or it will be taken from me by force. I'll give myself to Rey, pretending we are in love. It has to be today. Rey and I will spend time alone in our gang's secret training place. After tomorrow, we may no longer have a place to make love. Not even a mattress.

Sitting on the boxcar's floor around me are several exhausted-looking Starvillers. As the troops annihilate more small cities, the boxcars get emptier and the survivors become gossipers.

"The Commissioner said the 31st Battalion will arrive in two weeks," whispers a man.

I bury my head between my knees. It's the 36th Battalion, but I don't correct him. I've been having nightmares about that number since the announcement.

"I hope he's lying again. Patriots lost to the Nationalists near Montana, but the Commissioner made it look like they won," says a woman.

I close my eyes as though doing so will close my ears. I can't escape their buzzing.

"Rotten luck. My son turns eighteen the day of the recruitment ceremony. And my nephew and niece will become eligible for recruitment next week."

"Or they could get married."

"Too late. The Commissioner's not issuing marriage licenses anymore."

The troops are coming to exert their "constitutional right" to conduct recruitment. During the recruitment ceremony, they'll call non-married enlistees to join the army voluntarily. An enlistee will be at the service of the troops as a low-ranking soldier, a visitant, or a vassal. If the troops don't get enough enlistees, they are entitled to take them … in any way they see fit.

Unfortunately, this year there are only twenty people appointed as enlistees. Even during those years when we have hundreds of them, the ceremony ends with forced recruitment.

An old man murmurs derisively, "What's the big deal with rape, anyway? I'd take it over hard labor any day."

Easy for him to say. "Yeah, because you'd love it if they shoved a pistol up your anus with no lubricant," I mutter through gritted teeth. Childless old men like this idiot cannot sympathize. "After beating the hell out of you," I add. He doesn't hear me. I'd add more, but around Starvillers, the less you say, the better.

The whispering continues. "In Midian, they forced someone to abuse his brother."

"It won't happen here. The Accord Units arrive tomorrow, and Sergeant Gary Sleecket's coming with them."

"They won't stand against the troops. If the troops want to break the rules, they will."

"Maybe this time they'll stand up for the kids."

"Not with so few enlistees. If they're desperate, they'll assault you, too … and you're ugly. No offense."

"Then the crippled witch-doctor will be busy."

My head snaps up.

"*Shh*! There's his daughter."

Trembling, I stand up to lash out at these idiots. Before I can, a different voice distracts me.

"Hey! *Layla*!"

"It's *Lee-lah*. L-I-L-A, *Lee-lah*," I say in a warning tone. People always mispronounce my name, but Starville beauty queen Elena Rivers wants to taunt me.

Her brown almond-shaped eyes glint as she swings her shiny, dark hair.

"It's not easy being a *virgin*, is it, *Layla*?"

"In a country where rape is legal? No, it isn't," I retort.

"*Shh*! It's not … that," says Cara Winston, her blue eyes scanning the boxcar anxiously. "It's the army recruiting enlistees," she adds, running her hand through her short blonde hair. She of all people knows better than to speak her mind about recruitment. The half-concealed terror on her face shuts me up.

Elena's entourage laughs at me as she spits out sneering remarks. She is particularly nasty today, as her male cousins and two ragged-looking servants are with her. They'll come to her aid if I slap her, but if Elena insults my dad or my siblings, I'll take my chances.

I drown out her sneers until Elena says the word "troops."

"I bet they'll recruit you. You know why?" She doesn't wait for my reply, not that I plan on giving her one. "Because they usually take fat, fugly *virgins*."

"No need to be rude," says Cara. The V-word must sound noxious to a gang assault survivor like her.

Elena doesn't shut up, but I steer my thoughts back to Rey. The only person in Starville I consider a true friend. He's too attractive for his own good, but I got over my crush on him long ago. I wish I didn't have to choose between him or a forced deflowering.

The Starvillers around me whine about poverty, but it's their own fault. They renounced their American citizenship and embraced the Nat side—the side losing the war. Where were the charismatic Nationalist leaders who convinced the locals to support their cause when the Patriots occupied Starville? The Nat leaders still wear expensive-looking armor while Starville lacks the most basic services.

Despite the ruined state of the town, I have only two major complaints about Starville.

Pet peeve number one: Starvillers. Most are chauvinists and bullies.

Pet peeve number two: the smell. It stings my nose as the train reaches Starville's hills. The town reeks of stagnant sewage, fetid dirt, and musty mold.

If I could ignore those issues, I'd be happy here. Mother Nature has been generous with Starville's surroundings. The city was built in the area of the Lion Sierra that wasn't swallowed by the Californian sea after the last tsunami. Everything beyond the city limits is breathtaking: the vibrant green of the glades, the fields of orange flowers, and the thick, redwood forests. If you aren't afraid of finding genetically modified beasts, you can venture out to the lake by hiking up the river.

Starville, like other occupied cities, has banned technology—the Patriots' key weapon in the war. The prohibition of even the most outdated technologies has created a lack of electronic communications and decent plumbing. Starville doesn't even have a train station. The train slows down when it approaches the outskirts of Starville. This is the sign for the passengers to jump off.

"*Women with crinoline* and children first," jokes someone as Elena's servants assist her. Her ruffled dress billows as she jumps, but she lands with effortless grace. The other women jump, too, even in their ratty dresses. I'm the only one wearing pants. Still, I almost fall because I can't stop thinking about my emergency deflowering.

Elena and her cousins have horses waiting for them, ready to take them home. She may be a *woman with crinoline*, but all-terrain vehicles are reserved for the soldiers.

I walk up a steep path before I reach the crown of a hill. From here I see the entire city: a cluster of cramped, concrete houses—enveloped by vegetation—that seem to be mounted one above the other on the sides of steep hills. Patriots forced Starvillers to forfeit their minuscule dwellings. Most families cram inside ten decaying apartment complexes covered in moss that tower over the abandoned houses.

The weather goes from chilly to hot in an instant. The Starvillers peel off their cloaks, slipping them into their bags.

I take a detour into the wild that surrounds the east side of town. Soon, I can't see the others anymore.

Beads of sweat trickle down my face, and my curly, light brown hair tangles as I descend the steep slope. I need to make myself look beautiful for my sexual debut, and a bath would be a good start.

From noon to midnight there is no running water in my apartment, so we fill buckets from a nearby well. I'll take a better bath in the river.

The old soldiers who guard Starville won't come, but even so, it's dangerous to be alone this far from town. Bandits and beasts are a concern, but because of my tendencies, I'm more worried about being spied on while bathing. That's why I carry leather knife holders around my thighs. Besides, I hope to run into my personal bodyguard: my abnormally large dog, Poncho. He enjoys bathing on warm days. His acute senses will protect me.

My perfect bathing spot is partially hidden by old tree trunks. There's a colossal stone that acts as a wall, and a current so fierce that others prefer not to bathe there. I know which parts of the river are the most difficult to access and which spots are preferred by Divine Sawyers and Joey Waters, who love to have sex where there might be observers. Today, I'm not interested in watching them.

I don't see Poncho, but I decide not to wait for him. Ignoring the mosquitoes, I take off my clothes and put on my thigh sheath. Grabbing the soap, I walk into the current. The warm water sloshing against the rocks makes me sigh in contentment.

I wash my waist-length hair, wishing I could dye the gray strands that grow near my hairline. I soap up my body, watching the current drag away the bubbles. I take special care to wash the areas I hope Rey's lips will touch.

Despite my need to be on guard, my muscles start to relax.

The knives serve the dual purpose of defense and shaving instruments. I hesitate over whether to shave my pubic area. What would Rey prefer? Remembering his ex-fiancée and her spotless appearance, I opt to shave it all.

In the water, I forget that I'm behind on my plans. Most eighteen-year-olds I know have married already. This allows them to sport the tattoos that make them ineligible for recruitment. Some unmarried girls have been getting intimate with their fiancés. I don't have a fiancé, nor do I have the slightest interest in finding one here in Starville.

Rey's the only person I can think of who can serve my purpose. He's the only available man in town who doesn't despise me. Rey even protects me, and hopefully he won't feel the need to protect me from himself. He's been in my thoughts constantly since the troops announced their arrival, and I hate it. I don't want to develop feelings for my best friend.

To distract myself from these thoughts, I venture farther into the water. Now that I'm clean and shaved, my mood improves. I allow myself to splash and play.

A rumble takes me out of my reverie. My body springs to alertness and I pull out my knife.

I hear distant shots. It isn't possible. Nobody in town has access to gunpowder or explosives. You don't get caught with them unless you want to get executed. They have to be soldiers. Patriot soldiers.

Then I hear steps on the riverbank. I'm barely armed, not to mention naked. My knives might keep the Starville peeping toms at bay, but they'll be useless against soldiers.

I wade away, finding myself far from the spot where I left my clothes. The steps sound like they come from only one person, but I can't be sure. My best chance of escaping the situation is to avoid a fight. I can stay hidden if I move to the other side of the river, behind the rocks.

Trying not to attract attention, I distance myself from the steps. I submerge my body, leaving only my head above the water line. Several minutes pass. I hear nothing.

Once I determine that it's safe to leave my hiding place, I swim, splashing as little as I can.

At that moment, I notice something that makes my heart skip a beat.

I'm not the only person in the river. I can't see how many people are around, but I can hear someone treading water.

Panic rushes cold through my veins. Have they seen me? Are other Starvillers hiding from the shots as well?

For a moment, there's only silence. Then another shot startles me, and I force myself not to scream. I swim away as fast as I can, but the current slows my escape. I hide behind a trunk.

Then I see him.

A young man, so tall and built that for a moment I think he's a Sasquatch, minus the fur. No one in Starville, not even Rey, is this burly. Strong muscles reveal years of military training and hint at the use of drugs that makes soldiers inhumanly tall and massive. Long, wet strands of blond hair hang down his broad back, giving him a leonine look. The tattoos on his back tell me he has been in combat.

A soldier! He appears to be alone.

My stomach clenches in panic. Soldiers are sadistic giants and killing machines. The tonics they use to build muscle make them dangerous, violent, and horny.

I lose sight of him for a moment. He emerges in a different spot, where the water is deep. Sasquatch is so tall that the water stops at his waist while he's standing. He must be at least seven feet tall and, without a doubt, the strongest soldier I've ever seen. When he moves, I can see his private areas. Every part of him is enormous.

The soldier doesn't seem to be in attack mode. He's inclined and rubbing foam around his massive torso.

The possibility of being discovered with no one to witness him abuse me makes my hair stand on end. I could wait for him to go, but what if they plan to camp here? I won't wait for the coast to clear, risking discovery and a gang attack.

I force myself to remain focused. I suspect there's a reason he's unbothered by the shots. If he's not startled, whoever's making the racket will likely take his side.

Perhaps I should attack him while he's naked. I've been practicing knife-throwing with my rebel group, but Sasquatch's nakedness and relaxed behavior are deceiving. I'm armed while bathing, so he probably is, too. And what if he alerts his companions? I don't stand a chance, fighting against a trained unit of steroid-injected soldiers.

He's blocking the safer spot to exit the river. There's a gargantuan rock behind him that extends to a point not far from where I'm hiding. If I can climb it unseen, I can return to my clothes and escape.

The soldier repeatedly submerges himself for long periods of time. I pay close attention to my enemy each time he resurfaces. My eyes open wide when I see that Sasquatch's leonine face looks incredibly sad. Sadness isn't an emotion I associate with soldiers.

When he rubs his face with foam and closes his eyes, I silently approach the giant rock.

I put my foot on the base. It's smooth and slippery. There are few places that I can grab onto, but I manage to climb anyway.

When I'm almost at the top, I toss my knife over the rock to free my hands. From here, I see that the soldier is all by himself.

The higher I climb, the less visible I become to him. Sasquatch is back under the water now and hasn't resurfaced for a while. Despite the danger, I gawk, impressed by his lung capacity.

He finally emerges, but I hide until he goes back under.

I'm close to my goal when my feet become slippery traitors. I fall into the water below me.

Butt first. Straight toward the soldier's head.

CHAPTER 2

Unexpected

MY BUTT HITS WHAT I believe is the soldier's face, and I rebound directly into the current.

Something pulls me to the surface. The soldier, blinded by soap and startled by my sudden appearance, is already in defense mode.

One of my thigh knives is gone. I try to escape, reaching for my only weapon, but muscular arms catch me from behind. He doesn't have a weapon other than his powerful body, but he has the advantage of drug-induced strength and military training.

Water drips from our naked bodies as I writhe to escape his hold. I use my slippery skin and shorter height to my advantage and free myself from his embrace. I disappear under the water.

Adrenaline and terror give me speed. I swim against the current to the other side.

Disoriented by murky water, I don't get far. The soldier finds me and grabs my feet. Suddenly, I'm grappling with him again, but this time the water doesn't cover my torso.

As we struggle, one hand finds my left breast and squeezes. He freezes for a second, as if he was surprised. That second is all I need to launch a kick to his groin. But before I manage to do so, he grabs my arms, forcing me to face him.

If my nude body tempts the Sasquatch-like soldier, his face doesn't show it. He seems to care only about winning this fight.

"You …" His voice is menacing and accented. The scent of alcohol radiates from his mouth. His nose bleeds. "Why do you stalk me?"

I pant, unable to respond. Stalk him? What's he talking about?

"Talk or I'll kill you!" he yells.

My mind works at full speed. Unarmed and drunk. That's all I need to know.

I kick him in the balls, which are hard as steel. I do little damage. He's inhumanly resistant. He bends in pain for a brief moment but keeps a hand on my wrist and squeezes hard.

I cry out in pain. I lost the opportunity to knock him out while he was bent over. He grabs my other wrist and easily avoids the kicks I aim at his groin.

Sasquatch realizes that he has the advantage, and he relaxes his grip on my wrist. Then, as though he has just become aware of my naked-ness, his eyes travel all over my body. For a brief moment, I see the shock in his blue eyes as they melt into a different expression. His scowl vanishes and his eyes darken. I see something deep inside them that makes me blush.

I feel the urge to cross my arms over my chest. Much to my shock, he allows it, although he doesn't avert his eyes.

"You have … you have an incredible body," he says.

I'm paralyzed and unable to think straight. I would've preferred if he had gone in for the kill. Instead, he seems to want to force the violent sexual debut I was trying to avoid.

He mutters something under his breath as his enormous hands slowly approach my face. I think he uttered *ocean*, but it could have been something else. My body stiffens, but I find my voice.

"Don't touch me."

To my amazement, he stops. Our bodies are so close that my bare skin almost touches his.

His lower part draws my attention, and I notice something that takes me out of my trance. A bulging piece of veiny flesh, ready for action.

My body shivers. *No!*

I won't submit without a fight. Fortunately, his lust is distracting him.

With both hands, I grab his considerable length and twist. He doesn't double over, but I believe he's in pain. I free myself from his stone-like grip and escape as fast as the water permits. Soon I'm at the river's edge.

I'm running at top speed when I turn to see him. Sasquatch stands in the river, staring at me. He shows no intention of chasing me, but I can't let down my guard. Even for a soldier, he's remarkably strong and resistant. I applied all my force, and I'm not weak.

Soon, I'm back where I left my backpack. I put on my t-shirt, pants, and boots while I'm fleeing. Terror shortens my breath. My only thoughts are of escaping and making sure my family is safe.

My soaked body and hair dampen my clothes. I scramble up the river-bank, my clothes clinging to my skin. I spare a brief glance over my shoulder. No sign of the soldier.

Climbing the hill, I reach a winding stone path where I glimpse Starville's trash-filled sidewalks. I see no sign of recent combat, which only adds to my confusion.

I run down the path toward town, letting gravity pull me faster. People appear calm. Some Starville riders pass me, their horses prancing placidly. If the animals aren't scared, I shouldn't be either.

I haven't imagined the shots, have I? I ask the first stranger I see what's going on. He looks at me dismissively. "The soldiers got drunk, played with their guns, and lit fireworks. Aren't you *Laeela* Velez?"

I ignore the fact that he mispronounced my name. I'm still searching for meaning in his words. The occupation soldiers are close to retirement. With age, their bodies can't tolerate the drugs, so they turn to alcohol, and when they're drunk, they play with fire. Literally. Did I put myself through all that anguish for fireworks?

Sensing my confusion, he adds before walking away, "A reception for the Accord cops."

Accord cops. That explains my opponent's foreign accent and the alcohol on his breath. Annoyed, I spit on the ground. I hate cops. Sasquatch can't be older than thirty. His youth, long hair, and build are uncommon among the Accord Unit, so I mistook him for a soldier. I should've known. A soldier wouldn't have stopped when I said no. An Accord cop, maybe.

I walk home along Numbers Avenue, mumbling angrily, ignoring those who stare at me as I pass. How idiotic to use fireworks when the sun is still high.

The Accord cops are ex-soldiers who are part of an organization of "neutral" countries called UNNO. They're supposed to come for the recruitment ceremony to verify that the Nationalists and Patriots keep things civilized, and that they respect the international laws on human rights. When they haven't had too much to drink, they provide free medical services and food. They used to protect civilians. Nowadays, they don't do anything to stop recruitment. They're nothing but drunken idiots in black armor and red capes.

When I turn a corner that smells heavily of piss, a rat crosses my path. I can understand Sasquatch's desire to take a bath alone, away from this stench. If he didn't look like a soldier, I'd acknowledge his rugged handsomeness. But because he's a corrupt military man, I hope against hope that I've left him sterile.

Starville was built on hillsides, so moving around the city means climbing up and down steeply winding streets. I ascend a narrow asphalt street full of potholes near a cluster of abandoned, graffitied brick houses. I wonder how Starvillers build slums on such steep, tree-crowded slopes. The buildings seem to be standing not only against the hillside but also against the laws of gravity.

I'm walking up Judges Avenue, three blocks from the multi-family complexes, when the dog that sees the members of the Velez family as his pets hurries toward me. He almost knocks me to the ground with his enthusiastic welcome. "How come you didn't bathe today, huh?" I ask, scratching his ears.

Poncho may look like an overgrown Anatolian shepherd puppy, but he's a genetically modified dog I found by accident. Someone must have bred him for combat because, like Patriot soldiers, he barely eats and he's always horny. I trust Poncho more than I trust people. Having him by my side comforts me.

I should feel afraid, but I feel empowered. Escaping unscathed after my encounter with the gorgeous, naked enemy gives me some hope, despite my pessimistic nature. If I fight enough against it, perhaps I'll avoid recruitment.

My good mood lasts until I arrive home.

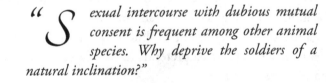

Chapter 3

"*S* *exual intercourse with dubious mutual consent is frequent among other animal species. Why deprive the soldiers of a natural inclination?*"

Barnabas Kim
Co-Creator of the Patriot DNA Modification Program

The Velez Family

WHEN I ARRIVE HOME, I don't enter our tiny one-bedroom apartment. To avoid a homeschooling session, I sit on the floor outside, leaning my back against the wall. I'm sure Olmo's watching Dr. Velez with wide eyes while my sister Azalea pretends to listen. Today's lesson transitions from biology to history.

I hear my father's voice. "Political differences divided what used to be America into The Nationalist States and The Patriot States. Then Nats declared war on the Patriots. Why?"

Olmo answers in an overly enthusiastic tone. "Because they couldn't agree on the division of *derrytories!*"

"Territories," corrects Dad.

"That, too," says Olmo cheerfully.

"At first, the Nats were winning, but knowledge means power," says Dad. "Patriots had the best scientists among them."

Being a doctor, my father admires science men, but I hate them. A scientist played a significant role in passing the recruitment laws.

"Scientists provided Patriots with a lethal weapon: genetically engineered soldiers. Their knowledge created invincible soldiers, thus engendered power."

Dad drills the message into our minds through repetition: Education is important. He never mentions that these so-called educated soldiers were the ones who left him without legs. Besides, education doesn't cure the troops of their superstitions. Some soldiers claim that there are women who can determine whether a girl is unsullied by touching the girl's arms. The fact that the polygraph sometimes proves these women right must be coincidental.

"Retaliation in the form of mass rape against Nationalist towns was expected because Nats used to enslave Patriots. But when the troops recovered Patriot towns from the tyranny of the Nats, the drug-filled soldiers didn't spare Patriot citizens," Azalea says in a bored tone. "Anyway, for the troops, every Nationalist child deserves punishment."

That was decades ago. I'm not to blame for whatever Starvillers did before I was born.

"Is that why Patriot soldiers do horrible things?" asks Olmo.

"Don't be naïve," says Azalea. She's grown up too fast and understands things better than Dad gives her credit for. "That isn't the only reason, is it, Dad?"

"Recruitment is their way of getting two things: retaliation and vassals," says Dad. The softness of his voice doesn't make the subject any less horrifying.

"But your pills and creams will stop them," says Olmo.

"No. My pills are contraceptives. The creams are to lessen the pain of an attack. However, they intend to see their victims' pain. They impale them with their male organs and other objects and—" Dad hesitates. "So the pills—"

"What does 'impale' mean?" asks Olmo.

Dad calculates his answer. "To pierce with a sharpened object."

Olmo giggles. I'm sure he doesn't grasp the repulsiveness of the subject.

In contrast, Azalea is aware of what is at stake with recruitment. Too aware. "Let's see if you find it amusing when they're doing it to you."

"Me? That's impossible," says Olmo.

"Not impossible. When soldiers break the recruitment rules, they abuse children, too," says Dad patiently.

In Starville, a few of the luckiest families, those who haven't experienced the worst aspects of the recruitment, may think that this is an inappropriate conversation between a father and his eleven-year-old children. Unfortunately, the twins have witnessed sexual violence and death. In wartime, you can't protect children from the cruelest facts of life.

Dad thinks his honesty will prepare them for the worst, but he's wasting his time. Olmo has the purity of a toddler seeing the world for the first time. The reality of war won't hit him in his self-created world. Azzy is intuitive and has managed to figure out the worst by herself.

"Someone's outside," says Azalea.

Poncho and I reluctantly enter the cracked-walled, barely furnished room.

"Lila! You're early today!" shouts Olmo, running toward me. I lift him and kiss his dark hair. He suffers from a rare form of fibrosis that messes with his growth; I've seen seven-year-olds taller than he is.

I take off my boots and clean my feet and Poncho's before walking farther into the apartment. We don't bring the dirt of Starville into our home.

Olmo pretends to shoot a gun. "Did you hear the shots? It was so exciting!"

Azzy and I exchange knowing looks. Olmo's delusions make him see war as a game. Perhaps his XY chromosomes make him see weapons as toys.

"You were outside, weren't you?" Azzy asks, tossing her light brown hair out of her face.

"I didn't want to interrupt homeschooling," I lie. Dad insists that my siblings get an education. I'd rather they get a gun.

"Are you hungry, Lila?" asks Olmo sweetly. "Oh! Your clothes are wet."

Dad moves the cart that has replaced his legs toward me. He has an illegal object in his hands: a solar reader. If soldiers discover it during their usual checks, they'll execute him.

"Lila, the Accord cops arrived today," Dad says.

I blush, remembering my naked opponent. "I've noticed."

"They're younger this year, so try not to catch their attention."

Too late. My bare butt on the face of one of them makes me more than noticeable.

"Perhaps it's time for you to take my pills," says Dad.

I look at him warily. Does Dad suspect what I'm up to? But his eyes show only the pride of a scientific experiment gone well.

"I finally made my pills and creams work. Safely." he says.

Dad and his scientific compulsion. He's been working to extract ingredients from plants to create two kinds of anti-rape pills. One pill
numbs your body. If you also put the medicated cream in your most
private parts, you'll get two bonuses: desensitization and lubrication.
You won't feel the complete pain of soldiers forcing themselves inside
you. The other pill is a contraceptive. He doesn't know it, but even
before Dad confirmed that they were safe, I've been taking those pills.

"We'll get more money selling the pills than we will from your salary,
so why don't you quit your job?" he asks. Dad's hopeful face breaks my
heart. "Besides, the Accord Unit will open the clinic soon and pay me a
doctor's salary."

I shake my head. Leave it to Dr. Velez to expect a positive change in
our lives. My dad, the eternal optimist. I'm sure the Patriots will send
their own staff rather than hire my dad. Soldiers and Starvillers call on
my dad's medical services only in extreme circumstances.

"People won't buy anything from us. I'll keep my Shiloh job," I say,
searching for something to eat.

Dad drops the subject and resumes his lesson. "The troops got out
of control, but the Patriot government wouldn't risk losing the support
of the soldiers, so they created the visitants service—people on the government payroll to attend the troops."

The apartment is small, and I'm forced to participate in the lesson.
Olmo and Dad have their cots in the room that we use to cook and eat.

"It was controlled: medical checks, STD vaccination, and birth
control. Rates of rape went down drastically."

Azzy yawns. We never pay attention to Dad's history lessons, but his
biology lessons are great. Olmo hums happily, and I make appreciative
sounds while eating carrots and a soy steak—no doubt a piece Dad
denied himself so that I could eat.

"Religious groups protested. They didn't want their tax money spent
on prostitution, so the Patriot government decided that the defeated Nats
would provide this service. Therefore—"

"Yeah. We know how things turned out," says Azalea, looking in
my direction.

I hate that my dad's talking about this while I'm eating, especially
since there's so little to eat.

Losing weight before recruitment may help, so I save some carrots
for later. From the last recruitment to this moment, I've blossomed.

My new womanly form isn't as attractively voluptuous as Elena's, but the soldiers might find it appealing.

Dad—finally!—wraps up his lesson and prepares to leave. He has house calls in the afternoons, or so he claims. In reality, Dad's job is to wait in line at the rationing board office to bring us food. The way he says goodbye to my brother reaffirms that he's my dad's favorite. Olmo is even bitchy Azalea's favorite.

Azalea looks a lot like me. As her green eyes scan my face, I squirm. My sister has developed acute observation skills and knows all about my plans. She blocks me as I approach our shared room, brandishing a carrot. "Why don't you put this inside you and get it over with?"

I sigh. I gave Elena Rivers a display of my patience not long ago. A family member deserves at least the same.

"It'd be easier than trying to seduce Rey," Azzy says. "He can have any girl he wants, but he keeps saying no, even to Elena. What makes you think he'd say yes to you?"

"Mind your own business, Azalea." She knows troops prefer V-girls, so she should be more supportive.

"What difference would it make? You don't want to be recruited as a *virgin*, right?"

I cringe at the insult. Everything you say—and even what you don't say—to Azalea can be used against you.

Her smile becomes a sneer. "You're wasting your time trying to make your first time memorable. You won't enjoy sex unless you can get into a romantic scenario."

"I'm not romantic."

"No? Haven't you always wanted what Mom and Dad had? Then get married? And reproduce like a bunny?"

"That was before *that day*."

Azzy frowns. She knows what day I'm talking about. Since that day, I've shuddered at the idea of love. Troops will hurt who and what I love the most. Deep down, I crave love so much it hurts, but love and marriage are out of the question until the end of the war, or I'll end up as broken as my father's legs. As broken as his heart.

If things were different, I would wait until I found …

I shake my head. What's the point of wishing for what you can't have? I can at least get lust, affection, and—most important—mutual consent.

Azzy's green eyes look through me. "So you're gonna go all the way to avoid falling for someone? You think having sex will help?"

I try to pass her. "Not really. There aren't enough men, and the good ones are taken."

"You didn't even share your plans with Rey, did you? Are you planning to get him drunk?"

I shake my head. If I give him time to think about it, he won't do it. I have to surprise him and appeal to his physiological needs. It's been a while since Angie broke their engagement. I can't imagine Joey going a year without sex with Divine. Rey must need sex right now.

I shrug. "Who knows? Surprise could be the greatest aphrodisiac."

"Not for Rey," Azzy says. "He hasn't been well since Angie—"

I ignore her as she tries to talk me out of my plans. Until my patience wears thin. I snap my fingers, and Poncho grinds against Azzy's leg.

Azzy is unfazed. She escapes Poncho's frenzy with dignity. I take advantage of the distraction and enter our room.

I peel off my wet clothes and take a long moment to stare at my naked figure in the mirror. My skin is uneven, tanned on my arms and face and pale everywhere else, except for the soft pink of my breasts. Despite the training and limited diet, there's unwelcome flesh in parts of my body where fat doesn't look good. At least I look well-shaved.

I remember the way the Accord cop caressed my skin with his eyes. I never thought eyes could touch me that way. My hands slide over my body, repeating what his eyes did. I've seen penises before, but never one so close or so ready. Such a strong, powerful man, and still he seemed affected by me. I'm used to seeing only contempt when boys look my way. Rey has never looked at me with desire in his eyes. We care for each other, but I don't think either of us wants, at the moment, the complication of love.

I search in my box of treasures—the box where I keep my mom's clothes and pictures. Her old school uniform will have to do because I don't have any sexy clothes. Most girls my age bind their chests with bandages and wear long cloaks, in part due to the unpredictability of the weather, but also to prevent provoking others with their bodies. It doesn't always work. Rey's ex-fiancée tried to avoid recruitment by hiding her beauty and getting a marriage tattoo, but soldiers still attacked her in public.

I won't wear my hideous bra. Instead, I button the white shirt, which is now tight in the chest in a way that enhances my breasts. Looking in the mirror, I knot the silky ties of the translucent underwear I've made for this occasion. My undergarment reveals enough to make me feel sexy, but not so much as to embarrass me. If my plans work, Rey's hands will snake up my thighs to reveal my legs and underwear. Then he won't care too much about the rest of my outfit.

The girl in the mirror purses her lips and looks uncertain. The mechanics of the act shouldn't be a problem because I've seen couples doing it. But my lack of experience may ruin my plans. Besides, Rey's a decent guy. He spent years in a religious order where he got the distinctive tattoo that spares him from recruitment. He slipped only because of love. He may not slip for an emergency deflowering.

I do my hair, being careful to hide the premature gray strands. After all my primping efforts, my hair cascades down my back in soft waves.

What I see in the mirror boosts my self-confidence. I'm not the standard Starvillian beauty. Otherwise, boys would turn their heads when I walk by. But I have enough self-esteem to like myself the way I am, despite what others think. I know I can turn Rey on.

After a final look at the mirror, I let go of my fears. I'm taking control of my sexuality. No recruitment law will take away my right to experience sex with the guy of my choice.

I put on my cloak and stride confidently out of the apartment. "Poncho! Let's go for a walk."

I'm ready to have what—in my inexperience—has to be the best kind of sex there is.

Consensual sex.

CHAPTER 4

Seduction

THE TORCH-LIT ROOM is empty except for the old, musty gym mattresses. Not the most romantic scenario for sex, but at least I can be sure soldiers won't come. Years ago, the museum was the scene of hundreds of beheadings, and now the soldiers think this place is haunted.

I'm more afraid of the living. Dead people can't rape me.

Privacy is a more pressing concern. There's the danger of Duque Diaz coming here with his fiancée, so I improvise curtains on the cracked windows and a lock on the door.

I make sure there are mirrors near the gym mattresses where I'll lose my innocence. I want to see how Rey deflowers me. I take off my cloak and lie on the mattress to test the old, cracked mirrors' view.

A girl like me, who has been kissed only once, and against her will, is supposed to be sexually ignorant. But I've learned a few sex tips by reading Dad's anatomy books. And watching.

After putting a coconut oil jar under the mattress, I lie down, fantasizing about Rey's amber eyes and Greek profile while the wind hits the museum ruins, producing ghostly sounds.

I get up when I hear him arriving.

Rey's shoulder-length black hair is wet, as though he has just bathed. It makes him look incredibly sexy. What makes him even more attractive is the knowledge that he's excellent at martial arts, knife throwing, archery, and … well … everything else we learn and practice here. He must be good in bed, too. But his beautiful soul overshadows his physical attractiveness.

I still don't understand how he doesn't have a fiancée. Since the end of his engagement, a lot of girls have offered him comfort, but he has rejected them all.

"Hey!" He greets me with a contagious grin that illuminates his amber eyes. "Why so early, Lily?"

I gauge his reaction to my outfit. I put so much effort into my primping that I suppress a pang of disappointment when he doesn't notice. But I still have cards to play. Today I need a grateful Rey who will give me something in return for my kindness.

"I made some clothes for Reyna," I say, taking them out of my backpack. I earn extra money by making clothes out of fabric leftovers. His three-year-old sister gets constant gifts from me.

"You're spoiling her too much, Lily. Thank you."

He looks so handsome, so innocent. I can almost pretend Rey's as inexperienced as I am.

As he sets some boxes on the floor, he notices that I'm staring at him.

"What?" he asks, puzzled.

"Lately, you've been smiling more often. It suits you."

"*Nah*! I only smile when you're around," he says, getting busy with the boxes.

I gulp. What does he mean? Is he flirting? Is he just being kind, as usual?

Rey's almost twenty-one. In addition to taking carpentry jobs—from guitars and flutes to ornate furniture—he carries heavy things in exchange for food. Those activities have made him muscular and alluring. Before love found him, he was studying to become a priest. Will he do the unthinkable? He doesn't expect what is coming at him, and I almost feel guilty for what I'm about to ask. Almost.

We talk about the Accord Unit's arrival and his grin disappears.

"Why don't Accord cops get hemorrhoids?" he asks while packing provisions in a box.

"Because they're perfect assholes," I say in a sing-song voice. I'm not at my wittiest, but he chuckles anyway.

"You hate them, doncha?" he asks. "They don't sit well with me either."

Our laughter echoes through the empty wooden walls. It's been a while since I've seen him in a good mood. He's been stressed out since he promised on his mother's death bed that he'd raise Reyna. I hope Rey will take a fleeting sexual escape from his problems.

When he isn't watching, I unfasten one button of my shirt.

His beauty and that *I-can't-imagine-what's-coming-at-me* attitude stir something in me. I want him. I do. I can't wait to feel the weight of his arms around me. I want him to undo my shirt and slide his hands up my thighs while lifting my skirt. I want him to carry me to the mattresses and hold me down with his weight. I want to wrap my legs around his body, let his hands and lips caress every inch of my skin. I want the pain of having him inside me. But I don't know how to start this. I don't know how to seduce him.

If I see something in his eyes that tells me he wants to be intimate, I'll invite him to take that route with me. At the first sign of arousal, I'll joke about my having no issue with the matter. Then one thing could lead to another.

As we move boxes to the basement, I make sure to brush my body against his. It takes two failed efforts, but this time, I can tell Rey has noticed. He blushes and tenses. Rey doesn't look unaffected like before, but he hasn't reciprocated yet.

Frustrated, I sit on the floor. We don't have the whole afternoon. It's time for Plan B: playing the damsel in distress. I hate this plan, but I've grown desperate.

I cut my thigh while he's not looking. When he sits beside me, I stand to give him another flash of my legs. Then, squealing, I pretend I'm losing my balance.

"Watch out!" His hands are on my body as he catches me.

Rey inspects my thigh wound, grazing it with his hand. The soft contact of his fingers with my skin sets my body on fire. Taking advantage of his closeness, I hug him. He's sweaty, but he still smells so good.

Rey tries to pull away, but I cling to him.

"Hey, what's wrong?"

"I'm afraid," I admit.

Rey's voice is soothing, sympathetic. "Of the recruitment?"

"Mostly."

He holds me close like he's trying to protect me. "It'll be all right."

It's an *I-care-for-you* hug, not an *I-want-to-have-sex* hug. I sigh. I have to keep up this farce. "My siblings—"

"They won't be eligible for seven years. Olmo may even skip recruitment because his fibrosis."

"They need me, Rey."

Rey understands. Troops won't recruit him because of his religious tattoo, but if I get recruited, my family won't have enough to eat.

"Is there anything I can do?" he asks.

Nodding, I bury my head in his shoulder and press my breasts against his chest. Every fiber of my body is buzzing with anticipation when I press my pelvis firmly against his. Rubbing him, grinding against him.

After what seems like an eternity, it happens. He gets hard. This is the signal I've been waiting for.

I hold the back of his head and pull him closer. I close my eyes and try to make my clumsy lip-work pass as an acceptable kiss. I don't know how to do it. Warren Lee-Rivers forced a kiss on me when I was ten. After that, no kisses at all. Perhaps I'm doing it wrong since he isn't moving his mouth in response.

I part his lips with mine. Then I suck his lower lip and caress it with my tongue. In the mirror's reflection, I see his eyes are open in shock.

He pulls away reluctantly. "Lily ... what ... why ...?"

I put my arms around him. One wrong word and I won't reach my goal. The right words and soon we'll be on those mattresses. "I don't want my first time forced on me by the troops. You're my only chance to have nonviolent ... s—sex."

His expression reveals confusion. "It'd be wrong. You may think you want this, but you're still—"

"A little girl? No, Rey. I'm not a little girl anymore." I slowly unbutton my shirt. He freezes. When I undo the last button, a visible trail of skin travels from my neck to my waist, hinting at the sides of my breasts. My cleavage is an invitation: *You can see it all. Kiss it all.*

He stands up, but not before I notice his lustful gaze. I can see he's restraining himself with all his strength. Rey avoids my eyes, his next words seem intended more to convince himself than me.

"You're not yourself. You don't want them to recruit you, but you don't want this, either. I'd be harming you. I ... I—"

I close the gap between us and kiss him again, running my hands all over his chest. "You would do more harm … if you … said no."

Rey hardens even more and can't hide it. I force him to sit on the mattress, straddling him. In this position, my skirt displays my thighs. Normally, I'm not so brazen, but the fear of recruitment dictates my actions.

I wrap my legs around him so that my most private parts press against his erection. Slowly, rhythmically, I move my hips in small circles, rubbing against him.

His body tells me I'm affecting him. He wants to reciprocate my touch. Still, he hasn't agreed entirely. Discomfort and uncertainty creep up on me. I want him to need this as much as I do. I won't continue if I don't get his full consent. Rey's expression is pained, revealing an internal battle with his conscience.

I don't know what he sees in my eyes, but his own eyes darken with desire. His face becomes a determined, lustful mask.

I lower my voice to a whisper, my lips caressing his. "Don't feel like you'd be stealing something."

Finally, he kisses me back. His lips are urgent, his arms tremulous against my skin. Rey ventures a hand to my waist and slides it up while the other hand grabs the nape of my neck, pulling me closer. The way his mouth and body explore mine tells me that Rey has surrendered. He gives himself to me with each deep, passionate kiss.

Rey takes off his shirt, and I gasp. A surge of passion courses through me at the sight of his abs, scarred by his religious tattoo. He encloses me in a tight embrace, constricting my breasts against his bare chest, making my nipples hard and sensitive. Our moans are muffled by the sound of our mouths moving in harmony.

Sparks shoot down my core as he places his hands on my legs. He moves them upward, caressing my thighs and revealing my underwear. He places me on a mattress like I'm a porcelain doll and covers me with his body. His hand trails down my side from my waist to my thighs.

Beads of sweat cover Rey's handsome face. His trembling hand caresses my hair and slides slowly from my shoulder to my chest before resting between my breasts. He slides down my shirt, exposing my left breast.

His lips leave my mouth and brush against my collarbone. They travel to my neck, sucking gently. I've always tried to imagine what a man's lips would feel like on my skin, but nothing could have prepared me for this wave of heat. It feels better than I'd imagined.

My entire body becomes a live wire when he kisses a path down my neck to the point where my heart is beating at full speed. My back arches, and I find myself begging for more. More of his hands, more of his eager mouth.

His hands find their way up my skirt to my underwear. My heart is beating so fast that it hurts. This is a side of Rey I hadn't known. Primal, sexual Rey. Rey the man. Rey the lover.

I take a look at our reflections in the mirror and pant. We're half-naked, my legs wrapped around his waist. His mouth hovers above my breast, and I writhe in anticipation.

I'm going to have sex, I think, feeling a mix of anxiety and triumph.

Rey's lips are about to cover my nipple when a crash startles us. Nothing to worry about. In the next room, chunks of the ceiling often crumble to the ground.

We stare into each other's eyes, saying nothing.

Then it happens. Something I thought I was prepared to experience, but I've overestimated my strength of will: his rejection.

"I'm sorry," he mumbles.

He doesn't push me away, but it hurts all the same when he, still erect, plucks his shirt off the floor and leaves the gym in a hurry.

Fighting the overwhelming feelings of humiliation and hurt, I button my shirt. He doesn't want me. I've only made saying *no* that much harder for him.

I was sure he'd say yes. There's a general belief that men can't think about anything else. Men need it all the time; men will jump at any opportunity. Why does Rey have to be the exception to the rule? This was supposed to be a blissful experience for both of us. His rebuff makes me feel so … cheap. So unworthy.

I try to conserve at least a little dignity as I put on my cloak and leave the gym. I fear I've lost my only friend. Outside, I whistle for Poncho.

It's not curfew yet, but the dusty streets are almost deserted, and visibility is poor. My dog sees through the darkness, so I rely on him to guide me.

I stop abruptly next to a broken lamp post. I can't shake off the feeling that somebody's watching me. Maybe I'm paranoid, but I prefer paranoia to the feeling of failure gnawing at me.

How will I face the troops now? I don't have enough time to meet anyone else before they arrive. I work long shifts at a clothing factory, after which I attend The Comanche Resistance training sessions where, incidentally, Rey is an instructor. Would it be possible to develop a crush on someone who would return my interest in five weeks? At this moment, I wish I were the kind of girl who could sleep with anybody at any time, like Elena.

Well, it is what it is. No use dwelling on this experience. I'll find a different route to having a consensual first time. If Rey won't cooperate, fine! That's his loss.

I arrive home and prepare to live through the loneliest night of my short life.

My loneliest night doesn't last long.

CHAPTER 5

The Accord Prince

PONCHO HOWLS WAY BEFORE the sirens start blaring. I throw my bed-covers to the floor, instantly alert.

The building rumbles, and I get up in a flash. Azalea is already on her feet.

I hurry into my usual pants and boots. Another rumble startles us. An air raid? Starville capitulated long ago. Why would Patriots do this?

A distant explosion makes the building shake. It has enough force to throw me to the floor. I take my emergency backpack and desperately reach for Mom's memories box.

"No time for that, idiot! Help Olmo!" shouts Azalea. She reaches for my cloak and throws it at me.

Dad is at the door, prodding Olmo, whose face is a mask of terror. I make him climb on my back, and we storm into the hallway. Dad knocks on the other first-floor doors as we pass them.

"Air raid! Go to the bunkers!"

A bomb hits the southern part of town, one mile from where we are. Rubble crumbles from the buildings in our neighborhood.

There's an eerie light illuminating the horizon, like lightning in the next town over. Only we know that it's destruction. When the local churches ring their bells, more Starvillers evacuate their buildings and head into the streets, running past us.

The bunker isn't far. Soon we see the air shelter entrance. The Starville Commissioner Kit Lee-Rivers, one of the few locals working for the Patriot government, stands at the bunker entrance. He's leading people inside. He lets me, Azalea, and Poncho in, but he stops my dad and Olmo.

"There's no space. Wait to see if there's still room once everyone's inside. If this gets too crowded, you'll have to seek refuge at the museum ruins."

"I won't go in without them!" I shout.

"Me neither, and I'm a minor. You're breaking the law!" shouts Azalea, pushing against the crowd to exit the bunker.

"As you wish."

Kit Lee-Rivers throws his hands in the air and moves on to the next group. I'm ready to force our way in, but local guards and soldiers are nearby. It's better not to risk a confrontation with them.

We head for the museum ruins, fighting our way against the masses.

I hear the rumbling and whooshing of missiles. It's total chaos—crying kids, terrified faces, screams, shouting. Finally, the anti-air-raid sirens go off.

Then I see him. The man I fought earlier in the day. He wears the standard Accord red cape and black armor. His long, platinum hair covers half his face. Towering over everyone, he looks imposing as he barks orders with a deep voice to help the growing crowd get into the bunker.

None of the other Accord Unit cops help Sasquatch organize the mess. They're trying to enter the building, but he doesn't let them.

"Prince Aleksey, please!" the smaller Accord cops beg, loud enough for me to hear them. Panic contorts their faces. Aleksey ignores them, focusing on getting in as many Starvillers as he can.

My family and I struggle to advance. Some people step on my dad's cart, and Olmo's out of breath. We won't make it to the museum.

I turn to Aleksey just as his eyes find me. He appears to recognize me. Given the situation, I shouldn't care that he was aroused the last time I saw him.

"Hey, you! That's the wrong direction!" he yells at us.

"They won't let us in," I shout back over the noise.

Aleksey strides toward us just as a bomb explodes in the distance. He's so intimidating that I instinctively cover Olmo with my body. Azalea seems ready to flee, but Dad is stupefied, frozen in place.

The cop grips Dad in one arm, as though my father is nothing but a weightless doll, and carries Dad's cart in the other. We gasp.

"No! Leave him alone!" Olmo shouts.

The cop ignores him and moves toward the entrance to the bunker. He pushes people out of the way, clearing a path for us.

"That man isn't allowed," Kit Lee-Rivers says. Aleksey shoots him a lethal glare. Kit, clearly intimidated, nods him forward, and we follow the cop into the dimly lit bunker.

Aleksey climbs down the steps to the secure area and gently—too gently for such a brutish-looking man—lowers my father and the cart to the floor.

I look up to thank him, but my eyes meet his glare—the most hateful glare I've ever seen. It lasts only a second, but it chills me as much as the chaos surrounding us.

Another blast startles us; something's exploded, and it sounds much closer.

Aleksey turns away. Before exiting the bunker, he instructs the crowd to give preference to kids, women, and the elderly.

I look around the square-shaped shelter. The Commissioner wasn't lying. There's not enough space, and more people are arriving.

Olmo looks terrified, and Poncho attempts to calm him without success. I give Olmo his inhaler and hold him close. I'm about to tell him that everything will be all right when he wraps his arms around my neck.

"Don't be afraid, Lila. I'll be your protector," he says, his arms shaking.

I kiss his hair and thank him. His fear intensifies mine. I'm not afraid of what could happen to me. I fear for my family.

The bunker doors close, leaving us in the dark. The crowd quiets down, as if silence might keep the bombs from dropping. I feel as though I'm in the midst of another vivid nightmare; only the sounds of a crying baby and my brother's trembling body convince me that I'm not dreaming.

The whole building starts to shake. A sharp whistle …

KABOOM!

Pieces of rubble fall over the screaming crowd. My ears ache and Olmo's grip on me tightens. In the dark, I feel Dad embracing Azzy. He murmurs a prayer that Olmo echoes.

At this moment, I envy others' ability to pray—to hope.

Somewhere in the dark, Baron Diaz's booming voice invites people to pray. The buzz of thousands of murmured prayers in the dark stops when the next bomb rattles the shelter.

❦

Three hours pass before the air raid winds down. The bunker is so crowded that the air has become thick and hot.

My protector sleeps in my lap while Azzy fights to keep her eyes open. My dad's eyes are closed, but I know he's awake.

We hear the doors open, and Kit Lee-Rivers' voice announces that the danger is over.

"Wait another hour before you exit the bunker," he commands.

Something compels me to look up. Ten feet away, Rey's carrying Reyna in his arms. At least a dozen Diaz relatives surround him, and he's staring at me. I almost close the distance to hug him when his rebuff replays vividly in my mind. Rey flushes as much as I do before breaking eye contact.

My godfather, Baron, fights the crowd to approach my dad, his sons Rey and Duque behind him.

"Dr. Velez! *Compadre!*" Baron's roaring voice matches his stoutness. "Thank God we all made it! A good reason to celebrate the Assumption Feast, isn't it?"

As Baron talks to Dad, Azzy notices Rey's discomfort. She shoots me a questioning look while I try not to look at him, which is hard. I need him. I could use a hug at the moment.

Duque Diaz is oblivious to our awkwardness. At eighteen, he is a slimmer, shorter version of Rey. He searches the crowd for his fiancée, Veronica, who is also a TCR member.

I wrinkle my nose at the stench of dirt and piss. "As soon as you two get married, leave Starville," I joke.

Even Duque's grin is the same as Rey's. "Yeah, if we had the tattoos and a j-device."

It's easy to get out, but we wouldn't survive outside. Not without a j-device: a trackable gadget shaped like a jewel that works as an ID and allows you to access money. The jewelry devices contain the owners' genetic code, so it's impossible to steal one. No Patriot or Nationalist city will admit us without one. The tattoos that brand a person as a citizen are also hard to come by. Only authorized Patriot artists can place tattoos. Besides, Olmo wouldn't do well with the merciless changes in weather. We'd need an all-terrain vehicle. And even if we could get the money for a vehicle, we'd risk the attacks of beasts and bandits.

Through Dad's illegal e-reader, I've learned how different life is out-side this town.

"I'd love to leave Starville and—"

Duque covers my mouth with his hand. "*Shh!* Are you crazy?" He whispers the following words in Comanche, a safe language to speak when one fears being overheard. "*It's they who should leave.*"

I refrain from rolling my eyes. The Diaz family is still fighting for the Nationalist cause.

Duque whispers something that chills my bones.

"*I heard the raid's target was Midian.*"

I freeze. Midian is a small city not far from here. Our gang exchanges information with Midian resistance through messenger doves.

Duque flicks his head toward the leader of our gang and goes to the other side of the bunker, followed by the rest of his family.

I understand his message. Patriots discovered the rebellion and re-taliated. If the Comanches aren't careful, Starville will face the same fate.

I hug Olmo tightly, hoping that our involvement with The Coman-che Resistance doesn't hurt him. I was a scrawny thirteen-year-old when I joined TCR. The bruises on my face infuriated Rey, and he always asked who my attackers were. They were usually Warren Lee-Rivers and his cousins, but I couldn't tell Rey. I knew he'd pick a fight with the Commissioner's son. Rey couldn't be my bodyguard all the time, so I asked to join his gymnastics club. I wanted to learn to fight back. I didn't suspect that his gym club was actually a resistance gang. TCR members learn combat skills that keep us able-bodied and fast enough to commit acts of sabotage.

These days, I'm part of TCR because not many people are standing against recruitment, but I don't give a damn about politics. I don't care about Nats—and if they weren't recruiting and murdering, I wouldn't care about Patriots either. They can kill each other if they want, so long as they leave bystanders alone.

The museum is my second home. What will we do if the bombs have reached the museum area? I can only hope the resistance hasn't been discovered yet.

At dawn, the occupation soldiers make us leave the bunker. Rocco Smith, their gray-skinned leader, asks the east-side families to gather at the town plaza in two hours. We live on the east-side so as much as I want to take the twins home, we must attend the meeting.

We lag behind so that Dad and Olmo can take their time climbing the stairs.

A slightly accented voice startles us. "Carry you outside?" A scowling Aleksey is staring at my father. His offer would be kind if his voice weren't so brusque.

My father hesitates before nodding.

"Thank you ... General ... *er* ..."

Aleksey mumbles something unintelligible. It sounds like *Fee-oh-st*. I eye him suspiciously. General *Fee-oh-st* is terrifying in his lethal, rugged beauty. He looks more like a lion than a guy coordinating evacuation efforts.

The cop carries my dad to a deserted street, and we run to keep up with his stride.

I scan my surroundings. At first I can't tell where the worst of the destruction is. Most of the multifamily apartment complexes are visible in the distance, apparently still in place. But smoke from the east and north is infiltrating the town.

Carefully, Aleksey puts my dad on his cart. Then he disappears into the crowd without acknowledging my father's thanks.

Dad picks up on scattered rumors.

"They say Patriots destroyed Midian. The bombs here were a mistake," he whispers, looking at the horizon. "But I don't think it's a mistake. It's a warning."

I agree. Patriot technology is too advanced to allow for this kind of mistake, and their bombs are needed in other places. Places where Nats are still powerful.

My eyes turn to the Midian hills, several miles from Starville. Two giant smoke columns swell in dark billows.

Ignoring my father's protests, I climb one of the highest hills in town to get a better view of the damage.

Some people stand at the crest of the hill, surveying the scene. The dark smoke makes ghostly forms above the skyline. Some Starvillers say they see the wicked smiles of demons in the smoke clouds.

At first, the smoke and clouds of dust block my vision. When I reach the top and scan the town, my heart clenches.

The apartment building where I slept only a few hours ago is no longer there. In its place is a gigantic crater.

I race down the hill toward the crater. The street is full of rubble. I stumble over scattered objects and fall, landing on a pile of lifeless bodies. Or more exactly … on severed human limbs. Horrified, I realize that my face is near a child's arm.

I fight down the carrots and bread from last night's meal. Suddenly and thankfully, my mind goes numb.

Chapter 6

"The false accusations of mass rape in territories occupied by Patriot troops, have hurt the feelings of an entire nation. A nation that has done nothing but support international causes since the twentieth century.

"We don't have such crimes in my country, thanks to an honorable institution in which we Patriots take pride: Recruitment."

Extract of Maximillian Kei's speech for the United Neutral Nations Organization Spring Conference

The clinic

I STAND WITH MY dad and my two siblings near the crater we once called home. It smells of burned flesh. I'd mourn the casualties, but at the moment desperation clouds my thoughts. Other than the clothes we wear and our emergency backpacks, we have nothing. Where will we live? What will we eat?

"We'll recover ... we ... we—" Dad forces a smile. "We'll replace whatever money can buy, eventually—"

He wants to cheer us up, but I know he's grieving his losses: Mom's clothes and pictures, his scientific records, his illegal solar e-reader, and everything else that made his life less difficult. His books were his source of hope. He always says that knowledge can make a difference in the world. Dad takes three deep breaths and blinks repeatedly. His eyes turn red and wet, but he keeps smiling. It breaks my heart to see him struggling to stay strong for us.

Olmo is bawling. His most valued possessions—notepads full of his stories, broken toys, a mouth organ—are gone. I hold him close, but I can't allow myself to grieve. At least not now, when Olmo needs solace. Not when Azalea and Dad are trying not to break down. I'll have to wait, as usual, to grieve by myself when nobody else sees me.

As we walk to the plaza meeting, I hear Dad thank God that we didn't lose our lives. I shiver when I see the path we almost took last night. We wouldn't have made it to the museum alive.

By some strange miracle, the bombs reached only three buildings— our apartment complex and two deserted buildings that saw their best days before the ban on technology: the library and the university research facility. Another bomb fell on the outskirts of the city and ruined the railroad. Not the modern one Patriots use, but the one that takes me to my job every day.

Monstrous soldiers wearing multi-terrain patterned capes arrive at the plaza. The Commissioner and the Accord Unit trail behind them. Some cops climb the trees surrounding the square for a better view; some stand near the stage. Aleksey is so burly that he towers above the crowd. The entire force of the local order is here. That's enough to keep the crowd silent.

The Accord Unit wears j-devices that appear to be rings. With them, the Accord Unit films what life is like in the places they visit. In theory, these films should inform the rest of the world when troops abuse unarmed civilians. In reality, they deceive. They give the false impression that everything in North America is civilized.

One of the Accord cops, a middle-aged, six-foot-tall guy, records the scene with his ring-shaped jewelry device. His gray eyes scan the crowd suspiciously. His black mane flows from a receding hairline, and although he looks athletic, he isn't as fit as the other cops are. Still, he's eliciting admiration.

"Look! It's Gary Sleecket," says the woman standing beside me.

"He's so … dreamy!" agrees her companion.

I recognize him. He comes to Starville every year for the recruitment ceremony. Commissioner Lee-Rivers addresses him in a respectful tone.

"Sergeant Sleecket, could you please get a good shot of Sergeant Rocco?"

Rocco, whose old, slate-gray face is covered in tattoos, addresses the crowd with a megaphone. His tone is deceivingly polite when he informs us that the families who have lost their homes will get new housing soon. He delivers a long speech, asking us to be strong and courageous. The camera focuses on Patriot guards holding hands with a group of local women and children. They must have rehearsed this message. Patriots and Accord Units share a passion for media manipulation.

Rocco asks Gary Sleecket to turn off his camera. When he addresses the crowd again, Rocco's voice loses the quality of a charismatic politician and becomes menacing. He states that they've discovered the rebel group in Midian. Therefore, Maximillian Kei, the Minister of War, condemned an entire city to destruction. Patriots will exploit survivors through forced labor, including visitant services. The rest will be killed or moved to camps.

"See? All that's left of the traitors is smoke."

It's as though he's speaking directly to TCR members. The Patriots are wasting their bombs when they need them to fight the Nats in the north. It's clear they're trying to make a statement.

They shouldn't have bothered. Most Starvillers are too afraid to participate in our resistance efforts. They tell the legend of an immortal soldier. Fifty Nats shot him repeatedly, but the multiple bullets failed to penetrate his strong muscles. The soldier killed his attackers single-handedly and built a palace in the mountains. His descendants are now part of the Patriot army.

It's a scientific fact: troops use genetic engineering and tonics to build their bodies. But mixing legend with reality leads to superstition. Starvillers say that even if we had firearms, we couldn't kill a single one of them.

Rey says the tonics are precisely the troops' weakness. Without drugs, they'd destroy themselves. When the Comanches sabotage a railroad, we cause a temporary shortage of tonics and the genetically modified snakes used to inject them. We're always careful to make it look like the fickle weather is responsible for the damage on the railroads. Otherwise, the Patriots' retaliation would obliterate all of Starville like it obliterated Midian.

Rocco addresses again the issue of the people who have lost their homes. "We'll assign new housing for these families in a month. *You* have two hours to decide who will accommodate them until then."

And with no further words, the soldiers leave the square.

Our former neighbors get shelter instantly. We, the Velezes, don't receive any offers. Most Starvillers loathe us, partly because Dad has performed abortions for soldiers' victims. The war and recruitment haven't diminished Starvillers' passionate support for prolife causes. The other reason is that Starvillers value purity of race because they say the soldiers are multiracial. They don't tolerate half-bloods, and we're evidently mixed.

Someone taps my shoulder. Mrs. Gibson, a blonde, pudgy, middle-aged Starviller, smiles at me. She could host all the families, feed them for a week, and still have plenty for herself.

"I can accommodate the two girls," Mrs. Gibson says.

She means the light-eyed Velezes. Despite our soft tans, Azzy and I resemble our fair-skinned Circassian mother. Olmo's and Dad's brown skin reveals the ethnic diversity that Starvillers hate so much. Mrs. Gibson's offer may seem nice, but it's insulting on a level of its own. Separating my family … how can she do this? Can't she see that Olmo needs shelter now more than ever? Dad has done nothing but heal the few Starvillers who seek him out, including *her*, and most of the time receives nothing in exchange.

"They gave you an order! You have to shelter us." I say, doing nothing to conceal my fury.

"All of us! Not only pieces of my family," Azzy shouts.

I point at the barracks. "Someone has to volunteer, or I'll tell the soldiers that you need motivation to carry out their orders!"

Angry voices confer. "You should do it, Gibson. You have no kids."

"Why me? Peter Rivers has more rooms in his house."

Similar discussions break out among the crowd. My mind repeats a litany as they fail to reach a consensus. *Everybody hates me. My family loves me because they have to, but everyone else hates me.*

I don't care. I hate them even more.

"Never mind! I'd rather be homeless than stay with a bunch of bigots who—" I can't continue because my voice is breaking.

We start walking toward the museum. All eyes are on us when Olmo trips and falls headfirst into the dirt. This makes the crowd erupt with laughter.

Sara Jenkins, a shy ex-Comanche, helps me lift and comfort a weeping Olmo. That's when I see Rey forcing his way through the crowd, his family with him.

"We'll take them," Rey shouts.

Nobody hears Rey's offer because they're still laughing at Olmo.

I look at Rey, conveying my gratitude with my eyes. I mouth the words *thank you* to him. True to form, Rey offers the little he has to help a person in need.

Suddenly everybody falls silent. Why are people staring at me in surprise, even fear? I turn to find Aleksey standing right behind me. He's so scary that I stumble away. In a menacing tone, he demands to know what's going on.

Nobody answers. People stare at Aleksey with morbid curiosity, as if he were a freak. Elena Rivers whispers something to Ava Peters and they burst into a fit of giggles. At first, I assume they're mocking his unnatural height. Then I realize with surprise that all the girls are ogling him. Aleksey's too brutish to be considered handsome, but he isn't unattractive. In fact, his bestial traits and roughness make him the most attractive man in the crowd. At least that's what the girls behind me are whispering.

"No problem here," says Rey. "We're just discussing something."

Aleksey glares at the crowd. "You were playing hot potato with the future of a family."

Olmo laughs, but this is a serious matter. A Patriot order is unquestionable. If Starvillers ignore it, the consequences will affect the whole town.

"You're wrong, General. I've just offered shelter to this family," says Mrs. Gibson.

Aleksey's eyes narrow. "So you offered your house to the *four* members of this family?"

"I offered shelter, too," says Rey, looking at me.

Aleksey glances at the toddler in Rey's arms. His eyes move to Duque and Baron, who scowl at him. "Is your apartment big enough, Starviller? Or would it be better for them to find different accommodations?" Before Rey can interrupt, Aleksey adds, "This family would be better off at the Accord clinic. I heard that this man is a doctor. We'll need his talent when the clinic starts operations."

Someone scoffs, and both Rey and Aleksey glare at the perpetrator. Kit Lee-Rivers deflates beneath their withering stares.

"Of course, we wouldn't deprive the clinic of Dr. Velez's … talents, General," says the Commissioner, his ears turning red.

Rey throws a protective glance over my family. "It isn't necessary. Dr. Velez's family and mine have a strong relationship. They'd be more comfortable in my apartment." Rey's eyes meet mine, making me blush.

Aleksey's tone is contemptuous. "You're deluded."

"Am I? Well, it's none of the Accord Unit's business; we haven't broken any treaties. Not that your people care much about treaties, anyway."

I look to my right. The clinic is two miles away, perched on top of a tree-cloaked hill. "We'll go to the clinic," I say in a firm voice, and the crowd whispers its approval.

Aleksey's blue eyes meet mine for a second. It's a strange look that I regard as hateful. Maybe he's still mad at the way I treated his penis.

"Lily, how could—?" Rey protests.

Aleksey interrupts him. "The lady said clinic. Everyone heard it. Now clear the space." His deep, authoritative voice discourages protests. Aleksey takes my dad in his arms and walks toward the west side. The crowd clears a path to let them pass.

I avoid looking at Rey and hurry after Aleksey. As much as I despise cops, Aleksey saved our lives yesterday. I hate to feel like I owe him, but my family is more important than my pride.

After half an hour of walking, we reach the base of the hill. Industrial buildings surround the bottom. A single trail of steps rises to the gray buildings at the top. Without a helicopter, the stone steps are the only way to access the clinic. I look up, already tired from looking at the endless number of cement stairs we have to climb. Aleksey lets Dad climb by himself and instead carries Olmo. The staircase is too much for my brother's diseased lungs to handle.

At the top of the hill are two L-shaped buildings separated by a large courtyard that doubles as a helipad. The clinic is well-equipped, almost like a Patriot mini-hospital. There's running water and electricity. The second building will be our temporary shelter.

Tristan Froh, a baby-faced cop with short, dirty blond hair, gives us our room assignments. Mine is at the end of a long, white-tiled corridor. From the window, I can see the helipad and the clinic's second story, which is still under construction.

"I'm sorry, Miss and Mr. Velez. These rooms don't have thermostats, but I will get you a fan and a heater," says Tristan. His accented voice sounds sincere, and he's blushing. The way he calls me *Miss Velez* is so formal, but endearing at the same time. That makes me wary. People who have hurt me have always been nice at first. We tell him we need no thermostat. We've adjusted to not having one.

Azalea regards Aleksey shrewdly as Dad makes an attempt at conversation. Aleksey answers in grumpy monosyllables. He uses full sentences only to inform Dad that several Patriot casualties and wounded civilians will arrive soon.

As if on cue, we hear the first of several helicopters approaching.

We stay in Dad and Olmo's room, listening to the ear-shattering screams and the hurried orders. Apparently, female soldiers are bringing in charred bodies on gurneys. The medics ignore my father, but accept Aleksey's help. Some of the victims died on the way to the hospital. The survivors, most of them soldiers, will be transferred to a real hospital once they are stabilized.

We fall asleep on the floor. It's dark outside when Dad enters the room to bring us food: leftovers from the soldiers. We finish eating quickly, still hungry, but I don't complain because I'm certain that Dad has given us his portion.

"That cop … Aleksey … is a medical expert," says Dad in a thoughtful tone. "He'll stay here instead of the Accord headquarters. I don't know why he's helped us, but it's better if you all keep your distance."

Well, he's a former soldier. He saw me naked and got a boner. Of course, I'll keep my distance.

In the darkness of an unknown room, I wake to a throbbing sensation between my legs. The dream was so vivid that I still feel the warmth of someone's mouth on my skin, and I continue to hear the somber tune from the dream ringing in my ears.

It takes me some minutes to remember that I'm here as a consequence of Midian's destruction.

Dad said earlier that all the patients had been transferred to hospitals, and the medical staff, too. So, if the clinic is deserted, where is the music coming from? I can still hear it, even after the last images from my dream loosen their hold on me.

In an attempt to forget the dream, I look out the window. A peculiar sight catches my eye.

In the middle of the dimly lit helipad, a group of tall, attractive women chat with Patriot soldiers. They wear orange unitards under their long, open coats. I recognize that uniform. These women are visitants.

Plastic and well-groomed, these women don't look like recruitment victims. They have to be Patriot citizens, serving the troops. Someone has to placate the constant hunger for sex that the drugs induce in the soldiers. Visitants volunteer for that in exchange of other privileges. They must be waiting for a helicopter after having provided their services.

One of the soldiers points to a room above his head, not far from where I'm spying. The most beautiful of the visitants, a curvy, long-haired brunette, climbs a scaffold and knocks on the door. Nobody answers for what seems like an eternity, but she's insistent.

The music stops. I crane my neck to get a better view. When the door finally opens, Aleksey appears at the threshold, scowling. He holds a double bass bow in his hand. The visitant smiles, evidently pleased with her client's good looks, and tries to enter the room.

When his door slams on the visitant's face, I decide I've seen enough. I return to my cot and cover my head with a blanket, fighting off waves of anguish. After recruitment, I may end up giving unpaid visitant services. As a vassal.

The music, replaced by moans and muffled screams from the soldiers being served, doesn't resume for the rest of the night. Partially because of the noises, and partially because I keep waking up after a stream of nightmares, my first night at the clinic is marked by anxiety.

When I arise in the morning, I'm forced to face the grim reality of my life.

I need an escape.

CHAPTER 7

A V girl

THE GLADE WHERE THE biracial couple makes a show of their love is a perfect circle of old trees, surrounded by grass and vibrantly colored flowers. Divine and Joey glue their mouths with slow, passionate kisses. He pulls her closer, holding her tight in his arms. His hands cup the flesh of her naked butt, and the sounds of their mouths mix with the sounds of the forest.

Joey isn't tall or handsome. He has rough features and, at thirty-six, he's losing his ash-brown curls. But he's got strong arms, hungry lips, and the remarkable skill of never leaving a single inch of her skin untouched. I enjoy watching him. His complete devotion to Divine, the way his face contracts in response to pure passion and love. I'm sure he'd give his life for her.

I sit with my knees tucked under my chin, behind a bush of orange flowers. I'm not hiding from them, but I don't want anybody else to see me here.

There's a French word for people who do what I do.

I'm a voyeur girl. Sort of.

No, I don't spy on people against their will.

No, I don't get a kick out of looking through peepholes.

No, I won't ever observe someone in the privacy of their own home.

What happens when they have sex in the wild, knowing that anyone can watch? On those occasions, I enjoy the show and feel no guilt. Why should I say no to their invitation?

Yes, I'm a girl with a kink. When I think of myself as a V-girl, the *V* is for *voyeur* instead of *virgin*, and I don't hate my nickname at all. I've come to terms with this part of my personality. I'm not hurting anyone, and I need a distraction from the horrors around me. I've been so busy at the clinic that I haven't had time for these shows.

Divine moans as her breasts bounce with each thrust. Finally, Joey grunts and quivers. His mouth forms a perfect *O* as he explodes. When they nestle in their post-coital bliss, I feel envy corroding my veins. I wish someone loved me like Joey loves her.

A noise startles me, but when I turn around with my knife drawn, I see nothing. I turn my attention back to the lovers. That's when Divine's eyes meet mine. She always seems to expect a standing ovation. Joey's so lost in his adoration for her, he never looks my way.

When I turn away from them, Divine shouts after me. "You! V-girl! Stop ditching meetings. Today at five p.m."

No way. I'd die if the Comanches heard word of my pathetic attempt to seduce our leader. I'm working out on my own.

Walking back toward town, I wonder why Divine and Joey keep doing this. Maybe it's because they can't get married. They aren't even allowed to live together because biracial kids like me aren't welcome. Even if they could get away from Starville, she wouldn't be able to get a new marriage tattoo, since her ex-husband left after the troops abused her.

A loud sigh escapes my chest. Perhaps if I hadn't seen the soldiers violating my mother, I wouldn't be a voyeur. Her attackers' faces haunt me at night, and whenever I watch Divine and Joey, my terror subsides a little.

Maybe I am trying to stop seeing what can't be unseen.

Distracted by these gloomy thoughts, I trip on a loose stone. That's when I notice *him*.

He emerges from the woods, not far from my hiding place. I can't decipher his cryptic expression. I doubt he could watch the show from where he was, but I'm certain that he saw *me* watching.

Of all people, why him? Aleksey unnerves me because he resembles my mother's attackers. Besides, he's seen me naked, and now he's seen another private part of me.

I'm about to say something, but then I remember who he is. A corrupt, drunk Accord cop—an ex-soldier with, most likely, a history of violence. They're the ones who should feel ashamed. Cops do nothing to defend recruits. Compared to that, my tendency to watch is nothing.

I take a breath and meet his gaze with defiant eyes before turning my back on him. I can feel his eyes stabbing into my back as I put more distance between us.

I have other things to worry about. The railway will take five more days to repair, and I hope I'll still have my Shiloh job by then. In the meantime, I have sewing jobs, and Dad has found a way to work on his pills again. The entire Velez family, even Poncho in his guardian role, fabricates the pills.

I cross town with Aleksey not far behind me. I don't jump to the conclusion that he's following me. Unlike the other Accord cops, Aleksey and Tristan spend a lot of time at the clinic, assisting every way they can. The rest are supposed to supply vaccines and run tests at the clinic for Starvillers, but most of the time, they drink on the streets. They come only when they need Aleksey to sign papers or to receive orders from him.

When I get to Exodus Street, Aleksey is still walking behind me. I take a detour, just in case.

These days, Dad has been working as though they're paying him a fortune, and I'm pleased to see him so motivated. Nurses and doctors come and go, leaving as soon as the wounded soldiers are stabilized and sent to bigger hospitals. Most of the time, my family is alone at the clinic. But when there are soldiers around, I don't leave my family alone, and I make sure the twins remain hidden.

Sweaty after the long walk, I arrive at the clinic and search for my family. I find Azzy making pills in an empty examination room. She's ditched the dull philosophy lesson that's taking place in another room.

We work on the pills together, hours passing amicably.

The soft music in Aleksey's room quiets down. Sometimes, Aleksey shuts himself in to play his double bass, and no cop or soldier dares interrupt. But whenever Olmo corners Aleksey, the cop listens with solemn patience—wearing his perpetual serious face—and answers Olmo's endless questions with nods and grunts. When I see this, I don't hate Aleksey as much as I should. I'm not always so patient with Olmo myself.

One day I overheard Olmo ask him, "Why don't you talk, Prince Aleksey?"

The cop tore a piece of paper from his journal, scribbled something, and handed my brother the note. Olmo grinned and regarded Aleksey with admiring eyes.

"Cool!"

Olmo showed me the note later. Only four words: *I don't want to.*

But when Elena Rivers, using a seductive tone, asked the same question while Aleksey was busy checking his j-device, she received an altogether different response.

"An experiment," he said curtly.

"Ooh! I love experiments," she purred. "What kind of experiment?"

He showed her the time on his j-device chronometer. "To see how long it would take an insufferable, nosy idiot to ask me about it."

Elena looked affronted. That day she'd been so nasty to my dad that I felt like Aleksey had avenged my family for me. Since then, Elena has recovered well. She often visits the clinic to try to get into Aleksey's pants. He's always rudely indifferent to her flirtation, but she doesn't take the hint.

Living so close to an ex-soldier scares me, but my family trusts him, perhaps because he's completely impartial. Neutrality defines Aleksey; I can't tell if he favors one band or the other. He gives the same care to all the injured soldiers, whether they're Nats or Patriots. And at the same time, it's as though he doesn't care about anybody.

"Well, he has to be nice to Patriot soldiers since they keep him fed. He eats a lot," says Azzy. She has an uncanny ability to read faces, hearts, and minds.

"Weird. Ex-soldiers barely eat." That's another desired effect of the tonics they take to build their muscles.

"He must have stopped taking the tonics after he left the army. Otherwise, he wouldn't be able to drink alcohol."

"Those aren't normal muscles. If he's not taking drugs, how is he so built?"

She stops mixing the ingredients to stretch her arms. "Because he trains every morning. Shirtless."

I look out the window. This room has a magnificent view of the stone staircase and the mountains beyond Starville. "You've been paying attention to him." Well, so has every other female in Starville.

Azzy shrugs. "There aren't many things to do around here. Maybe that's why he's always scribbling stuff in his notebook. I suspect he's writing music."

She stops talking and stares greedily when Aleksey appears outside the window. Poncho jumps around the cop as he climbs down the stone staircase. I nudge Azzy back to reality.

"I wasn't swooning, idiot! I was studying him."

I believe her. She likes to analyze people. "What's the verdict?"

"That man is dangerous. You're not considering him for emergency deflowering, are you, Lila?"

Azalea knows I'm still unsullied. When I arrived home feeling dejected that night, I thought she would give me the *I-told-you-so* speech. She didn't. With her talent for guessing emotions, she not only gave me privacy, she offered me support … in her own detached way.

I scoff. "No! He's kind of a soldier." *More like a beast.*

"Good. Just take a look at him!" she says. "He towers above soldiers, so his *truth* must be extraordinary. Too much for a tight girl."

Dad's biology lessons got us used to describing reproductive functions in clinical terms, but we use other words for fun. A penis is *the truth*. A vagina gets a different name every time. I wrinkle my nose. "Is that even possible? *Ginas* ought to have a stretch limit."

"A baby is the limit."

Remembering the monumental size I grasped in my hands, I shake my head. "That's different. Mother Nature prepares *ginas* and cervixes over the nine months of pregnancy for deliveries." *But not for unnaturally large penises.*

"That's why Rey'd be better for you. He seems well-endowed in a normal way. It won't ever happen, though."

I look away, feeling a mix of irritation and embarrassment. I couldn't see it, but I felt it.

"Bigger than normal … but …" She waits for me to elaborate, but I won't disrespect Rey by discussing his girth.

Azzy laughs. "Well, you know what they say: Penis is in the eye of the beholder."

I should stop this conversation for her own good. Discussions about sex are not uncommon with us, but Azzy is taking her adult act to uncomfortable extremes. I realize that I so *do not* want to talk about this with my sister.

It's Azzy who changes the subject. "Aleksey must like you. He sometimes stares at you."

I glare at her. "Then he must like everybody. He always stares at everyone with his *I-hate-you* attitude."

I need to distance myself from Azzy, so I take my batch of pills and enter a deserted emergency room. She follows me. "Forget about Rey; it wouldn't have worked. He isn't the only one with principles. You would've felt horrible."

She's right. If I can't have his complete acceptance, I'll feel as though *I'm* raping *him*.

"It was a stupid plan, doomed from the start," she adds.

I'm frustrated by her patronizing tone. All the tension from the past few days hits me at once. "You know what? Maybe one day you'll wonder what it'd be like if your best friend made love to you. Because you *know* he wouldn't ever hurt you."

She rolls her eyes.

My voice rises to a yell. "And you'll want to know what sex is like when it's not forced on you, so you'll make plans to lose your innocence, too! Even if there's nothing but friendship! Even if you'd rather wait 'til you met someone special … but you *know* that will never happen to you."

"Friends with benefits? No, thank you."

"Never say never, Azalea. Let's talk about it when *you're* the one eligible for recruitment."

Azzy ignores me, shaking pill dust from her dress. "It's too much trouble to erase it from my to-do list."

"You're eleven. You don't have a to-do list. It can't be Rey because—" I look at the floor and feel a lump in my throat. "I can't … *use* him." I look up. Her condescending expression makes me shout. "I'll find a way before the troops take me! Don't you dare judge me!"

I storm toward the double doors. I wrench them open and stumble into someone. Someone who may have heard my outburst.

Embarrassed, I stare at my feet. "Excuse me," I mutter, not daring to look up. But even without a view of his face, I recognize that colossal body.

At this moment, I want the ground to open up and swallow me.

Aleksey is looking at me with cold steel eyes. A wicked, humorless half smile crosses his face. He obviously listened to my diatribe.

"Dr. Velez?" he asks coolly.

I'm speechless. We saw Aleksey going to town, so why did he come back? I motion toward the aisle where I had heard Dad's voice. With no other words, I walk past him.

"So, if you won't use your friend, I have a friend who loves being used. By *virgins*," he says.

I want to make a dignified exit rather than show him that his words hit me like a punch. I keep walking, my head held high. My feet don't get the message, and I stumble. He responds with a strange breathing sound. Has this brooding man suppressed a laugh?

I can't take anymore and sprint to my room, slamming the door.

I'll make him regret that he used the V-word to make fun of me.

One day.

Chapter 8

Fly your flight, my dear dove
Sing your song, make it reach the ocean
I want my **freedom**
I want to live in **peace**
I want to sing your song
To have your wings
To be able to fly
I want my destiny to leave the path
that it is taking now.

The Dove—Eduardo Carrasco

The Comanche Resistance

AS THE DAYS PASS, I fight to mend my self-esteem. I can't get over my first failed attempt at seduction. My first failure, and likely not my last. There must be other options to lose my maidenhead, but masturbation isn't one. I want a shared experience. To feel that someone cares for me even in my most vulnerable state. Even under normal circumstances, that's difficult to find. I stand no chance as long as there's war, as long as there's hunger.

The air raid left Starville with little in the way of communications, so we have more food shortages. More people are enlisting for recruitment. Others scan the ruins for remnants of wallpaper; they say the starchy glue is edible. And I've noticed that the number of rats, stray cats, and dogs has drastically diminished.

The Accord cops distribute food, but it's never enough. Patriots say Starvillers should pay the costs of the occupation, so most of the Starville production, including food, goes to the war effort.

We can't use the provisions that TCR saved, and without my job, we rely on the ration coupons provided by the government. The rest of my family is starting to depend on Aleksey's charity, which I find humiliating. He brings us food, but I never eat it. Women mustn't take food from soldiers, as soldiers abuse the women who accept their food. Then they deny it was rape and claim it was prostitution.

If my family eats Aleksey's food, that's okay, but I won't. I don't starve, but I never get full. At least Olmo is eating better now, although he has this habit of eating only parts of the chocolate bars Aleksey brings him. Olmo hides the rest in his emergency backpack.

I could use one of those bars at the moment. My stomach growls as I walk down the steep, winding streets toward the museum.

Poncho growls when we reach Exodus Street, where some Accord cops are drinking. One of them, Gary Sleecket, leers at me.

"Why so lonely, pretty?" he shouts before they burst into laughter. I ignore them, hurrying on my way to TCR headquarters. I haven't been there since my failure at seduction, and I dread being that close to Rey again.

Buck Weaver founded The Comanche Resistance after he came across some solar e-readers at the museum ruins. He used them to learn survival and fighting skills, then shared what he was learning with his most trusted friends, including a fourteen-year-old Rey. As they got stronger, they began scheming acts of opposition, like hiding provisions and sabotaging the Patriot trains. Only a dozen of us remain because TCR has lost members to recruitment. My dad and Baron Diaz don't train with us, but they're members, too.

When I enter the foyer, I hear voices coming from the training room. Luke Rivers, Elena's brother, and Rey are arguing.

"Well, you're entitled to your *wrong* opinion, but you're mistaken," says Rey.

"You can't tell other people how to live their lives," retorts Luke.

"I didn't say *don't use visitant services*. I said *they deserve respect, too*. I couldn't care less where you stick your—"

Someone pats my shoulder, startling me.

"Hey! You're back! I missed you," says Duque, his amber eyes shining.

I smile timidly. It's good to know at least one person missed me.

Duque leads me to an empty room where his fiancée, Veronica, is talking to Cara Winston and her daughter, Holly. I don't join the conversation.

"It's too bad the law doesn't allow me to take her place," Cara says grimly. Like her mom, Holly is slim and blonde—exactly the kind of girl Starville bachelors prefer. And soldiers. But unlike me, Holly is not trying for an emergency deflowering because she hopes to marry a local boy someday. If by some miracle she doesn't get raped, and if she plays her celibacy card, she'll find a husband quickly.

As inconspicuously as possible, I return to the foyer. I take a deep breath before entering the training room.

Luke is already warming up in front of the mirrors, his straight black hair falling into his almond-shaped eyes. We ignore each other as usual. He's still arguing with Rey. I don't understand why a privileged boy like him even joined TCR when he doesn't get along with the leader.

"It's none of your business. I can live perfectly without *that*," says Rey from behind a half-broken folding screen.

"You don't even know what—" Luke fakes a gasp, "—*sex* really is, you prude."

Rey relays his sardonic comeback as he tosses his carpenter clothes over the screen. "You place your *small* penis inside a woman's vagina. Then you thrust continuously. After a while—*twelve seconds*, in your case—you ejaculate sperm. As simple as th—" He comes out from behind the screen and sees me. A mix of shock and embarrassment appears on his face.

"Lily," Rey says, blushing. He's shirtless, and his pants hang loosely from his hips. I don't know if he's embarrassed by what I've just heard or because of what almost happened between us.

"Hey, Rey," I reply awkwardly, making my way to the door. "I—I'll feed the doves."

The sunlight blinds me when I enter an adjoining room that has a partially collapsed roof.

First Nats, and later Patriots, used this room to behead their enemies. The room's tragic past and the strange sounds heard here at night are the reason for the rumors of a haunted museum. Here, a redheaded boy, Mathew Berkley, is using a contraband object: our outdated solar gadget. On sunny days, it gives us limited access to the Patriot networks.

"No news on … Midian?" I ask quietly. Until the night of the air raid, we kept in contact with Midian's resistance.

He shakes his head. "We haven't received pigeons either. Fanny has been praying for their souls."

Fanny is Mathew's pregnant wife. At twenty-two, Mathew has been married for six years and is expecting his second child. Starvillers believe engagement at thirteen and marriage at sixteen is natural. It's not. Those are aftereffects of war and recruitment.

Other than the Diazes, I don't feel comfortable around people. To avoid further conversation, I throw breadcrumbs on the floor, whistling "The Dove," my dad's favorite song. I step back as our messenger doves appear, fighting for crumbs amongst the dust.

When I return to the mirrored room, everybody is holding broomsticks.

"Duque will take charge," announces Veronica, kissing her fiancé's cheek.

TCR members are supposed to learn a combat skill and then *take charge*, training the rest of us. Today, Duque will train us in wooden sword combat.

We start with a warm-up and simple combat exercises, but when we pair up for more complicated exercises, the ditched sessions take a toll on me. I'm usually one of the top four fighters, but today I'm struggling to defeat Veronica, the most recent addition to TCR. When I finally manage to beat her, I'm sweaty and bruised; my lip is cut. It's humiliating. Ignoring the pain, I swear that I'll wake up at four a.m. every morning to practice.

Veronica notices my anxiety and taunts me in her annoyingly loud voice. "So, V-girl, will you ever take charge?"

I frown. What is it to her? I hate taking charge because I can't stand to have these people's eyes on me and … my mistakes. I know I haven't been the greatest contribution to the resistance lately, but neither has Veronica. Rey usually keeps the youngest members out of the most dangerous missions: Duque, Holly, Veronica, and me.

Rey scowls. "Leave her alone."

But I'm already sliding mattresses to the middle of the room. "I'll take charge."

"Not another first aid lesson?" asks Joey.

I shake my head. "Freestyle wrestling. Grab a mattress."

"Yes!" Luke exclaims.

"Work in pairs," I command.

Everyone stares at me. I have to demonstrate first. I feel less confident than I'm trying to appear, but I walk straight toward Mathew, who is in a defensive stance over the mattress.

He's strong, but I'm fast. In a sweeping move, I'm behind him, pushing his knees with mine and throwing him off balance. I punch his side, using my hips.

Mathew lands with a thud, but he smiles. "Way to go, Velez!"

From the corner of my eye, I see Rey smiling appreciatively. I fight the impulse to look at him.

"Take turns trying to knock your opponent to the ground," I say.

The group quickly splits into pairs. I circle them, giving feedback here and there before I instruct them to switch partners. I almost snort when I correct Veronica's technique as she struggles to keep her balance against Divine.

I'm giving some feedback to Holly and Duque when someone grabs me from behind. In a fraction of a second, my back lands on the mattress, and Rey's rock-hard body is above me, his face only an inch from mine. He pins my wrists above my head. I forget how to breathe.

Rey grins playfully. "Don't ever leave your defenses open."

His body lingers over mine before he stands up. I sit up, wondering if there's a hidden meaning in Rey's attitude toward me today.

We spend the rest of the afternoon scheming and plotting. With our rudimentary weaponry and the ban on gunpowder, the most we can do is mess with Patriot railroads. We're cautious. We sabotage trains only when storms and tornados erase our tracks. We don't want to turn Starville into another Midian.

Rey asks for volunteers for the next mission: an excursion to the electric wires that run north, sixty miles from the lake. There he'll create an untraceable server with a wireless connection to hack blogs that are free of government censorship. Bandits, weather, beasts, and soldiers are risks we have to consider. We don't have vehicles, so the five volunteers will have to hike for days. Some of us will stay behind. If the mission goes wrong and nobody survives, there'll be Comanches left to continue the resistance.

Everyone volunteers, and now it's Rey's call. He's not a tyrant but a leader who values others' opinions. The first opinion he asks for is mine.

"*Um* ... you and I should go ... Cara because she's great with weapons, and Mathew because he's our best hacker."

Others suggest a similar lineup. Rey will go along with Cara, Mathew, and Luke. There's only one spot left, and I fight for it, but in the end, Rey chooses Duque. Of course. Rey is always trying to protect me.

The meeting ends, and I hurry to gather my backpack. My bruises ache, but I can't help but think about achieving my goals. I have a new objective: becoming TCR's top fighter.

I find Poncho waiting for me outside, and we dart through the potholed streets.

We pass Olga Busko's house, which used to be Angie's. Angie was nineteen, a spinster's age, and afraid of being recruited. Rey put off marriage to raise Reyna, so Angie married Buck Weaver to get a marriage tattoo. Azzy gave her the cold shoulder after that, but I would have done anything to avoid recruitment, including marrying a man I don't love.

Loud footsteps sound behind me, and I turn to find Rey running to catch up. He doesn't look comfortable, and I'm at a loss for words. If I knew how to apologize, I'd say, *I'm sorry.* I tried to force him to do something he didn't want to do, and now he's acting awkwardly around me. But what's the point in apologizing? What's done is done. Words can't change the past.

"Hey! Can't we at least be friends?" he asks.

"I never asked you for more than friendship, Rey." I only wanted a kind gesture that would save me from recruitment.

He places his hand on my shoulder. "I wish we could go back to what we were before."

"Me, too. I just need time. I feel … embarrassed around you. And before I … I have to take care of some things."

He understands what I mean. "Some things? You mean you're still trying to … you know—"

This whole conversation feels wrong. I can't stand it. "I don't want to talk about this, especially not with you."

Rey grabs my hand before I can dart away. "Wait. Please … don't do *that*. You shouldn't do something you'll regret after recruitment when you're trying to find a husband. You don't have to."

Well, it's easy for Rey to say that. He's not in danger of recruitment.

"Yes, I have to."

CHAPTER 9

Drawn

THE COMANCHES COULD HAVE taken care of my bruises and cuts, but I was too proud to tell them that I didn't protect myself during training. When I open the door to an empty examination room, I expect to see Dad, but instead I find the idiot who made fun of me. He's leaning against a medicine cabinet, scribbling in his journal.

"Oh … *er* … I was looking for my dad."

Aleksey has barely glanced my way. He's still engrossed in his notes. I hesitate at the threshold, biting my lip and completely forgetting about the cut.

"*Ow!*"

I'm about to close the door when his deep voice stops me.

"Wait."

I turn to him warily. He frowns and, without saying a word, points to my bleeding lip. I answer his unspoken question with a lie.

"I … I … fell."

His cold blue eyes reveal a slight hint of concern. After all, he's a doctor. I look down, remembering that this isn't the first time we've been alone after one of my falls. Although this time we aren't naked, my cheeks feel warm.

"Come here," he orders.

I don't hesitate. Something in his voice compels me to obey. He must have achieved his General rank through his ability to make people follow his commands.

I stand near him, looking down. From the corner of my eye, I see him examining me.

"Sit," he commands.

My feet dangle helplessly from the examination table. As much as Patriots and cops deny it, this clinic was built for taller patients: drug-filled patients.

Aleksey gets closer, and my pulse quickens. With gauze, he skillfully cleans my bruises and cuts. I gasp when his colossal hand takes my arm. He applies ointment to the bruises and the pain disappears. I'm not used to this soft touch, and the sensation is nerve-racking and pleasant at the same time.

Aleksey hands me an icepack. "Keep this on your knee."

When he becomes interested in my swollen lip, his face gets dangerously close to mine. My heart beats in an erratic rhythm. I venture a glance his way and regret it immediately. I close my eyes to avoid his piercing blue stare, but I can't avoid his lingering smell. Or the sound of his breathing.

He must have brought his face even closer because I can feel his warmth radiating near my face. An intoxicating smell emanates from his muscular body: a mix of clean clothes, wood, and masculinity.

I shut my eyes with more force than necessary. Aleksey's mint-scented breath tickles my eyelids, then my cheeks, and finally my lips.

A soft humming sound escapes from my throat as I sense the heat that flows from Aleksey's mouth. It feels as though he's about to brush my lips with his. My stomach contracts, and every nerve becomes alert, but I don't pull back.

Before my lips touch his, the closeness is gone.

I refuse to open my eyes. My heart is pounding frantically, and I'm breathing at an abnormal pace. What the hell was that? Is that how he treats all his patients?

I hear him searching through the cabinets, then something meeting the examination table. I open my eyes and watch him scribble on a piece of paper. He hands me the folded note and leaves the room without a word.

My trembling hands unfold the paper. It's a prescription.

I take the medicines from the table and head to my room. My face is still burning, but I feel as though a heavy oppression has lifted from my chest. Now that I'm free of his intimidating presence, I can breathe normally again.

That night, I toss and turn several times before my eyes feel heavy. My mind is consumed by what happened. I must have imagined the kissing attempt; after all, he's a professional. Perhaps Aleksey is more decent than I give him credit for. This is the second time he could have overpowered me and didn't.

The imaginary kiss attempt has left me yearning, but I'm glad it was all in my imagination and that he didn't cross that line.

No girl can jump from thinking that a man can rape her to falling head over heels for him.

The sounds of shots and screams penetrate the walls, waking me. Terror surges through my body, paralyzing me. Somehow, I end up beneath the wooden floorboards. I can see everything from my hiding place.

My father injects Olmo and Azzy with a tranquilizer, and they stop crying. "Lila, as soon as the soldiers are gone, take them to Baron's." There's desperation in his voice.

Banging noises startle me. The door is about to fall off its hinges.

No!

The four colossal soldiers break into our apartment, seconds after Dad shoves Olmo and Azzy into a hidden closet.

Somebody! Help!

I can't scream. I can't close my eyes. Not even when they crush my dad's legs with their massive clubs. Not even when they viciously beat my mother's swollen belly.

Stop! She's pregnant!

"An eye for an eye! Retaliation!" yells one of them. His acne-ridden face, framed by long platinum hair, reveals that he may not be fifteen yet. He's less built than the other soldiers, but he boasts the same cruelty and sadism when he cuts my mother's clothes with his knife, slicing her skin along with her dress.

They take turns abusing her.

The teenage soldier isn't satisfied. His blue eyes gleam in the dark as he uses the handle of his knife to attack her.

Again and again. Her blood filters through the floorboards. The iron, salty smell of it makes me want to scream, but my voice has abandoned me.

Kill her! I'd rather you kill her … please … stop!

But she's still alive and partially conscious when they drag her out of the apartment.

My screams—not the tears dampening my pillow—jolt me awake. Somewhere outside the clinic, Poncho's barking overpowers the soft music in Aleksey's room.

Breathing so heavily that my chest hurts, I observe my surroundings. It's hard to convince myself that I'm back to reality. It's been five years, but the wet sensation of my mother's blood on my hands still makes me shiver uncontrollably.

The gloomy, barely audible music that comes from Aleksey's room finally convinces me that I'm awake. My dreams are always so vivid that this soothing, celestial tune may very well be part of them. Unfortunately, what I dreamt about was an exact recreation of *that day's* events.

To this day, I feel guilty for not closing my eyes. What kind of daughter witnesses her mother's most horrifying experience with her eyes wide open? I don't know what time it is, but I can't go back to sleep. I work out instead, trying to wash away my guilt with sweat.

My nightmare brings me back to the glade by the river. Watching the lovers may be a perverted act, but I need to remind myself that sex can be an expression of love. I may never feel that kind of love myself, but at least I can fantasize about it.

They're mutually inverted with respect to each other, and Joey is on the bottom. I can see the way their mouths tantalize the most sensitive parts of each other's bodies. I'm trying to imagine how warm and moist his mouth must feel on Divine's lips when I hear a sound to my right.

Three feet from me, Aleksey sits down on the grass.

My first impulse is to flee; he reminds me so much of the soldiers from my nightmares that I shiver. But I stay rooted to the spot, keeping my eyes on Joey and pretending that Aleksey is invisible. The rational part of me says that I shouldn't feel afraid. If he were anything like those soldiers, he would've attacked me by now.

Joey, as usual, isn't aware of anything that isn't Divine. She watches Aleksey warily without releasing Joey from her mouth, and something tells me that they have reached an unspoken agreement. Aleksey agrees not to disturb them; she agrees to let him watch.

From the corner of my eye, I see that he sits utterly still, the breeze ruffling his platinum hair. Why is he here? Should I leave? Should I say something? I don't move, waiting for his reaction.

And yet, I feel as though Aleksey and I are engaged in some sort of silent conversation. We're strangers with an inclination to watch when we shouldn't. For a while, it has been the lovers and me. Now it's the lovers and *us*. He'll leave and most likely never come back after recruitment, so why should it matter?

Aleksey stays where he is, watching the show for a while. Our eyes meet for an instant before he looks away. Unlike most soldiers, he hasn't tattooed the contour of his eyes. Even so, his eyes look beautifully piercing.

"An expanse, as green and deep as the sea," he says, as though he's talking to himself.

I can't make sense of his words "I … what?" He shakes his head, gets up, and walks away. His cape billows majestically behind him.

From that moment on, Aleksey becomes my voyeurmate.

Chapter 10

"In our duty to protect civilians, we often find ourselves between a rock and a hard place. When it turns out impossible to preserve both—civilians' lives and their integrity—it's not even a question what a good Accord cop must choose. Recruitment may not be a perfect institution, but it's an institution that helps preserve civilian lives."

Sgt. Gary Sleecket of the 25th Accord Unit.

Proposal

"HE'S HOT, ISN'T HE?" Azzy whispers. We've spent five hours in line at the ration center, and we've only just received our coupons. Poncho follows us closely along the dirty sidewalks while a dozen Accord cops patrol the potholed streets, flaunting their red capes. They're here to ensure that no one disrupts the delicate rationing system.

"Well, he's monstrously built, but he has an okay face."

It's better to not reveal much around Azzy. Otherwise, I'd admit that Aleksey is so ruggedly handsome that he hardly looks human.

"I meant Tristan. He's staring at you again."

Oops. She caught me thinking about Aleksey. My cheeks feel warm, and this time, it's not because of Tristan's stare.

I turn my head to find him leaning against an Accord ambulance. Tristan is lanky—thank God—so he doesn't resemble a soldier. Whenever I catch him staring, I blush. He always offers me a reassuring smile.

The soft drizzle forces Azzy to pull on her hood. "You need a boyfriend."

Azzy's more delusional than I thought. How am I supposed to find a boyfriend in a town where young people don't hang around members of the opposite sex unless there's a chaperone involved?

I try to change the topic. "We'll be late for physical education." I train the twins as much as Olmo's health and Azzy's stubbornness will allow.

"Lila, you never flirt because you don't like Starville dudes. You're kind of judgmental."

I snort. They're misogynistic bullies. By Starville's standards, if a woman takes initiative, she's a slut. Starvillers are even less sympathetic to recruitment victims when they are known to be flirts.

"You're always so paranoid when it comes to men."

I hold my tongue. She'd be paranoid, too, if she'd witnessed our mother's attack.

Azzy addresses my thoughts. "I didn't see it, but I heard it. And I have to live with it as much as you do. Anyway, there's no reason to assume that all men are bad. Not even all the soldiers are monsters." We pass a group of street musicians who are playing under the overpass, and she moves her hips rhythmically to their music. "Think about it like this: We're at war. Flirting could be another weapon—and you'll need all the weapons you can get. Try it. Next young guy we see. I'll give you my portion of bread today."

I pretend to ignore her, but maybe she has a point. Except I don't know how to flirt.

We turn a corner and see Luke Rivers riding his pinto horse several meters ahead of us. I can't believe I'm giving thought to this. He ignores me during TCR meetings, and now I'm supposed to flirt with him?

"So, am I supposed to say," I do my best impersonation of Elena's seductive purr, "*Hey stud, wanna make a baby?* Because if that's what you're saying, I'd rather—"

"You don't have to do anything special. Just don't act like you'll throw your knife at anyone who dares to look at you. Smile and be polite."

I cringe. "Me? Smiling? It'll look so fake."

"Fake, my ass! You shouldn't use the war as an excuse to not live your life. People are getting killed, but they're also flirting, finding mates, and getting laid."

I sigh. I may as well try it to shut her up. Although I'd rather jump into the river from the highest cliff than flirt.

Luke notices me, and my stomach somersaults violently. When he gets closer, Azzy nudges me. I almost back down, but I don't want to look too conspicuous by changing directions abruptly, so I tentatively smile at him.

"Hi, Luke." There. I did it. For an antisocial, quiet person like me, this is a triumph.

To my utter astonishment, Luke responds with a sincere grin. His voice is kind when he greets me, pronouncing my name correctly and with warmth. We pass him without uttering another word.

My jaw is on the floor. I can't believe it! I'm so used to bullies that I've forgotten there are good men around, even here in Starville.

Azzy looks proud of herself. "How was that?" she asks.

I hate her smug face. I shrug, trying to hide my smile.

"Try it again, Lila!" She looks genuinely happy for me. "Look, there's Aleksey Fürst."

Oh no! I won't flirt with Aleksey; he's always quiet and moody. I'm afraid he'll snap.

Elena Rivers and Ava Peters swarm around Aleksey, flirting covertly. They're what Starvillers call *women with crinoline*, which means that they can afford expensive, uncomfortable dresses. Starville rules stretch for girls like them. Aleksey ignores them, his focus on patrolling the streets.

I look at him, wondering how it's possible that this coveted man is now my voyeurmate. It seems unreal. The first time, I was too amazed to do anything. The second time, I thought about scaring him off, but I hesitated so long that he left before I did anything. By the third time, I stopped caring. Perhaps it's because I'm lonely here in this misogynistic town. I'd rather be alone than hang out with locals, but I still crave a different kind of company.

If only he didn't look like the soldier of my nightmares … perhaps … I …

Azzy brings me back to reality. "My bread portion for a week."

Aleksey strolls toward us. His cape floats around his gigantic frame, and his masculine face is set in its usual impenetrable mask.

When he turns, I grin at him, trying to put all the warm feelings I can muster into my smile. "Hi."

His reaction takes me unaware. Aleksey blinks and clears his throat. Then he turns his face away, making a strange gesture with his hand. The cop's version of a wave. He hurries away, disappearing down the street as Azzy grins, revealing an *I-told-you* expression.

I use my newfound charms on Tristan next, when he drives an Accord ambulance past us. He appears amused.

"Look at my sister, the flirter! You're the flirt ninja!"

"Look at you, Azalea. Teaching your older sister how to flirt to use men."

"Men don't care about being used."

I scoff. "You said that they're not all the same."

And that's what I want for myself. A man who is different. Not right now, but someday. When war doesn't threaten the people I love.

The trees that surround the glade seem to reflect the light of the sun. The balmy weather and the river's lapping melody have put Divine and Joey in a romantic mood. They've placed orange petals on the blankets and keep whispering how much they love each other.

My imagination has replaced Joey's body with Aleksey's. I have seen Aleksey naked only once, but I still remember every line of his chiseled body.

Imaginary Aleksey is now completely naked and sweaty, slowly planting kisses on her pointed nipples. His lips travel to her stomach, leaving kiss marks all along her torso. He gently bends her knees, exposing her completely.

Aleksey slowly kisses and licks her lower lips before he enters her with his considerable length. His broad back and shoulders cover Divine's entire body. Bulky biceps tense and bulge as his rounded, tight butt moves and clenches rhythmically. He thrusts into her again and again. At times in circular motions, at other times slowly, pausing. Sometimes in fast jerks that make her scream.

A deep, masculine voice growls behind me. "Miss Velez, you're under arrest."

Startled, I look up. I can't believe he's talking to *me*! His presence is imposing. The way he says "arrest" with a caressing, guttural *R* shoots bolts of electricity through my body.

"On what charges?" I ask, looking away. I'm afraid he knows that I was watching *him*.

He inhales deeply, like he's searching for a particular smell.

"Voyeurism. It's illegal in at least twenty states."

I'm still thinking about the undressed Aleksey in my mind as the real cop sits in his usual spot—three feet away from me. I glance at the couple in the meadow. The lovers, still ravishing each other's bodies, are oblivious to the new member of the crowd.

He takes a sip from his flask. I've never really *talked* to Aleksey before, and being in the situation we are in now doesn't make it any easier. At least today he's not wearing his *I-hate-everybody* expression.

I breathe deeply before speaking in a secure voice—a voice that I hope doesn't reflect the mess I am inside. "They'd arrest you, too. You're watching the same show I am."

"I'm not paying attention to them. Watching is not my kink."

What is his kink then? I search my mind for a witty comeback, but I can't think clearly in this situation. "Then you're watching *me* watching. That should be illegal, too."

He watches me appraisingly. "I'm a consenting adult. They're consenting adults, whereas you—"

"Hey!" I say defensively. "I'm a consenting adult, too. I may look younger, but I'm eighteen."

I shake my head in disbelief. Did I just exchange full-length sentences with this quiet man?

When the activity in front of us becomes too intense, I get uncomfortable. Divine's screams, the sound of bodies slapping, and this incredibly good-looking stranger watching me. I stare at my feet, feeling the weight of his penetrating gaze. The spectacle, the environment, and the sounds are quite sensual. It turns me on, so he must be turned on as well.

"Don't you have better things to do than watch me peep?" I ask. I receive no answer.

A loud wail and a series of tremors announce that Divine has reached the sky, the stars, and beyond.

"The little death," Aleksey mutters, looking fleetingly at Divine.

This is so twisted. How is it that I can't walk away? I should hate him, but my body welcomes the physical turmoil he creates in me. But the erratic heartbeats and the butterflies in my stomach don't come from arousal alone. They also come from fear.

The activity grows intense again. Now Joey's pounding her with so much force from behind that her breasts are bouncing. He digs his fingers into her hips and spanks her. Even though it seems like Joey doesn't care if he hurts her, I know he does. He possesses her. He's loving her with all he has, and it doesn't look romantic at all. It's primitive. Erotic.

After fifteen minutes, I realize Joey's exaggerating his ability to delay orgasm, and she's almost tapping her feet.

I won't watch anymore. "Come on! Just come already!" I mumble and suppress a laugh. Aleksey hears me. I swear he's trying not to smile.

I lie down, closing my eyes. "Why do they call you Prince?"

"My surname. Fürst in German is a kind of prince."

It suits him. If you look past his roughness, you can see a regal look that doesn't belong to an ex-soldier.

"My best friend's name is Rey, which means King; his sister's name means Queen, and his brother's name means Duke."

"*También hablo español, amor.*" His beautiful accent caresses the Spanish words. His voice doesn't sound guttural, and it's so sexy that the butterflies in my stomach go berserk.

The lovers are finally experiencing a mutual orgasm, but Aleksey has long since stopped paying attention. He's been scribbling in his journal and seems completely engrossed. He probably doesn't even remember I'm here. I don't want to be nosy, but he answers my unspoken question.

"I'm writing about the human touch."

"If I asked you, would you explain to me what the hell human touch is?"

His eyes turn to Joey, who is tenderly extracting twigs from Divine's hair. "It can't be explained; it has to be felt."

I sit up. "The human touch sounds like a concept that doesn't exist in Starville."

Aleksey shakes his head and mumbles something that sounds like, *Ask your brother.*

I look at him, wondering whether Aleksey is as skilled in bed as he is at playing music.

Is it my imagination? Or does scorching sexual tension crackle through the air every time we're together? There are naked people in front of us performing a sexual ritual I've been yearning to experience firsthand. Since Rey won't do it … why not search for a private place in this glade and …?

I shake my head. What a gruesome thought! If I had sex with Aleksey, I'd be giving myself to a soldier.

Then I get an idea. Maybe this voyeurmate thing can work to my advantage. "If you have so much free time to spare on your … hobbies, I was wondering if you … could do me a favor." He looks at me intently. Maybe it's my imagination, but his eyes seem greedy.

I inhale to gather courage. "It has to be a secret."

"I should not comply," he says. His theatrical tone doesn't match his grave expression.

My cheeks flush. "You don't even know what I was going to ask."

"It must be related to that conversation."

I grimace. "What conversation?" I ask, guessing the answer. *Ugh!* Voyeur *and* eavesdropper.

"The one with your sister. At the clinic."

I feel my cheeks burn … not only because of his awareness of my maidenhood status, but also because he looks like he'd say yes if I asked him that.

I take a moment to calm myself, but still my voice sounds croaky.

"It has something to do with that … in a way."

"I'd help if I could, but I'm too *intense* for an innocent girl. I prefer positions that are too deep, painful, and unromantic for an inexperienced maid—"

I bury my face in my palms. "Hey! I wasn't going to ask you *that!*"

Aleksey continues as though he hasn't heard me. "I've never had sex with a *virgin*. I never kiss during sex, and I prefer not to have sex in bed. I'm into perversions that are too advanced, kinky, and rough for you."

Whoa! How can he be so blunt with a complete stranger? Perhaps he's taunting me. Am I supposed to laugh? If so, then I'll rise to his challenge. "Everything you've said leads me to conclude that you're a bad lay."

Any other man would be offended, but Aleksey must be overly confident in his stud skills because he doesn't look affronted. Instead, he stares at me greedily, and I'm surprised to see a mysterious smile crossing his usual scowling face.

"Why would you think that?" he asks in a tone that seems to say, *You're too innocent to understand.*

"Because if intense is the only way you do it, and you favor only one position, then you're limited."

His now-hungry eyes reveal a wicked glint. He moves closer, staring into my eyes, forcing me to lean back. "I do all positions, well … I do everything. There's no way I could explain what I mean by *intense* without offending you. Your inexperience brought you to the wrong conclusion."

"If you don't kiss and you don't use a bed, how will you ever please your partner?"

"Oh, little Miss Velez, if only I could show you." His blue eyes look into mine mischievously. I force myself to maintain eye contact. "Of course, I wouldn't ever … otherwise, I would take you to a *quieter place*."

"I'd never let you," I retort, forcing my voice to sound casual. An angry tone would give away my true feelings: The fact that he has declined a hypothetical sexual encounter for which I haven't asked not only irritates me, but intrigues me.

I whistle, and Poncho appears, all wet from his bath. I don't look back as I make my way toward the trees.

Aleksey walks right behind me. "You were going to ask me for a favor."

"In fact, it's more than one favor." I turn around to look at him and glimpse Divine and Joey, who are eyeing us suspiciously.

"You'll have to whisper it in my ear," he says in a low, husky voice, looking at me hungrily.

I abruptly stop walking, and my jaw drops to the floor. He's flirting! I'm so impressed that I can hardly move.

He leans in closer, his eyes clouding over as he lends me an ear.

Chapter

11

"But if a man find a betrothed damsel in the field, and the man force her, and lie with her: then the man only that lay with her shall die: But unto the damsel thou shalt do nothing; there is in the damsel no sin worthy of death: for as when a man riseth against his neighbor, and slayeth him, even so is this matter: For he found her in the field, and the betrothed damsel cried, and there was none to save her."

Deuteronomy 22:25-27

Cops' fun

ASIDE FROM THE CHAIR and a full-length mirror that Tristan lent me, my room is almost empty. I sit on my cot before changing for a workout. I'm determined to improve my chances of defending myself against soldiers. Besides, I have plenty of pent-up frustration to release.

My face flushes, but it's not an effect of the workout. I feel humiliated by what I've asked of a perfect stranger, and by what he's asked of me in return. I don't have many choices, so it's natural that I asked ... but at his price? I have to think carefully about this.

I'm ashamed that Aleksey knows my secrets. I want to hate him, but the sadness in his face has kept me intrigued since the first time I saw him. I feel gratitude because he's helped me, but now I'm too shocked to keep up with all the conflicting emotions he incites in me.

Sunset overtakes the sky as I perform a succession of push-ups, crunches, squats, and jumps.

I take a break and look out the window. What I see startles me.

Aleksey sits on the clinic's roof, his back to me, his muscular legs crossed. He seems to be contemplating the vastness of the woods below him. It's not unusual for him to go there when the clinic slows down. What's peculiar is that Olmo sits near him, imitating Aleksey's everyday somber expression and pose. Olmo is eating an orange; it's evident that he's enjoying himself.

Apparently, Olmo has found a role model and enjoys his company, even though his hero rarely speaks. Poncho is with them, so I know that Olmo's relatively safe, but I hate the idea of my brother getting attached to this stranger.

When Dad calls him for another homeschooling session, Olmo disappears from view. If Aleksey hears Olmo's enthusiastic goodbye, he doesn't show it.

I stare at the broody General for a long time. Why is Aleksey always alone? How will he answer my requests? And how should I answer his? Perhaps it's best to be prepared for negative answers. I'm still considering his proposition, though.

I shake my head and return to my training. I practice knife throwing. I haven't given up hope of losing my maidenhood, so I also use Kegel exercises to work on my inner muscles. I'll clasp my partner's penis so tightly that he'll never forget me.

I don't know if it's an effect of my obsessive exercise, but that night, I have soldier-free dreams.

The steep streets are strangely deserted for an early, drizzly afternoon. My siblings and I had lined up for food earlier, but Olmo got sick while we were waiting. I sent them home ahead of me. Poncho went with the twins, so I carry a knife inside my cloak. Just in case.

On Ephesians Avenue, the members of the Accord Unit sit on the curb, drinking.

Damn! I wasn't expecting to see them here. This avenue reeks of sewage, so cops and soldiers usually avoid this area. I don't know why they don't go to the canteen. Hell, I don't know why they don't do what they're supposed to do: protect civilians. I wish they would return to their countries.

Their leader doesn't laugh with the others. Instead, Aleksey scribbles in his leather-bound journal.

I frown, recalling the events of the past few days. Aleksey discovered my secrets and made fun of me. Then, he made a strange proposal and hasn't spoken to me since. He hasn't even addressed my request. I hate seeing him surrounded by drunken idiots. I intend to pass them, pretending they don't exist.

Unfortunately, they don't extend to me the same courtesy.

"Prince Aleksey, isn't that the girl who, instead of eyes, has a pair of green oceans?" chuckles a man with a raspy voice. The cops respond with guffaws and catcalls. "No wonder she's blushing."

They are so drunk that I cannot make sense of their words. Aleksey remains silent.

"Sir Tristan," says Gary Sleecket, adjusting his belt. "The girl's rolling her eyes at us. You and Prince Aleksey should teach her some respect."

Someone drawls, "Sleecket, look at her. Isn't she more your type?"

Neither Tristan nor Aleksey participates in the mockery.

"Prince Aleksey is the one who saved her life, so she should compensate *him*. Of course, if Prince Aleksey wants to delegate that responsibility to me, I won't complain. Because—"

From the corner of my eye, I see Aleksey glaring at them. His icy stare shuts them up.

I briskly walk away after casting a scornful glance at them. This only makes them laugh.

The sky is getting darker, and hardly any Starvillers are in sight. I stop by the apothecary to buy excipient for the pills. Then I begin the trip home, taking a different route from the one I used before.

I'm halfway to the clinic when Gary Sleecket appears behind me. He seems to be in his late forties, and his stealth tells me that he must have been one of the best soldiers in his country.

I nervously glance at my surroundings. The other cops are nowhere in sight. Are they ambushing me?

"Where are you going, Sweetie Pie?" His speech is so slurred that I can barely make out what he says. "I can walk you home if you want."

I change direction several times but can't get rid of him.

"Why that expression? I've saved thousands of Nats like you from starvation."

I increase my pace, but he quickly catches up.

"I deserve a bit of gratitude. You're a sweet girl. I want to lick your nice, young cunt."

I gasp, feeling nauseated. My disgust is soon replaced by hot fury. The few passersby near the fallen overpass are oblivious to my distress.

"Are you a *virgin*? What am I saying? You obviously are."

I feel the insult deep in my heart. Maybe I can hit him. But what if I try to punch him and he calls his companions? Evasion is the best option. I drop my backpack and flee at top speed.

The chase seems to excite him.

"You're the juiciest bitch in heat I've ever seen."

My heart beats frantically. I take a route that's free of alleys. Fortunately, his companions don't appear.

The cop keeps chasing me, slurring obscenities. All of a sudden, he jerks his right hand and touches my lower back. I almost gag. I would have been less revolted if a slimy cockroach licked me. He traps me from behind and tries to force me into a deserted building.

"Get off me!" I scream, struggling with all my might. He pulls my arm. His touch almost makes me vomit in disgust.

I step to the side and lean in the direction of his arm. He has been pulling forcefully, so this movement throws him off-balance. Gary goes down. I hit his stomach first, then his groin. He shouts in pain.

I sprint toward the plaza, screaming, "Fire!" His legs are longer than mine are and still have a soldier's inhuman speed. Gary catches up in seconds. His arms encircle my body, constricting me. He lifts me into a chokehold, making sure I can't hurt his groin again.

My fire warning has attracted attention, but people aren't helping. They're fleeing.

I force down my chin to make room for air. I crouch and kick my legs to throw him off balance. I'm about to free myself when somebody pulls us apart and strikes Gary angrily.

"You son of a bitch! Stay away from her."

I've never been happier to see Rey. His face contorts with rage as he punches the cop again.

Gary recovers and counters Rey's attacks, his face twisting evilly

With the disparity in the amount and quality of their training, Gary has the upper hand. Rey can barely dodge his strikes. It's almost as though Gary's playing with a toy. He effortlessly avoids Rey's punches.

"You attacked me unprovoked. Are you this whore's pimp?" Gary asks mockingly.

I throw my knife, but I miss his neck by inches and hit his armor instead. The blade can't pass through it, but it gives Rey some respite. With renewed rage, Rey's fist locates Gary's jaw.

When the cop retrieves his pistol, the blood drains from my face. Rey pushes me behind him. His body forms a flimsy barrier between me and the gun.

"Rey, don't," I say.

"Rey, don't," mimics Gary. "Who's gonna miss a pimp and his whore when so many decent people get killed every day?"

He's right. Rey and I are less than third-class citizens to the Patriots and the Accord cops.

Gary's voice drips with disgust.

"You want this cunt so much? Huh?"

Rey's face doesn't display a single ounce of the fear that I'm feeling. I'm not afraid of dying. I'm afraid of what Gary has in store for us before he shoots us dead.

"Is she that good? Does she suck you well? Show me, bitch."

Panic dries my mouth and slows my movements. Perhaps I can buy us time. I need this guy to cool off. I kneel … slowly.

Unfortunately, Gary seems to be aware of my intentions.

"I don't have all day, you fucking whore!" he bellows.

My scream echoes through the empty streets. "No!"

Gary points the gun at Rey, takes off the safety, and shoots.

CHAPTER 12

Silence

THE BULLET MISSES REY'S face by a hairsbreadth. I'm sure Gary missed on purpose to make a point.

"I'll aim the next bullets at your foreheads, you pair of hole diggers. Hurry, whore, and show me how you suck it."

Blood runs down Rey's cheek. He looks at me fleetingly, then glares at the gun.

Panic has given way to numbness. My mind slows. Time stretches on like an elastic band. I'm deaf and partially blind. The only thing my mind registers is that Gary's finger is on the trigger.

Gary steps toward me. I take a step to the right, racking my brain, desperately trying to remember what I know about disarming guys. I'll throw myself at the gun when Gary gets closer. He'll shoot, but I'd rather take my chances than let him abuse us.

At that moment, someone arrives on the scene, but I keep my eyes on Gary. The newcomer wears the Accord armor and cape, so I don't expect help from him. Even without a gun, he seems invincible. We can't defeat two armed men.

My senses return the moment Gary's back hits the wall with a loud thump.

"Aleksey … Sir," whispers a white-faced Gary.

Aleksey looks enraged as he slams his fist into Gary's jaw. Gary wavers, nearly collapsing to the ground. His pistol falls several feet away from him.

"Get her out of here," Aleksey commands, his eyes fixed on Gary.

Rey is as shocked as I am. We are witnessing the full power of a bestial man like Aleksey in all his wrath. He hits Gary repeatedly. The older cop looks more surprised than hurt when he falls to the ground with a thud.

Aleksey forces Gary to stand before landing more punches and kicks amidst feral grunts. As though Gary were light as a feather, Aleksey grabs him from behind and throws him at the opposite wall. Gary's back and head smash against the bricks with a deafening sound before he lands on the concrete. The impact has left cracks in the wall. Brick particles fall to the ground.

This display of strength is spectacular for an ex-soldier. In fact, I'm sure that even active, drugged-up soldiers can't lift other military men like this.

A regular person wouldn't survive that kind of collision. But Gary is an ex-soldier, and his armor is sturdy. He slowly straightens, using the wall for support.

Aleksey doesn't seem ready to stop. "I told you to take her away! Run!"

We flee. I can't believe it. Aleksey has helped me again.

Rey and I approach the clinic, where he escorts me to my room.

"Are you okay, Lily?"

"No, I'm not okay." We've barely avoided sexual assault—the worst of my fears. It's frustrating to realize that the defense techniques I know are ineffective against military-trained men. I need to get stronger.

I close the door in Rey's face and spend the rest of the afternoon working out.

Conflicting rumors about the disappearance of an Accord cop spread throughout Starville. Some people claim that they saw Prince Aleksey crush Gary Sleecket's skull and throw his body into the river. Others swear that Sleecket is a Patriot spy who fled upon discovery. Regardless, Gary joins the group of soldiers who haunt me at night.

Aleksey has become a fort of silence; I haven't heard from him since that day.

I try to thank him the next time we meet at the glade, but he brushes me off.

"I didn't do it for you. I can't stand rapists."

He may as well have added *don't bother me* because that's what I interpret from his voice, tone, and demeanor. Still, even though he didn't do it for me, I owe him. If it weren't for the fact that he's an ex-soldier, I'd admit he isn't a bad guy. Besides, I can't hate anyone who says he despises rapists. Did he mean those words? Accord cops are experts in the art of lying convincingly. What if he's pretending?

I'm the only Velez who is concerned about his soldier-like traits, and I wonder how a man so burly doesn't remind Dad of the soldiers who brutalized his wife.

I warn my family of the dangers of befriending drunken cops, but they ignore my request that they avoid eating the food Aleksey brings. I expect Olmo to trust others, even the Starvillers who mock his skin color. My dad … well, he's the eternal optimist. But Azzy? She's too comfortable around Aleksey.

I ask her about it, and she only winks at me. "I can't be scared of a guy who is crazy about my sister."

I snort, but I wish that I could believe her. I need fondness, affection. Something to balance the darkness that surrounds me. Unfortunately, Aleksey is so reserved I can't see him giving me this. Whatever he feels, I doubt that it's anything more than lust.

It'll be better to devote my energy to more pressing matters. Like getting my job back.

Poncho and I ride the train back to Starville after a day of job-hunting in Shiloh. Since Gary's attack, my paranoia about men has returned. I don't go anywhere without Poncho, and any attempt to flirt is now unthinkable.

I take out my knife as soon as we jump off in Starville.

As I pass the mall ruins, I run into someone. Someone whose arrogant gait infuriates me. Someone who has yet to answer a certain request.

Instead of saying an ordinary thing like *hi,* he passes me as though he hasn't seen me.

"Aleksey *Furt!*" I'm almost positive that his last name is pronounced *fee-uh-st,* but I made it sound like *fart* on purpose.

He doesn't turn his head. I wonder whether he has even heard me.

"Mr. *Fee-uh-st!*"

Nothing. I'm okay with his broodiness, but I won't let him ignore me.

"General Fürst!"

Maybe he is as good as I am at tuning out annoying people.

Aleksey is now several feet ahead of me. What do the Accord cops call him? Oh, yeah! He has a nickname.

"Prince Aleksey, sir?"

He finally stops and turns around. His expression is haughty, but I see a hint of amusement in it. The guy has a sense of humor after all. Unfortunately, something in his eyes makes me uneasy. For a moment, they remind me of my mother's cruelest attacker.

Not knowing what else to do now that I have his attention, I curtsey theatrically and bow my head.

"I haven't received an answer, your highness," I say, hoping that he doesn't notice my trembling hands.

The cop's grave face reveals nothing. We stand in front of each other for an eternity before I break the silence.

"Prince Aleksey, you seem to be a bit bored. May I suggest a way to use the time?"

His wary look grows starker. I notice that he doesn't smell like alcohol today.

I venture a look. "I think you'll find it pleasurable to train me in fighting. And driving?"

He's listening, but he looks reluctant. "Pleasurable," he repeats, mulling the word. Then he shakes his head. "I can't."

"You told me that before, at the glade. May I inquire why not?"

"Neutrality."

That's true. Accord cops are supposed to be neutral. They shouldn't fuel uprisings.

"May I point out that I'm a little girl in a forgotten city, and the '*very neutral*' Accord Units have been covering Patriot crimes?"

He stares at the horizon, looking slightly annoyed by my use of finger quotes.

"Besides, you mightn't have noticed, but my loyalty isn't with the Nats." I shift my weight from one foot to the other. "I'm not a Nat. I'm an American, and I won't enter a political fight. I just want to learn how to defend myself from attacks. Like the one you saved me from a few days ago."

He hasn't said yes, but something tells me he might if I say the right words.

"I heard you tell my brother, '*Give people a trout—*"

"A fish."

I wave my hand impatiently. "'... *and you feed them for a day. Teach people to fish, and you feed them for a lifetime.*' So—" I swallow before continuing. "This is similar. Thank you for defending me, but you won't be around forever."

He looks at me. It's the same hungry, penetrating look from when we first met. It shoots sparks through my body.

Aleksey takes a step closer. I fight my impulse to look at my feet. Instead, I hold his stare. To my surprise, he sighs, nods, and mutters something unintelligible before walking away.

He said yes! We didn't set a place or time, but he'll have to make good on his word. And he didn't ask for anything in return!

I'm so happy that I prance my way back to the clinic, with Poncho jumping along beside me.

I'm passing Deuteronomy Street, in front of the Accord headquarters building, when I feel him.

Oh no! I stop my prancing. There's no way he didn't see my childish display. Did he come to establish a time?

Aleksey looks like a lion about to corner his prey.

"Miss Velez, I've agreed to your request. Have you considered the deal I offered you?"

I bite my thumb, looking away. My body language screams that I still don't have an answer. I'm ready to bolt.

He steps closer. "Let's discuss the terms of my offer."

I swallow hard. "Shoot."

He shakes his head. "Not now. The glade, in four days, at dawn."

I glue my eyes to the spot where he has disappeared inside the building. Then, I take a deep breath and begin a sprint. Why the glade? Why can't we discuss his proposition now? He's so confusing.

As I hurtle along the dirty sidewalks, the howling wind brings back my usual pessimistic thoughts. In a matter of minutes, the weather has gone from scorching to windy. I adjust the hood of my cloak.

When we reach the stairs to the clinic, Poncho becomes alert. Something's happening. I climb the steps at top speed and reach for my knife holder.

When I enter the building, I don't see anyone, but voices are coming from an emergency room.

Poncho isn't in attack mode, but something is wrong.

I approach the double doors slowly. I can't see anyone. Suddenly, an agonized scream pierces the air.

"Lila!" says an anguished voice.

I enter the room and freeze in horror.

CHAPTER 13

A V boy

THE WOUNDS MAKE THE body on the operating table unrecognizable. He lies on his stomach while Dad takes care of them. The floor under the table is smeared with blood.

A shiver creeps down my spine.

The sight reminds me of something I read recently on TCR's old gadget: an autopsy form. It's like I still have that report in front of me. In my mind, I create a checklist of possible causes of death. It matches the words that Dad's saying now.

Broken bones

Acute bleeding

Anal tearing

Rectum perforation

But the victim didn't die this time. He survived and is in unbearable pain, his clothes stained with blood and fecal matter.

In my shock and confusion, I can't figure out who he is. I do know that he's dealing with a form of castration. *He's lost a part of himself that he'll never recover.*

"It seems there was more than one attacker," says Dad.

I cross the doorway, my mouth dry. I scope out the room. Mathew, Cara, and Luke stare at the floor, wearing worried faces.

The survivor is shirtless. Someone has drawn on his skin with blood and dark ink. His mouth is bleeding and has all the signs that it was forced open against his will. Rey kneels next to the survivor as a seizure strikes his battered body.

Duque Diaz.

My eyes fill with tears. Why Duque? I care for him as much as I do for Rey.

I want to comfort Rey, but nothing comes to mind. What do you say to someone who has witnessed attacks on those he loves the most? First the woman he loved, and now his brother.

What if it had been Olmo? Or Azzy?

Duque's agitated jerks ease into an exhausted calm.

I timidly walk toward Rey, who appears physically unscathed.

"Are you ... do you have any wounds?"

He shakes his head.

I hate seeing him like this. Hesitantly, I put my arm around Rey's broad shoulders. It's my way of telling him, *I'm here for you.* He holds my hand and we stay like that for some time.

Nobody speaks.

After a while, a strained voice breaks the silence.

"I have to go." Cara leaves the room, fighting back tears. This scene must be a horrible reminder of the abuse she's suffered.

Luke Rivers answers my unspoken question. "We were almost at the railroad when we saw soldiers coming. We separated to hide in the trees. When the coast was clear, we couldn't find Duque. Then we heard his screams." He pauses. I swear he's shivering. "And we found him ... like this—"

"It looks like two soldiers attacked him," says my dad. "A female and a male."

Duque stirs. "Let me die," he whispers.

Rey's eyes are full of an agony we both know well. It's the feeling of powerlessness when the people you love are suffering.

Dad looks at Rey. "I stopped most of the bleeding, but—"

Baron Diaz storms into the room, demanding to know what happened. As he hears the story, his expression changes, from one of concern to one of disapproval.

"Why didn't he fight?" he asks, making us gasp.

"Father!" Rey's voice is a mix of shock and contained anger.

"All evidence shows that he did, and look what happened, *compadre*. Resistance made his attackers even more violent," says Dad.

I debate whether I should give Rey and Duque some privacy. I want to stay with them, but something tells me that Duque, unconscious though he is, doesn't want anyone to see him like this. Especially not a female friend.

Dad makes the decision for me. "Everyone, please leave the room. Duque's wounds will need particular care. Rey, you may stay."

Rey's gaze is intense. He reluctantly lets go of me and waits until he thinks I can't see him. Then he drops to his knees and covers his head with his hands. His despair breaks my heart. I feel desperate, too, but for different reasons.

If Duque's life is forever changed, I hope he at least had the chance to love Veronica physically. I hope he wasn't unsullied.

I close the door behind me and head to my room. The image of the broken boy on the table will haunt my dreams.

I make my way to the clinic after a string of unsuccessful attempts to get a job in Shiloh. Duque's attack isn't uncommon in Starville, but it still stirs the pot, so to speak. People who usually ignore me try to make conversation, but I know they're only being nosy about Duque.

According to Dad, his godson's anus was almost destroyed in the attack. Duque has had a colostomy and will remain at the clinic for a while, so the Diaz relatives spend a lot of time around, even though Duque has made it clear that he wants to be left alone. It cannot be easy for him. He must feel as though his attackers emasculated him. It doesn't help that Veronica and her father visited the clinic to ask him to liberate her from their engagement.

Baron's family is a tight-knit group. My aunt, Olga Busko, and Pastor Adriel Lee-Rivers were dismissed when they tried to visit Duque. Not even the multitude of Diaz cousins and aunts have been able to see him. I know that Rey needs space as well. I tried to comfort him once, and he acted as though he didn't want to see me. We've had more soldiers than usual at the clinic lately, so I remain out of sight. When Rey's ready, he'll come to me.

I can't stop thinking about the hell that Duque's going through. I can't shake the feeling that the next victim will be me. If my worst nightmares come true and someone violates me, will I be able to live a normal life? To enjoy love at an emotional level? A physical level?

At that precise moment, I hear a velvety voice. Turning, I find Tristan flashing a dazzling smile and hurrying to catch up with me as I pass a graffitied building.

"Hello, Miss Velez," he says, his accent thick. "Are you on your way to the clinic? May I accompany you?"

I look around nervously. "Isn't that fraternizing?" The punishment for Accord cops who fraternize can get nasty. They're supposed to be neutral.

He grins. "You're worthy of deportation, torture, and death."

I can't help but smile timidly. Tristan is so easy to like. Walking to the clinic with him by my side—and with him carrying my backpack—elevates my mood.

Tristan's twenty-one and has been a cop for four months. I'm usually tongue-tied around strangers, especially young guys. He doesn't mind the long lapses in our conversation, though. In between polite questions and his spilling the beans about Gary's whereabouts——he was sent to a hospital in Gyges before being deported——Tristan talks a lot about his boss. Evidently, he looks up to him. I'm surprised to hear that Aleksey is only twenty-five—he looks so mature. But hearing that he has never lost a fight and that he's a lone wolf is unsurprising.

"Soldiers and civilians admire Prince Aleksey, but they don't accept him because he's different. Most people don't see him as a human being, but the Velez family does."

"What are you talking about?" I ask, feeling intrigued. "Girls swarm around him all the time!"

Tristan stops walking and hands me a pair of headphones. "Yes, be-cause he's attractive, but they think of him as a stunning piece of flesh, not a person. They see him as a freak because he's a giant. Listen."

His j-device projects an image. I put on the headphones. Tristan has recorded his patrol and something more. I recognize Elena and her girlfriends talking about Aleksey in sexual terms. Admiringly, at first. But then ...

"Can you imagine having kids with someone like him?" a giggling girl asks.

"No way. What a creep! He's gorgeous, but there's no room for his freaky offspring inside me," answers Elena. *"His dick, on the other hand ..."*

Their words infuriate me. They'd be lucky if someone like Aleksey did so much as turn to look at them. Too bad I can't fight an untrained person because Elena has been getting on my nerves lately.

Tristan smiles, apparently pleased with my reaction. "Prince Aleksey rejects everyone because he likes his solitude, but also because women see him as a sex toy. He's been lonely forever, devoting every minute of his time to our missions. But I'm sure he'd be different, if he found the right girl."

I raise an eyebrow. "Why are you telling me this?"

"Because there's been some diplomatic turmoil. Nats and Patriots regard Gary Sleecket as a war hero. He saved many civilian lives from both countries. Now, many people around North America see Prince Aleksey as the bad guy."

Feeling irritated, I kick a pebble out of the way. Of course! Gary, the abusive cop, would become popular while Aleksey, the outlier, would be regarded as the villain.

Tristan doesn't like this either. I'd never seen him scowl before. "He doesn't care, but I wish people understood him more. He's saved my life twice, and yours, too."

I make a mental note to analyze all this later. That's when I notice some girls shooting me darker looks than usual. They're always lusting after the cops, and here I am, effortlessly talking to one. Unchaperoned.

"You Starvillers aren't exactly welcoming, are you?"

Tristan's offhand, friendly attitude makes it easy to talk to him. "They could be worse, Mr. Froh. I don't think you're ready to ask for a Starville girl's hand, are you?"

"Their hands?" Tristan chuckles. "Prince Aleksey and I are the only un-married cops in our battalion, but we can't marry Americans. If we married a Patriot citizen, Nats wouldn't allow us into their country, or vice versa. It'd be a disaster if Americans kept us out of occupied towns. There are enough abuses as it is."

"Because the UNNO does nothing to stop them," I say sharply.

His face becomes serious. "We've made mistakes, but the good out-weighs the bad. You don't have the official numbers, but I do. Americans need us, and we want to help."

Another delusional optimist like Dad, who sees only what he wants to see. Doesn't he know that most Accord cops turn a blind eye to Pa-triot crimes? Didn't a cop recently attack me? No point in discussing this with him. Let's see how he acts on recruitment day. When the troops break the recruitment protocol, will he risk his life to stop them?

I look around at some children playing on a deserted street. "So you'll protect Starvillers even if they aren't agreeable, won't you?"

Tristan observes me intently with an expression of fascination.

"Well, Starvillers have their fun side, too," he says. "I can't wait for the Assumption of Mary feast."

The Assumption Feast and the Anniversary of the Patriot Constitution occur on the same date. Starvillers pretend to celebrate a Patriot holiday when, in reality, they celebrate the religious party. One of the few liberties in the occupied territories is freedom of creed. Religious books are the only readings approved by Patriots, and the soldiers never miss a Sunday service.

I kick a piece of rubble. "How can people celebrate at a time like this?"

"They were going to cancel after the air raid, but we've never been to a town feast, so we pushed for it. Prince Aleksey took charge of the music. Are you going to the party?"

In response, I flinch.

"You should come," he says flirtatiously. "I can walk you home afterward."

It almost sounds like a date, but I won't read much into his invitation. Anyway, I'm glad that I got new information about Aleksey.

I understand his proposition now.

CHAPTER 14

His full consent

I CALL IT A DAY, exhausted after hours of training. I'm wearing only short white pants and a white tank, but the heat emanating from my body makes me feel as though I'm overdressed.

I'm about to go to the clinic shower when I hear steps outside my door. There's a soft knock.

"Can I enter?" asks a male voice.

I open the door to find Rey standing there. His amber eyes peer into mine. Rey needs me. His face reveals desperation and anger. I haven't seen him this distressed since the troops recruited Angie, and it's a heartbreaking sight.

"Duque." He blinks repeatedly. "He says ... he'll kill himself."

"Oh, no! Duque!"

I understand how Duque feels. I'd want to be dead, too, if they recruited me.

"TCR ... I convinced Duque to join ... to fight against Patriots, against recruitment—" says Rey, his hands in his pockets. "Look where TCR got him. Where *I* got him."

"I want to see him. I want to help," I say, but Rey shakes his head.

"He still doesn't want to see anyone. He just yelled at me that he wants to be alone."

I pull him into a tight hug. I know what it's like to have a family hurt by violence. I can't stand to see Rey so heartbroken again. I want to do something, say something, but I've never been good with words.

I wrap my arms around his neck and rest my head on his chest. He pulls me closer.

I don't know how long we stay like this.

Eventually, we move to lie on my cot. We're facing each other, talking softly. Not about TCR as we usually do. Rey talks about his pain and worries. He tells me how much he wants to kill Duque's attackers. He wants to protect Reyna, as he promised on his mother's deathbed, but now he thinks he's failed Duque. Rey doesn't mention it, but I know that he feels guilty about what happened to Angie, too. He says that he fears he'll never be free to start his own family. I feel the same. The war has hurt us both. His pain is my pain; his fears, my fears.

My hospital cot is too small for the both of us. Our bodies press together. I feel the rhythm of his breath, his chest rising and falling. He shifts to get a better grip on me and accidentally brushes my breast. The sensation of his body against mine makes me shiver. It feels thrilling and, in a way, arousing.

The atmosphere in the room changes. Rey must have noticed it. The tenderness in his eyes has turned into something else.

He places his hand beneath my chin, forcing me to look up before he kisses me deeply, his lips teasing mine apart. We're so close that I immediately feel when he hardens.

I'm so shocked that my first impulse is to reject him. But my slight push on his muscular shoulders doesn't stop him. If anything, his kiss grows more intense.

His trembling hand on my thigh slides down, bending my leg to bring it up. His hands roam around my stomach, my waist, and my hips. They gently move up and down my bare leg, stopping at my calf. Rey moans in my mouth, and I find that the sounds of his pleasure have an unwanted arousing effect. I don't want to feel like this now, not when he's vulnerable.

He removes his shirt and rolls me over on the bed so that he's on top. Rey's lips graze their way from my lips to my neck.

He started this. I might think he wants me, but he's not being himself. Should I stop him? But I don't want him to stop. My mind repeats a litany. *Recruitment. I should experience this before recruitment.*

Hesitantly, I trail my hands over the solid muscles of his stomach. He responds automatically, rubbing his body against mine.

"Rey, are you sure of this?" I need his full acceptance.

He smiles, but doesn't answer. He slowly rolls up my tank to kiss my stomach. I assume that's his way of saying yes.

I finally have his full consent. I'll lose my virtue tonight.

CHAPTER 15

Curiosity

WE'VE KISSED FOR SO long that my lips feel swollen. It's been a nice make-out session, but neither of us has dared to move things forward.

Rey's shirt and pants are on the floor, but I'm still wearing my white tank and underwear. We haven't seen each other naked yet, and my clothes feel like a barrier. It's evident his body is ready to take the next step, but his mind seems to need a little push.

Hoping that he doesn't laugh at me, I place his hands on the hem of my tank. Rey tenses but takes the invitation along with the top.

A rush of self-consciousness makes me blush; I have some imperfections here and there. What if he compares my frame to his ex's flawless figure? But Rey's eyes tell me he doesn't find any fault with my body.

He leans in to kiss the skin above the edge of my bra. His mouth follows the line of my undergarment. I close my eyes and moan. His hands on my back fumble to unhook my bra.

A sound startles us, and we pull away from each other.

Aleksey is in the entryway, looking at us with disapproval. His voice sounds casual but forced. "I was looking for Dr. Velez. Obviously, he's not around."

Rey jumps off the bed. Aleksey briefly glances at my pointed nipples showing under my bra while I fumble for my tank and shorts. Rey notices it, too, and his expression changes from one of surprise to one of anger. He throws a sheet over my body.

Aleksey points a finger at Rey, but his eyes are on me.

"You might not know this, Starviller, but this is my clinic. Dr. Velez—and, by extension, his family—can stay as part of the staff. But you're wearing out your welcome."

"This isn't your clinic, and you have no business in here," says Rey furiously.

"I'm the leader of the Accord Unit that built this clinic. Respect visiting hours."

Rey strides toward Aleksey, fuming. "I don't remember *you* carrying brick after brick to build the clinic."

Arrogantly, with an almost bored expression, Aleksey points toward the door, indicating that Rey should leave. It only irritates Rey further.

"You have no authority here! I won't take orders from you," Rey snaps.

Aleksey speaks in a derisive tone, "And I won't take seriously a guy who has his penis' head on full display."

I suppress a nervous giggle. In *truth*, the erect top portion of Rey's penis shows above the band of his underwear. If I weren't so embarrassed, I'd find it funny.

Rey's face is humorless as he slides his pants up, fuming. His muscles bulge in rage. Before I can blink, he throws a punch, aiming at Aleksey's massive chest. The Accord cop easily blocks the blow. That only infuriates Rey, who hurls himself against Aleksey. I never saw Rey attack anyone with such intensity, not even Gary.

Aleksey, on the other hand, yawns as he blocks Rey's attacks. It's as though he's only toying with Rey to enrage him.

"Enough!" I yell. Neither pays attention.

After several failed attempts, Rey lands a right hook on Aleksey's jaw. Aleksey's eyes turn murderous. I've seen those eyes before. If Aleksey uses his full force on Rey, he'll kill him.

I take a broomstick and swing at them. Both stop to stare at me.

"I said enough!" I force a measure of sternness into my voice. "Both of you get out!"

Aleksey shakes his head. "I won't go until he's gone."

I turn to Rey, the one I'm sure can be reasonable. My eyes plead with him, but Rey isn't looking at me. His eyes continue to glare at the mountain in front of him. "I won't leave you alone with *my* Angie."

Rey's words make me take a step away from him. Was he thinking about her while we were touching? Should I care?

When Rey realizes what he's just said, he blushes and seems ready to bolt from the room.

Aleksey turns to look at me, a malicious glint in his eye. "You want to give your *virginity* to someone who mistakes you for another?"

The V-word. So unnecessary. My fists clench, and hot anger courses through me. I miss those times when I couldn't picture Aleksey as someone capable of speaking in full sentences. If he's going to say things like that, I'd rather he shut up.

Rey's ready to fight again, but I stop him. He leaves the room after throwing a dark look at Aleksey—a look that says, *I'll get you back for this.*

"Now it's your turn to go," I say acidly. "As soon as you tell me why you're here—and don't give me that 'searching for my father' crap."

"I saw your friend coming up, but never saw him leave. I assumed he wouldn't stay with his brother. That maybe he needed a warmer bed." Aleksey looks me up and down. "Not that I blame him."

I glare at him. He knows I've been looking forward to my deflowering. Not only did he interrupt it, he also has the nerve to make fun of me.

He starts to leave the room, his red cape swishing as he turns around.

Aleksey is near the door when my knife almost hits him. Years of military training make him duck reflexively. The knife nails his cape to the wooden wall. I take pleasure in his look of surprise when he turns to me.

"You told me I could take this room, but that doesn't give you the right to tell me what to do with it!" My body shudders. "If you want, I'll move out. But never, ever, enter my room again."

I hear the sound of his cape ripping as he frees it from the knife, but by then I'm stalking down the corridor. I'm almost to the courtyard when I turn to glare at him one last time. He's glaring back.

He says loudly enough for me to hear, "Your curiosity will get you hurt."

"Curiosity?" I look at him in disbelief. I can't keep my voice down. "I'm not curious! I'm desperate!"

Seething with fury, Aleksey and I walk in opposite directions.

Chapter

16

"Among the fluctuation of the river currents, an abyss as green as the sea, its extension and profundity as immense as the ocean opened before me: the eyes of a beautiful girl.

I succumbed into that abyss instantly, like a man who falls from the highest cliff into the ocean ...

... and I drowned."

General Fürst's journal

Laying down arms

IT'S ALMOST DAWN, AND the sloshing of the river harmonizes with the loud chirping of birds. Excited, Poncho runs toward the water and jumps in. The orange flowers that frame the glade look more colorful than ever as a warm, soft breeze rustles them.

I don't come here just for Divine and Joey. I come for the peace and beauty of this solitary place.

Aleksey hasn't come to the glade in two days. Fine by me. Thinking about his arrogance brings a scowl to my face.

I lie down and let my mind wander.

That night in my room, Rey opened a door that I thought for sure we'd closed. But now that I know he won't reject me if I ask him to have sex, I won't.

I stretch my arms above my head and close my eyes.

Rey was stressed that night because of Duque. He should think it through, prove to himself that he wants me again. Maybe if we let things flow, I can have a magical sexual debut with him. It won't meet my idealistic expectations, but somehow it'll be enough.

I'm lost in my thoughts when the air charges with a heated magnetism. He doesn't make a sound, but I know that he's standing next to me.

I open my eyes. We aren't happy to see each other, but I want to keep things civil.

"General Fürst."

He nods briefly without looking at me and sits in his usual spot. I sit up, inhaling deeply. He doesn't smell like alcohol today.

His muteness lasts for an hour, during which we do nothing but enjoy the view.

Perhaps the key to his speech is booze; he must need alcohol to communicate. Well, that's unacceptable. He'll talk to me normally— no drinks involved.

"You know, that thing you said I ... *um* ... was curious about. What you rudely interrupted—"

He's still impassive, but I can tell he's listening.

"Curiosity isn't what motivates me. I know what *it* is about. Even before I became a ... you know ..." I'm trying to make him break his silence and complete my sentence. It doesn't work.

"I have plenty of reasons. None of which are curiosity. I was eight the first time I saw a couple doing it."

The tiniest twitch of his eyebrow tells me he's fighting to keep a poker face.

"It wasn't intentional. They were my parents."

He's preoccupied with his cape, but he has to be grossed out.

"I entered their room without knocking first. They'd quarreled that night, so I thought he was hurting her. They became awfully embarrassed and dressed quickly. Mom put me to bed, and, the very next day, I got the bees and flowers talk."

"From your mom?"

Ha! There! I got an answer. I grin. "Both of them. Don't wince. There was no morbid curiosity on my part. It took me years to realize what happened that day."

He finally looks up. A thrilling sensation runs through my veins when those perfect blue eyes look into mine.

"I'm not sexually ignorant. I've observed ... I've read books."

He looks at me intensely. "You're ignorant, Miss Velez. You just don't realize how much you still have to learn."

"Because I'm all theory and no practice?"

He nods and lies down on the grass with his hands propping up his head.

I throw a pebble into the current. "Mr. Fürst, I'm not so untouched anymore. I've been kissed in intimate places." My collarbone and cleavage are private places, aren't they? Though I wish my breasts had been kissed, too. And I wish this conversation didn't turn me on.

He looks frustrated. "If you're so determined, why don't you take a random guy?"

How do I explain that, for me, sex isn't just the physical act of rubbing together genitals for pleasure? I don't know why, but I want him to understand.

"Seeing my parents like that left a mark on me. When they were together, they became a single entity. Because of them, I'm convinced there should be a connection between sex and being one. Sex and being in a long, committed relationship. Sex and being in love. What I feel for my friend is—" Every time I mention Rey, the crease between Aleksey's brow deepens. "Nothing like that, but I care for him. And—" I shake my head.

The wind ruffles his long hair. "It would be a mistake. Your sister's right. You go through too much trouble to check this off your to-do list."

I sigh. I've never opened up like this to anyone, but something about him tells me he'll listen. "There's no to-do list. There's recruitment."

Aleksey nods. Maybe he's always quiet because he's a good listener. The word *recruitment* has elicited a look of disapproval from the cop. I know he understands me now.

"You might think I'm silly. All this love talk—"

Kind blue eyes meet mine. "Not at all. There's logic, even poetry, in your expectations."

At that moment, Divine and Joey arrive at the meadow. She smiles when she sees Aleksey's back. Immediately she jumps into action, showing off more than usual. "Enjoy it, sick perverts!" she shouts.

She practically tears off Joey's clothes. In seconds, they are both naked, and she's clinging to him, her legs wrapped around his waist. Joey presses her back against a tree and slides his hands down so that they rest on her buttocks.

I watch, fascinated. Out of the corner of my eye, I notice that he's looking at me. Then, to my disappointment, Aleksey takes out a flask. I reach for it without hesitation.

"Let me drink a little of what you have."

His voice is stern. "Just a sip."

Liquor tastes horrible. I use that as an excuse to drop the flask and let the liquid pour out. "Oops!" I put on my most innocent face. He doesn't look angry. There's a tinge of amusement in his eyes as he watches the lovers' antics.

My desperation to experience it makes me forget that sex has a fun side, too. The way they're clenching their bodies as Joey struggles to maintain his hold on Divine isn't as arousing as it is comical. Aleksey fights a smile. I openly grin.

Joey loses his grip on Divine, and his erection goes on full display.

"Small ..." Aleksey pauses as though he thinks he'd offend me if he said the word *penis*. "... thing." He wouldn't have offended me, but I don't want to remember *his* thing at this moment.

"Mm, let's call it *the truth*," I say quietly.

He bursts out laughing. "The *truth*? You can't handle the *truth*!"

I've never seen him laugh before. His joy makes him look younger, and God! He looks so damn hot when he's happy.

I'm done. So is Divine. I get to my feet silently and wind my way back home.

Aleksey catches up to me. Throwing him a sideways look, I see him smiling crookedly.

"So you want to discover the *truth*? The naked *truth*?" He makes it sound so dirty and sexy that I don't answer. Aleksey has an effect on me that alters not only my speech, but also the rhythm of my heart. It's a combination of forbidden attraction and the fear I have of soldiers.

Poncho gallops happily around us. As we make our way to the city, the road becomes uneven. A wave of heat travels toward my lower body every time Aleksey places his hand at the small of my back to steady me. Something I've been dying to know comes to my mind. Now that he's unusually talkative, I have to ask him. "Your proposal, the one you gave me a few days ago ... I'm still considering it. Do I have a deadline?"

He shakes his head.

"But even if I don't accept, will you train me in driving and parkour techniques?

Aleksey answers as if this should be obvious. "I've already agreed to that."

"If I accept your proposal but refuse to have sex with you, what do you gain?"

He gives me his hand to help me step on a rock as the road begins to climb up the hillside. "Hard to explain."

"What guarantees do I have that you won't try anything else?"

Aleksey pats Poncho's head. "No guarantees. Take it or leave it," he says harshly. "But if it makes you feel more secure, you can bring your dog."

"Why do you talk to me more than to others?"

He pauses before answering. "Maybe because you're a voyeur. I like that you've found a safe, harmless way to express a part of your sexuality. You may be inexperienced, but you have a kink."

"The same kink you have."

"This is not my kink."

I ask even though I suspect he won't answer. "What's your kink?"

He looks away, and we walk in silence for a while across a steep road flanked by trees. It's not fair that he knows so much about me while he remains a mystery.

"I hate that you're hiding the *truth*." I cover my mouth to suppress a giggle.

He stops walking and grabs my shoulders, forcing me to look at him. His hands cause a surge of warmth through my body. "Stop the jokes. You can't handle the *truth*. You need to start with basic training before moving on to heavier practices."

I want to say something, but my tongue refuses to cooperate.

His voice is raspy, low, and seductive. "I can teach you. If you want."

I break eye contact, feeling my face flush. Aleksey doesn't use words much, but when he does, sparks course through my veins. I force my voice to sound steady. "Only the basics?"

"Or whatever you want. You dictate the pace of our … lessons."

I look at him in disbelief. Is he serious?

"It will be educational for me, too," he says confidently.

"Educational? How?"

His accented voice comes out as a sexy growl. "I've always had it … rough. I've never been with a V-girl. Being gentle, taking my time *with you* sounds … incredibly sensual to me."

"You'd get bored."

He shakes his head. "Why do you care? This is about you." His eyes travel over my body. It doesn't feel offensive. It feels seductive. "Regardless, sex is an instinctive act. You may be one of those birds that can fly immediately, or you may be the bird that crashes to the ground because you stepped out of the nest when you weren't ready. You need guidance. My guidance."

His subtle, clean, masculine scent intoxicates me. I realize we've been unconsciously leaning toward each other. I step back, but he closes the distance again.

"I'm your best option. I have enough experience to guide you, teach you, and protect you from harm," he says huskily.

"What harm?"

He brushes my cheek lightly with his finger. The touch electrifies my skin. "Harm from other guys, from your friend, from yourself."

I think about his size, knowing that I'm not ready for this man. "If I don't want to go all the way—"

"Then we won't. If you want to, this could be an addition to the other skills I'll teach you."

I keep stepping back, shortening the distance between me and the trees. "Wouldn't that be fraternizing? You're not supposed to fraternize with Nats. They'll deport you."

He looks at me as though I'm crazy. "So? The world is full of places for us to go—if you wanted to come with me."

He's deluded. No country would admit me without a passport tattoo. But hearing how his deep, masculine voice carries those words is heaven.

"They'll execute you," I say.

"I've put my life at risk for others ever since I joined the Army. It would be a nice change to risk my life for something I want for *myself*." His humorless face smolders. "I crave you."

Aleksey craves me. My cheeks warm at his words, and I don't know what to say. He looks as though he has been dying to let out those words for a while. His eyes look at me expectantly. I can recognize his lust but … is there a difference between *lusting* and *craving*?

I shake my head. It doesn't matter, anyway. He's off-limits. Still, I'm overwhelmed with feelings I haven't felt before.

I look at him questioningly.

"I don't know anything about you."

The cop looks down at himself and smiles wickedly. "You know my feet are big. What else is left to know?"

"Many things." Like the people for whom he cares. For a few minutes, I bombard him with questions. *Who taught you to play bass? Who do you fight for? Is there anyone waiting for your return?* He moves closer with each question, though he politely refuses to answer.

We stand close to each other, and electricity sizzles in the air. I forget what I was about to ask.

My back hits a tree. I can't retreat anymore, so I tread to my side, stepping on a rock. This reduces our height difference a little. He presses his palms on the tree trunk next to my head, trapping me.

Looking at me intently, Aleksey takes a strand of my hair and twirls it, then tucks it behind my ear. The way his hand lingers at my earlobe leaves my skin tingling.

My voice comes out breathy. "I'll … have to think … your offer … through."

His voice is low, husky. "I'll give you something to think about."

Aleksey slips his hand around my waist, pulling me closer. He positions my body so that the height difference isn't an obstacle. He's building anticipation, making the wait for his lips deliciously torturous. His face slowly approaches, the deliberation clear.

When his lips touch mine, it's a soft brush that makes my body melt into liquid fire. Then they move against my mouth hungrily.

And everything that isn't his body vanishes into thin air.

He's showing me that he can be gentle, but I want more. My hands grab his shoulders. I press my body tightly against his. He mirrors my action with his pelvis, blending it with mine. Showing me through his erection the promise of greater pleasures.

I whimper. Automatically, the kiss deepens. His bulky arms tighten their grip on my body. My skin burns and tingles at all the points where our bodies are touching.

He kisses me deeply and lingering at times, playfully pulling my lower lip at others. Expertly, he moves his lips to my earlobe and neck before returning to my mouth. He doesn't make me feel like he's kissing me. He makes me feel like he owns me. I feel it in the way his hands move up and down my sides, the way his bulky arms constrict me. It makes my blood bubble deliciously with a desire I've never felt before.

I can't get enough of him.

Aleksey keeps kissing me like this until he finally pulls back, touching his forehead to mine and resting his hands at the small of my back. I struggle to control my breathing. My heart pounds in my chest, and I'm sure he can hear it. It's not embarrassing because I can see that I affect him, too. He's struggling to recover his cool, arrogant demeanor.

I've never been kissed like this. Come to think of it, I've never been truly kissed, until now. It was either Warren Lee-Rivers forcing me or Rey not being himself. It never felt natural—never felt like a ride to the moon and back.

"Surrender," Aleksey whispers, still holding me tightly. He skims his nose along my jaw to my neck. "Surrender to me and I'll …"

His lips at the hollow of my throat speak louder than words. If I surrender, the pleasure will be like nothing I've felt before. I can barely manage it now. If he makes me feel this way when both of us are fully dressed, how would I feel if we were scantily clothed, exploring our bodies in a private place? I'm dying to find out, but I can't overcome my reservations.

I've willingly yielded to a moment with someone I should consider an enemy. For all I know, he could have forced other girls into his wicked ways. Don't Accord cops ask for *compensation* in exchange for their help? He's helped my family, but that's not reason enough to lay down my arms. I don't know to what extent I can trust him with my safety and my heart.

But as I gaze into his eyes, which at this moment look kind and expectant, I decide that none of that matters. He might look like a soldier, but he doesn't act like one. He may have a past, but it's his present actions that count. He's a military man, but if we slept together, it'd be consensual. In my book, the word *consensual* is the key to my acceptance.

My breathing is still ragged, and my face must be all shades of red as his lips continue their exploration of my neck. Yet the overwhelming lust that Aleksey stirs in me can never match the history of mutual support Rey and I have. Besides, there's a certain arrogance in Aleksey that makes me think he might be mocking me.

I reluctantly escape the prison of his embrace. "You have to know that Rey … Come on! Don't scowl. Well, the guy you mocked is still my first choice."

He looks incredulous. Why would I prefer a regular guy over the quintessential super-soldier? The eighth wonder of penises?

"Him? You're like an ocean during a storm, whereas he's a slimy, moldy puddle," Aleksey says scornfully. He leans slowly to kiss my neck again. "You can't deny it. The way your body enjoys my touch … I can tell the sensations are new to you. He can't make you feel like that. He never has and never will."

I refuse to admit he's right. "I feel lustful with you because, apparently, every girl feels like that when you're around. And you know how to touch the right spots." His scowling face looks slightly smug, so I add quickly, "But that's not enough."

I stride toward the city, and he follows me.

"By the way, I'd appreciate it if you didn't mock Rey again."

He raises a cocky eyebrow "Or …?"

"I'll make you pay for it."

His only answer is a skeptical, crooked smile.

Chapter 17

"*Recruitment gives a choice to the hundreds of Nationalist civilians who would otherwise perish due to the consequences of a war **their** leaders started. Sixty-three percent of the recruits get married to our honorable soldiers, becoming Patriot citizens in the process. By contributing to the Patriot cause, recruits improve their living conditions.*"

Extract of Maximillian Kei's speech for the United Neutral Nations Organization Spring Conference

Hope

"OUCH!" I LICK THE finger I've just stabbed with the needle. The examination room fills with the laughter of my siblings. They've been repeating sexual puns all afternoon. Now they're competing to come up with the best stabbing accident joke.

The purpose of my embroidering efforts is worth the age-inappropriate jokes. I've been stitching the bridal sheets for the last authorized wedding before the recruitment. Sara Jenkins, an ex-Comanche, is engaged to a mysterious groom. I struggle to decorate the opening that will allow the husband to enter his bride without *offending her modesty* during the wedding night. The white sheets are a huge deal since they'll be displayed for the entire town the morning after. Starvillers expect that blood will stain the sheets.

It's tedious labor, but at least the Jenkinses will pay me well. I'm not at my best because I've been thinking about Aleksey's proposal. About his mouth on mine. A soft, sweet oppression constricts my chest whenever I think about that kiss. I can alleviate it only by sighing. Sighs and needles aren't a good combination.

Azzy covers her head with one of the sheets and puts her mouth through the opening, puckering her lips so that they look like a duck beak.

"And they won't see their bodies while doing it? Imagine if the groom is bigger than this. Poor Sara! I can't believe this is part of her '*thrust-oh*.'"

"*Trousseau,* Azalea. *Troo-soh,*" I explain.

"More like true-sore," says Azzy, tossing aside the sheet and giggling.

Dad enters the room and perches himself on a table for another homeschooling session. He's heard our sexual banter, but he's used to it.

I glance at Olmo, who, sitting on a stool next to the examination table, suddenly looks serious. Despite his mirthful nature, he's acting strange today. Perhaps it's because lately he's been struggling to breathe, even with his inhaler. Or maybe it's because today's lesson is about medicine, his least favorite subject. Having a disease like fibrosis type-Z is bound to create a distaste for talking about illnesses.

Lessons without our solar e-reader are tedious. To lighten them, Dad plays *Guess the Disease.* I have avoided homeschooling since I turned eighteen, but today I'll participate. I like medicine.

"The immune system turns against the patient."

"Lupus!" I say.

Dad nods. "Rigidity of muscles. Body functions slow down."

"Catalpsexy," says Olmo.

"Catalepsy," Azzy corrects.

"Inflammation of the bowel. It can be alleviated by a gluten-free diet."

I hesitate. "Cellist … Celia?"

Dad corrects me. "Celiac."

The game goes on for several rounds before Olmo interrupts. "Dad, I need to go to the washroom. It's urgent."

Dad looks concerned. "Are you struggling to breathe again?"

Olmo's tone is innocently serious. "No, I think I got my period."

Uh?

Azzy bursts out laughing while Dad blinks. Both twins know perfectly well the mechanics of the female cycle. Olmo is forgetful and imaginative, but this is ridiculous.

Dad climbs down from the table and sits on his cart. "Olmo, men don't have periods."

"*Eh*? The brown spots I have in my underpants … Azzy told me I should get a tampon and—"

Azalea plays innocent. "I never said such a thing."

When Olmo returns to the ER, my dad checks his blood pressure and temperature, then asks him several questions about possible bloody discharge. It becomes evident that Olmo hasn't really been spotting his underwear ... at least not with blood. Azzy has messed with his gullibility.

Dad shoots Azzy a *we'll-talk-about-this-later* look. "Olmo, diarrhea and periods are very different things."

Azzy smiles maliciously. "Diarrhea is hereditary; it runs in your *jeans.*"

My dad sighs. "Don't listen to her, Olmo. You've been eating too much of Mr. Fürst's food, haven't you?"

Olmo's face changes from slightly embarrassed to exceedingly confused. He opens his mouth to speak but closes it after a moment of hesitation. His attitude is unusual, and I realize that there's more to this than mere confusion. I'm getting worried about my brother.

Olmo looks at Azzy for a long moment before saying in a detached voice, "When you get your period, would you give me some blood?"

Azzy's face is priceless, but I can't find humor in her disgusted expression when I observe Olmo. What's wrong with him?

"*Ew!*" shouts Azzy. "You're crazy."

Olmo says something that makes my stomach twist into a knot.

"The blood of a V-girl heals, and I'm tired of being sick all the time."

My legs shake, and I sink to the floor. For a while, nobody moves or says anything. I desperately want Azzy to say something sassy that will make us all laugh, but she doesn't. The only sound comes from Aleksey's mournful music.

Olmo never mentions his disease. He goes to extremes to avoid it by creating all kinds of imaginary worlds. Not that we press the topic much. It's an uncomfortable reminder of a cruel reality—the reality that Olmo is living on borrowed time. We always treat Olmo as though he's healthy, but he's growing up. He can't keep reality at bay by making up stories much longer.

Dad comes to his senses first, and he hugs my brother. That stirs Azzy out of her silence. "No, you idiot. The blood of a *virgin* doesn't cure diseases."

There's bitterness in her irritated tone, and a tinge of unspoken misery. The misery of knowing that, as much as he wants to, and as much as we wish for it, my brother can't magically fight death. He needs medical treatment.

Olmo looks at Azzy. His voice is grave. "That's not what the soldiers told me."

I gasp. Olmo's interaction with soldiers is a terrifying revelation, but Dad looks at him tenderly. "They're superstitious, Olmo. Don't you think that if they were right, I would've already cured you?"

"I don't know. Maybe it has to be the first period. *Ow!* Don't slap my head, Azalea! Dad, look at her!"

Dad's voice is unusually stern. "Azalea, stop it."

Olmo rocks on his heels. "It's just … I want V-blood because … I don't want to die."

Nothing breaks the silence this time. It's heartbreaking to realize that Olmo is not only more aware of his illness than I thought, but that he's also sicker than I wanted to admit.

After what seems an eternity, Dad leads Olmo out of the room, his cart creaking. I know they'll have a conversation. Before today, Olmo has dismissed every attempt my father has made to explain his illness. Azzy follows to eavesdrop, but I stay rooted to the spot. I don't need to hear how Dad will address death with him. I know Dad will be honest as usual, but he'll infuse his explanations with hope.

I pace the room anxiously. Hope. The feeling that keeps my dad alive. Can hope save Olmo, too?

After a few moments, I clench my fists and dash out of the room. Perhaps there's hope for Olmo, but we have to be proactive. I'm not for passive optimism. There's something I can do.

I can and I will accept Aleksey's offer.

The metal scaffold that leads to Aleksey's room screeches under my weight. I knock nervously. He must be around. I heard him playing his bass recently.

Time goes by. Aleksey doesn't answer.

Perhaps he doesn't want to see me. This morning, because of the overwhelming sensation his kisses awoke, I felt the strange compulsion to grab his hand and hold it as we walked toward town. But he looked remarkably uncomfortable and retracted his hand from mine. As soon as we arrived in town, he disappeared, leaving me confused. It was a foolish, impulsive gesture. We're not a couple, and even if we were, soldiers are not known for their sweetness. Most don't relate to women unless it's for copulation purposes. Besides, in Aleksey's case, fraternizing with me could ruin his life.

I sit with my back against his door, thinking. Aleksey's a mature man who has seen the world. He must have understood that my foolish attempt was the result of my youth and inexperience. If he's not answering my knocks, there must be a reason other than that he's mad.

Tristan's lilting voice comes from below. "Miss Velez! He's not there. He's going to New Vegas on commission and won't return for some days."

I scowl. New Vegas is so far away. I can't wait that long. I climb down in a rush and almost trip on my cloak. "Tristan! It's urgent." *Please.*

Tristan smiles at me. "You have about an hour before he departs."

I call Poncho and sprint toward the staircase. I don't turn back, not even to look at Tristan when he shouts after me.

"He's at the canteen."

CHAPTER 18

Secrets and promises

NEAR THE PASSENGER STATION ruins is a two-story saloon that smells of alcohol, tobacco, and sweat. The round tables are full of men playing cards. At the large wooden counter, some local girls sit with their legs spread, showing their undies. Or lack thereof.

The canteen wasn't supposed to be this shrine of perdition. Starville volunteers built it to serve the Nat troops in a non-sexual way. Nowadays, it's frequented by soldiers and local males who might not have enough to eat, but who can always spare something for gambling, drinks, and sex. The soldiers won't come before the curfew because they hate mingling with the local customers.

Women aren't allowed here unless they're willing to give services. Under my closed cloak, I can pass for an unmarried young man searching for visitant services.

I don't need to scan the room to know that Aleksey must be upstairs. I let Poncho lead the way to the wooden staircase. He sniffs the doors along the torch-lit corridor and stops at one.

I hesitate, but before I knock, the door opens.

Three cops with Indian facial features stand in the threshold, holding drinks. The moment they see me, recognition shows in their faces.

I force myself to sound confident. "I'm looking for Prince Aleksey."

They exchange looks, and I swear they're trying to suppress smiles. I turn to leave.

"Don't go, he's here," says the oldest one.

When they walk past me, I hear them murmur something like "*Fürst Donnerkeil.*"

I ignore the stares I get, and the fact that all conversation has stopped at my arrival.

He's sitting at a round table. Two Accord cops and an old soldier are with him, playing cards. He's brooding as usual, scowling, focused on his cards and ignoring everyone.

Aleksey's eyes can't hide his surprise and disapproval when he looks up. His face turns a furious red that matches the anger in his voice.

"What are you doing here?"

Glad to see you, too, Aleksey. "I'd like a word with you before you go."

For a brief moment, he looks at me like he's trying to convey a message with his eyes. Then he turns to his cards, and his voice comes out curtly.

"I'm busy. Go back to the clinic, Miss Velez."

The men around Aleksey chuckle, but their smiles vanish when they see Aleksey's glare.

I force my voice to sound confident and firm. "There's an emergency at the clinic."

His voice is impatient, but his face remains expressionless. "Don't bother me."

I freeze on the spot, revealing an incredulous look. I feel unwanted and betrayed. We're not supposed to fraternize, but can't he at least be politely indifferent? Especially in present company?

It's then that I look around the room. There are two additional round tables where Accord cops sit playing cards, some stealing stealthy glances in my direction. On a bed in a distant corner, a dark-haired Patriot visitant straddles a barely dressed cop who looks as though he might have passed out. She wears an orange unitard. Her blue eyes shoot me a brief, scornful look. I recognize her. She *visited* Aleksey on our first night at the clinic.

She moves to sit on the edge of the bed, her legs spread wide. "Who's next?" she asks indifferently.

The zipper on the lower part of her garment is open, revealing her most intimate parts. How many times has that zipper gone up and down today? Has Aleksey used this woman today? The thought makes me frown. I thought he was different.

One of the cops gets up. "My turn."

"And then you'll serve General Fürst, Coco," says the soldier.

Coco's expression turns hopeful. My nose wrinkles in disgust. Fury and disappointment course through my veins, corroding my thoughts.

Aleksey growls without looking at me. "Are you deaf? Go away!"

In a heartbeat, I'm out of the canteen and running through the streets, Poncho trotting alongside.

As I cross the Judges Avenue overpass, I bump into a drunken man who tries to start a fight. I try to avoid him, but he's persistent. He throws a jab at my face, but I use his momentum to bring his chest against my elbow, making him lose his breath. When I use all my strength to kick his heels, the man tumbles to the ground with a loud thud.

My hood must have fallen during the fight, and my cloak opened. My long, bushy mane is on full display. The man looks at it, shocked.

"Holy Mary! You're a girl!"

Did he think I was a man? I wonder why girls, in his mind, couldn't be fighters. Are we only brides, baby carriers, or recruits? Or worse, visitants? I suppress the urge to kick him in the balls. Instead, I continue to run until my chest hurts. The ache in my lungs distracts me from other pains.

A big hand stops me. Of course, this bastard can catch up to me with minimal effort.

Aleksey's voice isn't breathy, but furious. "Could you stop that?"

I force my hand away and glare at him, fighting to breathe air into my lungs. "Stop what!?"

"Fraternizing with the enemy in public. In a canteen, of all places."

"You said you didn't care."

"I don't care if it's *me*. I won't risk *you*. My unit won't dare betray us, but there was a soldier in there."

He reaches for my face, but I step back and resume running.

Aleksey trots beside me. "What did you think you were doing there?"

"Your proposal." I stop my sprint and look at him. "You told me you'd arrange for Olmo's care in New Norfolk's Accord hospital in exchange for—"

"Yes," he looks surprised. "As long as Dr. Velez goes with him and both prove their neutrality in a polygraph test."

I glare at him again. "I came to say yes. You didn't have to be so rude."

For a fleeting moment his pupils dilate, and the corner of his mouth twitches. He almost looks … happy. I must have gotten it wrong because his voice recovers its angry tone. "I had to. Didn't you notice they were leering at you? Never go to that place again."

"Don't tell me what to do." My voice is sharp with anger. "This couldn't wait. You'll go to New Vegas soon, which I found out by hearsay. When were you going to tell me?"

He's taken aback by my fury, but his voice is harsh. "Why would I tell you?"

I suppress a gasp. It sounds like, *Who are you to receive any explanations?* Turning my back on him, I dart toward the clinic staircase.

I hurtle up some steps before he grabs my waist and forces me to turn around. I'm slightly taller due to the step on which I'm standing.

"What I meant is that I'm not used to giving explanations." His voice is unexpectedly kind. "I just received my commission an hour ago. I didn't think you'd care."

My anger is gone, replaced by a sudden shyness. I look down. He's making me nervous, but I do my best to sound nonchalant. "Aren't we both lone wolves and voyeurmates? That's almost like being friends, and friends tell each other things."

"Friends," he says, savoring the word. Apparently, it's not to his liking. With his thumb, he forces my head up to meet his gaze. "Ours has to be a discreet arrangement."

A tingling sensation runs through my skin as I stare into his eyes. "A secret?"

His voice becomes silkily sexy.

"Let's say we should avoid being conspicuous around the wrong people."

His face is getting closer and closer. I gulp. Not two kisses in one day. It'd be too much.

And yet my eyes are starting to close. My lips part.

Uninvited thoughts assault me, right when our lips are about to touch. His rudeness at the canteen. The visitant's beautiful, artificial face. *No!*

I disengage from his grip and ascend the steps at top speed.

By the time I reach the top, he's with me again. He looks at me with a tinge of puzzlement in his sky blue eyes.

"You can't be rude one moment and kiss me the next. Not even if we have to pretend we're perfect strangers."

He scowls. "You don't know how dangerous that place is. I was anxious for you to get away, but you stayed. You're stubborn! I would have lost it if someone had tried to attack you. I was enraged, worried, and … deeply uncomfortable."

His usual *I-don't-give-a-damn* attitude doesn't match this statement.

"You? Uncomfortable?"

"My unit was killing time, so I had to keep an eye on them. But I don't frequent the canteen, and I don't like to use visitants. The fact that you, of all people, found me there was uncomfortable."

"That woman … did you use her services today?" *Damn!* Now he'll think I'm jealous.

Aleksey seems genuinely pleased by my question.

"No. In fact," his eyes travel up and down my body in a sensual manner, "I won't ever require visitants' services again. I've lost interest in the opposite sex." He tilts up my chin, forcing me to look at him. "With one exception."

A sense of relief washes over me, but I don't know why. I can't hold up to his intense gaze. Should I believe him? I'll test his honesty. I ask casually, "Have you ever been with her?" knowing the answer already.

Aleksey shakes his head and guides me to his room. "I slammed the door in her face once. She has tried since then, to no avail."

The only acceptable option now is to believe both statements. I know he's being truthful about the former, so I'll buy the latter. He might believe my questions are rooted in jealousy, and I want to say something that will erase that impression. Perhaps a joke? I shake my head. No doubt an older man like himself must find my sense of humor too juvenile and lame. Then I remember that I have no reason to try to impress this guy.

At the bottom of the scaffold that leads to his room, I turn to look at him. "So, we have a deal now. Your first proposal. You'll get Olmo, Azzy, and Dad out of here."

"I'll make time for the necessary paperwork during my commission. They'll need a temporary visa to stay in New Norfolk. It'll take a while."

I purse my lips. "You said, in return for this, you want my company during nights in a non-sexual way."

He exhales deeply. "I've changed my mind."

My stomach does a somersault, and my voice turns desperate.

"Don't, please. Olmo needs help!"

"I meant that you don't have to offer anything in return. I already started arrangements, not knowing whether or not you would accept my offer."

"But if you're putting your own money into this, I want to pay you back. My dad suggested looking at this as a nursing job."

He frowns. "When did you discuss this with him?"

"The day after you proposed it," I say, shrugging. "Dad's an optimist. He believes that you're a gentleman and that we won't sleep in the same bed."

Aleksey runs his hand through his long hair. "Before proposing anything to you, I discussed the plan with him, and he said he wouldn't make any decision without you. I thought that an exchange of services would appeal to you better than if I offered you charity, but ..." He pauses and looks down at me meaningfully. "I don't want you to do anything you don't want to."

"I want to. I need a bit of ... company. It might be a good memory to take with me when the troops recruit me."

"They won't recruit you."

I won't argue with him. It's always better to expect the worst. If the worst happens, you are prepared for it. If it doesn't, you're surprised and grateful. Isn't that what's happening right now? I'm pleasantly surprised. The man I considered an enemy has become an ally.

"I'll give you the key," he says. "You'll start tonight."

"Aren't you going to be absent? What difference does it make if I start when you come back?"

He gives me a half-smile along with the key. "Roads are dangerous. Any danger I face will be easier to overcome if I know you'll be waiting for me."

My hand burns where his fingers touched it. "I ... don't know ... what I should wear."

"Whatever you normally wear to sleep. Remember, we'll be just sleeping. Our arrangement isn't about sexual contact but the human touch."

The human touch again. That concept that he refuses to explain. I steer the conversation toward more practical issues.

"I wonder how a soldier sleeps."

He smiles coyly with his lips closed. "I prefer to sleep half-covered by one my capes." Military capes have unique properties that protect against temperature changes, but it seems he's hinting at something else.

We remain quietly looking into each other's eyes. A pang of nervousness hits me. I drop my eyes and force myself to speak. "Don't you have a vehicle waiting for you?"

"Yes, at the canteen." His hands reach to touch my face, but he catches himself before touching me. His face is an adorable mix of manly confidence with just the right hint of vulnerability. "It's better if you go to bed. Sleep tight, Lila."

Lila. How intimate and melodic my name sounds in his raspy voice. I want to tell him to have a good trip, to be careful, to not get killed. I want to convey to him that I need him to return, rather than utter a clichéd, *"See you."*

He reluctantly steps back and crosses the helipad toward the staircase. Is this the last I'll see of him? Bandits, genetically altered beasts, and other dangers are lurking on the roads.

Impulsively, I run to him, and with a jump, I put my arms around his neck. He catches me by the waist, looking taken aback.

I plant a quick kiss on his lips before pulling away with a hop. The surprised look on his face gives me a warm feeling of satisfaction. "I'll be waiting for you. Under your cape. Naked."

I turn toward the scaffold without looking back. I feel the warmth of his gaze, like fire sweeping over my body, until I close his room's door behind me.

Chapter

19

We shall repulse the oppressors
Of all ardent ideas.
The rapists and the plunderers,
The torturers of people.

War hymn by Vasily Lebedev-Kumach.

The human touch

THE MORNING SUN FALLS over Olmo's bed. The room smells of medicine. Courtesy of Tristan, there's a humidifier and a thermostat. On a rickety table are at least twenty different medicines and several inhalers.

"Come on, Olmo! Just a little bit more," I plead in a sweet tone.

The way he looks at me, with wide eyes, his mouth half open and the tip of his tongue touching his lower lip, reminds me of when he was a toothless, drooling baby. Olmo looks exhausted. The olive skin of his face is mottled with patches of red.

"I can't … It hurts."

I insist gently. I've been massaging Olmo's chest and back since dawn to help him release the mucus that's keeping him from breathing normally.

He thrashes in his bed. "I don't want to."

"Please, Olmo. You'll feel better."

He finally complies and coughs up mucus, then spits it into a vase. I praise him and cradle him. What's happening to him lately? I miss his laughter, his smiles.

I try to distract him with a question that's been bothering me for days. "Olmo, what's the human touch?"

Olmo's face lights up.

"The human touch is that little snippet of physical affection that brings a bit of comfort, support, and kindness. It doesn't take much from the one who gives it, but can make a huge difference in the one who receives it. Like when you brush Azzy's hair or kiss my forehead. Or when you remove mine or Poncho's eye boogers."

I smile. Look at him, sounding so mature! "Did Aleksey explain all this to you?"

He swells with pride. "No, he wrote a small piece about human touch in his journal, and I figured out the meaning. He told me I got it right."

I stroke his hair. That must be another display of human touch. "Well done, bro! I was wondering how *boogers* would sound with his accent."

Olmo giggles. "He calls them *rheum*. More like *rrrr-rheum*."

It's early in the morning, but Olmo had a rough night. He falls asleep quickly. Azzy enters the room and we stand together in silence, watching him sleep.

"You know? I used to hate him. When we were six, I almost killed him," she whispers.

"Before or after … *that day?*"

"Before. I was tricking Olmo into taking a poisoned cocoa when Mom shouted *'Dinner time!'* I forgot my intentions and never tried later."

I say nothing, but I'm not surprised. The first time I saw Azzy, she was a newborn baby, searching blindly but determinedly for my mother's breast. Azzy found her objective and ate voraciously, making satisfied noises … only to get pushed aside. Mom's room seemed to shake with Azzy's deafening wails, but our exhausted mother needed to cajole Olmo, who was too weak, in desperate need of colostrum, and seeming to favor only one breast. Dad tried to get Azalea to eat from mom's other breast instead, but Azzy's wails were like a chant of protest. *I got there first! I don't want second best.*

Sadly, Azzy got seconds not only with food, but also with our parents' attention, multiple times. As a result, she took the term *sibling rivalry* to a whole new level.

The memory makes me smile. "I hope I never get twins. When did you warm up to him?"

Azzy strokes Olmo's hair. "Not long after *that day* when Mom—"

"I see."

"No, you don't. Olmo was wailing, desperate. Dad wasn't there to give him his medicine, mom would never come back … and I realized that he needed more people to take care of him than me, and that he kept losing those people each day. I gave him the damn medicine, and he looked at me as though I was the best."

"Because you were, Azalea."

"I'm the best still."

"Where was I?"

"I don't remember. Probably taking care of Dad's wounds."

Poncho's howl startles us. His loud barks are deafening. In the distance, the Starville churches ring their bells harmonically. It's a code we haven't heard in a while.

A public execution!

Azzy and I help Olmo put on his cloak, boots, and a mask. We must reach the university gym quickly. The consequences for my family after my parents refused to attend a recruitment ceremony were catastrophic. I won't risk being late to a public execution.

"Go ahead!" shouts Dad when he sees us at the clinic entrance. He and the Diaz cousins stay behind to prepare Duque for the journey to the gymnasium.

A soft drizzle falls on us as we take an unpaved road lined with trees down the steep slope toward the university ruins. From here, we see the crowd hurrying through the gym doors.

Of all days, I had to choose this one to wear a button-up dress. Olmo can barely move, so he has to climb on my back. It's the anguish, not his weight that suffocates me. Is the prisoner a Comanche? What if they've discovered us?

I shiver when we get to the gym, knowing I'll have nightmares tonight. They'll hold the recruitment ceremony here. The only illumination comes from the open doors. The wooden stage they used for the last recruitment is still in place in the center of the court. The basketball posts still show the bloodstains from people they abused in the past.

Some soldiers are already on stage, guarding two prisoners. I recognize Sara Jenkins, the dark-haired teenage bride for whom I was sewing trousseau gifts. She's an ex-Comanche. Incredibly, a young, curly-haired soldier is the other prisoner.

Public executions are reserved for acts of treason. The tonics make soldiers extremely loyal to their country. What kind of treason could have made them prosecute this soldier? And Sara? Did they find out about The Comanche Resistance through her?

War, starvation, and recruitment have caused Starville's population to dwindle. The gym can accommodate almost the entire town, and the rows of seats fill quickly. The soldiers are wearing jewelry-devices in the forms of rings and medals, which they use to call roll. Starvillers put their fingers on the j-devices, and an electronic sound indicates that their attendance has been registered.

The soldiers ask families with young children to occupy the front seats. They say this is educational for them. Olmo looks like a seven-year-old, so our family will sit in one of the front rows, but I try to find seats as far as possible from the stage.

Dad, Rey, and Rey's cousins arrive in the nick of time, pushing an emaciated-looking Duque in a wheelchair. His IV line is held by one cousin, his colostomy bag by another. Duque's appearance attracts impertinent looks and loud murmurs.

Azzy and I clench our fists, but our fury merges with fear when Rocco arrives, followed by dozens of soldiers. When did the younger soldiers arrive? Usually, we have fewer soldiers in town, and they're never the kind of soldiers who can still wreak havoc in the line of fire.

Dad joins us, dragging his cart painfully. The Diaz family sits in the front row opposite us. Rey's eyes find mine, and we stare at each other sharing our worries. If Sara's here because she was involved with TCR, we'll all be dead soon.

A disturbed-looking Tristan and other Accord cops arrive. It's their duty to try to stop the girl's execution, but they can do nothing against Patriot law if the charges against her include treason.

Today, Rocco isn't eager for the Accord Unit's cameras. As much as the old soldier tries to hide it, it's evident that he and Tristan are arguing heatedly. With a hand gesture, Rocco calls two soldiers to take hold of Tristan. The cop thrashes and struggles, but Rocco ignores him.

Megaphone in hand, Rocco tells the crowd that Private Petrov, the young soldier who stands stoically on the stage, has committed treason by fraternizing with Sara. I'm so sorry for her that I don't have time to feel relief that they didn't discover TCR. She was the only Starviller who didn't laugh at us the day we moved to the clinic. Sara was a quiet person during her time with the Comanches, and I wish I had known her better.

When they forcibly bare the accused's torsos, their engagement tattoos become visible. The couple resolutely looks at each other, holding their heads high in spite of everything.

A trial takes place, but it's nothing but a kangaroo court. Rocco uses a polygraph on both prisoners to interrogate them. He asks the couple dozens of questions, even intimate ones.

"Are you a V-girl?"

Sara answers defiantly. "No."

The polygraph attached to her arm confirms the answer with an electronic sound. A wave of murmurs and hissing comes from the crowd. Sara's parents, siblings, and countless relatives are openly crying.

"Was Private Petrov your first?"

"Yes. I love him."

Petrov declares his love for her, too. I never thought soldiers were capable of love, but here he is, completely devoted to Sara, about to die for and with her. Every time he answers a question, they kick him. Judging by the agony on his face, drugs don't make soldiers as immune to pain as everyone thinks. They're still human.

The soldiers announce their verdict. Except for two young-looking guys who get threatening looks from the others, most agree that the accused are guilty.

When they take a few moments to deliberate the penalty, terror courses through my body, making me shiver. Death, of course, but what before that? I know they'll hurt the person Petrov loves the most.

They might recruit her. It wouldn't be the first time they use recruitment as punishment. And the Patriot law protects them, even though Tristan is screaming against his restraints that they're breaking the recruitment protocol.

Not recruitment. Please don't recruit her.

Long moments pass before the soldiers reach a consensus. The tallest soldier whispers it in Rocco's ear.

No! Please don't recruit her.

I'm shivering violently. I grab my siblings' hands. They're trembling, too. *Olmo! Azalea! I don't want them to see this.*

Rocco's facial tattoos make him look sinister. He takes his time before announcing the sentence.

Not recruitment. Please, anything but rape.

Chapter 20

"*Godless, cruel, infamous tyrant,
are you not ashamed to despoil a
woman of that by which your own
mother nursed you?*"

Saint Agatha

With her and for her

I CAN'T HEAR ANYMORE. The foot-shuffling, murmurs, and soldier's voices have been replaced in my brain by an incomprehensible murmur.

Rocco announces at least a dozen penalties using legal terminology that my brain barely registers. Only one word from his discourse sticks with me, as that term represents the worst of my fears.

"… the consequence is recruitment …" Rocco's tone is the one you'd use to talk to a mentally challenged person to make him understand a complicated principle. "However, it's the recommendation of our leader, Maximillian Kei, never to recruit or kill a betrothed woman during full moons. It brings bad luck to our troops."

I sigh, momentarily relieved.

"We decided that *we* won't kill Sara Elizabeth Jenkins." The Jenkins family looks hopeful for a second before Rocco announces, "Instead, Private Petrov will kill her before his own execution."

The audience breaks into hushed conversations. Some men say Petrov is a fool. Petrov would be safe now if he had taken her and dismissed her. What do they call it? *Copulation without conversation.* He was going to marry her, so now both are criminals. What a sick moral code. They're punishing him for not raping her. For loving her.

At that moment, the sound of the gym doors opening draws our attention. A collective gasp courses through the gym. Three soldiers enter carrying a rack machine and place it next to the stage. I put my head between my hands before remembering that soldiers are watching the crowd, and that every gesture of horror or disapproval can warrant punishment.

My hands are cold and shivering. Dad discreetly gives Azzy and Olmo two pairs of plastic objects. Ear-plugs. I try to get strength from the fact that at least they won't hear. Everyone else seems to be paralyzed. The silence is acute, overwhelming.

Before Petrov can do anything, Sara is placed spread-eagled on the torture device. It takes three soldiers and several failed attempts before they force Petrov to push the button that operates the rack. Sara's shrieks mix with her family's wails.

Have mercy. Please! Somebody kill her.

Then Rocco jumps on the stage. When I realize what he's gripping in his hand, I sweat.

A pair of tongs and a metal dish.

"Saint Agatha," whispers someone beside me.

In this religious, conservative town, everyone knows the legend of Saint Agatha, a V-martyr, and the way she was tortured.

They are going to do the same thing to Sara.

The crowd murmurs, *"Saint Agatha"* repeatedly, and the buzz becomes so persistent that the soldiers call for order by firing guns into the ceiling.

Nobody moves. The crowd has become utterly still. The only sounds are muffled gurgles and cries from some babies.

I can't bring myself to watch what's about to happen. Soldiers can't punish all of the people who are averting their eyes, but even if they can, I'll take my chances. Unfortunately, I have no way to cover my ears without them noticing it. The crowd's stillness becomes a terrifying sound on its own.

A sizzling sound breaks the silence, mixing with Sara's loud shrieks of pain. The muteness that preceded her piercing screeches only accentuates their volume.

I don't need to see it to guess that Petrov is tossing against his restraints. His shrieks blend with hers, as though he were the one suffering the cruelty of the pincers that Rocco is using to torture Sara's chest.

A sound tells me that the dish is no longer empty; it now holds pieces of her mutilated flesh. I venture a look. Rocco holds up the dish for everyone to see. The sight of the crimson-soaked plate forces me to turn my eyes toward Petrov.

Petrov is an incredibly powerful soldier. He uses his strength to escape his captors and get closer to Sara. In a swift movement, he grabs her head in his hands and breaks her neck.

Sara's death is the cue the soldiers were waiting for to attack Petrov with all the force of their modified genes. All I can see is a mess of bodies in which I don't know which limb belongs to whom. It reminds me of the time when, during a TCR mission, we saw a wolf pack—genetically modified beasts, judging by their size and fierceness—falling upon a horse. But the horse wasn't on drugs and died in seconds. Petrov's drugs are prolonging his death.

To avoid the horror of what's in front of us, Olmo has been whispering the litany of his favorite self-created fantasy tale. Azzy has been stoically staring at her hands, and I suspect that she's coping with this better than Olmo is. I feel grateful for the blessing of her inexplicable self-sufficiency. I wish I were as strong as Azalea is.

Anything but rape, I think gloomily. Was this less cruel for Sara? Sexual assault is as painful and torturous as the pincers. They just used a different kind of torture device on her. If she'd had the option, what would her choice have been? I don't want to think about it, but my mind refuses to let these disturbing thoughts go as I watch how Petrov refuses to scream. To die.

Finally, it's over. Almost all the soldiers exit the gym, leaving the mutilated bodies there. They give the crowd permission to empty the gym. While the rest of the town, afraid of soldiers, pretends not to know the Jenkins family, the Diazes offer help. The Jenkinses don't accept it.

My legs wobble as my family and I make our way outside. I turn to look behind me. Only the Jenkins family remains to dispose of the dish … and the incomplete bodies of the bride and groom that'll never be.

CHAPTER 21

Epiphany

REY AND I LAG a little; our families are walking way ahead of us toward the clinic while the Diaz cousins are carrying Olmo, Dad, and Duque. I'm still trembling, so he puts his arm around my shoulders, subduing my fears slightly. *It's over for now. My family is safe.*

Rey stops and pulls me into a tight embrace. I lean my head on his chest and sigh, closing my eyes. This gesture of support and kindness must be what Olmo calls the human touch, and it is precisely what I need.

Let's stay like this for a while. Thankfully, Rey complies.

Sara's execution is the reminder of why love isn't a smart idea during war. Even sex might be dangerous. The fraternization rules should be stricter on cops. After all, they are foreigners claiming neutrality. What would happen if my arrangement with Aleksey was discovered? Would the two of us be the next Sara and Petrov? I shudder, and that makes Rey tighten his hold on me.

We finally break our embrace and hurry to catch up with our families. They're already on the clinic's staircase, talking to Tristan. The cop's warm eyes become cold when he sees Rey's hand on mine, but he recovers soon and waves at me.

I feel like I have to console Tristan, who keeps recriminating himself for not stopping the execution as Aleksey would have. "It was only you against several soldiers! We've never seen a cop come between Rocco and his victims before ... right, Rey?"

Rey doesn't answer. Throwing a dark look at Tristan, he enters the clinic, leaving me alone with the cop in the courtyard.

Tristan opens the door of the hospital to let me go in first. "You Starvillers don't like foreigners, do you?"

"Foreigners, yes. Cops, not so much. What you did is unusual for a cop. You risked your life."

He seems less gloomy, even determined. "You'll see, Miss Velez. On the day of the recruitment ceremony, I'll be stronger and make the troops toe the line."

"I hope so. I fear rape above everything else," I murmur.

"Really?" He seems pleasantly surprised. "Me, too."

My head snaps up, and I observe him intently. Maybe he's joking. But the hint of discomfort on his face, as though he is ashamed to have admitted an embarrassing truth, tells me that he's being honest. He's always surrounded by older, more experienced, and more dangerous soldiers. A lanky man like Tristan, who has a masculine yet vulnerable appearance— he, even with his military training, is also in danger of sexual assault. I never thought about it before. If not even the Accord cops are safe, I can't be optimistic. Without a doubt, the troops will recruit me.

Tristan winks at me. "We have more in common than you think, Miss Velez."

We enter an examination room where a dozen Diaz cousins, Baron, Reyna, and my family are about to share a meal. Due to the events of this morning, the atmosphere is somber, but they invite Tristan to take part in it. My eyes search for Rey.

"He went home to get some rest. Rey didn't sleep at all last night," says Duque. He sounds exhausted. It's evident that Duque got little sleep, too, and he doesn't seem to be enjoying the company of his relatives. I understand why he would rather be by himself. I share his feelings. The Diazes are great people, but I'm not a social person. I need to be alone. I have so much to think about.

I leave the room as discreetly as I can and head to the staircase. The wind forces me to pull on my hood as I stand at the top of it, contemplating the city and its surroundings. Aleksey's words play in my mind. *It'd be a nice change to risk my life for something I want for myself.* It's only now that I understand how much it would cost if we were discovered.

Sara's death has put me on edge, and Tristan's confession has hit me hard. No wonder the cops rarely face the troops. I wanted to see where things would go with Aleksey, but if even Accord cops can't escape recruitment … if Aleksey and I could get executed, then …

I descend the stairs in seconds, Poncho running behind me. I've had an epiphany. Even now that I have another option—a man who awoke in me a desire I've never felt before—Rey is still the safest choice for an emergency deflowering. *I'm sorry, Mr. Fürst, but I won't risk my life. Or yours.*

I can't wait anymore until Rey makes a decision, although I know that'd be the moral thing to do. I have to ask him once and for all if he will ever have sex with me. Perhaps it is a strange trick of destiny that Baron and Reyna will be at the clinic all afternoon with the Diaz relatives to attend to Duque. Rey and I will be completely alone. We can talk. We can make love.

The afternoon sun becomes scorching as I dash toward the multifamily complexes. I am ready for another attempt at having sex with my best friend.

CHAPTER 22

Lila's country

THE KEY REY GAVE me disappeared during the air raid, but Buck Weaver taught me how to pick locks without keys. I order Poncho to wait for me outside, and I enter the one-room apartment.

A table, a stove, and two bunk beds are the only furniture. Religious images and Bible quotes cover the cracks in the walls. Everything smells of wood and disinfectant. The Diazes keep the apartment clean, so there are no cockroaches, but the black ants sneak in anyway. Rey never kills them. Instead, he captures them and takes them outside.

I tentatively pull the curtain that divides the room.

"Rey? Can I enter?"

All I hear is deep breathing. Rey's taking a nap on the lower bunk. His long hair covers half his face, and he looks so peaceful that I can't help but stare. I keep looking until I realize that I'm wasting precious time.

I wish I didn't have to do this, but I undress. I couldn't press my breasts with bands this morning, so I'm topless in less than a second. My nudity makes me feel uncomfortable, and the image of Sara's bridal sheet invades my mind. At this moment, I wish I had it with me. Taking away the barrier of my clothes makes me feel like I'm letting down other barriers that protect me from showing my true self. How do other people have sex so easily all the time? It's nerve-wracking to let someone else see you inside and out.

I have to do whatever I can to avoid recruitment, so I don't understand why I'm hesitating. I'm shaking, and these aren't passion tremors.

I feel ashamed of my nakedness. I have to get dressed again. We can do it with clothes on, can't we? I begin to put on my dress when her name stops me dead in my tracks.

"Angie," Rey says, still sleeping.

Why do I suddenly feel dirty and cheap? I've known all along that he loves her, and that's one of the reasons I feel safe around him. What I need from Rey is sexual gentleness, not love. We won't hurt each other as long as he's unable to move on. But a bitter envy has killed the resolution that brought me here. When the war ends, will I find someone who loves me the way he loves her?

I look at his sleeping figure again. If he had tried to touch me while I wasn't sentient, wouldn't that have been abusive? This is wrong.

I'm about to leave the apartment, hoping he'll never know that I was here when I trip on my cloak and fall on my butt with a loud thud.

Rey springs up in a defensive stance. "Who's there?" He sees me sprawled awkwardly on the floor.

Dammit! Glancing up at his confused face from this position, I feel small.

He grins. "Did you trip, or are the ants explaining their plans to take over the world?"

There's the joking Rey I've missed. The one who vanished after Angie married Buck Weaver.

"I—I came to talk to you, but you were sleeping."

He takes a moment to look at me. I couldn't feel more awkward.

"I need to talk to you, too."

Rey lifts me from my tangled cloak, closes the door on Poncho's face, and lays me on the lower bunk.

For a while he says nothing. Then: "Lily, what will you do after the ceremony?"

"If they don't recruit me, I may leave Starville."

I see anguish on Rey's face.

"You can't go far without an all-terrain. Even if you could, they wouldn't admit you in another city without a j-device." His tone is urgent. "And you can't skip recruitment or they'll execute you."

"I prefer death to recruitment anyway." He's so horrified by my admission that I quickly add, "Shiloh is close. They'll admit me if I find a job. I can come here every year for recruitment until they—"

"Life isn't much better in Shiloh, and your family needs you. I need you."

I can't share Aleksey's plan with him yet. It sounds too good to be true. If my family leaves Starville, why shouldn't I try to leave, too? What if something ruins it?

I stare at my hands. "It would be difficult, but that's what I want and—"Out of nowhere, I have an idea. "Hey, why don't you all come with me? It would be the best for Duque—"

"The best? What about TCR?"

I purse my lips. I haven't thought of that. Who will take a stand against the Patriots if we don't? But there must be something we can do for Duque.

"You would flee the country if you could, wouldn't you?" he asks.

"Maybe." I'm not apologizing for that. "Anyway, fleeing the country is impossible, so what's the point of—"

"It's easier to run away than to stay and fight for a change in *our* own country," he says sternly.

I sigh and look at the ceiling. I won't engage in this discussion with Rey. He can go off on political rants for hours. Besides, I agree with him; I want to fight and improve the conditions of *my* country. Except that the Nationalist States isn't my country. If my country hadn't been divided, recruitment laws would never have been approved. And what could I do for the resistance if Patriots recruited me? When it comes to recruitment, I can't be idealistic.

"This city is our home," says Rey passionately. "It's not perfect, but these lands belong to us and we belong to these lands. They're the heritage of my ancestors and a loan from my descendants. Leaving my property to Patriots … I can't do that."

"What do you want to do?" I ask, eager to change the subject.

"That's what I wanted to talk to you about." For a few moments, there's only silence. Then Rey swallows hard. "Did you know that Angie's dead?"

Her name again. "Your dad asked us never to tell you."

"Everybody thought they were keeping the news from me. But as absurd as this sounds, a month after they took her, I felt like a part of me was missing. When I asked Mrs. Busko, she said she'd received *the letter*."

The letter includes a form of compensation that the Patriot Government sends to the families of those who die after servicing the troops. The recruits are part of the Patriot army, and their families receive coupons and a letter of condolence signed by Maximillian Kei when they die.

Rey holds my hand. "After I realized that she wasn't coming back, I thought I'd return to the seminary." The way he's looking at me makes me blush. "But you changed that."

"Me? Why?"

"I thought I loved you like a sister, but that night when you told me you wanted me ... I realized I wanted you, too. I never thought I could want somebody else. And I know I'm greedy and vain, but ... now that there's competition, I feel a greater pull toward you."

"Competition?"

Rey frowns. "That cop, the slender one. He kept coming between us today. Didn't you notice? I guess he was jealous, too. And the big one ... he seems to like you. I want them to stay away from you. I have no right to feel protective, but I can't help it. I want you to be my wife."

I gasp. "Wife?"

"After recruitment, when the Commissioner issues marriage licenses again, we'll marry, Lily."

"No! That's not what—"

"Listen to me. I was determined never to look at a woman again ... to devote my life to the resistance and to later become a priest, but I want to start a family, have babies."

Babies! I swallow hard and look at the door. Perhaps I should escape.

"It's what our creator wants." He blushes and inhales deeply. "Other guys make fun of me. They think that because of my years in the seminary ... that I'm against ... certain pleasures. But I'm not. Our creator told us, '*Be fruitful and multiply*,' but he must have known that we would disobey without motivation, so he created pleasure—"

His tone is so serious that I'm worried about what he will say next.

"—otherwise, why did he give us such sensitive ... *um* ... body parts? Why does it feel so good if he didn't want us to—?"

I cover my face with my hands to suppress a giggle. Rey has always had a bizarre sense of humor, but right now he's talking in earnest. I don't know how to feel about his mention of *sensitive body parts* in a religious context. Azzy would have a field day with this one, but Rey has never laughed at me, not even when I tried to seduce him. The least I can do is take him seriously.

He seems oblivious to my embarrassment and kisses my forehead.

"I won't lie to you. I'll love her for as long as I live, but I can't pretend that I don't have strong feelings for you. And you can't, either. You love me beyond friendship."

He's wrong. I care for him, but this is not even a shadow of my parents' love. If what I'm feeling were *real* love, my mouth wouldn't crave Aleksey's kisses. And if Rey *really, truly* loved me, his ex would be history. I wish there were a way to tell him *I don't love you* without hurting his feelings.

"I wouldn't marry you even if you loved me exclusively." Rey's face crumples, so I hastily add, "If the war doesn't stop, I won't marry anyone." I'm under no illusions that the war will stop in time for me to escape death.

He stands up abruptly and exits the room. Is he mad?

For a while, all I hear is the rain slamming against the window. Then a succession of musical tones blends with the rain. He's playing the guitar. The music is a soft mix of notes that convey innocence, sweetness, and longing. Like a child's song, but with a hint of sadness.

Rey doesn't stop the music when he pushes the curtain aside and reenters the room. His angelic voice sings a Spanish melody, and my heart melts. This song is evidently written for me. I love that each verse starts with my name.

My Spanish is rusty, but I understand the gist of the song.

> *Lila, you're so innocent and I want you,*
> *But now that I have you in my arms, I remember her.*
> *I'm not thinking about you, and I won't steal your first time,*
> *Your innocence,*
> *While I'm thinking about another girl.*
> *Lila, I beg you, I'm desperate here,*
> *Embrace me and make me forget her.*
> *Because I don't know who I am.*
> *Am I a dreamer? Am I a fool?*
> *Am I someone who wants to love you?*

I'm so moved, I cannot find my voice. How many men would not jump at the first opportunity to have sex, disregarding the girl's feelings? Rey's honesty is disarming. We'll never fall in love with each other, and we'll never be a couple, but if Rey deflowers me, we'll make a statement: The troops don't own our bodies.

We're wasting precious time. Rey and I should make love now; no more marriage talk.

"I won't ever marry, Rey."

"Then what do you want?"

"I ... want—"

"You want me to deflower you?" he whispers.

I nod.

His eyes ignite with desire. In a swift movement, he takes off his shirt. I end up pressed to the bunk.

Underneath him.

CHAPTER 23

Lila's sin

REY TRIES TO KISS my mouth, but I turn my head, so he kisses my jaw instead. His hands fumble with the top buttons of my dress while his lips slide to my neck. I enjoy the contact, but for a reason, I cannot offer him my mouth.

Suddenly, Aleksey's serious face flashes in my mind's eye. I shouldn't think about him at a time like this.

Rey doesn't notice. He takes my wrists and presses them firmly above my head. "Oh, Lily! I want to, but we'll get married first."

I finally allow Rey's mouth to find mine, but the raging storm that overtook me when Aleksey kissed me isn't brewing.

His hands slide down from my shoulders and search beneath my dress. A place he has never touched before. Rey stops right before he touches me, and I realize that he isn't really trying.

I put my feet on his stomach and push. He falls to the floor and looks up in confusion. My tone is accusatory. "If you won't do it, why did you touch me like that? I thought we'd make love, but you're just teasing me."

"I wanted to show you how good it'll be when we finally get married."

I cross the room, desperate for space. "I won't marry you, and I won't wait 'til after the Recruitment ceremony." I can't live following Starville's customs, and it's disappointing to realize that this life is exactly what Rey wants.

He's on his feet in a second, and there's a definite *no* in his voice.

"And I'll make love to you only after we marry—"

My hopes shatter into thousands of pieces. He's killed any possibility of my having sex with a person I know and trust. I turn my back to him and find myself looking into his wall mirror. "Then don't touch me like that again."

Rey's reflection turns its back on me and remains still for a long time.

"The other night, in my room, you acted as though you wanted me," I say, breaking the silence. "Why do you keep teasing me?"

Rey paces the room. "Because you're trying too hard to get rid of something you might value later."

Argh! That's the reason why the Comanches call him *Priest.* I run my hands through my hair in exasperation. "No, Rey. I'll never value *that.*" If he thinks my virtue is valuable, then he is as medieval as the soldiers.

"If you married me, you'd see how important waiting for the right person is and—"

I raise my voice. "No preaching. I don't value your religion's rules."

"But you value your own rules. Otherwise, you'd have been with someone already. If it weren't for recruitment, you'd wait." He turns to me, and our eyes meet in the mirror. "Your values don't stem from religion. You're a hopeless romantic. You want to belong to a man and only one man."

Rey knows me so well. At this moment, I hate that he's so right about my feelings and so wrong about our reality.

"Didn't you see what almost happened to Sara?" I ask in a shaky voice. "What does it matter what I want if they recruit me?"

"They won't. We hacked the 36th Battalion itinerary before the soldiers attacked Duque. We'll stop the ceremony."

I grind my teeth. "We've been trying that for years and—"

"Why can't you have faith?"

"Why are you trying to save me from '*sin*'?" I ask, emphasizing the word with air quotes.

"Please wait for me. Let me be your first."

"Can't you see that I *did* want you to be my first?" I yell. "But you won't budge, and that will earn me a spot at the end of recruitment. If they didn't punish the families of those who commit suicide, I'd kill myself first!"

Rey's face contorts in pain. I remember that suicide is a touchy subject with him because of Duque. I reach out to console him, but in a flashing movement, he grabs my hand and kisses it.

"I'll ask you again. So far, you've said 'no,' but we'll marry someday."

I storm out of the apartment, frustrated by his insistence. I'm almost at the front door when I hear Rey's desperate voice from upstairs.

"Wait. I'll walk you home, Lily."

"Don't call me 'Lily'! My name is Lila!" I snap, quickening my pace.

"Please! Stay away from the cops. They want you because you are—"

He doesn't say what is on both of our minds. Aleksey might be interested in me for the same reason the soldiers prefer inexperienced girls.

"—they'll lose interest after you … when you—"

When I lose my virtue? Rey would say that. He won't have sex with me, but he doesn't want me to sleep with anyone else. That's so selfish. I can't believe I've always thought of him as a selfless person. Almost a saint.

I stop, turning to look at him with a defiant expression. "Who are you?" My question takes him aback. "At what point did you lose yourself?" Or has he always been like this and I was too blind to see? It's incredible how little you know a guy until you try to sleep with him. But who am I to judge? I shouldn't feel disappointed. I'm more selfish than he is. I tried to use him for my deflowering, and now the plan has backfired.

Suppressing tears of fury, I open the door to Rey's apartment building and dart through the rainy streets. I make myself a promise—I won't ask anything of him again.

I'm still far from the clinic when Poncho barks, which keeps me from turning onto Numbers Avenue.

Danger. Poncho's warning me. I hide in an alley and get my knives ready.

The moments pass. Other than the afternoon rain, which has diminished to a light drizzle, nothing happens. I wonder if Poncho's survival instincts are still intact, and that's when I see them. About thirty soldiers pass the dark alley. They're focused on a drill, so they don't notice me.

Cold panic shoots through my stomach. These soldiers are new to

town. Have they come to start preparations for the recruitment ceremony?

I still have time to get home safely before the sun sets, but I have to
hurry. Taking a soldier-free route to the clinic, I end up near the south-
western border, where the ruins of the cinema crumple among a sea of
trees. I dart along a paved street partially swallowed by vegetation.

The place could be dangerous, though less so than the streets full of
soldiers. It reeks of the impoverished people who live beneath the ruins:
people who were never assigned housing by the Patriot authorities. The
plumbing in Starville is inadequate; here, it's nonexistent.

Poncho growls, urging me to move faster. Fear creeps up my spine.
I'm about to run away when I hear someone whispering. Not my
name. Not even 'Layla.' Someone whispers my Comanche nickname.

"V-girl. Come over here, V-girl."

The voice comes from behind a thick tree, where the grass grows
tall. I hesitate. It could be someone from the Comanche group. They
could be in trouble.

No, it can't be them.

I storm off, away from the trees, but the hesitation costs me a precious second.

"*Aaaaaaargh!*" I shout when someone takes me by the arms and
brings me to the ground. I lie flat on my stomach while the stranger pins
me down. I can't see my attacker, but I know my chance of beating him
is zero. Because my attacker isn't normal. His strength is inhuman.

I'm stuck beneath the weight of a soldier.

CHAPTER 24

Copulation without conversation

PONCHO IS ALL OVER the soldier, snapping furiously, and twisting the soldier's armor with his powerful jaws. Pieces of it fall to the ground beside me.

My dog's attack forces the soldier to search for his gun, but he cannot get to it. Poncho is incredibly fast, and only the man's armor prevents the dog's fangs from piercing his skin.

My attacker releases me and swiftly wraps his legs and arms around Poncho. They roll in a lethal embrace.

I'm on my feet and ready to flee when I hear something.

"Stop! If you flee, I'll make sure Azalea services the cocks of the whole battalion."

Panic freezes me to the spot. This soldier knows my family. "Order your dog to behave. Now!"

I whistle. Poncho breaks free and runs to my side. I scratch his ears and rub his muzzle, my eyes glued to my attacker. His Patriot uniform is falling apart, revealing his body. A middle-aged soldier. He's getting up slowly, his back to me.

"Long time no see, V-girl," says a drawling voice.

It's not possible. How is he even here?

"Gary," I whisper.

He finally turns around and points his gun at me. "So, you learned my name? I can't say the same about you."

His other hand goes to his slacks, and in a minute, he has his shaft in view. *No!*

"You'll cooperate with me, or your siblings will end up in a canteen. Your brother is the perfect age for a eunuch, and your sister will be very popular with the troops. Even your crippled father will be useful. Some soldiers aren't picky."

I glare at him. Disgusting cockroach. I want to kill him.

Gary laughs derisively. "You'd like to kill me, wouldn't you?"

I'm giving away my emotions, and this bastard will use them against me. I try to hide my disgust with a neutral face.

"Not happening, virgin. I've been on high doses of tonics lately. I'm as strong as a soldier, and I'll take you as a Patriot soldier should."

No one will hear my screams here. No one will care. This bastard attacked me before in front of dozens of Starvillers, and no one gave a damn.

I feel a sharp pain in my temple. He has grabbed my hair and is forcing me to kneel in front of him. "Keep your dog meek and do as I say. I don't trust you, so this little friend," I hear the pistol click, "will remain pointed at your little head while you and I enjoy private time."

Poncho is still, but he keeps growling at Gary. "Poncho, quiet please."

"In my time, it was forbidden for us cops to marry, fuck, or even look at Nat women. But copulation without conversation doesn't constitute fraternization." He chants his last words several times. "That's what Allied troops used to say when they attacked hundreds of women during World War II. You would think soldiers would have better things to do than rape ... but no."

He chants *copulation without conversation* again. "Do you want to know who taught us those words of wisdom? Every single Nationalist soldier we've met. You Nats love to rape, too."

The pain dulls my senses when he slams the butt of the gun into my head. "You know what? Thanks to the recruitment bill, I'll have any kind of fraternization I want with you."

He yanks back my hair to force me to look at him. I suppress a scream of pain.

"Stupid whore. You don't qualify as a person. You aren't subject to international human rights," he spits out. "You aren't any more human than a bitch in heat. You aren't better than a sow. Do you know why?" I don't answer, so he slaps me. A burning pain stings my left cheek. "Because the country where you were born doesn't exist anymore. The USA is nothing but an old fantasy."

He keeps stroking his shaft up and down. The white creamy liquid at the tip makes me want to vomit. I don't want it inside my mouth.

"You'll thank me for this later, when your face is covered with my cum."

I used to wonder why survivors like Divine didn't bite down on the men violating them. Now I know. I can't ignore his threat to my family. I'll endure whatever this asshole wants to do to me if he leaves them alone.

"Open your mouth. I know you want it."

Fighting the revulsion that threatens to overpower me, I clench my fists and open my mouth wide.

CHAPTER 25

Threat

THE CLAMOR OF MULTIPLE voices approaching makes me look to the right. Even Gary looks startled.

"It won't be today, virgin. But I'll give you something to remember."

In a heartbeat, he forces my body to the ground. The surprise of his weight immobilizes me while he gropes my legs and bites my left breast. The pain is nothing compared to the repulsion. It's over in two seconds, but those seconds feel like an eternity.

Poncho has resumed his barking, and Gary looks at him maliciously. "You'd better train your dog to obey me. He'll be useful when he becomes my pet."

His face is so close to mine that his saliva sprinkles me with each word. "You'll keep your mouth shut, and you won't let anyone except me take your virginity, you hear me? Don't cross me, or I'll make sure your whole family ends up in a canteen. You'd like that wouldn't you, little slut? You'd let your crippled father fuck you if you could."

I can't take it anymore. I spit at him. His face contorts in surprise and disgust. He slaps me again. This impulsive, almost involuntary act will lead to the damnation of my family. But before I can regret it, he stands up.

"One more thing," he says as he looks around, as though fearing someone might appear at any moment. "Don't be fooled by Prince Aleksey. He likes to possess women. You'll be only another one of them. He wants you to lower your guard; that way he'll hurt you more when he forces you. Oh, yes! He enjoys his wicked games. You'll see. He's a soldier and a rapist and—"

The voices interrupt him again. They're almost here.

"Ask him about the South Metropolis incident. Ask him about Clavel. See if he dares to answer. We'll meet again soon."

He races toward the woods.

I force myself up, shaking uncontrollably. I don't fear for my life. I'm afraid of what this asshole will do to my family.

In a remote corner of my mind, I notice black-clad people passing me, ignoring me. A procession. *They're heading to Sara's wake.* I barely register them because a dizzying combination of fury, fear, and nausea threatens to knock me out. But another emotion keeps me standing and eventually forces my mind to work: hatred.

He has to die. My mind repeats this mantra until I notice that some-one has grabbed my shoulders.

"V-girl! Snap out of it!" says Joey Waters, shaking me slightly. Divine and Cara are with him, looking at me worriedly. They must have been part of the procession. I wonder what they saw in my eyes that put them on edge.

I put my index finger to my lips to shush them. Gary seemed to know about my attempts to lose my V. *How?* I run my hands through my hair on a hunch. I don't cut my hair with my knife because the three Comanches keep looking at me like I've lost my mind.

A bug. He might've put a bug on me. It's the only explanation that makes sense. I search through my bushy, light-brown mane until my hands finally find it. When I raise the louse-shaped device for the others to see, they are aghast.

Starvillers used to spread rumors about Gary. I never paid attention to them, but now I know that they had a ring of truth. Gary Sleecket is a spy who might be working for the Patriot government.

A spy I'm determined to hunt and kill.

Right now.

Chapter 26

Prince Aleksey:

Gary attacked me today. I'll try to track him and kill him. If I don't survive, please, PLEASE don't let him hurt my family.

I hope you'll never forget me.

Lila Velez Tcherkassky

P.S. Thanks for everything.

Revenge

"DIDN'T I TELL YOU? We should've waited for the Priest," says Divine as we descend a steep slope toward the woods surrounding the city, leaving behind the crumbling walls of what used to be the music hall. The trees cover the moonlight, and we're advancing at a turtle's pace. The ever-changing weather has treated us to a scorching night, and we're sweating bullets.

"Didn't I tell you? You shouldn't have come," I retort. I'm acting impulsively. Without plans or a strategy, I'm reluctant to drag others into this.

"No time to wait," says Joey. "I couldn't find the Priest anywhere. And this is a now-or-never situation."

Now or never. That's an understatement. Gary didn't look like he had the Patriots' support. His armor was fake, and he acted as though he was afraid of someone. But if there's a slim possibility that he's a menace, I'd rather finish this now than give him time to act against us. My family didn't realize that I was saying farewell when I hugged them earlier. I may not survive my attempt to ambush Gary, but I would rather die than let him recruit my family.

It was supposed to be a solo attack, but Cara and the lovers insisted on joining me. When I told them what had happened, they revealed that Gary had touched Cara and Holly inappropriately, too. They were relieved when Gary disappeared. Now that he's back, Cara insists that we take care of this together. After preparing at the clinic, we followed Poncho into the woods.

I haven't trained Poncho in tracking, but he has acute senses and modified genes that tell him what to do. My dog stops to sniff some trees, and I pat him. I have always considered him family, and I fear for him.

"Don't get killed, little Poncho," I whisper. Then I look at our painfully rudimentary weaponry. Wooden swords, boomerangs, knives, and slings won't be of much use against real weapons. Drug-filled soldiers don't tolerate alcohol, so we've brought along small balloons filled with liquor. I've soaked my knives in alcohol. In combat, Gary will have the advantage, and not only because of his guns. An average person wouldn't have recovered so soon after Aleksey's bestial attack.

I left a note for Aleksey, asking him to protect my family from Gary's threats. A threat is only as strong as the fear of the threatened. Fear isn't clouding my judgment anymore, so I can see through Gary's lies. *I've been on high doses of tonics lately.* As if! There are hundreds of different tonics and they are used according to the level of the soldier's genetic manipulation. Using the wrong one means a slow, painful death. The same goes for stealing the drugs. No wonder he was on edge this afternoon.

The bug in my hair is a more worrisome threat. If those bugs have reached our headquarters, the entire town could face the same fate as Midian.

We reach a clearing surrounded by elms and oaks, and we're forced to crawl through it. The moonlight is so bright that we cannot hide. If Gary is on the lookout, he'll see us.

Our best fighters are Poncho and Cara. Crawling along the moonlit terrain, her short blonde hair shining, she looks like a lioness defending her cub. She crouches behind a tree stump, her bow already taut with an arrow. Poncho has sensed the danger and growls at an unseen enemy that only his acute hearing can detect.

I prepare my knives. Something is coming in our direction.

My heart beats with inhuman speed. I don't have time to wish that the danger is merely a bear. Poncho barrels against something I can't see while Cara shoots an arrow above Poncho's head.

The arrow rebounds and falls to the ground, as though repelled by an invisible force. Cara shoots a second arrow as the bangs of gunshots hurt my ears.

I press my head to the ground and roll over to avoid the bullets. The shooter is perfectly camouflaged, probably beneath a soldier's cape. A loud thud tells me that Poncho has collided with the invisible attacker.

"Kill the dog!" shouts a familiar voice.

Fear rushes over me. *No! Poncho!*

When I look up, I see that Poncho's attack has made them lose their camouflage capes. Gary and a younger soldier stand near the edge of the clearing. Poncho snaps and twists, but the soldier's armor doesn't budge.

Gary raises his gun, aiming for Poncho, but my knife reaches his hand first. He drops the gun and howls in pain. Divine and Joey throw alcohol-soaked rocks at Gary with their slings. Incredibly, this makes him retreat toward the trees.

Cara shoots an arrow at the soldier, and it almost hits Poncho as he wrestles the man. She shoots another arrow at our attacker's foot. The arrow lodges in his boot and snaps in two parts when the soldier steps on it.

Our only advantage is surprise. Gary and company weren't prepared for this. Soldiers would never have imagined that a few primitive, un-educated Starvillers could pose a threat.

I approach Gary close enough to drop a balloon full of alcohol over his head. Joey's boomerang collides with the bag at the right moment, causing it to burst. The cop ducks and avoids most of the liquid, but the few droplets he can't avoid make him scream.

The ex-cop uses his uninjured hand to shoot at us, but his aim is off. We are advancing in the fight, and now we're surrounded by trees.

Gary seems astonished when one of Cara's arrows hits its mark, dis-arming him. Divine catches the handgun and shoots Gary, but she misses.

My balloon reaches Gary's head, and he howls when alcohol drenches him. He loses his balance and falls headfirst. Divine shoots him at the same time Joey's stone hits his skull.

We don't have time to see if he's dead. The soldier, even with Pon-cho's powerful jaws enclosing his arm, manages to shoot at us. We seek refuge behind the trees, barely avoiding the incessant fire. We can't at-tack. Divine's gun skills are limited to theory and instinct. She has Joey, though. A silent message passes between them.

Joey's sling tosses stones toward a nearby tree, deceiving the soldier into shooting in that direction. Joey repeats this tactic several times, giving Divine enough time to carefully aim and shoot. The bullet reaches the soldier's forearm, which, thanks to Poncho's attack, is no longer covered with armor. His groan tells me that he's in pain, but he's a soldier, trained to fight until death.

Cara and I climb the trees at full speed for a better vantage point. I throw another balloon toward the soldier, and Joey follows with a stone to burst the balloon in the air, soaking our attacker. The soldier staggers, and Poncho throws him to the ground. Cara and I aim at him again. Some of Divine's bullets bounce, but our combined force is enough to finally incapacitate the man.

A manic, adrenaline-fueled smile spreads across my face. We did it! We defeated a soldier!

I climb down the tree at top speed. Gary doesn't have the full powers of a soldier, but he must have recovered by now. I find him crawling, trying to escape, so I kick him. Repeatedly.

We restrain and gag our prisoners with torn pieces of the soldier's shirt. The soldier is unconscious but still alive.

I kneel beside Gary, retrieve my knife, and echo his contemptuous words back to him. "You don't qualify as a person. You aren't more human than a bitch in heat. You aren't better than a pig. Do you know why?" I point my knife at his heart, but I intend to hurt him in a different way. "Because your penis is ridiculously small."

I laugh maniacally. The three Comanches look at me like I'm crazy, but I've guessed what Gary's weakness is. If I'm right, my words will cut through him as much as my knife.

I reach for his groin and squeeze forcefully. He screams.

"You're not as big as your comrades," I sneer. "The Accord Unit learned this and made fun of you all the time, not to your face, but you knew. I laughed at you, too. You're small. A pathetic excuse for a man."

I'm not an expert, but Joey isn't big, and he's fantastic in bed, so size shouldn't be that important. But I noticed Gary's reluctance to show his body in front of Rey when he attacked us. His size must be his Achilles' heel.

"You used to hire visitants frequently," I continue. "But when you got older, you couldn't get it up. You got tired of making a fool of yourself in front of them. And you still can't get it up. Not even with oral. Your wife cheated on you because—" I take a breath to yell, "YOU CAN'T GET THE DAMN THING UP."

He tries to spit in my face, but I dodge out of the way. It's clear that my guesswork has hit a nerve.

"You're old, and afraid to get older. Oh, poor Sergeant Sleecket, comparing himself to younger, better endowed cops all the time. That's why you molest girls, isn't it? And the older you get, the younger the girls you attack. You've even been eyeing my sister."

Cara puts a hand on my shoulder. Perhaps the other Comanches are worried about my sanity.

"You're pathetic; you're a creep. I've thought about castrating you to avenge the girls you've attacked." I point my knife at his groin. His eyes widen in fear. "I won't. There's practically nothing to castrate in the first place."

I slap his face like he slapped mine. "I'll kill you."

Cara glares at Gary, as though all the abuse in the world is his fault. "Not yet. He has to tell us about the bugs. And as for me—" She kicks his groin. "That's for my daughter." Her next attack is aimed at his face. "That one is for me."

Divine soaks Gary's groin with alcohol. "How many bugs have you planted?"

Gary shrieks but doesn't answer.

We haven't ever tortured anybody, and now that I see him defeated, I'm having doubts. I harmed his manhood both physically and—I hope—emotionally. I don't think he's a threat to my family anymore, so I wish things were different. I wish we could expose him to the world as the rapist he is. I wish that a court would punish him. But in a place where some parents are cajoling their daughters into enlisting, and where cops deliver food, who's going to punish Gary for his acts?

"Let's kill him. More soldiers might come," I say.

Poncho growls at the inert mass of the soldier, who must have regained consciousness. I approach the soldier and put the gun to his forehead. "This one first."

"Careful," says Joey. "Remember that the bullets might rebound."

The soldier struggles against his restraints. He has long brown curls, and his tattooed, gray face is dimpled. He can't be older than fourteen. A tattoo on his arm tells me that he was expelled from a military academy. This boy never completed training, although his genes must have been engineered for combat—perhaps before he was born. His Patriot armor is as fake as Gary's, which means he's also acting against military laws.

No wonder it took only four of us, and Poncho, to defeat him. He's massive, but he lacks the power of a well-trained soldier. The weather is still scorching, but I'm shivering. I force myself to put the gun to his chest.

There's something about the way he's fighting his restraints, about the way Poncho barks at him. Perhaps … *No!*

"Watch out!" Divine yells. But by then I'm already fighting for my life.

I fire the gun as the soldier throws his body against mine. My bullet rebounds off his armor as I fall to the ground beneath him. My head throbs as I try to scramble away. He has something in his hands that I cannot see, and he is lashing me with it.

"No! I need her alive!" shouts Gary.

The soldier stops moving, at which point an excruciating pain rips through my thigh. I scream in agony as my body jerks violently on the ground. I order myself to get a grip, but I've lost all control. The pain spreads quickly from my thigh to the rest of my body. It feels like a fire is burning through every single nerve ending.

Between the convulsions, I catch a glimpse of my leg. Something with two fangs is buried in the back of my left thigh. A genetically modified snake—like the ones the troops use to inject themselves.

The black snake detaches from my body and moves away. I'm in so much pain that I barely register the sound of a moving vehicle. More soldiers? Through a fog of agony and darkness, I hear shouts and stomping feet.

The pain worsens with each second. My eyes are open, although my consciousness has begun to drift away into a sea of darkness.

Firm, strong muscles scoop me up. Why is the soldier holding me to his chest? I struggle to push him away. My arm trembles upward an inch before falling limp at my side.

I'm about to pass out when I hear a taut, deep voice.

"Don't die."

CHAPTER 27

Near death experiences

"IF YOU HEAR ME, move your leg." The voice sounds distant and distorted. My leg doesn't move an inch, and the pain is killing me. I want to beg the speaker to take away the pain. Am I dying? If I'm going to die, I wish he'd stop the pain like Petrov stopped Sara's agony.

The hoarse, slightly accented voice is clearer now. "Sergeant Wong, go after Sleecket."

My eyes ache when I open them. A scowling, pained face looms above me. The darkness engulfs me, but I fight unconsciousness, struggling to hear everything.

"Her heart has stopped," someone says.

"She's so cold," says a feminine voice. "Her muscles are so rigid. Is she alive?"

I'm lying on my back on a flat surface. Someone cuts my trousers around my thigh wound.

"Oh no!" says a second woman. Cara?

"Prince Aleksey, look at this!" says another accented voice.

Aleksey? It can't be. He's far away. Is he already back from his commission? I want to tell him to take care of my family, but my voice fails me. All that I manage is a garbled mess.

"*Shh*, it's okay."

Tristan's voice is desperate. "He injected her with tonics."

With all my willpower, I open my eyes, again. Everything is dark, but somehow I see Aleksey's long, blond hair.

The next thing I know, I'm on my stomach. In a swift movement, he shreds my trousers to pieces. His lips find my thigh and suck harshly.

Stop! It hurts! But the pain starts to dull little by little as if Aleksey is sucking it out of my body.

A warm hand caresses my forehead and slides to my cheek. Aleksey whispers in my ear. How can he make his voice sound authoritative, worried, and gentle at the same time?

"*Meine mutige Kämpferin*. Fight death with all you have."

I can no longer stay conscious. I let the darkness envelop me.

I catch glimpses of my body lying limp on a clinic bed, attached to a tangle of tubes. I hear voices telling me that it's not my time to join them yet. Mom, Angie Weaver, Rey's mom. It doesn't matter whether I'm having a near-death experience or losing my mind. All I know is that I can see and hear everything that's happening around me. That's how I learn that the Comanches and Poncho sustained only minor wounds.

I've read once that people feel peaceful during near-death experiences. Sometimes they see dead relatives. Not me. I'm all by myself, desperately fighting to return to my body and afraid that I'll die if I don't. Plus, the pain doesn't match my idea of peace. My heart has stopped four times, and the pain of the electric charges they use to make it beat again is excruciating.

I float over my inert body. My family is here, and so are Rey and Aleksey, leaning against the tiled walls. Rey is openly concerned, while the brooding general conceals his emotions behind a scowl.

I need to make sure that Aleksey helps my brother, but I continue watching the clinic's ER from above.

Olmo pats my shoulder, his voice hopeful. "Come back to us, Lila. You can do it."

Azalea looks from me to Aleksey as she holds my hand. "You really like your drama, don't you? Wake up, idiot, so I can kick your ass for frightening us."

"Hey! Her mouth twitched. Are you smiling, Lila?" asks Dad. "Are you listening?" I want to answer him, but the drugs drag me back into a dark tunnel.

The drugs have another undesired side effect. They give me double dreams. I've had dreams within dreams before, but the tonics have made them more frequent. My dreams are vivid, a combination of every recruitment ceremony I've ever witnessed. Gary stalks me in my dreams, but nothing wakes me. I'm lucid. Completely aware that I'm dreaming, but the terror is still there until darkness engulfs me again.

Among darkness and recruitment scenes, I dream about Aleksey. When no one is around, he lets himself reveal a wounded expression.

He grabs my hand and speaks quietly. "*Kämpferin. Meine kleine Kämpferin.* I don't want to lose you."

The darkness overpowers me, but I'm awake. Time loses its meaning, and I'm no longer sure what's real and what's not.

When I open my eyes, I don't recognize my surroundings. Then I realize that my hospital cot has been moved into Aleksey's room.

I give myself a once-over. My wrist is connected to an IV line rather than to multiple tubes, and I'm naked beneath the hospital gown.

"Finally, you're awake," says Dad brightly.

He shoots me the kinds of questions a doctor needs to ask his patients to gauge their health.

I look at the door wistfully. I need air. I yearn to escape this room, but my eyelids feel heavy, and I'm not sure I can get up.

I force myself to sit and scan my surroundings. I slept here once and hardly remember the spacious room. The large walls are bare except for a digital torch. Aleksey's double bass leans against an abnormally high chair. There's a mirrored wardrobe next to a door that leads to a bathroom, and a nightstand that wasn't here a few nights ago. No pictures, no personal items.

What stands out is his gigantic bed—perfectly made and covered by one of his red capes. How can a soldier's bed look so proportionally similar to a regular single bed? I measured it once, out of curiosity. Height: fifty inches. Length: eighty-eight inches. Width: forty-four inches.

"Why am I here?" I ask, still staring at his bed.

"You were delirious and kept screaming about soldiers coming," dad answers calmly. "I thought that the drugs had worsened the symptoms of your post-traumatic stress disorder, but you were right. We've had plenty of injured troops. I didn't want you to wake up surrounded by them."

"The bugs ... Gary threatened us—"

"*Shh.* It's okay. Mr. Fürst has a battalion hunting him down. The young soldier was found dead. Sergeant Sleecket was tried in absence by a Patriot court and sentenced to death."

"Death? Why?"

"Sleecket stayed in the country illegally, stealing and faking army items. He coerced an underage Patriot citizen to attack you. When he left the hospital before his deportation, he disobeyed a direct order from a general. That's equal to desertion and treason."

"Where is Aleksey? What about his promise? And Olmo?"

"Don't worry about it, Lila. It's been arranged, but don't ask him until you thank him. We owe him so much already. He read your note and found you in the nick of time. And he's been taking care of you as much as his Accord cop duties allow him."

"It was ... close ... my death."

Dad nods. "You were lucky, Lila. Soldiers using tonics on regular people is something I've never seen. I didn't know how to treat you. They don't use drugs indiscriminately. Genetic engineers prepare their bodies for years before receiving those drugs. They keep strict control over the chemicals that enter their bodies. Anything that alters that balance, like alcohol particles, could have—" his eyebrows knit together. "I was afraid of even starting the IV."

He removes the catheter that connects the IV line to my wrist.

"Rey took care of you, too ... until you sent him away." Dad looks at my puzzled expression and explains, "You were screaming for him to go away. Extremely rudely, I might add."

"Oh, no! I didn't mean to—"

"*Shh.* Don't worry. My godson knows you meant no harm. I explained to him what PTSD means, what you've been suffering since *that day.* The drugs might have worsened your symptoms. I can't tell for sure."

I lie down, looking at Dad. Long moments pass in peaceful silence.

His eyes take in the cop's bed before falling on mine. "Rey doesn't know you're here, though. He is overprotective, so let's keep this sleeping arrangement a secret, shall we?"

I sit up, ignoring his question. "I need air."

"Not yet. Take it one step at a time."

Dad crosses the room in his cart and takes in the bed again. "You should never act against yourself."

He always says that when he thinks I'm not taking care of my health.

I collapse back onto the bed, staring at him in wonder. For some reason, I think he may be talking about something else.

Dad changes the subject.

"You know, the twins will be so happy to hear you're finally awake."

Am I, though?

The soldiers have inspected the clinic, but didn't dare check Aleksey's room. He clearly intimidates them.

The only window in the room reveals a ruby-red sunset. I know I've been awake enough to feed myself. To go to the toilet and to fool the twins. But Dad keeps giving me sedatives, and the grogginess never goes away. He says three days have passed since the incident, but it feels like years. The out-of-body experiences have stopped, but I have false awakenings all the time. I dream that I'm sleeping on this bed, then I dream that I wake up feeling dazed … but it's all still a dream. Dad says the soldier's drugs led to "mild schizophrenic symptoms."

I get up woozily, surprised to find myself alone. Where is everybody?

As I make my way to the door, an angry voice stops me.

"Don't. The soldiers are still around."

I flinch in surprise. I didn't notice Aleksey's seven-foot, one-inch frame at first, as the sedatives make me inattentive. He's in a chair, his bass between his legs, adjusting the strings. He's wearing black slacks and a white shirt that opens at the chest.

I continue my slow walk toward the door. I need air. Badly.

Aleksey storms over to me, irritated by my defiance. "Stop! Return to bed."

He sounds so commanding that the grogginess disappears. "Nobody will see me if I'm careful."

"I'll drag you to bed, Miss Velez," he growls threateningly.

I'm almost at the door now, more awake than ever. I've just remembered how much I like him. Defying him creates a special energy between us. He wants me to obey him, and I want to see how far he'll go to stop me.

I barely have time to turn the doorknob when he scoops me up and carries me to the bed. His voice is angry. "If you're going to act like a brat, I'll tie you up."

He lays me on the bed softly, checks my blood pressure and temperature, and returns to his seat. He plays a fast and furious melody, his eyes closed, completely engrossed in his music.

Disappointment curls through me. That's it? The way he's just treated me makes me feel as if, to him, I'm just a little girl.

I sit up and look at him. The way he skillfully works the strings makes me aware of the contrast between us. He's older than I am in more than one sense. The man is not only the leader of his unit, but also well-traveled and skilled at music, medicine, and the art of seduction. I'm just a regular girl and hardly a leader. I have yet to seduce anyone, or even leave my hometown. For me, attending medical or music school is only a dream. In short, he has lived his life. Whether he has led a good life or a bad life, at least he has lived. My life is based on survival, which means I have yet to live at all.

But I want to.

Aleksey has offered to teach me the basics of sexuality, but at the moment, he's ignoring me completely. I am stirred by a yearning to make him pay attention.

I rush toward the door. I don't take two strides before my back slams against a hard surface. His palms are pressed against the wall, and my head is enclosed between them. Aleksey kneels on one knee. We're face to face now.

"Lila."

The hoarse sound of Aleksey's voice makes me shudder. Nobody has ever said my name like that, with that breathy, lustful quality. I don't want to admit that I love the way my name sounds on his lips.

I close my eyes. *Please say my name again.* All I want is to hear him say my name.

My mind reels, and for a moment, a black haze overcomes me. I feel that I'm about to faint. The sedatives are keeping me from thinking clearly.

I try to escape, but I find myself caged in the prison of his strong arms. Eager anticipation courses through me. Something is about to happen. I want *it* to happen, but insecurities riddle my mind. *Am I safe with him? Will he be gentle?*

"Let's start your training." The way his breath caresses my face sends sparks all over my body.

I'm trembling. "I … *uh* … parkour training?"

A half-smile appears on his face.

I realize what kind of training he's referring to, and I shiver.

"Don't be nervous."

"I'm not nerv—" I gasp when he puts his hands on my hips and roughly presses them to his hardness. Rubbing. Grinding.

The sensations overwhelm me. I shove his chest in an attempt to put distance between us. "Let me go."

He ignores me.

I try to use one of my self-defense moves, but he dodges it easily and traps my wrists with one hand. I use all my strength trying to free myself, but I can't.

Aleksey's lips caress my ear, which makes my skin ripple with goose bumps. "Breathe, Miss Velez. Inhale." He inhales against my neck greedily. "Exhale." He blows his hot breath on my ear. "Even an aroused little girl like you can do that."

I try to push him. Is he mocking me? My body trembles with a mingled feeling of desire and anger. I insult him with every swear word I know.

I shiver when he gently nips the lobe of my ear. He sucks, nibbles, and pulls. I try to conceal my enjoyment, but my body squirms under his touch. I feel Aleksey smirking against my neck. He knows what he's doing to me, and he's enjoying it.

His tongue trails from the hollow of my throat to the side of my neck. Aleksey is acting as though he knows he'll get what he wants and is taking his time to savor his prey.

He trails light, teasing kisses over my collarbone, to my jaw, down to my neck. When Aleksey nibbles on my tender flesh, I realize that I'm panting. He's marking me. I don't want to admit that I love his animal-istic touch and the way it sends warm, tingling sensations all over my body.

Aleksey is still restraining my wrists above my head with one hand. The other forces my legs apart and reaches under the hem of my hospital gown. He caresses the back of my thighs, my hips, and my waist. I can't think of anything but the way an unknown heat is spreading over my body.

Big hands slide to the small of my back and yank my lower body to-ward his hardness. He harshly grinds against me and resumes his assault on my neck.

His smirk against my skin tells me that he's amused by my arousal. I don't want him to make fun of me. Aleksey won't hear me respond to his touch. I stubbornly bite my tongue to suppress a moan each time he nibbles my skin.

He rises to the challenge and unties my gown. My right shoulder is bare now. He trails soft kisses there, driving me crazy. I never thought my shoulders were an erogenous zone, but they seem to have a direct link to other nerves. Waves of pleasure course through me and gather in a spot between my legs. His hungry kisses slide my gown to the ground.

I can barely breathe. His eyes travel up and down my body. I instinctively try to cover myself, but his grip is firm. My nudity makes me feel extremely vulnerable.

He teases my hardened nipple with his nose, inhaling deeply and then blowing on it before his hot mouth takes it in. My head falls back abruptly, and my body squirms. My throat burns from the exceptional effort of suppressing my moans. I've never felt pleasure like this before. This feeling is foreign and overwhelming.

Aleksey's teeth tug at my nipple. When his tongue flaps quickly over it, I reach my limit. I try to kick him away, but his muscular arm blocks my attack. He sucks at the tender skin like his life depends on it. I writhe to free my breast from his greedy mouth, but he ignores my attempts to escape his torture.

Aleksey speaks, my breast still in his mouth. "Not a chance. I'll hear you moan, little girl."

He pleasures the other nipple before brushing my lips lightly with his. Stubbornly, I refuse to part mine. But nibbling his way in, he eventually forces open my lips, and I lose myself in his kiss. His mouth has never been more possessive.

I can't take the onslaught anymore. I come up for air in desperate pants. Aleksey attentively watches my pathetic attempts to regain control of my body. He must be enjoying my inexperience.

Just when I'm about to lose my mind, Aleksey throws me over his shoulder and crosses the room swiftly.

He slams me down on his enormous bed.

CHAPTER 28

Claimed and taken

MY EYES ARE WIDE and fearful when he takes off his shirt. I didn't appreciate how magnificent his body is when I saw him in the river. Strong masculine chest, muscled stomach, and a perfect V line. Tattoos and scars enhance his rough beauty. Unlike the soldiers who look too beefy and artificial, Aleksey's muscular frame is perfect.

I try to lift myself up, but I gasp when he pushes me down with his body. His weight restrains me. The contact of our bare skin feels glorious. I'm immobile, under his control, and—despite myself—exceedingly turned on.

Aleksey traps my wrists above my head with just one hand. His breath tickles my neck as his nose skims it up and down. He inhales deeply.

The moment he parts my legs with his knee, I look up at him wide-eyed. His face is intense, and I know that this time he'll take me. I don't want him to stop, but a part of me is trying to bring myself back to my senses. I barely know him. I'm still recovering. I fight his hold, but it's as though I'm fighting a marble statue.

Aleksey looks down at me sternly. "Don't fight me, little *Kämpferin*. It'll be worse for you." He grinds against me, making me tense. I shiver when he breathes against my ear. His commanding voice has a raspy, husky quality. "Just relax."

He slowly runs his hand downwards, reaching that intimate, soaked place between my legs that nobody has touched before. A satisfied groan builds in his throat.

"*Hmm*. So responsive."

A deft finger circles a sensitive spot gently, and I bite my lip so that I won't cry out. *Oh, God!* I never imagined it'd feel this good. I feel the need to writhe in response, but his weight is holding me down, unyielding.

His pinky finger enters me, and he gasps when I contract my inner muscles, constricting it.

He smirks against my neck. "You've been doing Kegel exercises. *Hmm*, inexperienced but naughty. I love that."

Shocks of pleasure run through my body when he rhythmically moves his finger in and out. His hand is so big that each time his finger is in, his palm presses my most sensitive spot.

He curls his finger, massaging another extremely sensitive spot inside me. I can't suppress my whimper. I'm going to explode into thousands of small, soaked pieces.

My heart pounds. I speak through heavy pants.

"Please ... I ... need to—"

He lifts his muscular body slightly, giving me room to writhe and breathe. Our eyes meet.

His voice is hoarser than usual, full of desire. "You look beautiful ... underneath me like this. Naked ... helpless ... aroused ..."

"Please ... give me a moment to—*Ahh*!" A loud moan interrupts me when Aleksey takes my most sensitive spot between two fingers. He doesn't stop. He strokes it sensually, deftly. I can't hold back anymore. I whimper loudly, and my response encourages him to increase the pressure. He's an expert in the art of giving pleasure, and he's playing me with the same deftness with which he plays his bass.

His fingers leave my body, making me feel bereft. I groan in protest. Then his hands grab my waist. He sits on his heels and brings me up, putting his arms around me. I'm straddling him now. My face is squeezed tightly against his collarbone. Involuntarily, I press my lips to it and run my hands up and down his muscular chest.

A vibration from his throat tells me that he likes my touch, but he stops me violently. Aleksey grabs my hands and puts them behind my back, clasping them in his hand. Obviously, he won't give me the slightest bit of control. He leans, pushing me down until I'm arching my back on the edge of the bed. My head falls back.

In this position, I can see us in the wardrobe's mirror. He's hovering over me; my breasts are lifted up and dangerously close to his mouth. The way he keeps my hands prisoner makes me look defenseless. Seeing us like this ignites my desire. The contrast between our sizes, our ages, and our power becomes evident. I'm the prey, and he's the predator. I'm about to be devoured. I'm about to be taken.

When his lips clasp my breast and suck, my eyes open wide as incredible pleasure washes through me. He looks confident when he takes off his slacks with just one hand, and the mirror reflects his full erection. I wiggle nervously. What he's about to do will hurt.

His hardness brushes against my pulsating lips. Once and again and again, drenching himself in my wetness. Massaging in the right places. Ripples of pleasure shoot through my body and pool between my legs.

He murmurs softly against my neck. "I adore your innocence. I love the few things you know. I love the many things you ignore. And above all I love … everything you'll learn … with me."

Using his ex-soldier strength, he turns me over and bends me until I'm crouching on all fours. One of his hands holds mine behind my back while the other keeps my torso down so that my breasts press against the mattress. I wriggle, and his grip strengthens. Oh my! I haven't ever felt so exposed. So helpless. Dirty. Used like an object.

He keeps teasing my lower lips with the tip of his erection. His voice is husky, sensual.

"How will I take you, sweet girl?"

Aleksey's fingers dig into my butt cheek's tender flesh, and his mouth descends on my engorged lips, devouring them hungrily.

"*Ah!*" I'm sure the sound of my moan will reach the town. This position is so animalistic, so raw. It feels wrong and pleasantly erotic at the same time.

"Will I take you this way?" he asks without stopping his hungry attack. His breath tickles that sensitive area and hot pleasure washes through my veins.

As though my body is a toy, he turns me again, and now I'm under him. One hand holds me immobile by my throat. The other grabs my left knee to force my leg to bend.

"Or this way?" he says as his now-soaked tip presses against my entrance, bringing agony and ecstasy into my weakened body. I whimper loudly, and the hand on my throat slides to cover my mouth. My already-wide eyes open impossibly wider.

The tip retreats, and Aleksey sucks and bites all over my shoulders. My breasts. My stomach. Marking me.

Whatever he intends to do with me, he won't do it gently. At all. I have to lose my virginity, but … like this? He's taken full control of my body and won't share it with me. He'll take me in any way he wants.

And, yet, because my body is yearning for him, I can't bring myself to ask him to stop.

Putting his hands on my waist, he lifts me. Aleksey sits on his heels and forces me to straddle him just over his erection. Our faces are closer now. I look at him nervously, and I see no affection in his blue eyes. Only a lustful determination to possess me.

"Wrap your arms around my neck," he says gruffly. I comply feebly. And soon I'm holding on for dear life, because, with the tip of his erection, he's teasing my entrance while making my hips sway to and fro.

He circles them upward.

He sways them downward.

Circling, swaying.

Each time his tip at my entrance opens me more and more.

Each time brings a fresh surge of pain.

And I know it won't be long. He'll enter me.

"Look at me."

I obey. His face displays a cold, harsh, calculating expression. He slides inside me millimeter by millimeter, then stops. I'm panting, knowing what will come next.

"I'm going to take you—" In a swift movement, he pushes down my hips and his full length is inside me.

"*Ow, ow, ow!*" I yelp against his chest.

"—this way." He growls and doesn't move for a long moment. My nails dig into the back of his neck in an attempt to diminish the pain. I'm breathing harshly. Beads of sweat cover my skin as my body struggles to accommodate the intruder.

It infuriates me to notice that he's looking down at me with a mechanical, triumphant expression.

Why does it have to hurt *only* me?

I furiously hit his chest with my fists. The movement brings more pain, but also an uncomfortable kind of pleasure.

"Get out of me!" I shout.

Aleksey pulls back until only his tip is inside me, and I breathe in relief before he slams back, making me flinch and whimper.

He doesn't stop this time. With his hands on my hips, he keeps moving me up and down, picking up speed with each thrust.

I cling to his neck with all my strength, and the pain, little by little, gets intertwined with a pleasure I could never imagine existed. The fullness, the connection between our bodies, the way my breasts bounce, making my nipples brush his naked chest—it's intoxicating.

Still inside me, he stands up. I instinctively wrap my legs around his torso and strengthen my grip on his neck so that I don't fall. He chuckles.

With brutal strength and confidence, he hooks his arms under my legs so that the backs of my thighs rest on his forearms.

His hands grab my waist to move my body like a puppet master. With each of his thrusts, he pulls my pelvis against him … farther from him … and against him again. Each time, he works my body in a different way. Each time, he seems to try out which angle makes my body react the most.

When he finds the best angle, the pounding begins. I'm weightless, defying gravity, supported by his arms and his erection.

He thrusts in a merciless, accelerated rhythm, and my head falls back. I can't decide if I'm in heaven or hell. Is this pleasure? Is this pain? All I know is that the most intense sensations are coursing through my body and pooling between my legs.

The dizzying, glorious sensations are too much. I squeak and desperately clench my nails into his shoulders.

My hips start to move on their own, adjusting to his rhythm, and that only makes the pleasure increase. He speeds up into a punishing pace. It's driving me mad.

Deep within me, the pleasure builds, making me whimper uncontrollably. He's pushing me closer and closer to the edge of an unfamiliar sensation. A sensation that my body knows is coming, even if this is something beyond the limits of my experience. And I want *it*. I want *it* badly.

"Don't fight it, little girl. Let yourself go."

My muscles stiffen before my body bursts in waves of unadulterated bliss. I repeatedly scream as shattering pleasure makes my body spasm. A white haze is the only thing my mind can register. And ecstasy. Sheer, delicious ecstasy.

I struggle to catch my breath and come back from my paradise. I open my eyes and see that we're on the bed. My shoulders and head are hanging off the edge and I can see myself in the mirror. He pounds into me with a relentless rhythm while his hand covers my mouth.

He's so rough that my breasts bounce, and my reflection looks closer to pain than pleasure. I'm gazing at him with eyes full of wonder. Every time his thrusts become painful, I flinch and whimper. He looks so in control, so violent. In contrast, I look so young and vulnerable. But the mirror doesn't reflect how much I love this. The fullness, the roughness of it.

I like it. I like him.

Aleksey's thrusts become erratic. His body jerks into mine in short, swift bursts before he goes rigid and growls. I feel his heat radiate inside me. I feel the pulsing throb of his virility as he plants his seed.

He rests his head in the crook of my neck. His hot breath burns my already-overheated skin.

Oh, God! That was fantastic, but also scary as hell and confusing. I wonder why a part of me feels slightly ashamed. I enjoyed it, but I feel taken rather than loved.

Aleksey hasn't moved. If it weren't for his ragged breathing, I would think that he was dead. Has he fallen asleep while still inside me? I lie under him for a long time, trying to collect my thoughts, his weight and my post-orgasmic weakness keeping me prisoner.

I feel sore, wet, and groggy. My reflection in the mirror is swirling and turning into a mess of shapes. Am I falling asleep? I force my heavy lids to open and shake my head.

The mirror reflects my thoughtful self again. I examine my reflection. Do I look different now? Will people notice the change in me? How am I supposed to talk to Aleksey now? I didn't think about anything at all when I ... *Oh, God!*

I need time to digest what happened.

I compare this first experience to what I've seen. Sometimes Joey is rough, but never like the cop. Aleksey didn't act like a lover. He acted as though it didn't matter how much I resisted; he would have taken me anyway. I know that I surrendered willingly, but he still took me as though I had no choice. He didn't have a way to read my mind, to *know* that I didn't want him to stop. Even so, he irrevocably possessed me. While inside me, he didn't kiss me or ask me how I was. Not once.

I haven't seen enough to know the difference, but isn't that the way … soldiers … recruit … people?

Oh, no!

He didn't act like a lover because he was acting like a … Gary's words replay in my mind: *he's a soldier and a rapist.*

Panic constricts the pit of my stomach. *Did I lose my virginity … to rape?*

"NO!" I scream at the top of my lungs. I fight against his hold. In earnest, unlike before.

He comes back to life and looks down at me before covering my mouth with his hand.

"*Shh!* Don't be difficult," he whispers.

His eyes bring back a painful flashback of *that day.* The soldiers, my mom. Almost the same blue eyes.

And exactly the same malice.

CHAPTER 29

Consent

WITH ALL MY STRENGTH, I try to push him off me. The mirror doesn't reflect my attempts. Instead, I see three people who shouldn't be here. Rey's mom died during childbirth. Angie Weaver died serving the troops, and Mom … *Oh, Mom!* Seeing these women means I've either lost my mind or I'm near death.

"Come with us. You prefer death over rape," says Angie.

"And he recruited you," says Cecilia Diaz.

I scream silently against Aleksey's hand. I must wake up.

A different voice echoes in my ear. "Hey! Wake up!"

I order my mind to obey the voice. Little by little, I gain control of my eyelids and open my eyes.

Divine leans over me, looking concerned. I'm gasping and shivering violently. I look down and am relieved to see that I'm wearing my hospital gown. The sheets are moist. That's undeniable evidence that my arousal was real, but I can't find any blood.

I need air to quicken this slow awakening. Fighting to control my unresponsive legs, I get up and search desperately for the door. I open it, making sure nobody sees me. The grogginess subsides as a cold breeze brushes my face.

"Where is he?"

Divine points to a colossal chair next to my bed. "Prince Aleksey? He was sitting here, but he left as soon as I arrived."

"Was he dressed?"

She walks over and places her palm on my forehead. "What? Of course he was dressed."

I close the door and stagger toward the chair. "Divine, this will sound weird, but did he look … different? Strange?"

She blinks in confusion. "Well, he was … flustered. Like I'd caught him doing something—Hey! What are you doing? You wanna move this chair? I'll do it. Where do you want it?"

"Next to the mirror. I think I might've been … attacked."

Her beautiful dark skin fills with goose bumps.

"Please turn around," I say. "I need to see whether I still have—"

She lifts a hand to interrupt and turns her back to me.

Sitting in front of the mirror, I part my lips and take a look. Dad's anatomy lessons pay off. The damned membrane is still there. Not that a hymen is proof of virginity, but there aren't any signs of tearing, reddening or bruising in my intimate spots.

The whole thing was a dream, though one so vivid that I'm surprised to find no marks except some bruises on the back of my thigh where the drugs entered my body. My skin still tingles in certain places—the spots where Aleksey's lips tortured and pleasured me. I put my head between my knees as I struggle to organize my thoughts.

Why did I have such a dream? In my dream, I didn't feel violated. A little scared, perhaps, but I was enjoying the thrill of it and internally gave my consent. I know I'm willing. More than willing if I want the guy. And I want Aleksey in a way I have never wanted anyone before.

The fact that Aleksey acted like a rapist turned what should have been a blissful dream into a nightmare. He would have taken me whether or not I had given him permission. I tell myself that if he were like that, he wouldn't have stopped when I rejected him at the river. He even protected me *from* rapists. But that doesn't mean he won't do it, does it? What if he is just trying to make me trust him? I've heard stories about criminals enjoying the challenge more than the crime. What if Gary's right?

This dream has reminded me of how little I know about Aleksey. How far we still have to walk on the path toward trust.

The worst thing is how much I … enjoyed it. I cover my burning face with my palms. I feel guilty and ashamed. Does this mean I subconsciously want to … want to …? *No!*

I rock back and forth on the chair. I can't control my dreams, especially not with the drugs affecting my mind, but I hate how turned on I was.

Divine's hand on my shoulder interrupts my thoughts. "V-girl? You want me to call Dr. Velez?"

I shake my head. "I'll take a bath." Dad said baths are allowed, but Divine insists on acting like a nurse, and she enters Aleksey's bathroom with me. After the bath, I finally feel awake.

Divine and I share complementary kinks, but we're not friends. Sisters in arms … maybe. She's an abuse survivor, so she might understand what's going on. I explain to her my problems with deflowering and my guilt-inducing dream. Normally I wouldn't discuss my intimate secrets, but the medications are messing with me.

"Kiddo, it's not as if … you wanna get … raped. No woman wants that. You just had a rough sex fantasy. I have those fantasies, too." She looks flushed. "In those, my man doesn't ask, he takes me forcefully … and uses … and discards. My Joey turns them into a reality whenever he can. That, ironically, makes me feel in control. *Rats!* I'm horny just thinking about it."

She changes the wet sheets. "I didn't have any control when the soldiers … I was terrified, and it was painful as hell. I hated every second of it." She inhales deeply and shakes her head as if trying to erase the memories. "I hate to think about it."

I'm at a loss for words. I put my hand on her shoulder as if to say, *I'm sorry they did that to you.*

"For two years I bathed five times a day. Couldn't get rid of their smell. It was on my mind all the time. I still have scars on my body and in my soul. Joey's love helped a lot, but I'm still trying to recover the part of me that died when they—" Divine pats my hand, which is still on her shoulder. "When my man takes me roughly, I always feel in control. I have the power to stop him … but I never ask."

She theatrically fans herself. "Rough sex is awesome when you're doing it with the right person. The rougher, the better. *Hmm!*"

"Well, not for me. I prefer loving, sweet, delicate sex. Slow and with plenty of kisses."

She blushes. "What do you know if you're still intact?"

It's funny how she's completely shameless about showing her body to strangers, yet she still reddens when discussing sex.

"I may be inexperienced, but I know that I need a partner who cares for me, even if it's only a little. Nothing of that *use and discard* business. And the boundaries should be well-drawn beforehand—what's acceptable and what's not," I say.

"Then draw the lines! Set your limits."

"How, if I hardly know the guy?" That's why I went for the safest option first. I feel a pang of frustration thinking about my unfulfilled plans with the only man I trust one-hundred percent.

"Then keep those hormones in check until you find someone trustworthy. I trust my Joey with my life. *Heck*! You've seen us. He's very harsh at times. How much … *um* … intimacy do you think we would have if each time he was like, 'May I touch you there, please?' 'May I fill your mouth with my cum?' Or, 'May this finger enter your'—"

"Stop! I got it," I say, suppressing a cringe. "The difference is that Joey knows he has your eternal permission. In my dream, the guy didn't know or care if I was willing or not."

She shows me the moist sheets. "You were willing."

"How would he know that? He assumed. The fact that he continued even after I said *'Get out of me'* is what scares me." I raise my hand to stop her when she tries to argue. "I know it's just a dream, but for all we know, that could be his style." He's said so before. *I'm into perversions that are too advanced, kinky, and rough for you.*

"I don't know. In real life, the guy could've done harm long ago and—"

"Maybe he's taking his time, and he'll eventually take off the mask." My knees shake, so I sit on the cot. "Can you tell me it's one-hundred-percent impossible for him to prefer rough sex in real life?" She shakes her head. I sigh and look away. "If rough is what he's into, I'd rather not have sex with him."

Divine looks at Aleksey's bed thoughtfully. "He looks like the rough-sex type, but I think he'd never hurt you. You should've seen him when he found you and thought you were dead. He looked as though the world had ended for him. I haven't seen that kind of agony in a man before. It broke my heart to see him so sad. He must be in love with you."

I raise my eyebrows. "That's impossible. Horny for me? Yes. In love? No. The guy barely knows me and at times can barely stand me. I don't know him, either." What do I really know about Aleksey's moral code? If I had second thoughts just when Aleksey is really at it, would he stop if I asked?

I put my arms around myself as if that will keep me whole. "How can I trust him with my body and be sure he'll stop when … if … I say so?"

Divine sits next to me. "There's always a risk with any man. I knew my first husband since childhood, and he forced me whenever he was drunk."

Her words make me wince. "Any other man … I'd fight him and have a good chance of overpowering him if it came to *that*. Not Aleksey. Not the man who even the soldiers fear."

I lie on the cot, and she half covers me with a sheet. "You always expect the worst from people, Velez. If the guy scares you, don't have sex with him. But if it turns out he's an honest man, you'll regret that you missed your chance. You won't find a better man for pleasure. A manly man who can do all sorts of tricks with his strength. He'd make you feel full and stretched. *Hmm*, you don't know what you're missing."

I remember how he played with my body, manipulating it into different positions. He had sex with me aloft for a long time, and he never grew tired. Even in real life, a stud like him wouldn't tire so easily. Now I understand why he said he doesn't need a bed for sex.

Divine's next words bring me abruptly back to reality. "I have an idea. The Priest is your friend, and it's obvious you trust him. Why don't you two hook up? *Huh*? You're wincing. What's wrong? Are you in pain?"

Not that kind of pain. In my desperation to feel safe, to have sex on my own terms, I've done things that I now regret.

I turn my back to Divine. "No, I'm not." I've promised myself that I won't think about Rey in that way anymore. He may be the only guy I trust who can control himself, but he isn't an option.

"Thanks for your help, Divine. I'll doze a little."

This vivid hallucination has put everything in perspective. The sex wasn't real, but my fear is. It's not Aleksey's fault; it's not my fault. It's just that Aleksey and I are not compatible.

And there's nothing we can do about it.

CHAPTER 30

Human touch vs. sexual touch

WHEN I WAKE UP, I'm not surprised to see that Divine is gone. My family is here, about to have a medicine lesson. Dad makes Azzy and Olmo check my blood pressure, temperature, and respiration rate. They're supposed to take notes and compare their charts.

Olmo is gauging my blood pressure when a sound makes me turn my head. How could I not notice him sitting in a corner, lazily stroking Poncho's head?

"*Aah!*" My skin heats up and I blush fiercely. I'm incredibly self-conscious to see Aleksey here after my orgasmic hallucination. My heart and breath speed up. The twins discuss the contrast in their charts, and Dad says that Olmo must have made a mistake. I hope that Aleksey, being such a skilled doctor doesn't associate my symptoms with sexual arousal.

I try not to think about it, but a dream that gives a girl her first orgasm is bound to leave a mark. Maybe parts of the dream were real. I'd better ask him now that my family is present. I don't think he'll answer testily in front of them.

Aleksey dismisses my shy attempt to thank him and acts as though he hadn't done it for me, earning an incredulous look from Azzy.

"Were you here when I woke up last time?" I ask.

He nods without looking at me, still scratching Poncho's ears.

I try to sound casual. "Did you—call me a *brat*?"

Aleksey's eyes meet mine with a malicious glint. Then he returns his gaze to his stroking hand. "I did. You were acting like one."

"Yes!" exclaims Azzy enthusiastically, putting her fist into the air. "Lila *is* super stubborn." She turns to look at Aleksey, who nods at her with a hint of amusement on his otherwise humorless face. "I'd call her a brat myself, but you saved me the trouble."

I scowl. Look at her talking so breezily to this pervert! I envy her so much. Aleksey doesn't intimidate her at all.

"Don't call her a brat!" says Olmo defensively. "Lila isn't a brat! She's just as unreasonably pigheaded as a mule."

"*Um* ... thanks?" I say, shuffling under the bedspread.

Olmo smiles proudly. "You're welcome, sis. I'll always defend you." He sticks out his tongue at Azalea.

Azzy laughs while adjusting my cot. "Keep defending her, bro!"

I'm not much of a smiler, but the twins' joking exchanges never fail to make me grin.

The feeling of being observed makes me look at Aleksey again. I catch him staring at me. He looks away before I can react, so my attention turns to Poncho. He seems at ease in Aleksey's room, placidly accepting his petting. I haven't seen my dog since that night, and now I love him more than ever because he saved me and the others. I blow him a kiss, and he wags his tail. I force my dad to promise that he'll spoil Poncho with extra food.

Poncho's the reason I don't drown in nervousness when my family retires, leaving me alone with the brooding general. My dog won't let him get too passionate without my consent.

Silence extends between us. Aleksey looks angry and doesn't make any attempt at conversation. I wish he'd play the bass and end this uncomfortable silence, but with so many injured soldiers in the clinic, he won't. I wish he were at least writing in his journal and not sitting there, trying to avoid looking at me. Maybe we can bond only through voyeurism and alcohol.

He wanted me to sleep here; it was part of his deal to save Olmo, but as the time to go to bed approaches, I feel like an intruder.

"Sleep in my bed," he says curtly.

I shiver. I was ready, even eager, for that before the dream, but now it feels wrong. Aleksey notices my discomfort and quickly adds, "I mean that you'll be more comfortable there. I can sleep somewhere else—for tonight."

What does he mean *somewhere else*? A visitant's bed? I shouldn't care, but I do.

"No, don't go. This cot is fine," I say, patting the mattress. "I'll sleep here."

"No. Your bed is unacceptable. Sleep in mine. I'll go if you want," he says brusquely.

I scowl. I think there's another reason for his insistence. "You really want to sleep *somewhere else*, don't you? If I weren't here, you'd go anyway. Guess what? Whether or not you're here, I'll sleep on this cot."

He steps angrily toward me. "I'll put it like this, Lila. You'll sleep in my bed. You can go to bed meekly, or I'll drag you to it." His voice is so authoritative that before I know it, I've slid under his bedspread.

The bed may look huge, but it's only the equivalent of a soldier's single. There will barely be space for the two of us. He sits on the opposite side with his back turned to me. "Now that you're in the bed, the question is, will you be more comfortable if I stay or if I sleep elsewhere?"

"What do you prefer?"

"I asked you first," he says impatiently.

"That depends …" I begin, blushing. He looks at me as if waiting for me to elaborate. "Where would you sleep? The canteen?"

"No. I have a bed at the Accord headquarters." He continues looking at me questioningly. "Why?"

My lips remain sealed while I look down. How can I tell him that I don't want him to go to a place full of eager visitants? I don't want to sound like I'm jealous because I'm not even sure that I am.

Aleksey seems to find the answer in my long silence. "You don't want me to go to the canteen, do you?"

My reddening face shows my affirmative answer. Something flickers in his blue eyes, and his face loses a bit of its customary hardness. It seems as though the thought of me being jealous has moved him.

"I wouldn't go to the canteen," he says in a less harsh tone. "Unless my men caused any problem there, I'd stay at the Accord head-quarters."

He gathers things as if packing to spend the night out. Perhaps he prefers the Accord headquarters to my company after all.

"You're healing. You must get the whole bed to yourself."

I realize at this moment that Gary lied about Aleksey. He can't be a rapist if he's so willing to give me space. My initial reluctance to share a bed with him disappears.

He's almost at the door, his back to me when my longing voice deceives me. "Stay."

Aleksey stops. He doesn't turn or say anything. *Damn!* I beat myself for asking. He'll probably leave anyway, but by now he knows that I want to spend the night with him more than I should.

I fiddle with the sheets, looking down. "Never mind, you ... you need to go somewhere to sleep comfortably ... call it a night ... wake up early. Forget it."

But Aleksey closes the door and walks toward me again. He starts getting ready for bed.

I'm going to spend the night in a man's bed for the first time in my life. For some reason, this feels even more intimate than the dream.

Aleksey's lack of modesty when he undresses borders on the indecent. He doesn't ask me to turn around. He doesn't even turn off the lights. I try not to watch, but from the corner of my eyes I see him taking off his armor and every piece of clothing underneath it. His movements are as feline, masculine, and gracefully rough as they always are. I read somewhere that soldiers never undress completely to sleep, but Aleksey doesn't seem to care.

When I look at his shirtless figure, a wave of heat courses through my veins. Aleksey is wearing only short-legged undergarments that leave nothing to the imagination. The moment is so intimate that I get butterflies in my stomach. He turns off the light, and the only illumination comes from the dim glow of the digital torch on the wall. As he lies under the bedspread, he puts a gun under the bed.

The bare skin of his leg briefly brushes my calf. The contact feels strange and deliciously warm, but I pull away as much as the bed allows. I force my mind to ignore his proximity. I think about something else instead. "When will we start training?"

He tries to give me as much space as possible by lying on his side.

"When I say so," he says.

"When will you say so?"

"When you promise that you'll do everything I ask during training.

No questioning. If you still want me to train you, I'll be aggressively strict. Harsh. Downright severe."

"I'll take everything, I promise. Just make me a good fighter."

He remains quiet for so long that I think he has fallen asleep.

"When will we start training?" he asks in a hoarse tone that implies he's talking about the sexual training he offered not long ago.

"When I say so. Perhaps after you answer my questions. What's your kink? Do you love someone? Your parents? A girlfriend?"

He turns his back. "Girlfriend? That's a ludicrous idea."

"Why is it ludicrous?"

"I'm not into girlfriends, courtship, or fiancées." His scornful voice reflects his hatred of those concepts. Tristan once said that Aleksey had never devoted time to women.

"Mr. Fürst, obviously you don't have time for a girlfriend, but all of your men are married. Are you telling me that you have commitment issues?"

"No. It's atonement. I've done terrible things. I don't deserve to be loved," he says unemotionally, as though he's explaining a scientifically proven fact.

My eyebrows rise in disbelief. I'm used to seeing a hint of arrogance in his severe stance, one that screams *I deserve everything and always get it*. Maybe he's being pragmatic. Love in the time of war is not a wise emotion to feel.

"Why?" I ask. As usual, he answers my question with a shake of his head.

My hand reaches out to touch his muscular back but retreats immediately. "Mr. Fürst, you may think you don't deserve love, but I'm convinced that you believe you deserve to be admired."

Aleksey turns on the bed, his eyes shining with humor. It makes me smile. He's just made revelations despite himself.

"Is that why the day I tried to hold your hand you …?"

He nods. "I don't want you to get false expectations about me. My offer is exclusively for pleasure. I'll make you feel so good that you'll feel like you won't ever need love in your life."

His words are both tempting and disappointing. No love means no pain. No fear that someone who is important to you will end up dead. But how can he go through his life denying himself love? If I were as powerful as he is, I'd feel safe enough to love, and I'd fight for it.

I shift under his bedspread. "What I want is a mix of human touch ... with a more ... *um* ... kinky kind of contact. I'm not exactly expecting romance."

Aleksey nods, his expression unreadable. "I said I won't give you romance, but I can give you human touch." He stays quiet for a while, then inhales deeply. "Tell me. According to you, what is human touch?"

I try to remember Olmo's words.

"*Um* ... if it were a dictionary definition, it'd go like this: Physical affection of a non-sexual nature that provides comfort, warmth, support, and humanity," I say, imitating the preachy tone of voice that my dad uses during home-schooling.

Aleksey turns to look at me. "And kindness. And recognition. That is exactly what you need, Lila, and what I need from you. Only from you."

I don't know why his words elicit a warm, pleasant feeling. *Only from me.*

"Why me?"

He shakes his head. The topic, like many others with him, is closed.

I try a different question. "What does human touch have to do with us?"

"At the glade, you talked about a connection between sex and love. I'm so averse to love that I won't even pretend I'm not. If you accept my training, I won't give you love." He looks down at his superb body. "But I can offer you the rest of myself and plenty of human touch."

I like his offer. We don't care for each other as much as we should, but if we had sex, it would involve more than just two people using each other. There would be *something*.

"Besides, Miss Velez, I won't stay here for long. We won't have any contact after the recruitment ceremony."

I pout, but he doesn't seem to notice. "You can always send me a letter or a messenger dove."

"That would be like giving the Patriot authorities a written confession that I'm fraternizing with Nats. They'd kill you."

I've known all along that whatever we have together would be short-lived, but hearing that he'll completely disappear from my life makes my heart constrict in pain.

"I'll show you the basics only if a temporary arrangement works for you. If you want to," he says.

I can't find my voice. Our silence extends uncomfortably for what seems like hours.

"Why don't you want me to sleep on the cot?" I ask, breaking the silence.

"It's partially moist."

My head snaps toward him. "How do you know?" I search for answers in his silence. If the *brat* insult was real, perhaps other parts of my dream *did* happen. "Did you ... touch me right after you called me a brat?" He shakes his head.

"Why not?"

"You were too intoxicated to give your consent."

"And?"

He frowns. "And? If, while you were drugged, I had touched you like I wanted to, I wouldn't be able to call myself a real man."

That's true. He'd be a rapist, but that's not what I was implying.

"What I meant is ... I have vivid dreams, and I had one that ... I don't know what was real and what wasn't. I won't call you a liar, but I think we had some ... physical contact."

"Only to stop you from hurting yourself. I trapped you against the wall, but not for long. The moment I said your name, you melted."

Oh no! "What do you mean by *melted*?"

"You had the strangest hallucination. You fainted, tossed about in your unconsciousness, and ... said my name."

I cover myself with the sheet, feeling the skin of my face burn. I'd give all the money in the world to evaporate on the spot. "You aren't a gentleman—" My voice is barely a whisper. "Why didn't you leave the room? You shouldn't have stayed and watched—"

He answers as if, for him, a girl having a sexual hallucination wasn't worth his attention. "I'm your doctor. I kept checking your vital signs. You seemed to be having a reaction to the drugs."

Dammit, Aleksey! "How long ... did you observe me?"

"An hour."

I almost fall off the bed when I try to put more distance between us.

"Don't feel ashamed, Lila. The genes of non-military people aren't prepared for the effects of the tonics, so their bodies react in strange ways to repel the drugs. The triggering of certain body functions is only natural." There's a certain pride in his voice when he adds, "You had an orgasm."

I groan. Such an intimate moment … in front of him, of all people. I hate that he knows that my dream about him gave me my first orgasm. "Don't flatter yourself. As you said, I was under the effect of the drugs. Rey appeared in my dream, too," I lie.

Fury replaces the smugness on his face.

That first night together, we fall asleep facing away from each other. But I wake during the night to find myself resting my head on his chest while he lies on his back with his hands under his head. I pull away, but before dawn, I feel the warmth of his muscular arms leaving my body. He must have wrapped them around me to keep me from falling out of bed.

Later in the morning, the last helicopter taking soldiers to a hospital leaves. I put on my cloak and visit a slightly less depressed Duque.

Tristan arrives at noon to take a blood sample. The lab test proves that I'm free of the drugs. To celebrate, we have lunch in the ER with Duque, the Diaz aunts, and the twins. I'm behind in my embroidering, so I spend the rest of the day trying to catch up.

When I return to Aleksey's bedroom, I notice a change. Something has replaced his old single bed. The engraved four-poster bed is a work of art that seems fit for a king. Is this bed for my comfort, or his? Why does he insist on this arrangement when he can get sleeping companions so easily?

Confusion makes my muscles tense, so I take a shower, still wearing my hospital gown. Since I moved to this clinic, I've always showered partially clothed. It makes me nervous to be undressed when soldiers can arrive at any minute. I try to relax under the hot water, but I can't. Anything can happen between a man and a woman who share a bed. I keep thinking about my dream. I don't want to feel that uncertainty, guilt, and shame again. As much as I'd love to repeat the blissful sensations of my first orgasm, I need to feel that I … that we … If only I could talk to him. Set limits. Get to know him and trust him.

One thing is certain: I won't ask him. I asked for sex from another man, and it didn't work. If things flow naturally, we'll have intimacy, but I hope the sex won't be like it was in my dream. I hope he'll control the beast that lives inside him and be gentle with me.

Can he really?

Chapter 31

"Even if there is some truth to women being raped in Germany when the Allies came, these were soldiers whose wives have been killed, raped, houses burned, cities and villages flattened, for no good reason. So yes, maybe SOME of them retaliated. It doesn't mean it's right to retaliate, but neither is calling Allies horrible. There was only one horrible side in that war.

Nats aren't that different from WWII Nazis. Patriots are treating Nats better than they deserve. Patriots limit their retaliation to sporadic recruitment ceremonies."

Comment on an article about Mass rape in WWII.

Downright severe

"WAKE UP."

"*Mm.*"

A harsh, angry voice disturbs my sleep. "Do you want me to train you or not?"

"Tomorrow," I mumble.

The mattress disappears abruptly, and I land on the floor.

"*Ouch*! What the hell?"

"From now on, you'll speak only when spoken to," says a commanding voice.

I look up to find Aleksey towering over me. He looks down at me so harshly that I recoil. "It's three hundred thirty hours. We'll train every day from three hundred forty-five to five hundred forty-five."

He doesn't want me to answer everything with '*Sir, yes sir!*' does he?

"You'll nod and shake your head in reply," he says, using his unearthly ability to read my mind. "Now get up." He doesn't offer his hand to help me. I feel dizzy, but I won't tell him. I need to prove that I can do this.

To my surprise, he kneels and lifts the hem of my gown to check on my thigh. His face gets close as he examines my skin, but he doesn't touch me.

"Your thigh wound is still in bad shape, but soldiers drill and fight even when wounded. If you want to survive the war, you'll have to give your best even at your worst."

I nod. I have a fever, and my head is killing me, but I'll take any pain if it means the slightest chance of getting better.

"You have ten minutes to get dressed, make the bed, and meet me at the top of the staircase."

With no other words, he leaves the room.

Making the humongous bed is a challenge. Poncho keeps pulling the bedspread for fun, and the posts don't help. When I finally meet Aleksey at the top of the staircase, he's looking at the time on his j-device.

"You're a half second late. Fifty push-ups."

I'm taken aback. Is he serious?

"NOW!" he yells, startling me.

I crouch and circle my wrists.

"What the hell are you doing, Velez?"

"I never do push-ups without warming up my wrists first—"

"No warming up. Now you'll do sixty push-ups."

I obey. By the time I'm at number forty, my arms ache, and I struggle to keep up. I'm used to doing fifty push-ups easily, but the wound and bed rest have messed with my endurance. To make things more difficult, he puts his foot on my lower back, adding weight to the last five push-ups. I remember his words: *I'll be aggressively strict. Harsh. Downright severe.*

I knew he meant it, but I didn't know that I'd resent him for it. Still, I won't let him scold me for not completing the exercise.

My chest burns and sweat runs down my face. *For Olmo*, fifty-six. I feel stabs of pain in my wrists, arms, and chest. *For Azzy*, fifty-seven. I feel like I'm going to collapse. *For Dad*, fifty-eight. My arms feel like lead, and I'm trembling. *For everything I love*, fifty-nine. *I won't make it.* I groan loudly. *For me.* My arms burn and tremble, but they manage to straighten, lifting me off the ground.

Sixty!

I want to do nothing more than collapse. Instead, I stand up to confront Aleksey's inexpressive face. Although my head is killing me, I feel proud of myself and submit to his warm-up routine obediently. Stretching, jogging, hopping on one foot.

I hold my ground with dignity until he tells me that I have to descend the infinite stairs, then climb back until I reach the clinic roof in less than a minute. I frown. That doesn't seem humanly possible.

Without a word, he hands me his j-device. It projects a minute countdown. Then he jumps and plants his feet down several steps only to immediately ready himself for another leap down.

Jumping several steps at a time, he looks as if he's flying. His biggest leap is the last one and covers what looks like twenty steps. When he reaches the bottom of the stone staircase, he drops to the ground and skillfully rolls on his shoulders. Then he barrels his way up again, several steps at a time.

It's taken him nineteen seconds—the kind of stunt only soldiers can do. I force myself not to gawk at him.

"It's all about balance and using the right techniques," he says in a steady voice. He's not even short of breath.

I step to the edge of the top step, feeling vertigo invade me.

"The impact of the landing should be in the muscles of your legs, not your bones. Tense your muscles a little, but don't get too stiff. When you're nearing the bottom steps, use your leg muscles to decelerate the fall. Don't bend your knees past a ninety-degree angle, and roll to the ground on your shoulders."

I look down the staircase, trying to hide my apprehension. A single mistake, and I'll fall and perhaps even die. But the fear of falling is nothing compared to the fear of recruitment. Perhaps if I attend the recruitment ceremony with two broken legs, the soldiers won't take me.

Aleksey climbs down several steps and reaches up his hand to grab mine. "I'll be with you to prevent any accidents."

That is if I don't make him fall, too. Looking at the bottom step hundreds of feet below me, I take a deep breath and jump off.

My stomach drops as I descend at top speed, spotting the place where my feet should land. Staggering, I manage to plant my feet several steps below my starting point. I struggle to maintain my balance, but Aleksey's hand helps keep me steady.

Heart beating fast, fighting the waves of vertigo running through me, I jump off again. This time, if it hadn't been for Aleksey, I would have fallen for sure. Each jump gives me momentum and accelerates my fall. Each drop makes me feel as if my stomach is clutched in an iron fist.

"Decelerate! Roll your body on your shoulders!" shouts Aleksey when I'm nearing the bottom steps.

I lean forward and take the last fifteen steps with my largest leap yet. I remove the pressure from my legs by immediately rolling on the ground. The hard surface connects with my shoulders, bringing acute pain. I still have momentum, so I use it to get up and sprint.

I don't have time to feel pain or gratefulness; I have to return since Aleksey is already on his way up. He didn't say I couldn't use the staircase railway to propel myself, so I do this as I take five steps at a time.

Breathless, I reach the roof, but I don't get time to recover before I'm forced to throw myself to the ground and out of the way of a wooden sword. I cry out as Aleksey attacks again. I roll on my side and manage to jump to my feet in time to avoid a third onslaught.

A wooden sword is propped against a metallic fence, but he blocks my way to it with a blow to my head.

"There are plenty of things you can use against an enemy," he says sternly. "Look at those loose bricks over there. There's a broomstick right next to you. During combat, you must resort to whatever you have at hand. Attack me with a pebble if you must."

The sense that I'm being rightfully chastised overcomes me, and I'm ready to kick myself. Why didn't I attack him with the broomstick? It seems I can't do anything well today.

Aleksey hands me the wooden sword. After an hour of drilling, we start a sparring match.

At the end of the session, my body aches almost as much as my pride. I'm drenched in sweat. With each attempt to bring air into my lungs, my chest burns. I'm sure Aleksey didn't use his full force, and even so, I was dreadful.

"How many times do I have to tell you to use your peripheral vision?" His cold, arrogant tone hits me harder than a punch. I'm sure he never yells at his trainees; his harsh, disapproving voice alone must keep them toeing the line.

"You focus too much on the enemy in front of you and don't pay attention to your surroundings. In real combat, that would be a fatal mistake."

I look at him with resentment, but he's right. Soldiers wouldn't give me time to breathe in a real fight. I won't waste my energy complaining about his training methods. I'll prove to him that I can improve.

Aleksey hands me a list of assigned exercises and orders me to train on my own later today for at least four hours. Then he escorts me back to his room. I remember Azzy mentioned that Aleksey directs his unit drills at six every morning.

His eyes turn to me. I'm surprised by their intensity. "A contingent of a dozen soldiers will arrive at five. Stay in the clinic."

He seems to silently demand, *Be careful. Don't go near the soldiers.*

Aleksey takes a step toward me. His eyes smolder. They are full of an emotion that doesn't match his detached, authoritative voice.

"I'll be patrolling from three to eleven p.m. Make sure to sleep early."

Both of us are surprised when he leans in to kiss my hair. He looks as though he has just lost an internal battle. A battle to prevent himself from being gentle. For the first time since I've met him, he has shown an almost imperceptible hint of nervousness. A bit of the vulnerability hidden under his tough exterior. It suits him. It makes him seem human.

That is, until he frowns. It's as if he realizes that he's been too kind with his trainee.

He spits out a single word, a word more in tune with his *aggressively strict* role.

"Brat."

He walks away silently, leaving me confused and blinking at the door.

After a few moments of dazed silence, I giggle, covering my mouth with one hand.

He said *brat* in a way that implied he didn't mean it. It was as if he felt that he had let his barriers fall and was building them again by adding a harsh word. Was I supposed to feel insulted? I feel flattered instead. He's shown me a bit of human touch.

That kiss on my hair is the sweetest gesture he's made since I've known him. I touch the spot, smiling widely. In an instant, my emotions have changed from slightly resentful to giddy.

I'm really looking forward to seeing Aleksey again tonight, although he might be mad at me by then because I won't obey him. I can't stay in the clinic. I need to find a job, and I have to teach the Comanches everything I learned today. But I'll be back in the clinic before the soldiers' arrival.

I'm preparing to take a shower in his bathroom when I notice that he left his journal open on the desk.

I feel tempted to look, but when I'm about to do so, I stop. I want him to talk about his secrets; I don't want to pry them out of him against his will.

Still, my eyes have glazed over the page enough to make out some letters that repeat themselves.

C.N.

I keep thinking about something Gary said. *Ask him about Clavel.* A female name. What if C.N. are the initials of someone he cares about? A sister? A lover?

My fuzzy feelings disappear, and my usual distrust of Aleksey returns as I stand under the warm water. I realize that as much as he seems to like me, he might never open up.

And that means I'll never be able to trust him.

CHAPTER 32

Preoccupations

THE WIND BLOWS THROUGH the train's open door. It's almost noon, and if the thunder over the ruined cities is any indication, a storm is approaching. The boxcar carries more Starvillers than usual, but I claim a seat next to Poncho on the trash-strewn floor.

My head is killing me and my muscles ache. I lean back against the wooden wall and close my eyes. I want to forget that my job search today in Shiloh has been fruitless.

Joey is standing somewhere across the boxcar, the wind caressing his sandy curls. As usual, we pretend that we don't know each other for the sake of concealing TCR.

Duque's ex, Veronica, is here, too. Sitting next to her chaperones—two aunts and two cousins—she isn't discreet about her engagement to Mr. Gibson. He's a man old enough to be her father, but with enough privileges to compensate for his age. How can she be engaged when it's been only a week since she broke up with Duque? I rationalize that she never loved Duque. She and Duque got engaged two weeks after they met. It takes only a bit of tragedy to destroy insta-love.

Unfortunately, her roaring voice forces us to listen.

"How was I supposed to marry him after that? As what? Would he have been a husband or a wife?"

Mr. Gibson grabs her hand. "He's not a full man. He's a fag."

I close my eyes and count to ten, breathing heavily to subdue my anger. Dad has taught us that there's nothing wrong with homosexuality, but Starvillers have very traditional gender roles. Aside from the V-word, *fag* is the worst insult a Starviller can muster. Well, according to Dad, there's nothing wrong with being a maiden either. But Starvillers think of V-girls as spinsters—females not attractive enough to get husbands. Even worse, V-people are considered the troops' bitches. Not that Starvillers' opinion should matter. It's not the use of the word *fag* that infuriates me; it's the maliciousness behind their words.

One of Veronica's aunts tries to shush her.

"Drop it, Aunt Shelly," says Veronica. "If my man lets himself get attacked, who will protect me? I need a *real* man. One who can fight back."

"Good riddance," agrees Mr. Gibson.

If Duque were here, what would he do? How would he feel?

Mr. Gibson touches Veronica's knee, and she bursts out laughing. "Yeah, can you imagine it?" says Veronica. "A marriage with two wives, *ha, ha, ha.*"

I don't make a conscious decision to slap her or to kick Gibson's groin. One second I'm sitting on the floor and the next second Joey is restraining me while Veronica and Mr. Gibson lie on the floor. He is grabbing his balls while she is shooting me a look of incredulity and fury.

"You didn't like it? Come and slap me back if you can," I say, thrashing against Joey's grip. I don't care that all eyes are on me. Duque is family—I have to avenge him.

Joey won't let go of me, so I make Poncho attack Veronica's legs, hoping that his sexual appetite humiliates her like she wants to humiliate Duque.

The train screeches as it slows down, the sign for Starvillers to prepare to jump off, but nobody moves. I push aside Joey. The train hasn't lost enough speed, and there are steep slopes all over the road, but I'm already at the door.

My voice is acidic. "That's for Duque." And my mom. And every recruitment victim who has been ridiculed in Starville.

I glare at them one last time and jump, letting my fury escape with the wind. I land on the balls of my feet, on eroded terrain, and roll the way Aleksey taught me to do this morning. Veronica's words have helped me make a decision: if I get to leave Starville, Duque will come with me. Whether Rey and Baron want to come with us doesn't matter. No assault victim should endure this kind of mockery, especially not an innocent boy whom I consider family.

When I arrive at the clinic an hour later, I head straight to Duque's room.

I look proudly at the final touches I've put on my creation. Sleeping with Aleksey in my hospital gown makes me feel self-conscious, so I have created for myself a martial arts-inspired gown that is comfortable yet not entirely uninviting. A jacket of white translucent fabric with a fuchsia satin belt and black pants made from a soft, stretchy material. I didn't sew the sides of the pants; instead, I joined them with hook-and-loop tape. I'm still confused, but if we get in the mood, he'll be able to undress me in seconds.

After training on my own and taking a shower, I feel a sexual vibe sizzling through the air. The anticipation is killing me. I've spent the whole afternoon thinking about what's in store for me tonight.

It's only seven, but I'm tired, and he won't be back until eleven. I trained so much that I have no energy left. My eyes close of their own accord.

I wake when I hear the doorknob moving. Poncho greets Aleksey with exuberance, jumping on him and barking happily.

"Welcome," I mumble.

"*Shh.* Don't wake up." He looks at my translucent jacket, his eyes approving.

I pull up the bedspread to just below my eyes. "I want to wake up. I was having a nightmare."

He starts to undress, and I force myself to look away.

"Sergeant Gary Sleecket is haunting you again?"

I try not to look surprised that he knows. "Yes. Is he still alive?"

Aleksey's scowl deepens. "Not for long."

"If even Patriot forces haven't found him—"

"Sleecket saved thousands of civilians from starvation and death." He waves his hand impatiently at my incredulous face. "Even here in Starville. That's why we haven't found him. Civilians all over North America are protecting him." Sheer hatred taints his voice. "He didn't want to hurt you. When he attacked you, he wanted to get to me."

"Why?"

He shrugs. "I kept an eye on him so he wouldn't sexually abuse civilians. Other generals didn't have the guts to stop him, but I almost killed him."

I sit up, a tight knot forming in my stomach. "No, I mean why ... why hurting me ... would hurt *you*?"

He looks at me, as though trying to convey through his eyes what his lips don't dare say. "Can't you tell?"

A powerful feeling constricts my chest. "I've made assumptions in the past, and I've been painfully mistaken. I'd rather hear it from your lips."

A strong emotion shows in his blue eyes. "My lips. I'll tell you with my lips."

Aleksey leans in slowly, his face nearing mine. At first, I close my eyes and lean in, too. Then I notice the alcohol on his breath, and all my reservations about him swirl through my mind. *Who is* C.N.*? Can I trust this guy?* I pull away. We're not a couple, so we shouldn't act like one.

He looks at me intently, reading into my refusal to kiss him more than I'd like. A scowl emerges on his face.

"Haven't I treated you right, Lila?"

Totally. He has offered me the human touch in abundance lately. Taking care of me while I was sick, cuddling with me through my nightmares, kissing my hair after a training session that stole hours of his limited sleep. But more importantly, he'll help Olmo. "Yes, you have."

"You want me. If I touched you—and don't worry, I won't—I'd find evidence of your arousal."

I drop my eyes, feeling overheated. "That's the problem. My body responds reflexively ... but ... I don't trust you."

"Because I'm an Accord cop?" he asks, his tone angry.

"It's partly that you look like ... *er* ... a certain soldier, and I'm afraid that your touch will trigger bad memories."

"You don't mind while you're sleeping," he says, placing his thumb beneath my chin to force me to meet his gaze. "I try not to touch you, but you always end up sleeping on my chest."

I blush and fidget uncomfortably under the bedspread.

The fury in his eyes turns to warmth. "I'm not complaining, Lila."

I know he's not complaining. This only makes me more flustered. "I told you that I'm not accountable for what I do in my sleep. But I'm talking about—" I look at my fingers. My blood rushes to my cheeks. "A more intimate kind of touch."

I can't describe the way he looks at me. It's like my words have moved him. As though he feels real affection, even admiration, for me.

"You implied that there was another reason."

"I don't know you. I don't want love ... at the moment, but I need to trust my first sexual partner. How can I trust you with my body in my most vulnerable state when I know nothing about you?"

He lies down under the covers, and I resist the urge to curl against him. "What do you want to know?"

"I won't ask you anymore. You always refuse to answer," I say, scowling at him. "If you don't want to talk, you must have your reasons."

"But then you'll never trust me, right?"

I nod.

He puts his hands under his head, looking thoughtfully at the ceiling.

"Sleep, Lila. We have training tomorrow. I won't wake you up this time."

Time passes, and I can't fall asleep. I toss under the covers. My sore muscles constrict, and my mind runs on overdrive: Recruitment, Olmo's health, TCR, Gary, Duque, getting a job, protecting my family, Veronica's malice, C.N., and, of course, the disturbingly handsome man resting beside me.

Aleksey hasn't moved, but I know he's awake. He gets up, and before I know it, he's playing his bass.

He usually plays solemn, furious pieces. This time is different. His skillful hands produce a sweet, soothing melody that seems to tell a personal story of tenderness and passion. I open my eyes and look at him, fascinated. He works the bow skillfully over the cords, his eyes closed, looking far away from here. He takes deep breaths that ruffle the blond strands falling on his face.

My muscles relax. Finally, I can't fight sleep anymore. I don't know if I'm dreaming, but I think I hear him speaking in a soft voice.

"Sleep now, *meine kleine Kämpferin*. Everything will be all right."

As the tornado approaches the Patriot railroad, we plant our bombs in holes we previously dug. Manipulating the bombs with the wind working against us is difficult. Mathew, Luke, and Rey lie flat on the ground to avoid the debris. In the meantime, I attach the detonator, being careful not to blow myself up.

We've hiked through woods and valleys for hours to reach this point several miles north of Starville. Patriot battalions don't keep watch over the cargo train routes in the highest points of the Lion Sierra region. The tornado will scare anyone who is foolish enough to try. The soldiers haven't mastered the art of tornado chasing like we have.

The bomb explodes in a series of *booms* and *bangs*. This will delay the drug supplies that keep the soldiers strong. With a little luck, the engineers won't notice the road is damaged until it's too late, and the train will derail.

It takes us a few hours to get back to Starville. Nothing lifts the spirits more than blowing up a Patriot railroad with nothing but handmade bombs. Protected from the stormy wind by hundreds of skeletal buildings, our group of four laughs as we jump the potholes that cover Deuteronomy Avenue.

"TGON," says Luke. This stands for *"The Glory of Our Nation."* The others parrot the acronym, but I can't join the chants. The troops are idiots for punishing innocent civilians with recruitment for what the Nat leaders did, but I agree with the Patriots when they say that the Nat army is evil. Unlike the other Comanches, I'm not doing this for the glory of the Nationalist States. I'm doing this because someone has to take a stand against recruitment. I might not save myself from the ceremony, but perhaps other people will benefit from my attempts at opposition.

During the hacking mission that nearly killed Duque, Rey got the itineraries of many trains. This has made our attacks more effective, as we no longer blow up the roads blindly. Rey even got information about the train that will carry the 36th Battalion. For the first time, we have a real shot at stopping the ceremony. Now it's all about waiting for stormier weather to take the blame for what we'll do. I don't want to allow myself to hope, but the enthusiasm around me is contagious.

With more and more soldiers arriving for the ceremony, Rey insists that he has to accompany me to the clinic. He drapes his arm around my shoulders, and we walk behind Luke and Mathew. It's been a while since we've chatted like friends. It helps that I no longer expect that he'll be the one, and that he hasn't mentioned his proposal again.

Miraculously, we don't meet soldiers, but when we turn onto Genesis Street, we run into the Accord Unit on its way to the canteen. In front of his men, the gigantic German general pretends that he doesn't see me. In fact, as if they have been ordered to do so, the dozen or so cops act like we're invisible. The few who look at us do so derisively. Even Tristan.

Ours has to be a discreet arrangement. I didn't understand Aleksey's words until Sara's execution.

Rey scowls and clenches his fists. "That was rude, even for Accord cops. Idiots! To be asses like that on purpose is—"

I'm not offended by the cops' demeanor, but I'll play Rey's side for now. "They're not being asses on purpose." I look at him, and he grins. "They were born that way."

Rey turns to look back at them, and his grin disappears. "That *Fee-uh-st* guy, he just wants the novelty of untouched flesh. I told you, Lila. They're playing games."

He's right, but what he doesn't know is that I'm playing games, too. And it seems that I'm going to lose them all.

Chapter 33

"*Our troops haven't ever forced the consent of anyone. Nationalists have learned it's better for them if they cooperate with the war efforts on **our** side. They gladly and consensually enlist for visitant services. They exchange their bodies for food. That isn't rape. Is it prostitution? Maybe, but it's one hundred percent consensual and ninety-nine percent legal.*"

Colonel Rocco Smith, Leader of the occupation forces
in the 31st military district.

Gyges

WHEN I FINALLY GET a job in a Shiloh clothing factory, my already-busy schedule becomes hectic. Every morning, I work out before the sun rises. The rest of the day is filled with pill-making, going to work (sometimes double shifts), TCR meetings, more pills and then dressmaking. Some nights, it's well past midnight before I get some sleep.

I haven't had a proper conversation with Aleksey since that night. If I didn't know better, I'd say that he was mad after seeing me with other guys. Lately, he speaks only during training, and he's been coming to bed after I've already fallen asleep. I sleep facing away from him, but somehow I always wake up with my head against his chest. And he still keeps playing that same melody when I'm restless. It keeps the night-mares at bay.

I jump off the train after working a short Sunday shift. The noon sun falls ruthlessly on the hood of my cloak as I walk toward Starville. When I hear a vehicle roaring toward me, I prepare to bolt. In the occupied terri-tories, only soldiers drive all-terrain vehicles.

Before I can find a place to hide, the vehicle levels up with me.

"Go away," I shout, reaching for my knife.

The passenger door opens. I'm ready to throw the knife, but then I hear Aleksey's deep voice. "Are you coming?"

I suck in a breath, forcing my stress to simmer down. "Where?"

He ignores my question. "Do you want to come or not?"

My head sways in hesitation. Aleksey doesn't wait for my answer. He slams the door shut and says, "Take care, Lila."

I watch in disbelief as the ATV rolls away. His manners don't match his last name.

The vehicle is several yards away. An impulse overcomes me, and I run to catch up. Aleksey doesn't stop to let me in, just slows down and opens the door again. I sneak sideways glances at his coy smile as we ride in silence. I wonder why he's in such a good mood.

After an hour, the old highway becomes rugged and bumpy. Trees and rubble force Aleksey to venture off the path, where the terrain is anything but smooth. The humongous ATV was designed for military men, and the buckles that are supposed to fasten me to the seat don't work as intended. I'm bouncing and struggling to keep my balance.

Aleksey answers my unspoken question without looking at me. "I have business to attend to in Gyges. I thought you'd like to get away from Starville for a while."

"You could say that." I grin, stopping myself from bouncing on the seat like a child. I've never traveled past Shiloh. Nats aren't allowed beyond occupied territories unless they have two things I won't ever get: money and a j-device. Gyges is part of the Californian territories, so it's only a few hours from Starville. Still, it will be a welcome change from the monotony of my life.

Aleksey stops the vehicle near a lagoon in an arid, almost treeless landscape.

"Why are we stopping here? Isn't this area full of beasts?"

Instead of answering, he hands me a box. My eyes widen when I open it to find what looks like …

"Patriot clothes?"

He nods and exits the ATV.

I gawk at the lilac halter dress. In pure Patriot fashion, the long skirt opens at the front to showcase the legs. In addition to the dress, there are purple fingerless elbow-length gloves, a purple satin belt, and tights that complement the crinoline dress. In another box is a pair of purple high-heeled boots and, to my embarrassment, white underpants and a corset.

Where did he get his knowledge of women's garments? I suspect that General Fürst has been more involved with women than he cares to admit. Did that C.N. woman teach him about women's clothes? Not for the first time, I feel a trickle of jealousy over a guy with whom I'm not even in love.

Getting dressed takes a while, as the corset is difficult to put on. As I fumble with the clothes in my seat, I glance outside the window. The sun is hidden by ominous, gray clouds. Without the protection of the mountains, the winds have become ruthless. Aleksey is standing next to a solitary, leafless tree and his red cape is dancing wildly.

Finally, I open the door and call to him.

Aleksey looks me up and down. His pupils are dilated, and he nods approvingly. "Doesn't *my* Lila look absolutely gorgeous?"

I smile and punch his bulky arm. "*Your* Lila? Only in your most perverted fantasies."

"Not really. In my most perverted fantasies, you're naked." It's funny how this dangerous man is one of the few people who can make me laugh.

He leans into the vehicle to adjust the buckles, fastening me to the seat. I gasp when his face lingers near mine. I couldn't get away even if I wanted. Our closeness creates a whirlpool of overwhelming sensations. My heart beats painfully against my chest. I don't want Aleksey to hear it, so I try to distract him.

"These clothes … they won't be enough. They won't let me in because I don't have an identity tattoo."

"I'm your identity tattoo."

"A foreigner and a Nat? They'll arrest both of us."

"They could try," he says, smiling crookedly as he tightens the last buckle. "There. You're all tied up and have nowhere to run now. *Mmm*, the possibilities—"

He leans in slowly. His breath washes over my face, and I realize that I'm effectively trapped and paralyzed. I won't be able to stop him from kissing me. I look up and receive the full force of his penetrating gaze.

I'm short of breath, and shivers run down my spine. Well maybe it'd be better to go with the flow. I close my eyes and lick my lips, waiting for his mouth to meet mine.

But our lips never touch. Instead, he runs a finger through my hair.

I open my eyes, unable to hide my disappointment when he leans back. His serious face reveals a hint of smugness.

"For someone so young to have so many gray strands," he says mischievously.

Bastard! He knows I was eager for a kiss.

We don't talk for hours as we ride through the solitary highway. Other than soldiers, few people risk traveling on roads full of bandits, tornados, and beasts.

The buildings scattered here and there tell me that we'll arrive soon. At that moment, the ATV shakes, and a mechanical buzzing strains my ears.

Aleksey looks at me, unfazed. "It's the Gyges dome. They're taking it down because the weather is stable."

When Gyges finally comes into view, my jaw drops.

The skyscrapers shine in the distance, reflecting the blinding light of the sun. A circle of giant firs that rival the height of the skyscrapers form a wall around the city, framing the revision post. A flashing billboard welcomes travelers, warning them to prepare their documents and have their tattoos on full display.

My anxiety worsens as we get closer. I'm dying to go inside those tree-walls. It'd be disappointing to be turned down by the guardians at this point.

To my surprise, the two guards at the revision point look briefly at Aleksey and then wave us through.

"Welcome to the City of Blinding Lights," Aleksey says, brushing my gray strands aside.

CHAPTER 34

New experiences

FOR A SMALL CITY, GYGES is breathtaking. I've seen Patriot cities in TCR's old gadget, but visiting one is surreal. The glassy skyscrapers disappear into the clouds, and a bridge passes over a turquoise river that reflects the afternoon light. There are gigantic holograms, almost as big as the sky-scrapers, advertising all kinds of products. There's also political propaganda: a hologram of General Maximilian Kei towers over the buildings, soliciting support for the war efforts against the Nats.

Some holograms advertise the love district: a place full of repose places where couples can have privacy. The ads showcase barely-clad couples kissing and touching. The imagery isn't too graphic, but it's erotic and definitely tempting. How many couples are there doing what I long to do before recruitment?

Aleksey appears delighted by my awed exclamations. I'm taking in everything with no dignity whatsoever. He chuckles whenever he hears an "*oh*!" escape my mouth.

"Enjoying the view, voyeur girl?" he asks in a deceptively indifferent tone.

After Aleksey leaves a parcel in what looks like a UNNO office, he drives through downtown Gyges and parks in an underground lot.

We stroll down an alley in what looks like a commercial district.

Gyges has a booming military industry, and the financial benefits are evident. I see nothing that resembles the poverty of the occupied cities. There are luxury stores and game centers. The most recent models of jewelry-devices shine from garish storefront displays.

Gyges people are tall and beautiful in a plastic kind of way. There are plenty of *women with crinoline* wearing long, open dresses in gaudy shades of blue, orange, and fuchsia. Men wear outfits that resemble the multi-terrain-pattern army uniforms. Our wild, long hair contrasts with their stylized, short bobs, and I suspect that's the reason they keep staring at us. I hope they think I'm a foreigner. If they thought I was a Nat, I'd be in trouble.

Several holograms show footage of nasty war-related events: a group of Nat women torturing a Patriot prisoner; a bridge collapsing after a terrorist attack, sending thousands of vehicles into the sea; a group of scarred women showing the rifles the Nationalist soldiers used to rape them. I can't blame these people for hating Nats, but I wish their leaders didn't use that hate to make them support recruitment.

"Here," Aleksey says, handing me his red cape.

"If I wear this, they're going to stare even more."

"So what? You're shivering."

I look up and see that the dome is still down. I've been so distracted that I didn't notice when the temperature dropped. In Gyges, the temperature changes more drastically than it does in Starville. No wonder the Gygeans built a dome to protect the city.

Aleksey stops midstride to scribble something in his journal, before leading me into a well-lit alley.

"Why are you always writing?" I ask.

He shrugs. "Maybe I don't want to forget."

"Forget what? Is it military stuff you write in there?" Perhaps C.N. is a military term.

"Mostly."

"Can I see?"

A look of irritation crosses his face.

"No way. Not a chance, Lila."

I groan and look away. I don't get him. He gives me a bit of human touch by lending me his cape, then he acts like I'm annoying him. If he doesn't want me to ask about his writing, he should keep the act private.

He stops in front of a three-story building.

"Let's eat," he grumbles, leading me inside with a hand on the small of my back.

The restaurant is shaped like an octagon and spins around a column of small screens. Each screen projects a live image of the most beautiful places in Gyges. We sit in a private booth near a window. From here, I have a great view of the alley below.

Slices of fresh, sweet, and juicy fruits that are impossible to get in Starville distract me from the meat-based courses. Starville greenhouses produce plenty of fruits and vegetables, but we can't keep them. I eat avidly and moan appreciatively with each bite.

"Do you always make sexual noises while eating?" There's not a single trace of humor in Aleksey's voice.

"No. I just don't always have enough to eat," I shoot back.

But as the meal progresses, I realize that my joy brings him satisfaction. Aleksey encourages me to eat more, but I put my hand on my bloated stomach.

"I'm full. Can we take these desserts to the clinic? My family will love them."

At that precise moment, a round of applause erupts in the restaurant. A group of people wearing spectacular civilian clothes strut toward a booth. A standing ovation receives them. Everyone is beaming, and some people are trying to take a picture of the newcomers with their j-devices. The new arrivals must be celebrities. When I recognize the tattoos on their necks, I drop my fork.

Visitants

Three women and three men, most likely sponsored by the people who are eating next to us, judging from their expensive-looking crinoline dresses and armor. They're beautiful, tall, and athletic. Visitant job descriptions include military drillings since they travel with the troops. I wasn't expecting this air of physical power and professionalism that the Starville visitants lack. These visitants look more like warriors than prostitutes.

For an experienced general like Aleksey, dealing with gorgeous visitants must be as natural as breathing. He hasn't even bothered to look at them, focused as he is on eating his food. Aleksey eats a lot.

"They're not recruits. They're enlistees," I say, frowning.

"How do you know?"

I peer back at them. "They look well-groomed."

Most recruits become vassals: sexual slaves with no sponsors. Patriots think Nats are less than animals, so troops treat recruits as such. On the other hand, visitants *volunteer* to satisfy the troops' sexual needs. They're war heroes. The government doesn't pay them. Religious groups don't want the taxpayers' money spent on prostitution, but hundreds of donors sponsor them.

"They're beautiful," I say in an admiring tone.

"Top-paid visitants are always surgically altered," he says indifferently. The rest of the men in the restaurant are ogling.

"How do you know?"

He shakes his head as if to say, *You really don't want to know.*

I stare at him defiantly. "Oh no, you'll answer this one, General Fürst. You leave most of my questions unanswered. I'm sick of that."

He sighs. "Their breasts don't bounce during sex."

I blink and then look down at my empty plate. It hits me how little I know about sex, and how much he seems to know about the matter. This disparity between us makes him even more attractive … and dangerous at the same time. I understand momentarily why Starville men are so obsessed with unsullied women. If both of us were inexperienced, we'd learn at the same time. We'd be on equal ground, and I wouldn't feel the pressure to keep up with another woman's sexual standards.

I look at the visitants again. They're receiving the royal treatment.

"Have you … *um* … been with a lot of them?" I immediately regret my words. That's none of my business.

"Free visitant services are considered a perk of military life, but I don't have time for those distractions. Besides, I told you. I don't like to use visitants."

"Why not? Let me guess. You don't need them because you have a lover waiting for you in every town."

"We don't fraternize with women in the countries we aid," Aleksey answers, shrugging.

"Don't you have a sexual partner? Not even in Germany?"

"Not at the moment."

I purse my lips thoughtfully. At the moment? As if he's had plenty of flings in the past?

He said that he had rejected the visitant from his first night at the clinic. And Tristan mentioned that Accord missions are Aleksey's first and only passion. Yet, Aleksey doesn't have a marriage tattoo, and he's a young, healthy man. He must have needs. I'm sure that, of all the women who have thrown themselves at him in Starville, he must have accepted one or two. Perhaps Elena? The thought makes me uncomfortable.

"How is it?" I ask in a low voice. "Sex with visitants?"

He shoots me a brief look before turning his face to the window. "It's cold. I've received more affection through a handshake."

That makes me smile.

"How so?" I ask, extending my hand as if asking for a shake.

Aleksey ignores me and takes a sip from his flask. "Visitant services are mechanical, efficient, and satisfactory. In a way. But that kind of sex leaves some people feeling empty."

"It'd leave *me* feeling empty," I say, and his head snaps back in my direction. No humanity, no connection, just pleasure from someone who doesn't care for you. If it weren't forbidden, I'd try to save him from his solitary existence. Aleksey deserves to know the joy of sex in a committed relationship. Like Joey and Divine.

He finishes the rest of his meal in brooding silence. When it's time to pay, he hands over his ring. Jewelry-devices are the only way to access money in the Patriot States. We've eaten a lot, so the bill is two thousand Continentals. Accord generals' salaries must be high if he's paying such a fortune without blinking.

As we head back to the ATV, I decide to ignore Aleksey's mood and give more weight to his acts. He's rough around the edges, but he is the reason my family is still alive. He makes time in his busy schedule to train me. And his bringing me here feels almost like a date.

I grasp his hand as if it were something we do all the time.

He tenses.

"I'm not the holding-hands kind of person," he says warningly—but he doesn't pull away.

I grip him more firmly. "Neither am I. We'll learn."

He hesitates, and then squeezes my hand softly. After that, he keeps a firm clasp on it. It's evident that neither of us is used to physical kindness. I've never walked hand-in-hand with anyone before, and it feels wonderful.

Next, he drives over to the love district, where the skyscrapers seem to reach the crystal dome. Gygeans aren't prudes. Flashy holograms and billboards invite couples to come inside and have "relaxing repose time" for an hour. *Repose.* Sex. It's all the same. I look at the holograms with fascination. My voyeur side wishes that I could see what they're doing.

"Have you thought about my offer, Lila?" he asks casually.

From the corner of my eye, I notice that Aleksey is watching me as my eyes move nervously from one repose-place to another. When I gather the courage to look at him, goose bumps cover my skin. Aleksey is looking at me with a greedy expression. I blush deeply. Has he brought me here for my sexual initiation? The thought makes me fidget in my seat.

"Are you ready, Lila?"

He drives the ATV into a discreet, underground parking spot. A repose-place entrance.

CHAPTER 35

Exclusivity

"AH! YOU PROMISED WE'D go slowly," I say as I try to recover my breath.

"I couldn't help it. I can't think clearly when we are this close. And you can't deny it—going fast can be stimulating."

He's demonstrated the correct use of the gear stick through speeds that should be illegal even on a highway. In this empty parking lot, under the metallic repose-place building, his speed is insane.

Following his instructions, I start the ATV.

"You're ready to upshift now. Depress the clutch again and slot the stick into the second gear," he says, pressing his hand over mine to move the gearshift. His skin on mine makes me shiver. "Ease the clutch slowly. There it is! Good. Add a bit of gas."

The manual transmission of military ATVs is easy to master. The military instrumentation that comes with the control table is another matter.

Aleksey's hand shoots out to stop me from touching the panel buttons.

"I never agreed to teach you how to sabotage Patriot vehicles."

"You're breaking the rules anyway," I say. "Teaching a Nat girl the functions of a technologically advanced ATV? That's taboo!"

"Forbidden is good. Taboo is good."

Sexual innuendos. This whole lesson has been full of them. Of all the places in Gyges where we could have started the driving lessons, he chose a parking lot under who knows how many people having sex. A ride in the elevator next to us and we'd be rising toward the sex-rooms. His intentions are clear, but I'm undecided.

After an hour of practice, driving becomes easier, but I'm still distracted by sexual thoughts. It's thrilling to think of what would happen if he rented a room. We're already sleeping together, but he promised that he wouldn't make anything sexual out of our arrangement. He said nothing about a repose-place, though.

"You're ready to drive on the open highway, Lila. Let's go."

I get out of the ATV to walk around to the passenger seat so that he can take the driver's seat and drive us outside the city limits.

Aleksey grabs my wrist to stop me. His intense expression makes me feel a tickle traveling up my tummy.

"Come with me," he says in a seductive, throaty voice.

Oh no! Does he intend to take me to one of the rent-by-the-hour rooms? A primal part of me screams its approval, but the rational part of me needs to know him better before taking this step. Am I ready to have sex with a man who may hurt me? I worry about not being able to stop him if I have second thoughts.

"Don't overthink things, Lila."

Effortlessly, he lifts me off my feet and drapes me over his shoulder. The way he displays his strength by manipulating my body makes heated blood course through my veins. Before I know it, we're in the elevator.

I gasp when the elevator doors open, not to a repose room, but to a breathtakingly beautiful sight. An infinite stretch of twinkling city lights extends before me, and the tallest skyscrapers shine dazzlingly as if they were made of diamond. The sound of the wind beating furiously against the crystal-like dome shielding Gyges becomes rhythmic—almost like a sensual melody.

Placing his hand on my lower back, Aleksey leads me to a railing at the edge of the roof. I look down. A gorgeous sculptured bridge stands over a sparkling river. I realize that the reason he chose this repose-place was not because he wanted to get intimate. He chose it because this building has the most beautiful view of the city. I can't take my eyes off the stunning sight, but I'm vividly conscious of how close our bodies are. A warm feeling gradually spreads through me, leaving me speechless.

When I finally turn to Aleksey, his gorgeous blue eyes stare into mine. The words stick in my throat, struggling to come out. "Thank you for—" The driving lessons, saving my life more than once, bringing me here ... I can't pick just one thing for which I owe him. "—everything."

We look at each other for what feels like an eternity. He must have seen something in my eyes because his face warms up. It's the first time I've seen him grinning boyishly with no hint of wickedness or arrogance.

"What?"

Aleksey turns his eyes to the majestic view. "The way you looked at me. You haven't looked at me like that before."

"Like what?"

"With warmth. Like you care for me."

"I c—" I'm about to say *care*, but stop myself. "*Um* ... have I ever treated you badly?"

He sits with his legs dangling over the railing. I imitate him. "You always act so cautious around me. I wish you weren't afraid of me."

"But I am. That's the reason I can't accept your ... training proposition. But thanks for the offer."

The grave expression on his face speaks louder than words. Evidently, he isn't used to hearing the word *no*. Rey's not an option anymore, but I'll make Aleksey believe that he still is.

"I think it'd feel better with my friend." I look up to the dome. "I know him well, and I trust him. I wouldn't be nervous, and it wouldn't be a one-night stand." I shake my head. "I don't have anything against casual sex, but I have expectations, and I won't accept less."

Aleksey's good mood is gone. His face reddens, and his scowl reappears. Everything about him, from his clenched fists to his cold eyes, speaks of contained frustration and anger.

"Fine," he says curtly.

I look at him in confusion.

He looks up at the dome and then at me. "Fine. Tell me exactly what your expectations are, and I'll adapt."

"You'll *adapt*? I don't understand."

"I want your *exclusive* attention. I'm not having sex with anyone at the moment because you're the only girl I want. You want me, too. You have my exclusivity. Give me yours. I'll meet your expectations if you tell me what they are."

"What's the point? You said that you're interested only in sex, and that's not enough for me."

"That was before I saw how determined you were to be with your friend."

He saw what? After his marriage proposal, I haven't thought about the Priest in that way. Is this because Aleksey saw Rey with his arm around me? He can't be that possessive, can he?

"But what is it to you? If Rey and I—"

His scowl deepens. "I'd rather you didn't, Lila. I've noticed that you don't want me to have sex with other girls, either." He takes my hand and kisses my fingers. "Let's be exclusive."

My mouth opens in surprise. For a while, I say nothing, struggling to find the right words.

"One of my expectations is to know my ... partner. You're a mystery, and I don't get you, Mr. Fürst. What you are asking for sounds like a boyfriend-girlfriend relationship, and you said you didn't want that."

"I don't understand either, Lila. That day at the river, I knew I had to get you in my bed, under me. I yearn for you like I've never yearned for anyone before. I yearn to possess your body, but I also yearn for every bit of human touch you can offer me."

I take his hand. "I'll give you a good share of human touch, but ...*um* ... se—sexually ... I won't ever meet your expectations. You can't pretend that you aren't more interested in the sexual touch than the human touch."

A soft breeze plays with his hair. "At the beginning, my interest in you was one hundred percent sexual. I thought you'd be an adventure like any other. I would have given you the kind of pleasure nobody but me can give you. You would've been grateful and satisfied even if you hadn't seen me again. You would have preferred that to the alternative of never getting to know what a man like me can offer."

The way he speaks confidently about his sexual plans awakens my desire.

His eyes scan the horizon. "I wanted to use you and then return to my normal life as though you had never existed. But you're anything but easy. There's no middle ground with you. It's either your way or nothing at all. And I started to like you more because of that. Sex won't be enough for me now. I want more."

My stomach is full of butterflies. If this isn't a declaration, then what is?

He lifts my chin, forcing me to look at him.

"I gave you time. I thought you'd come around on your own. But you won't be convinced solely by desire. It's evident that you want a mutually exclusive relationship, but I don't know how to be with you in that way. I haven't ever had a non-sexual relationship with a woman. And Lila, whatever happens between us, I won't ever forget you."

"So for the time you are in Starville, you want … a relationship?"

He looks at me with an intensity that makes me melt. "I want exclusivity. I want your body, Lila. Badly. I want your consent even more. But don't mistake exclusivity for romance. I want the sex part. The bestial part. This is a means to make you crave the sexual touch as much as I do. What do I need to do?"

My first impulse is to dance with happiness. It should have been evident before, but now I can be sure: Aleksey Fürst not only wants my company and human touch, he also wants my consent. And he'll fight for it!

I take a deep breath and try to sound casual. "Let me know you. I hate that you know all my secrets, but I know nothing about you."

"Then do you agree not to have sex with that Diaz boy?" he asks, evidently disgusted by the thought.

"I won't sleep with him, and you'll have my exclusivity as long as you stop leaving my questions unanswered and—"

I gasp when he pulls me into his arms in a firm embrace. I snuggle against his broad chest. It's incredible how easily we have moved from a sexually charged conversation to a display of human touch.

Long moments pass, and the feeling of being small and protected in his arms leaves me cozy and content. He seems to be happy that I've accepted his deal.

"What do you want to know?" he asks without breaking our embrace.

I'm dying to know who C.N. is, but I begin with basic questions.

"Do you have a family? Parents? Children?"

A hint of the sadness he had the day I met him appears in his eyes.

"I don't have children. I haven't seen my mother in years. I'm not as close to my father and siblings as you are to yours."

I feel a pang of sympathy as he speaks. He's not close to his family, he never stays in one place, and he shuts himself away from other people. Aleksey is the quintessential lone wolf. I reach up to touch his cheek. We stay like that for a while.

Later, he gives me a tour of the roof-garden while I attack him with more questions. His favorite color is purple. His mother taught him how to play the double bass, and he's part of the Accord Unit orchestra. After the war ends, he'll return to his residency in neurosurgery. He's supposed to live in a cottage that the UNNO provides for high-rank officers on the Californian coast, but he hasn't been there for over a year.

He makes me laugh when he describes the first time he trained Tristan in Kung-Fu techniques. His funny side is adorable. Plenty of details come to the surface, and for the first time since I've met him, I feel as though there's no barrier between us.

When we reach the elevator doors once again, the wall I've built to keep him out has collapsed. I'm ready for everything.

I look up, and the smoldering expression on his face sends warmth through every nerve inside me.

Aleksey softly runs his hands through my hair, his sensual gaze interrupted only when he pulls me close and touches my lips with his. He starts with a deep, intimate kiss that I don't return. But the kiss turns possessive when I kiss him back, molding my body to his. Strong hands cover my hips and slowly move their way up to my neck before cradling my face. Soft touches of his tongue caress my lips. I can't get enough of his heady, masculine scent, of the way his long arms easily encircle me. Waves of desire run through my body and concentrate in intimate places.

"Let's go to a quieter place," he whispers breathlessly in my ear, raising goose bumps all over my body.

"Quieter?"

"Where we can … relax and have some privacy. I know you're dying of curiosity to see the rooms."

"That's neither here nor there, and I think we better … *Whoa*! Put me down!"

He carries me toward an elevator. I don't resist. My body is burning with need, so it'd be pointless to play hard to get.

The elevator ride takes us to the sultriest place I've ever been.

CHAPTER 36

Sex training

I NERVOUSLY SCAN THE lavish, dimly-lit room. It must cost thousands of Continentals per hour. From the red little sofa at the entrance to the marble mantelpiece, every piece of furniture looks elaborate and expensive. There's a long bench made of translucent material. Gadgets that resemble video cameras move in circles under the bench and around the four-poster bed.

Multiple screens on the walls project various images: ocean waves on one, a beautiful lake on another, and soft rain in a forest on the biggest screen. Some screens show couples performing sexual acts on translucent benches in rooms that look like this one. The sexual imagery not only turns me on, it makes me acutely aware of Aleksey's muscular arms around my body, of his massive chest near my head. Being so close to him ignites sparks that spread deliciously across my skin.

The widest screen projects a live image of everything that happens on the bed. I can see my wide-eyed face when Aleksey makes me stand on a plush velvet stool next to the four-poster bed.

The tension paralyzes me. He walks confidently around the room and turns off all the screens except the one that reflects my trembling body as a mirror would.

Aleksey points to the camera circling the bed's canopy.

"If it makes you feel more secure, I can turn that one off, too."

"Don't," I whisper. I'm a voyeur; I want to see what we're going to do. Whatever that is.

For what seems like an eternity, I stand timidly next to the bed, not daring to look at him, but all the while feeling his burning gaze on my body.

He takes off his cape and walks toward me intently. "Maybe we can work it out … your lessons."

He kisses me slowly, deeply, biting my lower lip with a sensuality that takes my breath away. "Relax," he whispers in my ear, making me shiver. "You can stop me at any time."

"Mm … how … would it work?" I ask breathlessly between kisses. "If you … teaching me stuff … with your hands on me … may trigger bad memories?"

His face and stance are hungry. Predatory.

"I guess I'd have to show you," he whispers in a husky voice.

He leans in slowly as if waiting for my permission. His cheek touches mine before his nose nuzzles my face. My head falls back when his lips graze the skin of my neck and collarbone. A tingling, warm sensation radiates through my body.

Aleksey inhales deeply, as though trying not to lose control. I feel his breath, but not his lips, on the skin of my shoulders. It's as though he's deliberately prolonging the moment. Every millimeter of my skin has become ultra-sensitive. The sensation of his breath on my skin creates a delicious current of electricity that washes through me.

Finally, his mouth brushes lightly against my shoulder. I never knew my shoulders could be such a source of pleasure. I bend my head to the side, exposing my neck. His lips barely touch me. They move from my shoulder to the pulse point on my neck, to my collarbone, back to my shoulder, then up again to repeat this exquisite cycle.

My dress falls to the floor, and I'm wearing nothing but a corset and underwear. I'm extremely turned on by his ability to use his lips to undress me.

"You're feeling it, too. You want my hands all over your body as much as I do," he whispers huskily while gently sucking the pulse point in my neck.

My trembling, inexpert fingers fumble with his leathered armor. My voice comes out in a whimper. "How do you take this off?"

Smirking, he scoops me into his arms and places me on the bed. Standing near me, he takes off his armor, and his naked torso comes into view. I stare in fascination at his bestial size—the chiseled lines of his strong muscles, his tattoos, and scars. Every part of him exudes a brutish, feral beauty.

I can't bring myself to look at him anymore. I turn to the screen. The difference in our heights, builds, and sexual expertise is evident. I look like a scared doe about to be devoured by a lion.

With feline movements, he climbs on the bed and crawls until he's on all fours over me. For some moments, we stare at each other, breathing forcefully. What will he do?

He places his hands on my waist and waits. When he sees that I don't panic, his hands smooth up my sides, sending shivers across my skin. A maelstrom of pleasant sensations curls inside me when he slowly nibbles my ears. His husky whisper caresses my earlobe as his lips do, making me shiver. "It's okay. Just relax."

His nose tentatively skims my neck, tickling me with his breath. The loud beating of his heart and his jagged breath tell me that he enjoys this as much as I do.

He alternates between kissing my mouth and kissing the hollow at the base of my throat as his hands run over my thighs slowly. Aleksey lowers his body, being careful not to crush me with his weight. I run my hands over his abs, chest, and shoulders, enjoying the contact. I can feel his erection pressing against me.

When I timidly trace his tattoos and scars with my fingers, he shudders and rolls me over him. Expertly demonstrating that he knows what he's doing, Aleksey loosens my corset's ties and takes it off. The only obstacle between our naked bodies is a flimsy piece of tie-side underwear.

Showcasing his considerable strength, he lifts me above him and takes a moment to caress my body with his penetrating gaze. It's nerve-racking and erotic at the same time. I've never been so naked and vulnerable in front of anybody. Except *him*.

I cover myself with my arms, shivering slightly. He realizes that I'm getting scared and pauses to give me time to adjust. For a moment, he cradles me against his chest. Then, with his hand firmly against my head, he kisses me gently. It doesn't take long for me to invite him to continue.

"Look at me, Lila."

His eyes become dark and unfocused. I can see that he's fighting hard to control himself so that I don't run scared.

He moves my body so that my breasts are hanging dangerously close to his face, to his lips.

When he sits up and makes me straddle him, my arms wrap tentatively around his neck. He tips my head back and trails kisses all over my chin, my jaw, my neck, down my collarbone and to the top of my breast.

"*Ah,*" I moan loudly when he takes my breast into his mouth and sucks it softly. Waves of hot pleasure travel from my breast to my core. I've never felt anything like this before, not even in my dreams.

"You're so beautiful," he whispers in a hoarse, deep voice while my breast is still in his mouth. His cool breath and soft lips tickle me deliciously. He nibbles my erect nipple before flicking his tongue over it.

"Oh, God!" I whimper. If the throbbing pulse between my legs keeps building, I'll lose my mind.

With his mouth still on my breast, he rolls my body so that he's on top.

Aleksey's eyes search mine eagerly, as if looking at them gives him the same satisfaction as touching me. His mouth moves to my stomach, my hips, and my underwear.

The sensations are becoming so overwhelming that my mind flips and my thoughts disappear into a strange haze. Something is happening to my brain.

When his fingers tease the ties of my underwear, time loses its meaning. I have difficulty breathing as the room disappears.

The Accord Unit tells the international audience that everything was done according to Patriot law. They turn off their cameras and flee the university gym.

Fifty recruits, the majority of them girls, are placed on big stones.

I close my eyes, revolted by the spectacle, but I can hear everything. What is happening on that stage is making Starvillers gasp and groan in horror.

At times, troops use a different kind of violence: the victim is drugged and forced into an orgasm. Nobody will believe later that she wanted none of it.

Just when I think it's over, Angie Weaver screams. A sergeant drags her to the stage. Buck Weaver shouts that there's been a mistake. She's his wife. She has a marriage tattoo. The soldiers shoot him in the leg before taking turns debasing her with delicate, mechanical precision, massaging her in front of the whole town.

They make her come twice.

A hand rests on my shoulders. I turn around and see Gary. "It's your turn."

I writhe and scream at the top of my lungs.

"*Shh*! It's okay," a masculine voice says, bringing me back to reality.

I'm trembling. I study the cape covering my nudity. Somehow, I'm still wearing my underwear.

He is very careful not to touch me when he passes me a hot beverage. "Drink this. Dr. Velez has to know you had another hallucination."

I blush intensely. "No!"

"Don't worry. I won't tell Dr. Velez what we were doing. But it's important that he knows you're having PTSD episodes." There's a sliver of concern in his blue eyes. "How are you feeling?"

"I'm okay. I want to drive back."

He nods and walks out of the room to let me dress.

This wasn't a hallucination. For the most part, all those things have happened. I'm not sure whether it was his touch or the look in his eyes that triggered the memory, but I'm sure he caused it. If his touch brings back memories of events I want to forget, I can't have sex with him.

If Aleksey is disappointed because he'll get blue balls tonight, he doesn't show it. When we arrive to the clinic, we get into his bed even though we haven't exchanged a word since we left the Gyges love-room.

He reaches his hand to touch my cheek, but I pull away. I won't risk another hallucination. His face remains impassive, but my rejection, after everything that happened today, is a huge step back in our friendship. Does he suspect that I'm about to tell him that I won't have sex with him because I won't risk having another flashback?

Even so, I need to know more about him. I have to ask him. Gary's voice replays in my mind. *See if he dares to answer.*

Tomorrow. We'll have to talk tomorrow.

CHAPTER 37

Aleksey's secret

THE WIND ON THE roof of the clinic hits me with force.

"Watch out! Your balance is feeble," Aleksey says after five minutes of battle.

His wooden sword descends hard on me. In a swift move, I slide around him and attack him from behind. He dodges easily and brings his sword down on my head. I lift my sword arm above my head to block the attack and stagger under its force.

"No. Plant both of your feet firmly on the ground. Slide your feet. Don't lift them." His voice is stern. He's been repeating the word *balance* since we started the spar.

I manage to block the thrusts of his sword as I try to attack his legs. That's usually the weakness of taller opponents, but his movements are as fast as lightning.

I jab forcefully at his right leg one last time. My sword finally finds his shin as I dodge another swing at my side. He's so stout that the blow doesn't do any damage, but he takes it as a sign to stop the sparring match.

I fall to the ground, exhausted. I don't care if it's not sunset yet, I'm ready to sleep on this roof if necessary. It's my second training session of the day, after a morning parkour session. I also had a stressful shift at the factory. I was supposed to take charge of a training session with TCR, but Aleksey insisted that we make our remaining time together count. I didn't think he meant training.

Aleksey scoops me up in his arms and carries me to his room. I want to talk to him, but I'm worn out.

I'd love to skip a shower, but exhausted or not, I never go to bed without washing my feet. I've always felt self-conscious about them, and after all the exercise I've had, they're in worse shape than usual. I stagger to the bathroom, wash myself paying close attention to my feet, and change into my sleeping gown.

When I return to bed, I'm surprised to see that Aleksey has undressed. It's too early for him to go to bed.

He surprises me with a quick kiss. When he pulls back, I'm wearing something I wasn't wearing this morning. A rose-shaped pendant. It's orange, the color of my favorite glade flowers. Nobody except my family has ever given me a gift.

"It looks lovely with your green eyes."

I want to say something, but I'm overwhelmed by an emotion that makes my chest swell and that forces me to sigh. I blink, trying to find my voice again. He'll appreciate action above words. Before I know what I'm doing, I lean in to kiss him.

Our kiss starts sweet and innocent until he rolls me down. I'm under him while his erection rubs against my thigh.

It happens again. A fleeting flashback to a different set of blue eyes. They belong to my mother's young attacker. He was so unfair, so violent. Mom was such a kind, pacific woman. She never hurt anyone. *Retaliation*, the soldier yelled while he was attacking her.

I push Aleksey away. We're quiet for a long time as I try to catch my breath. He turns to glance at me for a moment before looking away.

I wish it were a coincidence that every time things get intense, I have a PTSD episode. We can't go on like this. I might overcome the flashbacks, but we need to talk. There are so many things I want to tell him, and there are even more things I want to know. I'll start with Gary's accusations.

"Clavel," I say in a sharp voice.

Aleksey's head snaps up.

"Gary said you wouldn't answer questions about Clavel."

At first, his eyes show a hint of surprise, then annoyance.

"For once, Sleecket didn't lie," he says in a harsh voice, scowling at me.

Another step back in our *relationship*—or whatever it is. It stings, but it makes me feel good about my decision to not have sex with him. I can't lose my V to a man who not only gives me flashbacks, but who won't open up to me.

My voice comes out edgy. "Clavel. Spanish for 'carnation.' Is she your lover, Mr. Fürst? A member of your family?"

He sits up. "No, she's nothing of the sort. And I'd rather not talk about her."

Her. I knew Clavel had to be a woman, but even so, this confirmation rubs me the wrong way.

"Just answer *yes* or *no*. Are Clavel's initials C.N.?"

"No," he answers curtly.

"I never read your journal, but I did glance at it. There were several notes that I didn't understand."

He sighs, exasperated, but I feel entitled to know. After all, he knows all my secrets.

"You mentioned C.N. a couple of times. Why?"

Long moments pass before he answers in a gruff voice, "I use those initials to write erotic poems."

My anger subsides, replaced by curiosity and admiration. Poems?

"Will I get to read them one day?"

To my surprise, he nods, although his tone is stern. "As you are the one who inspired them, it's only fair that you read them. But not yet."

I inspired him to write erotic poetry. A part of me feels flattered, though another part feels scared. What if C.N. is something too kinky for me?

"At least tell me what C.N. stands for."

He lies down again and turns his back to me. "Sleep. Mental breakdown won't save you from an early morning," he says impatiently.

Hot fury curls its way inside me. Is he implying that I've been having too many PTSD episodes? As if I'd offer an excuse for not waking up? I've trained even with a fever and a headache. I've trained even when my thigh wound causes me pain. As immature as this is, I'll ask more questions just to irritate him.

"What's your kink, Fürst?" I ask him again and again in the loudest voice I can manage. Silence is his answer.

"Is it so terrible that you can't tell me? Or are you hiding that you're into men, too? Because that's not bad and—"

In a swift move, he wraps his left hand over my mouth. The other hand traps my wrists above my head. I'm pinned to the bed, immobilized by his considerable weight. It reminds me so much of my dream that desire spreads through my body.

"I told you to go to sleep, Velez. You're wearing out my patience, and you of all people shouldn't provoke me into losing control."

My eyes are open wide in surprise, excitement, and a little bit of fear. The atmosphere of the room is charged with sexual energy. His breathing becomes uneven.

I struggle to get free, but his grip is too strong. It turns me on, but, above all, it confuses me. It's one thing to dream about his physical power taking away my control and my having an orgasm because of it. It is a very different thing to fear not only that he'll lose control in real life, but that his touch will bring on another hallucination.

He inhales intently. I'm sure that, with his soldier's sense of smell, he has noticed the scent of my arousal.

"You want me to take you like this, don't you? Blink once to say yes. If you want me to let you go, blink twice." My eyes open even wider. A part of me wants to have sex with him, but I don't want another flashback. And yet …

I blink once.

Without releasing his grip on my wrists, he unties my translucent sleeping gown. The back of his hand trails from my waist to my now-exposed breasts. Aleksey touches them in a way that's more like squeezing than caressing. His touch is almost rough, but it makes me writhe in pleasure. He places kisses on each breast.

I whimper under his touch. My nipples harden so much that it hurts. The tingling, smoldering sensation between my legs is overcoming my fears. His erection grows harder, if that's even possible.

Aleksey's mouth clasps my nipple while his eager fingers tear apart my pants. His lips move south all over my torso, my stomach, my hips. I know where he's heading. The dizzying sensations threaten to make me lose my mind.

And then, another flashback. "*Ah*! Stop!"

He collapses on the bed. We stare at the canopy, taking a moment to normalize our breathing.

I close my sleeping gown. "I told you … I need to know more … and you keep avoiding … my questions," I say breathlessly.

He looks at me with eyes full of fire. "I'll answer everything you ask, except questions about Clavel. She is a secret that is not mine to tell."

I use the bedspread to cover my bare legs. "It's your kink that worries me the most."

"You have nothing to worry about. I wouldn't ever expect you to take part in it. When I become your first lover," he says this so confidently that I gape at him, "I'll be gentle and start with the basics."

I cover half my face with the bedspread and look at him with huge eyes. "Do you get to … live your kink as often as I live mine?"

"No. It's difficult to find women with the right mindset."

"Even among visitants?"

"Especially among visitants."

I muse about this for a moment. "If this mindset is not found among visitants, where would you find it?"

He looks at me and then at the ceiling. It seems that he won't volunteer more information.

"Correct me if I'm mistaken: Visitants don't participate in your kink, but regular women sometimes do."

He nods.

Why can't visitants perform his kink the way he likes it, but other women can? If he had even the slightest trace of romance in him, I'd say it's because visitants don't have feelings for their clients. I would never hire a visitant, even if I could afford one. But I'm the kind of girl who thinks that love and sex should always blend. Aleksey cares about the human touch, but he's still an extremely sexual man who seems to follow a practical approach toward satisfying his needs. He has used visitants even if they're not into his kink. There must be a reason.

"Why is your kink not good for visitants, but good for non-professional partners?"

He looks away, and I'm starting to think the worst. *Oh no!* This is bad. Positively bad.

I have to repeat my question several times before he reluctantly answers.

"Visitants always act as though they enjoy it."

No. A shiver runs through my spine. So, his kink is women who don't enjoy it? *Oh no!* Because of the recruitment ceremony, I've watched many women engage in sexual activities that they don't enjoy, and it's the saddest, most horrifying vision I've ever seen. What kind of man likes something like that? *Oh.* I know what kind ... the worst kind.

No. It can't be. Perhaps his kink is to have sex with shy women? Yes, that must be it.

I'm trembling violently. "You're saying ... you like it better when your partner ... doesn't ...respond?"

He doesn't deny it. *Dammit!* C.N. I didn't understand the meaning then, but I do now because I've just remembered something that I read in one of my dad's books. Still, I want Aleksey to confirm it.

"Just answer yes or no. Your kink has to do with hurting your partner?"

His scowl deepens. "Lila, listen—"

"Tell me what C.N. stands for."

He whispers the meaning of those initials, and I freeze. I don't want to believe it.

I'm not breathing. My stomach clenches in panic, and I know that I will remember this moment for the rest of my life.

Aleksey's kink is ... *to rape.*

CHAPTER 38

A father's feelings

MY BREATH COMES IN ragged intakes of air. What a foolish girl I am! I was so attracted to him that I wanted to believe that he wasn't a monster.

For the first time since I met him, hints of desperation show on his face. I sprint out of bed. Aleksey reaches to stop me, but I jerk my hand out of his reach.

"Don't you dare touch me!"

Poncho growls and puts himself in a defensive stance in front of me. I take Aleksey's bow and point it at him. "You're a rapist! You know how I feel about recruitment, and still—"

Aleksey takes a step toward me cautiously as if I were a doe about to flee, scared at any sudden movement. "It's not like that. Women love it, hence the name."

"Consensual non-consent is the name! *Non-consent*! That's rape."

His voice is even and low. "Nobody gets hurt. It's only role playing, Lila."

"The roles of a rapist and his victim. A rapist! *Dammit*!" I spit at him, but he easily avoids my attack.

Aleksey runs a hand through his hair. "It's just another expression of—"

"Don't try to make it look good!" I kick his double bass case, which crashes noisily to the ground. "You know *that* is what I'm afraid of the most. You know what I saw when the soldiers attacked my mom! How could you—?"

He paces in front of me, frustrated by my reaction. "I won't try this on you."

"The hell you won't, you disgusting, creepy freak!"

A fleeting expression of hurt appears on his face, but he soon recovers his usual confident attitude. "Lila, C.N. is an activity that—"

The bow in my arms trembles as much as my voice does. "No. It's rape."

"It's not."

My nose wrinkles in disgust. "Struggling with a woman so that you dominate her is—You're a rapist!"

He steps back and walks toward his wardrobe. Red capes and armor are neatly hung up, but what he takes from the wardrobe makes my stomach tighten in panic. It's the most illegal object in Starville: a firearm.

He strides toward me pointing the gun. What is he going to do? Force me into submission?

I'm shivering violently. I look around the room, racking my brains for a way to escape. That's when he throws the gun at my feet.

"Kill me. If you indeed think that I'll take you against your will, it's the only thing you can do to stop me."

I reach for the gun. It feels heavy in my hand, but I take off the safety and point it firmly.

He waits a few minutes before saying in a defiant tone, "If you are so convinced I'm a rapist, why don't you kill me? Shoot the gun, Lila."

Even with all the emotions that are hazing my mind, I know I won't kill him. The last thing I want is to face charges of arms possession. They'd kill not only me, but my family as well.

His glare is as cold as his voice. "You don't need to flee, Lila. Stay here. Sleep with the gun if you prefer." Aleksey strides furiously toward the door. "I'll see you tomorrow in training." He slams the door shut behind him.

I remain glued to the spot for a long time, still pointing the bass bow and the gun.

Just when I thought we had connected. Just when I was starting to feel secure around him. I sit on the bed, putting my head between my hands.

A whirlpool of emotions threatens to make me pass out. Fear, disappointment, disgust, regret, and self-loathing. How could I have been so stupid? I should've known better than to trust an ex-soldier.

I curl up, still trembling. Why do I feel scared and betrayed? He never lied to me. He never betrayed me. We weren't even friends. There was sexual attraction, but hardly anything else. After all the things that have happened between us, we're still perfect strangers.

Even so, I thought we had bonded. Both of us are outcasts, both of us crave the human touch, both of us have felt lonely while surrounded by people. I thought he was a voyeur. Then I remember that he said voyeurism isn't his kink. I never imagined that his kink would be something so disgusting. How can he justify something as horrible as non-consent?

The worst thing is that he has ruined me for other men. Nobody has touched me so intimately. Nobody has made me feel the way he did. I'll always think about how it would have been to lose my virginity to him.

In light of his confession, the memory of the day I met him takes on a whole new meaning. Now I get his attraction to me. If non-consent is what he's into, the reason he became aroused by our fight at the river was because I was resisting him with everything I had. Visitants never fight a soldier. They're supposed to enjoy everything the soldiers do to them. He mustn't be used to find fighters among regular girls. Everything makes sense now.

I don't think he'll force *me*. During the date at Gyges, he was fighting for my consent. Even so, the fact that he has used his considerable force on other girls and enjoyed it scares me. As much as he has helped me and my family, a man who has raped is completely irredeemable. I won't be able to sleep with him again. Actually, I don't think I can live in this clinic anymore. I'll convince Dad that we should find another place to live.

After putting more clothes into my emergency backpack, I look for my father.

As soon as I enter the clinic, Azzy pulls me toward an office, gesturing at me to remain silent. Olmo has his inhaler in his hand and his ear pasted to the wall, listening attentively. Voices come from the ER.

"Daddy and Uncle Baron are mad at each other," Olmo whispers. "That's weird, isn't it?"

It is. They call themselves *compadres* because Dad is godfather to

Baron's children, and Baron is my godfather and Olmo's. This union is more than a friendship; it's co-parenting.

"Lila, you're the reason behind their argument," says Azalea.

Baron's next words prove her right. "*Compadre,* what is my god-daughter doing sleeping in that man's room?"

Dad's voice betrays hints of tension. "She was unconscious, and soldiers were coming to stay in the clinic. Lila would've become a temptation for them so—"

"A temptation for what? For taking away her innocence? That man will do exactly that! Her own father is delivering her V on a silver plate to him!"

"Baron, Mr. Fürst is a gentleman. He's also a doctor. She's had night episodes, and I can't take care of both Olmo and Lila. Olmo hasn't been well lately."

I look at my brother. Although he eats more than ever, he's been losing weight.

The sound of furious pacing accompanies Baron's words.

"He's too old for her, and she's inexperienced. What if he gets her pregnant?"

"He won't get her pregnant; he's her doctor," says Dad irritably. "Besides, Lila's taking my pills, and the cops are on contraceptives. I've injected the Accord Unit myself."

"Other things might happen."

"Not unless Lila wants them to."

"If she *wants them to*? She's too young to know what's best. You're supposed to keep her away from anything that endangers her purity!"

"Like what? Like the recruitment? I can't keep her away from that."

"That's different. In that case, it wouldn't be her fault if her V … um … every future husband would understand that *she didn't want to* and—"

"Stop! Lila is eighteen, and I trust her. I've raised my daughter to become her own best friend and to do nothing that goes against herself. Whenever she decides to start her sexual life, I'll respect her decision."

"You can't tell me that this is what you want for your daughter."

"Recruitment isn't what I want for my daughter," says Dad brusquely, his cart making squeaking sounds. "I want Lila to have control of her life and to be happy."

Baron's voice is calmer. "Ethan … *compadre* … I wouldn't meddle if I didn't care for her as though she were my own daughter. She might not want to marry now, but she'll have to get a husband in the future, and by then there'll be no way to recover what she's lost. Even Camilla would agree with me."

"Don't mention my wife!" Dad's furious voice startles us. He's never been so angry. I'm getting furious, too. My father always pretends that Mom's still alive somewhere. I'll go ballistic if Baron says something about her that breaks that illusion.

"I'm mentioning her because she wouldn't have given Lila permission to—"

"Drop it!" Dad yells. "I'll put it this way, Baron. I'm a doctor and a father. As a doctor, I know that the vaginal corona doesn't have a function. What people call the *maidenhead* is nothing but a set of elastic folds of mucous tissue. As a father, I would prefer that she didn't marry a man who values tissue more than Lila's distinctive personality. Any guy should consider himself lucky if a girl as noble as my Lila accepts his proposal."

"But—"

"If she's going to tear that stupid membrane, I'd rather Lila make that decision herself, as opposed to the soldiers making it for her." Dad lowers his voice. "Do you get it now? Or should I bring in Duque to explain it to you?"

A thumping sound tells us that Baron has left the ER. The squeal of Dad's cart follows.

"That was fun! *Vaginal corona,*" says Olmo, giggling as he leaves the office.

I don't find any humor in the situation. I'm on the verge of tears. My father's support moves me. Whatever else is missing from my life, I'll always feel grateful for the honor of being his daughter.

I look at the window and see my godfather storming down the stairs.

Baron means well, but the Diaz family's decisions are situated in the territory of *have to* rather than *want to*. I can't live like that. I need a balance between the two. And right now I *have to* prioritize Olmo's health. I can't drag him out of the clinic to a homeless existence. Wasn't he the reason I shared a bed with Aleksey in the first place? I *want to* make my family leave this clinic, but I *have to* accept that they're all better near medical help. I'm the one who can't live here anymore.

"And?" Azzy asks with a malicious look on her face. "Have you lost the *stupid membrane* yet?"

I ignore her question and share with her my plans to leave. Azzy's incredulous but supportive. She promises to tell Dad and Olmo about my decision.

I still have time before curfew. There's only one place in Starville where I can spend the night.

Chapter 39

"*Some soldiers believe it shouldn't be considered a crime unless the victim is a married woman. That point of view sees recruitment only as a violation against a woman's husband, not the woman herself.*"

Edith Hayes, ex-leader of the 021st Visitant Division

The wounded lion

I WAKE UP, STARTLED, in a bed I don't recognize. A chiming clock announces midnight. A ray of moonlight filters through the window, giving the place a strange glow. Then I remember where I am. This is a bed where Rey has slept countless times.

My eyes scan my surroundings. Thanks to Rey's carpentry talents, the brick hut is full of furniture. He's made pieces of ornamental art out of chairs, cupboards, and cabinets, giving the small one-window room a cozy look. Fine woodworking that was supposed to be a surprise for his bride.

Olga Busko, Angie's mom, is my only living relative in town. While my father was recovering from the amputation of his legs, we stayed with my uncle Flint Velez. We fled when Azzy told me that our fifteen-year-old cousin had showed her his penis. We lived with Aunt Olga for a while. She's always been kind to my siblings, but she's still on bad terms with Dad. She can't forgive him for marrying my pure-blood Circassian mother.

Aunt Olga is relatively safe living by herself. No soldier would dare come near a hut so close to the museum ruins and their ghosts. Just in case, she has three dogs that are almost as big as Poncho, though they're not genetically modified. They're so meek that they treat Poncho as an old friend.

With my loyal Poncho beside me, I drift back to sleep. As usual, vivid dreams assault my slumber. A beautiful, deadly lion howls in pain, searching for the mate it has lost. Its search around the wood becomes frenetic, desperate. He searches inside a cave and then whimpers when he finds nothing. He hurries to look around rocks. He howls again. The lion's mate won't come back, and the predator's agony is evident. The pain of its loss breaks my heart. I want to reach for him.

The lion starts to race toward the cliffs at supernatural speed.

At that precise moment, I wake up. I've developed the habit of waking up at exactly three-thirty for training. I toss in bed for a while, thinking about recruitment.

Aunt Olga gets up and lights some candles when the clock chimes five o'clock. She's in her early forties, but the blonde, green-eyed woman looks older than her age as she moves around her stove. I accept the piece of bread she offers me as I get ready for work. I won't abuse my aunt's hospitality. I'll work my regular schedule and later return to the factory for a night shift so that I can spend the night there.

"Only ten days until recruitment," she says, interrupting my musings.

A shiver runs down my spine. I never forgot the date, but being around Aleksey gave me a false sense of security. Even though I'm afraid of him, I'm sure he wouldn't have let them recruit me. After his C.N. confession, I think he wanted to reserve the privilege of raping me for himself.

Suddenly, Poncho whimpers, springing to alertness. He's sensed something. It takes longer for my aunt's dogs to detect the enemy. When they bark and snarl, Poncho remains utterly still, angling his body toward the door. Ready for combat.

I take a cautious look out the window and freeze. There are no words to describe my shock.

"Aleksey," I whisper.

The cop is scanning the entrance of the museum ruins fervently. A genetically modified hound accompanies him. My scent must have led the dog, and it won't be long until he follows my trace here.

Aleksey looks as confident, regal, and fierce as he's always been, but there's something different about him. There are hints of despair in his stance. In the way he storms through the museum entrance, shouting my name. In the way his fist hits the unhinged doors when he finally comes out, making them fall to the ground with a crash.

"Is there anything wrong?" asks Aunt Olga worriedly.

I peer outside one final time. As he runs his hands through his blond mane, Aleksey's face reflects anguish. Even pain. I've never imagined that such a strong, expressionless man could show despair like this. He reminds me of the lion in my dream.

Except that lions don't mate for life. For Aleksey, I'm not a long-term mate. I'm prey.

I lower my voice. "An Accord cop will come looking for me. Please tell him that I visited you two days ago and that you haven't seen me since."

"I knew you had gotten yourself in trouble," she says as she peers outside.

The barking becomes deafening; Aleksey must be getting closer.

Aunt Olga looks at me knowingly. "What have you done to that man?"

"I wish I knew," I whisper. With a closed-up man like Aleksey, I might never know.

Knowing full well that Aleksey is never at the clinic in the afternoons, I return to leave a false trail and to check on my family.

I find the twins trying to cheer up Duque. All of us thought that Duque was feeling better and was determined to rejoin TCR after Sara's execution. But the Diazes are taking turns staying with him night and day as a precaution.

Olmo sings at the top of his lungs in his chiming voice. Totally out of tune. "You are a chiiiiiiiiiild of the universe, no less than the trees and the staaaars, you have the riiiight to be here. And whether or nooot it is clear to you, no doubt the universe is unfoldiiiiiiiiiiiiiiiiing as it shouuuuuuuuuuld."

Azalea makes a gagging expression and, behind Olmo's back, mimes the act of vomiting on her hand. She has caught Duque's attention and is making him smile. Still, though Duque is trying to look cheerful, the agony in his eyes indicates that he's anything but.

Duque's eyes fall on me. He knows me well and realizes that I'm nervous.

"Do you want to tell me something?" he asks.

I nod. The twins protest, but eventually agree to give us a few moments alone.

"Duque, you used to say that you'd never leave Starville."

He inhales deeply and shakes his head. "Not anymore. I hate this place. Here, everybody … knows. Everybody laughs—" He doesn't need to say more. I haven't forgotten how I beat his ex-fiancée because of her cruel comments.

I pace the room. "If they don't recruit me, I'll try to find a place in Shiloh. Why don't you come with me?" In Shiloh, Starvillers don't get good jobs, and it's difficult to find housing when you have only coupons to pay the rent, but it would be a change.

"Shiloh isn't far enough. I was thinking of a farther place," he says. His tone implies that he thinks his only way out is through death. Not now, as he has to be here for the ceremony. Once you're eligible for recruitment, you can't escape by suicide unless you don't care if the troops recruit your family in retaliation.

"Nobody knows you in Shiloh, and you're the best musician in town. There are '*Musician Wanted*' signs all over there."

"I don't know, Lila. Maybe. It sounds better than … I dread the moment I'll have to walk those streets again with all the gossip and girls looking down at me and—"

I pat his arm. "*Shh*. I know." Starvillers' comments about my mom still resound in my nightmares. "At least you'll consider it. Rey would never leave."

His head snaps back, and there's venom in his words. "Well, Rey won't have trouble finding a wife, will he? What woman would want me after … *that?*"

"I know of one."

He sighs and looks out the window. "I hate your jokes, Velez."

"I couldn't be more serious." I planned my actions and words carefully before coming here.

His eyes grow wide when I take a jar of ink from my dress pocket and kneel beside his bed. It's not the official tattoo that only government artists can issue, but it's valid enough to count as a binding promise.

"Duque Charles Diaz, would you marry me?"

CHAPTER 40

Hiding

DUQUE'S AMBER EYES OPEN wide as Azalea's voice startles us.

"MENSTRUANTING MOTHER OF GOD!"

A crashing sound, like breaking glass.

"I'm sorry," says Olmo, his voice loud and apologetic.

I leave the room briefly to scare off the eavesdroppers. When I return, Duque's still in shock. I wait patiently for him to recover. He bursts out laughing, his outburst mixing with winces.

"You shouldn't make me laugh like this. It hurts."

"I'm serious, Duque." Although I'm doing this only to divert his suicide plans, I know him well, and I'm sure he'll say no. Still, I need him to consider himself worthy again. Even if he calls my bluff, this plan has advantages. We could get a marriage tattoo when Kit Lee-Rivers starts to issue marriage licenses again. In theory, that would protect us both from recruitment next year.

"Marry me and start a new life with me in Shiloh," I repeat.

Duque smiles sadly and gestures toward his colostomy bag.

"Thanks, but no thanks. I don't want that kind of pressure. I'll never … lay with a girl. I'm broken … I can't perform groom duties while my waste is on display."

"Who cares about that? You're beautiful, loyal, smart, and kind."

He considers this for a moment and sits up straight. "You can't imagine how good you're making me feel. I know I have competition. The tall cop … and my own brother … You prefer me over them?"

"Absolutely!" I say, and Duque smiles at my sincere enthusiasm. One is a rapist, and the other is in love with a ghost. Duque is a boy as inexperienced and afraid of the troops as I am.

"You'll make a better husband than either of them."

"You're wrong. They are too strong to be … overpowered … whereas I—" He sighs and turns his back to me. "I know why you're doing this, Lila. Thank you. I'll have to think about it."

Duque will decline, but I hope my proposal has made him consider other options for stopping his pain.

Options that don't include his death.

⁂

Time at the clothing factory flies by, and before I know it, the morning light filters through the factory windows. Around me, dozens of seam-stresses sitting at two large tables embroider the crinoline dresses that Patriot women love.

I caress the dress that I'm embroidering, unable to stop thinking about the day I got the chance to wear one of these. Would I feel better if I could wear beautiful dresses every day?

Finally, my shift is over. I put my backpack around my shoulders. I'll come back at sunset for another shift that will keep me in the factory all night.

"What are you girls looking at outside?" asks our female supervisor.

There are tall windows in the square-shaped plant, and my coworkers are fighting to get a look out of them.

"A mutant is pacing at the entrance," says a high-pitched voice.

A short-haired blonde girl nudges her way through the giggling girls to gain a spot near the window. "A mutant?"

"He has to be a mutant. Otherwise, why is he so handsome?" another girl answers in an admiring tone.

"Look! He towers over the guards!" says a girl, bouncing on her toes.

I stop dead in my tracks. Tall and handsome?

"I didn't know the Accord cops could be so strong," says another admirer.

I don't need to hear any more. I dash toward the stairs. I reach the roof and jump from building to building, using the parkour techniques that Aleksey taught me. I find Poncho at Shiloh's plaza and together we make for the railroad.

Aleksey is going to be extremely difficult to avoid. I barely managed yesterday morning. There's only one place where I can spend the night without the risk of being found.

I wake up curled against Poncho in a dark attic. Broken-beyond-repair artifacts, black armor suits, and dusty cardboard surround me. A story below me, the Accord cops end whatever business it is that keeps them busy in the evenings before they head for bed. The sound of conversations in foreign languages filters through the loose floorboards.

The Accord headquarters are in an old three-story house. Soldiers won't come here, as they consider this building to be UNNO territory. And the lion never hunts in a lion's den, much less its own. Aleksey won't search for me here.

The murmurs fade, and the night watch starts; I hear steps going back and forth in the dark. I hope that the watchman's rounds don't include the attic.

I spend most of the night dozing. I have no way to determine the hour, and I have to leave before the cops wake for their 0600 drills.

Just when I thought I could relax, Poncho snaps up his giant head. Someone is climbing the attic stairs. We hide behind some huge cardboard cartons, perfectly still.

To no avail.

The dim beam of a flashlight points directly at us. A confident, heavy stride approaches.

"Lila Velez," says a beautiful, accented voice.

CHAPTER 41

Last chance

PONCHO WAGS HIS TAIL and walks enthusiastically toward the new arrival, leaving me alone in our hiding place.

The accented voice sounds closer. "I saw your dog's silhouette when I pointed the light. The cardboard is translucent."

I reluctantly step out of my hiding place and am momentarily blinded by the flashlight.

"It'll be better if my comrades don't find you here." He grabs my arm. "Come on. Let's go to my room."

Tristan's room is so small that the door collides with the nightstand. The wardrobe is almost as big as the room, and there's barely any walking space next to the single bed. A candle provides faint light.

The lanky cop helps me take off my cloak, and I sit next to the bed's headboard. "Have you been hiding here all this time, Miss Velez?"

"No. Please don't tell Aleksey that I came here."

Tristan sits on the bed next to me. "I can't promise you that. He's my general, and I'm supposed to inform him of everything. Besides, we're very close, and it breaks my heart to see him so afflicted." He looks at me, relief and his trademark friendliness dancing in his eyes. "I've been worried, too."

I shiver. "I've been so terrified. It's only eight days until recruitment."

He smiles reassuringly and hugs me, but I'm still trembling. I can't rely on Rey or Aleksey for emergency deflowering. I'm alone with a young man who seems to like me and who is neither a priest nor a sexually dangerous man. What if …?

A strange impulse overcomes me. Blushing furiously, I lean in.

"Tristan, let's … have s—sex. I … don't want the troops … to recruit me," I say.

He looks surprised, but doesn't pull away.

"Miss Velez," says Tristan timidly.

Slowly, our lips get closer, but I fear the contact. Why am I hesitating? Why do I miss Aleksey's lips now?

He puts his hands on my shoulders and softly pulls away.

"Miss Velez. I can't make love to you."

Not that again! I look at the floor, defeated. I've heard that before, and I know it's not in my power to convince him. Why are my options so limited? I keep finding rapists or guys with medieval moral reservations. This was my last chance before recruitment, and I don't know what I'm going to do now.

"You fear recruitment, too. Let's have willing, consensual sex while we can."

He shakes his head. "I wouldn't make love to the woman Prince Aleksey loves."

I stare at him, incredulously. Aleksey's words come to my mind. *I'm so averse to love that I won't even pretend I'm not.*

Tristan swallows before continuing. "But more importantly, I don't want you. Not the slightest bit."

My face reddens in humiliation. I lean against the wall. It's not like Tristan to be rude in this way.

He looks at me apologetically. "I didn't explain myself well."

Avoiding his gaze, I reach for my cloak. "Don't. You don't have to say anything."

"I don't want you at all because I don't want *any* woman."

Any woman? As if …?

I fight the impulse to gasp. "You … prefer men?"

"*Shh!*"

Wide-eyed, I nod. It makes sense. Homosexuality is forbidden in the Patriot military, and it's punished with recruitment. No wonder Tristan fears for his integrity. As long as they're in Patriot territory, the cops submit to the same laws.

"Don't tell Aleksey that I tried to ..."

He rubs his earring absentmindedly. "I'm sorry, Miss Velez, but I can't promise you that. I told you; I'm obliged to tell him everything because we're family."

"But—"

"Literally. We are first cousins."

My jaw drops, and I cover my mouth with both hands. Why didn't Aleksey tell me? Oh, right! Because he always hides the important details about his life. My first impulse is to ask Tristan about Aleksey's family. Perhaps it would explain why he's into C.N. But something tells me that Tristan's unbreakable loyalty to his cousin will keep his mouth shut.

Tristan sighs. "Miss Velez, I don't know what happened between you two, but please don't judge Prince Aleksey so harshly. You haven't seen him in the past two days. Your absence is hell for him. Even other cops have noticed that he's in a bad place. He misses you terribly and is worried about you. Go back to him, please."

"Tristan, I can't. Because of my mom, because of Duque. Aleksey represents everything I fear and hate."

Tristan looks horrified. "Miss Velez, never say that again! If you tell him that you hate him, you'll destroy him. You hear me? Completely, irrevocably ruin him."

My eyes shoot upward in disbelief. "You're exaggerating. I'm a temporary thing. He said so himself."

"He's a good man, and life hasn't been kind to him. He deserves to find his happiness, and he'll never come out of his shell if the only girl he's ever loved—"

"Love?" I shake my head. "Since when does obsessive lust mean love?" Tristan tries to argue, but I ignore him. "He's full of dark secrets, and he never—"

"He shared one of them with you, and you left him." Tristan's velvet voice is unusually recriminating. "I never thought he'd open up to anyone. It must have been difficult for him to be honest, and he did it for you."

Tristan's right, but ... why? Why does Aleksey prefer a violent form of sex? I would have understood if it were something else. Anything goes as long as we're talking about *consenting adults*. I'm a kinky girl myself. But forcing himself on a woman who has to struggle with him? Isn't there enough violence around us?

It doesn't matter if it's not me. It doesn't matter if it's role-play. A kink like that makes us incompatible. The worst thing is that I can't explain this to Tristan. Aleksey has kept the secret of my voyeurism. I won't expose his kink.

My voice comes unsteady. "I can't … rescue him from … whatever it is that makes him close his doors to the world. We won't see each other after recruitment. I can't stand rapists and—"

Tristan winces. "Whatever he is, he isn't a rapist, and it angers me that you say so."

I purse my lips thoughtfully. What if I'm taking Aleksey's kink the wrong way? Perhaps Tristan knows information that can help me understand Aleksey. "Did he tell you … *er* … about … C.N.?"

He looks confused. "C—what? What are you talking about?"

I sink to the floor, grabbing my head. Tristan clearly doesn't know Aleksey's secret, and I can't bring myself to expose it further. *Damn!* I was really hoping to hear that C.N. isn't as bad as I fear it is.

"Miss Velez, I'm sorry, but I can't let you go yet. Aleksey is on his way."

I spring to my feet. "On his way? How—?"

"I called him. My earring is a j-device."

I hurry to the exit, but he blocks the door.

"Tristan!" I squeal.

Tristan shushes me. "I beg you to listen to him. You have to talk out your differences."

"No! You don't understand—"

"You think all he feels is lust, but you're wrong. Prince Aleksey can deal with lust. You won't find a man more skilled in giving women pleasure. But he's not used to dealing with … other emotions. It doesn't help that you're being too hard on him," he says in a calm tone. "At least listen to him."

"Not yet! I promise I'll talk to him one day, but the last thing I need so close to recruitment is—" He doesn't budge. "Tristan! If you force me to stay and talk, I'll hate him. I swear I will."

Tristan looks crestfallen when he finally lets me pass. Poncho and I run down the corridor to get to the attic. I knock over some of the garbage and old armor, but I don't have time to worry about the noise.

The wind is howling furiously when we climb out of a window and onto the butterfly-style roof. We jump to the adjoining building.

That's when a colossal form hurls itself against me and pins me to the ground.

CHAPTER 42

The sweetest word

IF GENERAL ALEKSEY FÜRST has been impatiently looking forward to our reunion, his tone of voice doesn't show it. The stormy, furious quality of it could break stone.

"If after listening to me you still want me to leave you alone, I will. I'll leave Starville tonight if you want me to."

I struggle helplessly under him, but he's solid rock.

He whispers in my ear, his breath making me shiver. "And I'll give you the chance to get your revenge on what the soldiers did to hurt you. I won't lift a finger to defend myself."

Poncho jumps anxiously around us, whimpering. He's not sure if he's supposed to defend me or welcome the cop. The General whispers something in German, and my dog sits placidly. Some guard dog he is. But if Poncho's instincts say there's no present danger, I should placate the fear Aleksey's toughness stirs in me.

"Okay. Let's get this over with," I say, although I keep struggling.

He looks at me with narrowed eyes as the howling wind plays with his blond hair.

"I'm not a rapist, Lila. It infuriates me that you think of me as one. I told you once: I can't stand rapists. I wouldn't ever do what someone did to my mother."

The surprise paralyzes me, overcoming my desperation to escape. *His mother?* My curiosity is piqued, but I say nothing. I wait for him to elaborate, but instead he attacks the problem that worries me the most.

"C.N. Consensual non-consent *isn't* rape. It's an activity between *consenting* adults. It's just role-play. The women I've possessed in that way enjoyed it and *always* came back for more."

I frown at the mention of other women. "Have you ever hurt them?"

He shakes his head. "There's always a pre-established sign if I become too intense. My previous partners rarely used it, but when they did, I stopped."

"How do you know they weren't too intimidated to tell you to stop?"

"I did this only with women who were into C.N. Middle-aged women who knew what C.N. was and asked *me* for it. They were the ones who initiated these encounters because I didn't even have time for it."

"But ... C.N. means rape role-play. Doesn't it?"

His face is grimmer than usual.

"I would never put the words 'rape' and 'play' in the same sentence. If there's rape, there's no play," he says.

I think about this for a moment and nod. I've witnessed recruitment, and there is nothing playful about it. As much as I hate to think about it, his explanations have begun untangling the strands of a disgusting crime and a consensual activity between willing adults.

"C.N. works only when you trust your partner and have experienced at least the basics. Evidently, that doesn't apply to you," he says.

I'm no longer struggling, so he eases the pressure from my body. "And I've told you several times that I won't try C.N. on you, but you still treat me like I'm a criminal."

His enjoyment of this kind of role-play scares me, but I have to admit that I've never been particularly nice to this man. He's never done anything to harm me. When it comes to Aleksey, I've taken my usual paranoia around military people to unfair extremes.

"I'm not your toy, little *Kämpferin*. I thought you were a woman, not a little girl who is so flattered that someone has finally paid attention to her that she plays cat and mouse."

Scowling, I turn my face away. His words sting because he's partially right. I adore the attention he gives me, and I don't manage that feeling well. Still, it's maddening to have him call me out on that. I didn't escape on a whim. I have every right to fear military people. And C.N.

"Did I ask you to chase me? No! If you're the adult here, you should know when an immature *brat* like me needs space. Otherwise, *you're* the one playing games."

Aleksey looks cool and possessed, though his voice reveals his anger.

"Or perhaps it's *me,* the adult, who doesn't want to find your corpse in a Shiloh dumpster," he says, his scowl deepening, his body tensing, "showing signs of a gang attack. You could have stayed in the safety of the clinic, and I would have given you space."

"News flash! There's no place in this country where I'm not in danger of a gang attack. I wasn't in more danger than usual! I'd never put myself at risk just to avoid you."

We stare at each other in silence. I'm trying to control my emotions, but it's difficult when he's looking at me so furiously. He's unnerving.

He finally breaks the silence, his voice full of controlled rage. "You risk your safety, and then you jump into Tristan's bed." Aleksey's body is trembling. He can't be jealous of his homosexual cousin, can he? "I understand why a distrustful girl like you would prefer someone she has known for years over someone like me. Even if you don't love him. That Diaz guy doesn't even have to try, does he? He only has to be there, and you'd prefer him." He looks away and shakes his head. "Because he will always have the advantage of being the one who was there for you during your darkest moments. But Tristan Froh?"

I'm not flattered by his possessiveness. Instead, I find it irritating. We're not a couple, and I agreed to our exclusivity deal only because I didn't know about C.N.

"I don't have to explain anything to you."

He releases my arms and leans on his elbows, easing the pressure off my body.

"Yes, you do. You're not a spoiled little girl. You're a woman who fights for what she wants and talks about her needs. You want something that I can give you and—"

"Not the way I need it." I remember his words. *I prefer positions that are too deep, painful, and unromantic for an inexperienced maid.*

"Then tell me what your way is," he says, glaring at me. "I thought we had agreed on that. I told you that I can make adjustments. You want me. What's stopping you?"

My long silence irritates him further. His face contorts in frustration.

"I'm new to this. I'm going out of my comfort zone for *you*, and you don't seem to care either way." He looks down at me again, piercing my eyes with his stare. "You have to get your hands dirty, too, Lila! Take risks! But you say nothing. You run away from me. You keep me hanging." His fist slams into the concrete roof. "Damn it, Lila! Give me something to work with."

My reluctance to talk to him turns into a longing to make him understand the feelings that constrict my heart. I want to tell him that he's being unfair. That a kink like his would scare not only secondary rape survivors like me, but also regular women. How do I tell him that I wish I could feel safe enough to trust him and that, despite everything, I care for him more than I should? I can't find the right words.

He runs a hand through his hair. "At least say something! Anything would be better than your silence."

My body squirms underneath him. His sincere, passionate speech has moved me.

"I'm not toying with you. I can't be with you if I feel threatened and you're a threat ... for reasons that aren't ... easy to put into words."

"Try," he commands.

"You—" He waits patiently for me to continue, but I can't say anything that he can't figure out himself. He's aware that his touch triggers painful flashbacks. He knows that I don't trust him, and that being together means risking our lives. Not to mention that after his C.N. confession, I fear he'll take me like he took me in my dream. That's enough for me to feel the need to stay away from him. But there's something more that I haven't admitted to myself until now.

"You'll leave. I'd prefer to lose my innocence to someone who will stay."

He shoots me an incredulous look.

"And Tristan? You don't have reservations about him. He'll go away, too."

I take a deep breath and avoid his piercing stare.

"If it were Tristan ... it wouldn't hurt."

Aleksey understands that I don't mean physically. The coldness in his eyes melts into an ocean of the warmest blue. For a long moment, he says nothing. His arms pull me to his chest as we roll so that I'm on top. I can hear his heart beat beneath my cheek, a soothing rhythm for my nerves.

He lifts my chin with his thumb, forcing me to look at him. His deep, low voice sounds serene. "It would hurt you more to say goodbye to me than to him?"

Yes, I'd miss you. "Let's say that when the Accord Unit's time in Starville is over, I'll happily say goodbye to Tristan ... but saying good-bye to you will be ...." *Torture.* Even thinking about it makes me cringe because my heart feels as though somebody is squeezing it force-fully. And now he knows it. Aleksey has heard my unspoken words. I blush, knowing that I just declared my feelings for him. They might not account for much because we will soon be separated, but now he can be sure that I'm not indifferent. And so can I.

Aleksey exhales as if an internal conflict has been relieved. When I glance at him, his eyes are bright and kind. Perhaps it's my imagina-tion, but he looks different. Have my words moved him?

He tightens his muscular arms around me. Our chemistry has be-come tangible, electric. I look down and force myself to continue.

"As absurd as this sounds, it'd be easier to stay away until recruit-ment day than to get more attached to you ... only to say goodbye in a week." I glance up and catch a delighted flicker in his eyes. "But that's not the only reason. I can't explain everything now—"

"Tell me more," he says with poorly concealed eagerness under his somber tone.

"When I met you, I thought you were a soldier. You resemble my mother's attackers and your kink ... puts me on edge ... so—"

"I can't change the way we met." A tinge of frustration shows in his blue eyes. "But have I ever done anything to make you think I don't care about your safety?" I shake my head, and his hold on me strengthens.

"Don't fear me, Lila."

I remember what Tristan said. People fear Aleksey or lust after him, but they never love him. I don't want to belong to the former category, although it's impossible, with a man like him, to not belong to the latter.

"It's hard to feel relaxed around any man, because of my fears ... but with you ..." As I continue speaking out long years of distrust, little by little, my reservations about Aleksey begin to evaporate. But there's still the C.N. aspect. "I'm also afraid of discovering my darkest side. You stir in me a feral need … to be taken, to be claimed. I'm worried that the consent lines between us might get blurred."

"Don't sweat it, Lila. I understand when no means no."

I believe him now. I should have realized that after our first encounter because I asked him not to touch me, and he complied. Yet my fear of him is more nuanced than that. Because part of my fear of him is fear of myself.

"But I don't," I say.

The confusion and shame that my orgasmic hallucination has brought on prove it. I thought I was well-versed in the theory, even though I have had no practice, but Aleksey has challenged all that I thought I knew and wanted. As much as I think I'm ready for sex, there's still a part of me that will feel extremely vulnerable when the moment to get naked and go to bed with a man comes.

He cradles me and considers my words carefully. "Do you mean you're afraid to push boundaries?"

I bury my head in his chest, relieved that he not only listens, but understands. "I'd rather go safe and sweet."

"In Gyges, I could tell you were scared. So I took care of you." My body rises and falls along with his chest as he sighs. His hand caresses my hair. "I proved to you that as much as desire drives me crazy when I'm with you, I'm in control, so rest assured." He pulls me up so that our faces are closer. We look into each other's eyes for a while as the atmosphere continues to spark. "You're safe with me."

As if trying to prove that he can be gentle, he kisses my forehead and rubs his stubble against my cheeks before placing gentle kisses all over my face except my ready lips. His touch transmits tenderness, longing, and reverence. It also has just the right amount of desire to make me feel wanted without scaring me.

I raise my hand to touch his cheek and he leans into it, evidently enjoying the contact. I'm surprised to see him smiling. It warms me to think that I'm the one who has brought that grin to his brooding face.

"You rarely talk," I say. We'd avoid misunderstandings if he talked more about himself.

Several minutes of silence pass before he answers. "That's partially your fault."

"How is it my fault?"

"I only talk right after sex. And since you refuse to have sex with me ..." He winks at me, and I grin. Playful Aleksey always makes me smile.

He gets up, scooping me up with him. "Come on. There's a place I want to show you."

Poncho gallops toward the hot springs. During our time on the run, he couldn't get his daily bath in the river the way he loves to. The water in the pools is crystal clear and offers a good view of the sandy bottoms and rock walls. Some feet ahead of the springs is a noisy, steamy waterfall that creates a sparkling mist. Green moss blankets the rocks surrounding us.

We sit on a rock, and Aleksey drapes his arm around my shoulder, his fingers grazing my face tenderly. It has taken a long ATV ride and a difficult hike to get to this place well north of the river, but it was worth it. I got to drive on the bumpy roads, and the sight before us now is beautiful.

Aleksey watches me fixedly as he plays with my hair. "There's no time now, but before I leave Starville, I'll take you to see the Pacific Ocean," he says in a low voice. "There's a UNNO refueling point only a few hours away. Three more hours of driving and we'd reach the California coast."

Aleksey must have ditched plenty of his leadership duties to spend time with me. That makes me feel like he's honoring our reconciliation. Reconciliation must be the sweetest, yet most underutilized, word in the English language.

There's barely any time left for us to build good memories. After the recruitment ceremony, we'll see each other only in our minds.

"We'll become the lovers that never were," he murmurs as though reading my thoughts. By this time next week, I may be on my way toward a life of sexual slavery as a vassal, and he'll be on his way to another occupied city. The thought makes my chest constrict painfully, but I won't dwell on what can't be changed. It'll be better to take advantage of the time we have left.

Not saying anything, he gets up, and I follow him toward the waterfall. We end up in our underwear under the hot water, back to back, the water sliding from our bodies. This is how we met, but unlike that time, when sadness was evident on his face, I can feel a lighthearted mood exuding from his hulky frame. Even if he's not smiling.

I turn and wrap my arms around his waist, pressing my body firmly against his lower back. The contact of my breasts against his bare skin feels glorious.

For a long, delectable moment, I revel in the feeling of being so close to him. I like his solid muscles, his extraordinary height, and the strong arms that make me feel like I'm small and safe whenever he embraces me. I love that he protects me, and I love how he's silent to everyone except me. I won't let him leave Starville without telling him how I feel about him.

My voice doesn't come out in a seductive purr as I intended, but in a girlish chime. "Sir, I like you so much, sir."

In answer, his hands graze my arms, which are still around his waist. My cheeks flush.

"Sir ... before you leave Starville ... I'd like you to become my first, sir."

Aleksey's body tenses. His head snaps up and to the right. I admire his perfect profile. His face is expressionless, but there's a definite hungry determination in his eyes.

His voice is husky. "Now?"

I shake my head. There's something I have to take care of first. Something that will allow me to start my sexual life out of willingness, not out of fear. "In three night's time, sir. In your room."

He nods. We have a deal now, and the promise of the pleasure that will come makes my body buzz in anticipation. I'll have a hard time not thinking about what's in store for me.

That is, if I survive long enough to act on my plans.

CHAPTER 43

Love

THE RATION CENTER BUZZES with activity. The entire town is in line at different vaccination stands. Two dozen cops call people alphabetically according to their last names: *Bronte, Andrea; Brown, Joseph; Busko, Olga.* Aleksey told me he isn't usually part of these activities, but with only six days to go until the recruitment ceremony, he's making the process speed along.

People won't suspect that we spent a good portion of last night kissing. He said once that our arrangement must be discreet, so we aren't even looking at each other. Still, I wonder if it's a coincidence that my family will receive their vaccines from him.

While waiting in line, Olmo stares longingly at Elena, who is wearing a floor-length blue dress and has made several attempts to approach Aleksey. One of those attempts has included pastries. My eyebrows shoot up at her tenacity. Elena knows that he's busy, that she'll be rejected rudely—this time in front of witnesses. Does she think he might take her just so she'll leave him alone?

When Aleksey calls for *Velez, Azalea*, Elena approaches him again. "I asked for Miss Velez, not for her bitch." The force of his derisive tone makes me wince, even though I'm not the one receiving his cruelty.

Azzy laughs loudly. Elena acts as though she hasn't heard, but she hurries away, and we don't see her after that.

There's a huge contrast between the way he treats Elena and the way he treats Olmo. "If it makes you feel better, I will inject myself first," he says softly when he sees my brother's reluctance. Aleksey plunges the thick needle deep into his bulky bicep without wincing. Olmo stops crying.

A look of self-realization crosses Olmo's face after Aleksey injects him.

"It hurt like hell, but I'm a tough dude," says Olmo proudly.

It's not the first time I've seen Olmo feeling good about himself after Aleksey gave him a challenge to overcome. Clearly, Aleksey makes Olmo feel capable.

Later, after he's finished with his afternoon duties, Aleksey takes me out for a stroll around the woods that surround the city slopes. This time, he's the one who reaches for my hand. *Ha!* And he said he wasn't the holding-hands type.

"You're too cruel to Elena, Mr. Fürst."

Her name brings a scowl to his face. "She's been abusive to your brother."

Fury boils inside me, reddening my face. "Abusive?"

"While you were on bed rest, your brother declared his feelings for her. She laughed at him and pushed him aside. He fell back, and I had to tend to a few cuts and bruises."

Molten rage runs through my veins.

"That bitch!" I try to storm back to town, but Aleksey stops me. "Let me go! I'll find her and—"

"Don't waste our time together, Lila. I've been avenging your brother with my attitude ever since."

"You're right, keep snapping at her. Only not on account of her sluttiness."

He arches his eyebrows questioningly.

"Starvillers always slut-shame Elena," I say, scowling. "As much as I want to slap her for the way she treats us, I hate slut-shaming." Getting engaged at a young age, getting scorned in public if the bridal sheets are not stained with blood, making fun of spinsters ... all those customs are not the best examples of sexual free will. Elena never follows Starville's sexual rules, and that's earned her slut-shaming insults.

Amused admiration shows on his face, but his voice comes out lustful. "Is there any topic you don't have a strong opinion on?"

Aleksey stops and wraps his arms around me to pull me close. His touch sears my skin.

"I'm not snapping at her because of her sexual life. I'm mistreating her because of her cruelty to your family."

All thoughts of Elena disappear when he slides his hands around my waist. We stare into each other's eyes intently. The atmosphere between us has suddenly changed into something palpable—hot and magnetic.

Aleksey abruptly pushes me against a tree and presses his body against mine. I look at him in wonder. What will he do? He answers my unspoken question when he slowly, sensually leans in.

I forget everything except the way he's making me feel. The way his lips are grazing my neck, charging my skin with zinging electricity everywhere they touch. Aleksey takes his time to inhale and then gently slides his lips all over my neck, the hollow of my throat, my earlobes. I tip down my head as waves of warmth make my skin tingle from the roots of my hair down to my toes.

His hands slide their way up from my waist until he's cupping my face. My eyes get lost in his for a while before our lips touch. Softly at first. Then he kisses me at length, lingeringly and passionately.

An hour passes as our mouths dance in a slow, ardent rhythm. At times, he whispers my name in my ear before he returns to my mouth. Aleksey's teaching me that many things can be said not with words, but with the language of two mouths moving in unison. His sweet, lingering kisses convey longing, tenderness, and admiration. When his mouth turns ravishing, it's as if he's passing along a message of passion, eroticism, and possessiveness. As our mouths speak silently of emotions I didn't even know existed, I fear that no one else will make me feel like this again.

His hands are starting to roam freely under my shirt when the overwhelming emotions become too much. Aleksey realizes, that even if my body refuses to stop, I've reached my limit. He breaks the kiss and pulls me into his muscular arms. For a while, I snuggle against his chest. Being this close to him, I notice that his heart is beating as wildly as mine.

I can't help but feel nervous. When the moment comes, sex between us will be difficult. I keep getting overwhelmed. It won't be comfortable, and there's the risk of flashbacks. He'll have to be extremely patient and caring. Perhaps we should practice beforehand. But right here, right now, his concern is not his pleasure but my feelings.

"I'm being selfish here. I'm putting an innocent girl at risk of getting too attached to a man like me," he says in a self-reproaching tone. "The last thing I want is to hurt you."

I playfully punch his arm. "I'm not at risk of falling in love with you ... or anyone. It's impossible to fall in love in a matter of days."

His head snaps down to look at me. "Is it?"

"Of course. Divine and Joey have been friends since childhood. My mom and dad spent years getting to know each other before—"

His serious face becomes more somber. He doesn't like this conversation. "For such a young person, you're incredibly opinionated."

"I'm not so young. I'm an eighteen-year-old spinster."

"Your body might be eighteen," he says, not trying to be discreet in how his eyes rake my frame. "Your face stopped aging at thirteen. And you're fairly inexperienced and unworldly." He kisses my forehead. "Like a child. All you Starvillers are."

"I'm not a Starviller!" I say indignantly. "I'm an American." I look at him in wonder. "Do you agree?"

He looks away as if pondering heavy thoughts. Then he drapes his arm around my shoulder and leads the way home. "With your political affiliation? I do. I still regard Patriots and Nats as Americans."

"No. I mean my opinions on love. My *insta-love isn't real love* statement."

His voice sounds distant. "I've seen men lose their minds over women they've just met. My men call it the *donnerkeil.* 'Thunderbolt' in German. When a man looks at a woman and gets hit by the *donnerkeil,* the rest of the world ceases to exist for him. And no other woman holds a millionth of the pull that his *donnerkeil* holds. He'd kill before letting anything–anyone–take her away from him. She becomes everything and—" Aleksey seems to suddenly realize that he's being too intense. He looks away from me and recovers his cool demeanor.

"That's passion ... lust ... possessiveness," I say. "I'm no expert, but I think thunderbolts aren't true love." I pull up the hood of my cloak. "When there's a storm, the thunderbolts illuminate everything but die in seconds before leaving an even darker sky. They're replaced by other short-lived thunderbolts. When the storm ends, they leave nothing."

Aleksey's eyes turn to me as if asking, *What is love for you, then?*

"It would take all afternoon to explain it."

In response, the back of his hand grazes my cheek. "We have all afternoon and, if you want, all night."

All night. "Bear with me; this will be boring." I inhale deeply. "I think true love transcends time. The thunderbolt does not. Not if it strikes men the way you described."

I start a sprint toward a glade where my favorite orange flowers grow. He catches up with me easily.

"Most girls prefer flowers over trees." I brush my fingers on the petals. "These flowers blossom quickly. They speak of passion, of beauty." I take a withering flower that has dropped to the ground and fondle it between my fingers. "But flowers don't last. They wither easily and have limited growth. A tree speaks not of passion, but sturdiness. Yet, it grows higher and lasts longer. Some of these trees were here before I was born, and they'll be here once I'm gone."

My head falls back as I look at the highest tree. "Real love ought to be more like a tree and less like a flower." I sigh loudly. "That's the kind of love my parents had. It wasn't as consuming as it was everlasting. And you see that tree over there?" I point toward a cluster of trees across from us. "Now it's showing only green leaves, but in spring it's covered in flowers. Because as reliable as trees are, they can also speak of beauty and passion."

Aleksey contemplates the tallest tree in silence. "I prefer trees, too. Let's go back." He scoops me in his arms the way people carry toddlers. I don't protest. This position has advantages. It makes it easy to wrap my arms around his neck and peck his cheek. He tenses. His eyes show a tinge of wonder, and I smile. I never imagined that giving affection would feel this good.

"Why do you despise insta-love, Lila?"

"To love somebody, you need to know them. That takes time."

The wind becomes violent, so he covers me with his cape. "Lila, can you honestly tell me that I haven't seen through you? That I haven't told you things about yourself that you didn't suspect?"

My voyeurism, my fears, my dreams. Not only does he know me better than most people do, he understands me.

One of his hands plays with a gray strand of my hair. "You have seen past the barriers I built to keep people away. You're the only person who sees the boy inside of this man. Nobody knows me better than you do."

His voice turns husky. "And you'll know me even more in due time." He must mean sexually, but he seems to imply something else.

As we get closer to town, we split apart to take separate roads for the sake of discretion. I haven't walked two steps before his hand grabs mine to stop me. I turn to look at him. His blue eyes are piercing into mine, dazzling me for a moment.

"I'm a proud man, Lila. It's not easy for me to admit feelings I've never felt before, knowing that you're going to dismiss them. My pride would take a blow. With a girl like you, I prefer to show and not to tell."

Except that he *has* just told me. Indirectly. Through the implications of his last words. And it seems that he hasn't even realized his own admission.

He walks away, his red cape billowing to the rhythm of the wind. I remain frozen to the spot, trying to collect my thoughts.

To show and not to tell. I rack my brain, trying to remember the number of feelings that Aleksey has demonstrated so far. Undeniable passion and mind-consuming lust. Lascivious possessiveness and insane protectiveness. Gentleness and sweet obsession. But above all that respect and commitment.

How could I not have noticed before? And now that I can't keep denying his feelings, I don't know how to love him. Whatever this is— thunderbolt, lust, insta-love—there's only one undeniable revelation from the last words he's said.

Aleksey Fürst has fallen in love with me.

CHAPTER 44

The 36th Battalion

REY SCANS THE RUDIMENTARY map. "Turn to the right, Lily."

The visibility is minimal, but Aleksey taught me well. Before I learned how to drive, none of us could operate a military vehicle. Unfortunately, I'm the only Comanche capable of driving a Patriot ATV. These vehicles could have been a valuable weapon.

The valleys surrounding the Lion Sierra are facing a tempest, as my dad predicted. Ideal weather to blow up a train; Patriots assume that the damage is caused by the storm, and they never investigate. We can trust the downpour to erase our tracks.

"Are you sure this is the right way, Priest?" asks Luke, wiping the fogged up window with his sleeve.

"No. I'm trying to get us lost on purpose," answers Rey sardonically.

The soldier-like owner of this ATV is sleeping, her head resting on Mathew's knees. She's a drunken veteran who was my supervisor at my former job. If soldiers track the vehicle, she'll be our best cover. Nobody will press charges against a veteran for getting lost on the road after too many drinks. After they stop receiving the drugs, ex-soldiers not only tolerate alcohol, they crave it.

Under normal circumstances, we attack railroads without knowing when the next train will pass; this delays the drug supplies, but hurts no soldiers. Today, for the first time in five years, we have a real chance of stopping the recruitment ceremony. Duque's integrity was a high cost to pay, but thanks to that hacking mission, we now know exactly what intersection to attack.

After hours of driving, we reach an intersection lost in an ocean of trees. The only path is the railroad itself.

I find a spot to conceal the vehicle among the trees. We get our rudimentary weapons ready. Luke will remain in the ATV, turning on the ignition and letting Poncho run free when he sees the first explosion.

Poncho seems tranquil, which means we have the clear to go. I don't join the collective prayer that Rey directs. It's too late to start believing. With great effort, we get out of the ATV and hike along the railroad until we leave the woods and enter a valley.

We're soaked, and we have a hard time advancing against the wind. It doesn't help that we have to tread through streams of mud. Thanks to the storm, there's a good chance that any security system will record only blurry silhouettes, but just in case, we've covered our faces with masks.

With the roar of the storm, we can't hear one another. Our bodies tremble. The other Comanches are worried that the violent movements will activate our homemade bombs, but I trust my father's designs. I know the bombs won't explode on us.

After hiking a mile, we reach the foot of a mountain. I look up. At the top, there's a section of trail road.

We climb. With steep, eroded slopes on each side, the overpass hovers dangerously over a deep chasm. We'll set our bombs here and trigger them when boxcar number thirteen reaches the overpass. If my dad's calculations are right, that'll make the soldier-filled train derail.

It's almost impossible to keep our balance while the wind is threatening to throw us off the cliff. Perhaps some of us won't live to tell the story. Some soldiers will survive because of the strength of their modified genes. Knowing that this is sabotage, they'll chase us. We can't outrun the soldiers, and we can't escape by climbing a tree. They'll climb after us. Throwing ourselves into the nearby lagoon won't do, as they swim at incredible speeds. They'll have the advantage in a fight.

Rey and I set the bombs while the rest of the Comanches form a human cocoon to protect us from the wind.

A vibration startles us. The train is approaching.

Holly and Mathew glance down nervously at the abyss. The bottom is far below, and the trees are death traps. There'll be rocks and falling rubble, but I've trained them hard in Parkour techniques. We're as fast and agile as non-soldiers can be. The rest will be in the hands of destiny.

I manage to work out the detonator just as the mechanical giant is getting close.

"Let's get out of here!" shouts Rey.

We sprint on the railroad. The train is right behind us about to run us over.

I feel the power of the machine about to consume me before I jump out of the way.

Aleksey's training pays off, and we make our way through the slopes as if flying, picking up speed on some ridges and slowing our descent on others. My stomach drops as I approach the bottom of the cliff at top speed. We roll on our shoulders at the bottom and make a dash for the place where we left the ATV.

Rey, still making his way through the slopes, activates the detonator. *BOOM!*

The boxcar explodes, and the 36th Battalion's train rolls down the cliff, making a loud noise that drowns out the sound of the storm. Hurtling rubble and shrapnel fall from the sides of the cliff with the force of a meteor shower, but we've managed to put some distance between the wreckage and ourselves.

I run across the flooded trail, splashing. The way the water slows me down only increases my desperation to reach the ATV. I don't look behind me, but I can feel them. They're chasing us already.

When we get closer to the ATV, Poncho runs past us, barking frantically. The wind stops, as if turned off by an invisible switch, and the pouring becomes a soft drizzle. I see the place where we left our getaway vehicle.

But it's too late.

I turn my head. They're difficult to make out because of their camouflage capes, but I see them. Two gigantic soldiers are following us, accompanied by a genetically modified dog.

When the first shots sound, we hit the ground and roll, trying to avoid the bullets.

CHAPTER 45

Combat

SURPRISE, THEIR ARROGANCE, AND our luck work in our favor when Cara's arrow disarms a soldier. My knife hits the hand of the other before he can draw his firearm. The guns go flying as both soldiers charge us. At the same time, Poncho leaps, colliding with the soldiers' dog in mid-air.

Cara, Holly, Divine, and Joey all fight a single soldier, while Poncho does his best to keep their dog from attacking us.

The bigger of the two soldiers darts toward us. I don't have time to aim and can only roll to the ground to avoid him. The momentum and his big bulk give me a fraction of a second's reprieve before he skids around and charges again.

Mathew, Rey, and I avoid the soldier's attacks. We try to hurt his legs, but the soldier is too fast for us.

Luke has abandoned the ATV and joined the fight. He's brought with him a spear and a set of wooden swords. He throws the spear but can't penetrate the soldier's armor; at least it creates a second of respite for the rest of us. As the soldier raises his hands to intercept the weapon, each of us grabs a sword and attacks his flanks.

Poncho snarls and snaps. His opponent yelps in pain and stops moving. Poncho doesn't hesitate a second, turning and hurling himself against our soldier. I'm afraid of throwing another knife and hitting my dog.

We're barely coping and our defenses won't last long. There's only one thing I can do.

While Rey and Mathew try to attack the soldier's legs, I climb the nearest tree. I jump and wrap my legs around our enemy's back, clinging desperately to his neck as he fights to shake me off.

I try to bury my knife in the only place that is not protected by his helmet: his nostrils. The soldier shakes his body violently, and I fly backward. I tuck into a ball in the air and try to break the momentum by rolling in the mud. Even so, I feel a searing pain in my shoulders as I smash into a tree trunk.

My attack gives enough time to Poncho, Luke, Mathew, and Rey to finally throw the soldier to the ground and soak him with alcohol.

I see Holly, Divine, and Joey cover Cara so that she can aim another arrow. My movements feel slow and my lungs burn when, from the ground, I throw a knife at their soldier, aiming at his nose. The knife doesn't penetrate his skin, but it makes him stagger.

Cara manages to insert her arrow into our enemy's armored heel. It throws the soldier off balance, and he crashes to the ground. While falling, the soldier takes Joey down, too. Joey screams in pain as his right leg breaks. Divine and Holly throw alcohol-filled balloons into the soldier's face as Cara shoots another arrow.

"The pills!" shouts Rey. We force a pill into the mouth of each soldier—cyanide and alcohol. We've never had the chance to use these pills on a soldier before, and we won't have time to see if they're dead. We throw our weapons into the murky streams and dart toward the ATV. More soldiers might arrive any second now.

In seconds, we're driving as fast as the uneven roads permit. It's not fast enough to lose a new pair of soldiers who are chasing the vehicle.

I accelerate, trying to ignore the sound of their guns. Suddenly, the ATV starts acting on its own, slowing even though I've mashed the gas pedal to the floor. With a pang of panic I realize that the strange button in the ATV is a remote control.

The soldiers have taken control of the ATV and bring it to a stop in a clearing surrounded by deep forest. Their armor looks cracked, and their helmets are missing, so their gray-skinned faces are on full display.

"Get down, pigs!"

We're forced to lie down with our faces and stomachs on the ground. They search the ATV for weapons.

My muscles freeze in panic when the soldiers use knives to cut our shirts in search of the tattoos that indicate our professions, places of birth, and citizen statuses. Rey has one from his religious order. Luke has the tattoo that indicates he's about to gain Patriot citizenship. They might skip recruitment as punishment and be executed immediately. The rest of us won't have that luck.

I force my brain to overcome the panic and think hard. If I'm going to die, is there a way to take them down with me?

The tallest soldier points his gun at my cheek. His shouting voice sounds artificial, almost robotic. "Not even a marriage tattoo, little sow? Are you a V—?"

A vehicle screeches to a stop near us, splashing us with mud and water. Three people get out of the vehicle. From the corner of my eye, I see their boots.

CHAPTER 46

The person she shares her tears with

"I'M GENERAL FÜRST, REPRESENTATIVE of the United Neutral Nations Organization."

Aleksey! My heart beats at an impossible speed. He'll get himself killed while trying to save me! As strong as Aleksey is, he's a regular man who doesn't consume tonics. He's no match for two genetically engineered soldiers who survived an attack that would kill normal people.

"These people are civilians, protected by the 25th Accord Unit under my charge," says Aleksey. "You! Stop pointing that gun at them. They're unarmed."

The soldier must have obeyed because Aleksey orders us to stand.

I look at him. He's scowling at the soldiers, and his red cape is billowing in the wind. Aleksey is flanked by Tristan and a beautiful, Asian-looking female cop. The Accord General emanates confidence, command, and power. The soldiers are not used to facing enemies who tower over them, and they're looking at Aleksey with a mix of curiosity and hostility.

The tallest soldier steps forward and yells, "I'm Sergeant McCarthy from the 36th Battalion. A Patriot States of America train suffered a terrorist attack. Every Nationalist-born citizen in the area will be interrogated."

"Not happening, Sergeant. The international convention of Basel prohibits the use of torture to interrogate civilians."

McCarthy warily eyes the earring-shaped device Tristan is using to record the scene. "No torture. But they'll at least tell us why they're traveling in an ATV. Vehicle usage is illegal for Nationalists in Patriot territory, Mr. Fürst."

"Not when the life of a Patriot citizen is in danger. As you can see, the owner of the vehicle is a Patriot woman in no condition to drive."

Aleksey turns to Tristan and the woman beside him. "Colonel Froh! Sergeant Wong!"

They step forward and salute Aleksey. "Sir, yes, sir!"

"Take the civilians back to Shiloh and the ATV's owner to an Accord clinic."

Wong takes us to the Accord Humvee. The inside is warm, and she gives us some blankets. I stick my ear to the window, straining to listen.

"You're interfering with national security procedures," says McCarthy, his tattooed face contorting in rage.

Aleksey ignores him and strides confidently toward the ATV we stole.

"Sir, those Nats—" insists McCarthy.

Aleksey looks at him impatiently. "You searched the vehicle yourself and found no weapons. As you can see, these people are not genetically engineered. They pose no threat to your country."

"You're a foreigner. You have no jurisdiction over Patriot troops."

"Wrong." Aleksey's ring-device projects the hologram of a map. "As you can see, Patriot territory starts twenty feet from where we're standing. These lands are entrusted to the UNNO until the Nationalists and Patriots reach an agreement."

He turns his back to the soldier and walks around the ATV.

I see McCarthy's features change. Everyone gasps when he pulls out his gun and aims at Aleksey. But Aleksey grabs McCarthy's wrist and disarms him.

McCarthy escapes Aleksey's grip and hurls himself against the cop.

"No!" I yell. I open the Humvee's door, but Tristan stops me.

"He's not in danger," Tristan says "He has never lost a brawl."

I look up again. Just like the time when he fought Rey, Aleksey seems to put little effort into blocking McCarthy's attacks. His speed is as inhuman as his foe's.

McCarthy's face contorts when Aleksey wraps a muscular arm around his throat. In a swift movement, the cop tips back the soldier's head and twists it forcefully to the left. The crackling sound of McCarthy's neck sends shivers down my spine.

My face is frozen in shock. Until now, I've never given much thought to why Aleksey's so strong. I assumed that it was simply because he's naturally tall and that long hours of training did the rest. Why, even without drugs, is he stronger than the soldiers?

The other soldier has his gun pointed at Aleksey, but it looks more like a defensive maneuver than an attack.

"Look at me, Sergeant Stevens," says Aleksey, glowering at the soldier. "Don't you recognize me?"

Stevens' tattooed eyes open wide and shine with recognition. "Sir! You are ... Prince Aleksey."

Aleksey murmurs something that my damaged hearing can't make out before he raises his voice again. "Remember, the camera recorded everything. Now go!"

Stevens disappears, and Aleksey strides toward the Humvee. He ignores everyone as he addresses me in a scolding tone. "The existence of a resistance group will remain hidden for now. But you're playing with fire, Miss Velez, and you'll get burned." He grabs my arm. "Come with me."

He pulls me toward the stolen ATV, yelling orders. "Froh! Dispose of the body! Wong! Take the Starvillers back to town and straight to the clinic. Make sure only Dr. Velez treats their wounds."

Aleksey takes a sip from his flask before he starts the engine. He doesn't talk during our journey to Shiloh. I'm used to his silence, but the fury brewing underneath it baffles me.

I look at him with arched brows. "How did you find us? Why are you stronger than the soldiers? Where did you meet Sergeant Stevens?"

He ignores my questions.

The only reason I don't get irritated is because I know he loves me in his own strange way. When someone has gifted you with one act of love after another, it's only fair to ignore their bad moods and concentrate exclusively on the many things they've done for you. Acts and feelings should always prevail over moods and words.

We return the woman and her ATV to their rightful place in Shiloh before boarding an Accord ambulance.

We're passing Midian's ruins when Aleksey finally speaks in an even tone. "I've just broken my neutrality pledge. I can't call myself a cop."

"Are you in trouble?"

He shrugs. "They may banish me from the North American territories if they find out. I shouldn't have taken sides, but—" He turns to look at me. "The side you support will be my side."

I realize what's eating him. Guilt. Neutrality is part of who he is, and now he has broken a vital principle that has ruled his life. All for me.

I shake my head. "You haven't taken sides. Nats have done nothing to deserve my loyalty. They started this mess of a war. And for what? Useless lands where nobody can live. You're not feeling guilty because you killed that man, are you?"

His grip on the steering wheel tightens. "No. He was going to recruit you."

Since yesterday, I've been thinking about Aleksey's feelings for me. I can approach the situation in one of two ways: I can grieve that I've found a man who loves me but who's not going to be part of my life, or I can feel grateful that I met him at all.

His eyebrows are still furrowed as he accelerates, making the tires squeal.

A yearning to alleviate his worries surges inside my chest. I want to kiss that scowl until it disappears. Maybe my next words will change his somber mood. "You know why I asked you to wait some days before we—?"

His eyebrows arch.

"Because when we're—" I fidget in my seat, unsure how to continue. "—in that bed together tomorrow night, you'll know that I'm not giving myself to you because I have to. Not because of fear, not because of curiosity. I'll give you my body, my trust—my v— virginity—because underneath that red cape and grim look, there is the only man I want."

He says nothing, but offers a cocky half-grin. I'm covered in mud, and my hair is a bushy mess. Even so, he's looking at me as though he couldn't get enough of the sight of me. Wide, shining eyes and dilated pupils illuminate his face.

By the time we reach the clinic, word has spread. Five days before the recruitment ceremony, the majority of the 36th Battalion is en route to New Vegas hospitals.

Aleksey examines my hearing in one of the ER rooms. He says it'll take a few days before it returns to its full capacity. He acts like a true professional in the way he makes me lie on my stomach so that he can examine my thigh wound, which reopened during the fight. Still, forbidden thoughts take over my mind. *I want you to suck on that thigh. I want you to make love to me.*

While he's taking care of my bruises, he receives a call on his ring-device. Rocco won't make the news official until tomorrow, but he informs the leader of the Accord Unit about an important piece of news.

The recruitment ceremony has been canceled.

I collapse into a chair and bury my head in my hands. I haven't slept in two days, and I've felt tense all along. A whirlpool of emotions replaces the tension. Relief, uncertainty, pride, joy, weariness, and the overall feeling that it's too good to be true. Until next year, I'm free from the pressure of recruitment. I'm finally free to make love to a man who loves me. I don't even realize that tears are rolling down my cheeks until Aleksey cradles me in his arms.

"*Shh*, don't cry, my *Kämpferin*. Allow yourself to hope."

And at this moment, I realize that I'll never forget him. You usually can't recall all the people you've shared laughs with. But you rarely forget the people you've shared your tears with.

CHAPTER 47

Family and farewells

BY THE TIME MY dad takes care of all the Comanches, it's way past curfew. They'll have to spend the night at the clinic.

I sneak out and cross the courtyard, hoping that no one notices. As I'm about to climb the scaffold to Aleksey's room, I hear a voice.

"Lily, where are you going?"

Rey and I look at each other awkwardly. Comprehension dawns in Rey's amber eyes. He grabs my wrist with force. "No. Stay with us."

I don't notice when Aleksey leaves his room and jumps from the scaffold until he lands gracefully in front of me. He assumes a protective stance. "Get your hands off her, Diaz."

"What have you done to her, beast?" Rey asks, scowling.

Aleksey ignores the question.

"Nothing I didn't want him to do," I answer for him.

Rey throws a punch that Aleksey easily avoids.

"She doesn't want to," says Rey. "She's young! She's scared! You're taking advantage of her fear of recruitment!"

The general looks at Rey the way someone would a slimy insect.

"She loves me, Fürst."

Aleksey turns to me, his expression questioning. He sees something in my eyes that makes him scowl.

"I offered her marriage," says Rey. "What have you offered? Pleasure? She deserves more."

"Stop being a jerk, Rey!" I shout. "Aleksey has helped us and—"

"You're after the joy of exploring unclaimed territory, being the first," says Rey, ignoring me. "But when you're gone, I'll still be there for her. As her husband."

Although I feel his fury brewing, Aleksey maintains a cool, distant attitude. Rey throws another punch, and the cop looks as though he couldn't care less. I'm not sure whether Aleksey considers Rey a worthy rival, but I won't risk things escalating between them.

"Aleksey, if you hurt him, you'll hurt me."

Aleksey looks at me with an unreadable expression.

"Give us a few minutes. I need to talk to my friend," I say in a conciliatory tone.

"No, you don't," Aleksey says tersely. "I'll settle some things with Diaz. Wait for me in my room."

I mean to make my voice soft, but I can't. "You can't boss me around. I'll talk to Rey."

Aleksey wraps an arm around my shoulder and glowers at Rey. "If you need to talk, go ahead. Pretend I'm not here."

I look at the stars above the clinic, feeling suddenly weary. I don't want to talk to either of them anymore Surprising both of them, I lower my body until I'm sitting on the ground with my head between my knees.

"You look pale," says Rey in a concerned voice.

I yawn. "Can't we *all* celebrate the news of no recruitment and take a well-deserved rest?"

"In which bed, Lily?" asks Rey, his tone sarcastic. "Mine or his?"

"That's it, Diaz," growls Aleksey. "Get out of my clinic."

I hear footsteps. Someone is approaching, but I won't look up until I'm sure my emotions are under control.

A voice I wasn't expecting pulls me out of my trance.

"Leave her alone, Rey! What did you say to her?" Azzy pushes Rey with a broom. "You don't have any claim on her. You're hot and cold and don't even know what you want! You have to sort your shit out and stop messing with her."

At that moment, Aleksey puts his palm on my shoulder. "Lila, I need to talk to you. Now."

No! Not now. I just want to gather myself.

Azzy puts the broom over her head. "You won't start a fight here, Aleksey Fürst. You don't have any claim on my sister, either."

She swings the broom menacingly before tossing it aside. "If she wants to do or dump both of you, you'll either accept it or clear the space for someone else." Azzy points a finger at the men, who watch her in awe. "She'll do whatever she wants with her body, and you won't have any right to be judgmental. Because you—" she jabs her finger at Aleksey, "—have screwed visitants, and you—" she turns to Rey, "—you weren't so eager to wait until marriage when you screwed Angie, were you?"

She takes my hand and leads me to her room. I'm shaking, and my stomach growls. Aleksey offered me food earlier, and I declined. Now I regret it.

Azzy storms from the room and returns with soya bread and tea.

"Eat this; it'll increase your pheromones."

"You're making that up." I ravish the bread and swallow the tea in one gulp. "But thanks." And I don't mean just for the bread.

She shrugs. "Somebody had to shake up the Priest a little. In your emergency deflowering triangle, he became the weak link."

The support of my annoying sister warms me. I might not have much in life, but I have my family. Acknowledging this is enough to make me feel better.

I smile and pat her shoulder. "No triangle. My deflowering dilemma was never a matter of *who*. It was a matter of *how*."

I won't sleep with Aleksey tonight. I'd rather spend the night with my siblings in Azzy's room. I'm emotionally exhausted, and I need time with my family before they leave Starville. Thanks to Aleksey's contacts, Dad and the twins will get temporary IDs and move to New Norfolk, where there's an Accord hospital. I'm not sure I'll survive to see them again, so I worry that tonight is my last chance to say goodbye.

We use sheets to build a makeshift tent. Blankets become our sleeping bags. We pretend we're camping outside, in a place without war.

Olmo, as usual, sings and makes animal noises in his sleep. Mostly soft coos, but every so often he growls like a lion, startling us awake.

"Let's slap him until he wakes."

"Come on, Azalea."

We finally fall asleep. I have blissful dreams for the first time in a long time. A starry sky over a sleepy blue lake. I dream about a pair of magnificent angels deep in conversation as they fly to the moon.

"She looks so young like this."

"I blame the war. Sometimes I think Lila hasn't developed emotionally. After all, she was forced to skip all the rites that let other girls reach maturity because she had to take care of herself, of her siblings ... of me."

"She developed well. She's a woman, a fighter."

"But in many aspects of her life, she's still growing up."

"She looks so peaceful."

"You thought that she sleeps peacefully only with you, didn't you?

"Dr. Velez, I know it's customary in Starville to ask the father first."

"Ask?" For a while, the only sound is the murmur of the wind under their wings. *"No. It's customary to ask the head of the family. You'd have to ask Lila."*

The angels soar toward the sun until one of them breaks the silence.

"... Farewell."

"Farewell?"

I can't listen to the angels anymore. By the time I open my eyes, the sun is high in the sky. We haven't overslept since the twins were toddlers.

I make my way toward Aleksey's room. Giving him my virginity will be my way of saying goodbye.

When I enter the room, I freeze in shock.

For a moment, I think I'm having a vivid nightmare. The room is unrecognizable. Where his bed, his bass, and his desk used to be, there's nothing. Nothing that could convince anyone that he ever lived here.

I enter the room. Each step echoes against the empty walls. Did he move his things to the Accord headquarters? Is that what he wanted to tell me last night?

At that moment, a female voice sounds from outside. "V-girl! Come here!"

It's Divine. Her lips are pressed together and her body is tense.

"General Fürst and the Accord Unit left Starville."

"Oh!" I shrug. Well ... he's constantly out on commissions. "When are they coming back?"

She avoids my inquiring gaze, and hesitates before answering. "Never."

I blink in confusion.

"Don't you get it? They were expelled from the country. They're never coming back."

Chapter 48

I carry the woes of those who don't know

where they're going

My dear dove; bring me my freedom from

those remote lands.

The Dove—Eduardo Carrasco

Missing him

I PUT THE SOLAR gadget in its usual hiding place under the museum floorboards and enter the beheading room. I've been hacking the wireless connections all morning and found the evidence that Aleksey won't come back. A couple of notes mention that the 25th Accord Unit is on its way to Bern, an European city that holds the UNNO headquarters. Some military blogs that question the neutrality of the Unit show a picture of General Aleksey Fürst boarding a military hovercraft. Patriot military sites wonder whether other units in Patriot-occupied territories should be forced to leave the country, too.

I whistle "The Dove" song and take my favorite pigeon, Cher Ami, between my hands to pet her. The soft contact with the pacific creature soothes my feelings of loss. Aleksey broke his neutrality pledge for me. The cost we'll pay is that he won't make love to me tonight. Or ever. *The lovers who never were,* he said once. His words were foreshadowing. I thought I was ready to lose my ally, my voyeurmate. The only man who has made me feel loved. But why so soon? Why like this?

"It's logical. No recruitment ceremony means we don't need them here," says Divine, who is helping me feed the pigeons.

I look away and inhale sharply. "A goodbye would have been nice." I've been told that Aleksey spent an hour talking to my father while workers took his things to a Starville orphanage. Later, he took a helicopter to the soldiers' headquarters and disappeared from my life. "If he could say goodbye to Dad, why not say goodbye to me?"

"He said he didn't want to wake you up."

I raise my hands in front of me, open my palms, and release Cher Ami. She flies through the damaged ceiling and disappears into the blue sky. I wish more than ever that I could fly with her. I still can't believe that I won't see Aleksey again. But what can I do to change what happened? Nothing! It is what it is.

"Gary Sleecket was part of several ceremonies. Perhaps the handsome Prince—"

"Gary returned only because he was a popular cop," I say. "A lot of Starvillers wanted him back. That's not the case with Aleksey."

Divine tries to push the topic further, but I don't let her. I'm trying not to think about him. It hurts, and I can do nothing to change the situation.

"Who's in charge of the clinic now?" she asks.

"My dad. Provisionally. But the soldiers have assigned us a new dwelling in the same building as the Diazes. So … I don't know."

It's pointless to move. My family will transfer to New Norfolk, in the Atlantic Coast, and I'll leave Starville soon, but we can't disobey an official order. Besides, moving out might help me get Aleksey out of my system. I can't mourn when there are many things to do.

That afternoon, I take our scarce belongings to our new provisional apartment. My family has always had keys to the Diazes' apartment, so, in a reconciliation gesture, Dad has given copies of our keys to Baron. Yet, I turn down their offer to help me. All we have are some mattresses, a mirror, and boxes full of Olmo's medicines. It's not much, but it takes a few trips to get it all into our new home.

After returning from one of my trips, I decide that this is a good moment to talk to Duque again about our plans to move to Shiloh.

Duque hasn't mentioned suicide since the day I proposed, so I internally congratulate myself. I lost my voyeurmate, but perhaps Duque and I will become like brother and sister while we live in Shiloh. I'll do everything in my power to heal his broken heart.

I decide not to knock first. What if he's sleeping?

When I open the door, I freeze for a second, during which all my nightmares pass through my mind.

I haven't seen a more revolting, soul-breaking spectacle in my life.

CHAPTER 49

Losing a part of herself

THE MONSTER HAS PRESSED both of the girl's hands against the cot. His hospital gown is open from behind, giving me a view of his rear moving rhythmically. His face is unfocused, like he's in a trance.

The girl is fully dressed, her eyes open wide.

He hasn't entered her; the friction is against her stomach. She's as paralyzed as I am. So unresponsive that she might as well be dead.

But she's not dead. Her entire body emanates disbelief.

She never agreed to this. She's too young to have agreed to this.

The girl suffering Duque's frenzy is Azzy.

The monster stops his attack. Duque runs his hands through his hair. It's as though he's coming out of a trance. He says something loud enough to take me out of my paralysis. "What am I doing? Why am I—?"

I ram against him; he falls from his hospital bed and howls. I smile as I realize that he fell on his wounds. I'm glad it hurt.

I yank his gown toward me and slap him hard. "She trusted you! *I* trusted you!"

His face contorts in agony. "I'm sorry, I don't know what happened. I was hurting and—"

"STOP THE EXCUSES!" I slap him again, harder. So hard that my hands burn in pain. A blinding rage numbs my senses. "My father, Cara, Divine. They aren't lashing out at innocent people!"

I don't know if it has been seconds or hours, but I keep thrashing at Duque. Eventually, someone pulls me away.

"Let go of me!" I scream.

"Easy, Velez," says Joey. It takes the combined efforts of Joey and Mathew to restrain me.

Cara helps Duque to his feet, her face paler than usual. I'm about to order her to stop helping a brute when I hear a whimper. I turn to look at Azzy. She has just sat up on the bed. She's red-faced and immobile, looking as though she were the one who has done something wrong.

I stop struggling and gag. If I hadn't found him, how far would he have gone?

"I won't hit him … let me go to Azzy."

I hold my sister, cradling her tenderly. Because the Comanches won't let me hurt Duque physically, I resort to verbal violence.

"I knew you felt castrated. You felt like less than a man, and *damn* if I don't doubt your masculinity this very moment. You impotent freak!"

Azzy covers her ears. Duque is leaning on Cara's shoulder, a pained expression on his face. The others look at him sympathetically, but I can't. He might have castrated my sister—because that's what this is, even if we're talking about a female victim: a form of mutilation. Losing a vital part of herself that she'll never recover.

"You're not a man. You're nothing. You of all people should know what you were about to destroy." I glare at Duque, who isn't returning my gaze. "I love your family, so I won't hurt you as much as I want to. But you'll stay away from us."

Tears fill his eyes. "I'm sorry. Believe me, I'm sorry. Kill me to repay the damage."

His tears only enrage me more. My eyes are wet with the intensity of my anger, and I'm trembling. "Oh, yeah? What about your family? Stop hurting people, goddammit!"

Still pressing my sister against my chest, I lead her to the doors.

I turn to look at Duque. His eyes are full of tears as he's staring at his feet. I haven't hurt him enough. It's my sister we're talking about. He should have tried to protect others from the pain he suffered himself.

I steady my breath and add, calmly, "I pity you so much. Taking out your pain on the people who love you most. Or, should I say, on those who used to love you? You're so broken, so pathetic. I pity you."

My words hit him harder than my fists. I can tell he's in agony as I leave. I drag Azalea straight to her room.

"Don't say anything to Dad," she says in a shaky voice.

Azzy is always so clever and strong that I sometimes forget she's still a child who needs protection. The guilt that corrodes my veins forms a lump in my throat. My head bows, my shoulders hunch. How could I have failed to prevent this from happening? *Damn!* Maybe it's because there was a sense of security when Aleksey was around. Besides, I thought the danger would come from the military staff. I hid the twins from them, but I didn't see the need to protect my sister from a friend.

I slump next to Azalea on her cot and wait for her to say something. She doesn't.

"There were other Comanches around," I say in the kindest tone I can muster. I don't want her to think that what happened has anything to do with her. *Why didn't she scream?*

Her green eyes are unfocused.

"I … my mind went blank and I couldn't move," she says, her voice detached.

Dad has explained this to me. When someone attacks you, your instincts take over. One instinct commands us to fight. Another orders us to flee. But more often than not, our instincts tell our bodies to freeze.

"Starting tomorrow, you'll train with the Comanches."

Usually, she gives me a hard time about the physical education component of her homeschooling. This time, she doesn't.

Rey clenches his fists and takes deep breaths as he strides around the small room. "I won't let a monstrosity like this go unpunished." He turns his eyes to the bibles that crowd his apartment. "And I swear to God I won't let him harm anyone else. I'll get help for him."

"I know he wouldn't have done it if he hadn't been attacked … I wish him well," I lie. "I want him to recover, but I hate him. I—"

"I'll never hate my brother, but he should have risen above the circumstances. It's not like he didn't have other options. I'm so sorry he hurt Azzy."

"What now?"

"He needs treatment. Spiritual treatment. I'll convince him to join the seminary. And—"

A loud knock startles us.

Rey opens the door to find Cara looking disgruntled. It's evident she's been crying. "Priest, it's over. They …"

Rey's eyes widen with confusion. "What?"

Cara wraps her arms around us. "The recruitment ceremony … they just announced … it's still on."

"*No!*" I pull my hair with both hands, hoping the pain will overcome my anguish. "They can't! The ones who aren't dead should be badly injured! They—don't have a train!"

"Half of the soldiers survived. They've recovered already and will arrive in two days by helicopter. The ceremony is—"

I close my ears to her words, already knowing the cruel reality. Recruitment is not only still on. They've pushed the date ahead.

The day after tomorrow.

CHAPTER 50

Broken illusions

WEAK CANDLELIGHT ILLUMINATES THE room. I look at my reflection in the cracked mirror. My outfit is the same one I once wore to seduce Rey: a button-up shirt over a tank top, a skirt, and tie-side underwear. It's been weeks, and I'm different now. Only one thing hasn't changed: I still dread what will happen tomorrow during the recruitment ceremony.

Tonight I'll explore and get to know my body for the first time before the troops take control of it.

Closing my eyes, I lie on some old hospital mattresses and partially cover myself with Sara Jenkins's bridal sheet. My hands slide slowly over my thighs, my hips, and my breasts, but the spark is missing. I pucker my lips. I yearn to be kissed, and I need to kiss *him*. If only these hands on my body were *his* hands.

I stop the touching. It's pointless if he's not here. His grunts, his ragged breathing, his erection pressing against my body. The heady sensation that I was the only girl in his life. It's not practical to yearn for what I can't have, but I can't help it.

At that moment, someone touches my cheek. I sit up, startled.

Rey's flushed face and leering stare tell me that he's turned on. His voice has a breathy quality. "I kept calling you and you didn't answer."

I hastily cover myself with the sheet as though I weren't still fully dressed underneath it. My family is spending the night at the clinic, so I thought that I was alone. I forgot that Rey has the key to my apartment. I try to get up, but he grabs my wrists.

Before I know what's happening, he's kissing me, forcing me against the mattress.

I push him forcefully. "Whatever you saw, I'm not needy."

"That doesn't make me want you less," he says, climbing back to the mattress and hovering over me. "I want you to know that ... I'm willing."

"I told you, I'll never marry you."

"I've accepted that. I'll take whatever part of you that you want to give me." He presses his lips against my neck. "Let me make love to you. Now."

I look at him in shock. "Why did you change your mind? Charity work, Rey? You don't have to ..."

He talks with emotion, his eyes brilliant. "No. I can't think of a life without you." His fingertips brush my cheeks. "I don't have much in my life. No money, no future to offer a woman, but you ... you're one of the best gifts life has given me."

I shake my head. "I was thinking of *him* when—"

"Don't you have feelings for me, Lily?"

"I love you as a friend. You and I ... it'd be so wrong because there's someone else ... in your heart and—" I swallow. "—in mine."

"But they're not here." His face reveals an internal battle. "They're the past." He sits me on his lap, and his arms encircle me. "You still want to lose your innocence before the troops come. Don't you realize that I want to be with you in that way? In every way?"

"Rey, I have strong feelings for another man. I'll leave Starville. I—"

"Then why don't we not waste the limited time we have together?" he whispers in a deep voice. His lips brush my earlobe, sending a thrill throughout my body.

He takes off his shirt and places my hands on his shoulders. He presses his lips against my collarbone. From there, he places kisses all over my neck.

"If you want to, it would be only tonight. Tomorrow, I'll be your friend again."

His lips move urgently on my mouth. As his hands travel up and down my back, my mind repeats: *The recruitment is tomorrow. This is your last chance.*

But my lips refuse to cooperate.

Rey takes off my shirt, sliding his hands up and down between my waist and neck. His mouth is still ravishing mine. He pulls up my skirt, and it becomes a messy bunch of fabric surrounding my waist. I can't think straight. This doesn't feel right in my heart, but my body responds as if by reflex, and my mind keeps telling me that this can't be worse than recruitment. *Recruitment!*

He is still all hands and lips when he lays my body on the mattress and removes my skirt.

I suddenly feel naked, although I'm still wearing a top and my underwear. I cover myself with the bridal sheet—the one that, by design, should allow him to enter me, but that won't allow him to see my body.

In the blink of an eye, his body is over mine. "You want me to continue?"

His question provokes internal turmoil. This is war, and it's not the time to hesitate. But my heart becomes an enemy working against me. I wish Aleksey were the one I could trust with my mind, body, and heart. I almost expect to see him burst through the door and interrupt us as he once did.

Rey's beautiful face is sweaty, his breathing is ragged, and he can't hide the look of hurt in his eyes at my hesitation. I know it would shred him if I said no at this point. Unless … What if he's the one who changes his mind? The thought scares me. This is my very last chance.

I order my heart to cooperate, and I put my arms around his neck, pulling him closer. Still covering my body with the bridal sheet, I untie my underwear and toss it to the floor. Shivering all over, I force my hips to express my consent.

Rey understands and positions his body between my legs.

❧

I feel a strange sensation on my face, and I run my hand over my cheek. Moisture. I must have shed a tear or two.

Rey kisses my forehead.

"Are you okay?"

I nod, although my heart feels heavy. The whole thing felt like an out-of-body experience. My body overrode my brain, and my hormones cooperated, but it was as though another girl was on this mattress, and I was watching the scene from another place. I barely remember how it was, except that physically I felt something close to relief. In my heart, I know this was a painful victory. I'm not emotionally satisfied. Not at all.

I run my fingers over my thighs and find some of his release.

I look down at the white bridal sheet and a strange compulsion to burn it runs through me. I settle for tossing it to the ground.

Why am I so irrationally upset? It's absurd. I made a decision, and I shouldn't second guess it. Perhaps it's the events of the last few weeks that have left my feelings raw and exposed.

Later, Rey wraps me in his arms and falls asleep. I wonder if it's normal to be thinking about someone else while I'm in the arms of another guy.

I cover my eyes with both hands, feeling a pang of sadness for the lovers Aleksey and I could have been. We both fought hard to share this moment together, and we failed. Those illusions are broken, irrevocably dead because I let the opportunity slip through my fingers.

I turn my back to Rey.

Knowing that, as much as I wish things were different, Aleksey will never come back makes me feel as though an iron hand is tearing my heart to pieces. He marched away thinking I feel nothing more than a girlish crush.

Of all moments, my traitorous heart had to choose this one—when I'm in bed, wrapped in a different set of arms—to realize that I'm in love for the first time. In love with a man who will never become what I need him to be: the first man who makes love to me.

His red cape, his half-smile, those strong arms that wrapped themselves around me when I had nightmares. The man who played a sweet melody on his bass to lull me to sleep. The one who told me he loved me without realizing it. All those memories of him come to my mind, accompanied by pangs of longing.

"I love you, Aleksey," I whisper to my mental picture of him.

As much as I struggle to fight them, a few tears make their way down my cheeks. The sobs that I'm repressing are burning down my throat.

I inhale as deeply as I can, enjoying one last instant of regret. After I exhale I promise myself that these are the last tears I'll ever shed for Aleksey Fürst.

That's when I hear the helicopters.

The troops have arrived.

Chapter 51

In warfare in ancient times, the spoils of war included the defeated populations, which were often enslaved, and the women and children, who were often absorbed into the victorious country's population.

World Heritage Encyclopedia

Spoils of war

NAKED AND SCARED, I rub my intimate areas with a desensitizing cream before swallowing Dad's pills. My father's inventions—the cream and the anti-rape pills—are my only protection against what I'll face today.

In an attempt to calm my nerves, I inhale and exhale deeply in Aunt Olga's bathroom before I don the recruitment uniform: a tank top and white pants made of an almost translucent fabric that reveals my white underwear. My thigh wound is bleeding, and I'm struggling to keep the uniform clean. Today we're not allowed to wear anything that isn't white.

Dad must be at the university gym, but my siblings are waiting for me outside the bathroom. I open my arms, and the twins take the invitation to hug me. Olmo cries while Azalea buries her face in my shoulder. I'll leave the twins in the care of Aunt Olga. Will I be the one who will pick them up after the ceremony? Or will Dad be forced to do so because I'll have become a recruit?

"Come back to us," says Azzy as she pulls back from my embrace.

Rey, dressed in the recruitment outfit, meets me in front of Olga's. Together, we head to the gym.

When we pass through the gym doors, the sight makes my bile rise. Fifty stone benches are scattered around the wooden stage. They'll hold the bodies of recruits while the soldiers attack them. The wooden stage is lit by a set of lamps suspended from a metallic structure above. Three soldiers in the middle rows are pointing moving lights toward the stage. The ceremony has the vibe of an inoffensive occasion: a music concert, a sporting event, or a graduation.

A huge crowd is already filling the rows when Rey and I line up with the other potential recruits. A section of the rows is left empty.

As they get their cameras ready, the new cops look old and fragile compared to their predecessors. One tired-looking cop is talking loudly enough for me to hear. "I looked it up on the wireless yesterday. Prince Aleksey is a world away from here."

"Good! He would've made us face the soldiers," answers a Mexican-accented voice.

Silence spreads throughout the crowd when Kit Lee-Rivers climbs the stage and welcomes the 36th Battalion.

Herds of soldiers meld into a single unit as the troops enter the gym through the east doors. TCR's efforts have dwindled their numbers, but even so, there must be hundreds of them, marching in ultra-coordinated, perfect formations around the court. They're human, but their tattooed faces, artificial heights, and inhuman build make them look demonic. They emanate a stench that burns my nostrils. At the order of their superiors, the soldiers cease their military choreography and become statuesque.

A claustrophobic sensation courses through me when the doors close. I shiver.

The leader of the 36th Battalion is Sergeant Landry, a red-haired soldier whose gray, tattooed skin shows recent scars from the derailment. He addresses the crowd without a microphone. "In accordance with the protocol established by sections seven to eighteen of the Twenty-first Amendment, before the recruitment ceremony begins, we welcome the enlistees to our glorious Army."

The first enlistee, a ragged, scrawny girl, walks toward the stage like she is trying to force her feet forward. "I pledge my allegiance to the army of the Patriot States of America," she exclaims.

The crowd, which has filled the gym rows, applauds halfheartedly.

Several people follow her example. Enlistees are people so poor that they say it is better to serve than to starve. Enlistees who please the troops earn a meager salary and Patriot citizenship. Some families would die if it weren't for the contributions of their enlisted relatives.

Recruits, on the other hand, end up as Vassals—unpaid visitants and, in the case of girls, baby carriers. The strongest boys enter as low-rank soldiers, those who will be on the front lines during battle.

Over the last weeks, the number of registered enlistees has increased. The air raid left many people in a dire situation. One hundred and sixty people enlist. They climb down the stage and form a line backstage.

"Starvillers, this is your last chance to submit voluntarily and improve the living conditions of your families," shouts Landry.

When no one else enlists, they divide us into groups according to our ages. Rey is about to join the twenty-one-year-old group when his eyes meet mine. "Take care," he mouths.

Landry tells the rest of us to parade around the gym's court. As we do so, the troops take a good look at us. I frown. They must be choosing their favorites. Some take videos with their j-devices. This makes my blood boil in fury.

I'm not an animal.

I'm not an object.

I'm not a spoil of war.

Finally, they make us line up at the right side of the stage. They usually take thirteen recruits among unmarried boys and girls of each age group. Because they're superstitious, the soldiers refuse to take more recruits from a group. They say it brings bad luck.

A murmur spreads through the crowd when a group of female soldiers enters the gym from the east doors. The Starvillers keep repeating, *Witches, witches.* These women are as tall as the male soldiers, though less muscular. They will determine the V-status of the potential recruits. They have brought digital polygraphs, even though they rarely use them. The troops are convinced that the witches need nothing more than to touch the arm of a recruit to determine his or her celibacy status. The witches join Landry on the stage.

The lights go out, and I cover my mouth to suppress a scream. The darkness lasts a couple of seconds. I can hear the collective breathing of the crowd surrounding us. A huge beam of light illuminates Landry's massive figure.

"On August twenty-fifth of the twenty-first year of the Patriot States Era, in the name of the Minister of War, General Maximillian Kei, I declare the eleventh recruitment ceremony officially inaugurated at exactly 1400."

CHAPTER 52

G class recruits

THE TWENTY-THREE-YEAR-OLD group steps onto the stage as a monstrous-looking captain reads their names from a list. The lights make their white garments look almost transparent. Because most of them have marriage tattoos, it's obvious that the four eligible women will be recruited. They are spinsters in a town where women outnumber men and bachelors are scarce. All of the recruits will be assigned to the *G* category. The lowest rank in the military.

Landry calls the first candidate from the group. "Ingrid Philomena Wisniewska."

A blinding beam of light follows Ingrid as she approaches Landry with faltering steps.

Landry shouts, "You will join the Patriot army as a *G*-class recruit." Ingrid's face remains impassive, but I could swear that her legs are trembling.

The four new recruits are flanked by the soldiers and descend the stage to form a line in the back. The non-recruits occupy seats in the section of rows that was left empty.

Mathew is part of the twenty-two-year-old group, but he skips re-cruitment because he has a marriage tattoo. In his group are fifteen eligible people. One boy, fourteen girls.

"It's the witches' call," murmurs Holly Winston, who stands by my side.

The witches touch the arms of the fifteen. Two girls are declared non-virgins and Landry spares them from recruitment. The thirteen new recruits join the enlistees. It seems like they're fighting tears. I want to shout at them to stop crying. Looking vulnerable isn't a smart idea in the army.

The twenty-one-year-old group steps up. Because his religious tattoo is evident under his nearly translucent, tight-fitting shirt, they spare Rey immediately. In this group, only twenty people are eligible. The witches touch the arms of all the potential recruits. None of the boys in that group is declared unsullied, so they're spared.

When the girls are particularly good-looking, the witches skip the test. The troops will take the most attractive girls no matter what their V-status is.

Landry's eyes go back and forth between the candidates and the troops. There's a silent communication among the soldiers that reaches the stage, indicating their preferences to Landry. From that group, they recruit thirteen scared-looking maidens.

The twenty-year-old group is next, forty-two people.

Elena Rivers' magnetic Asian features and curvy body have caught the attention of the troops. Reluctantly, Landry spares her because her tattoo indicates that she's about to get Patriot citizenship. The V-status of thirteen girls earns them each a spot among the recruits.

I shuffle uncomfortably. It's almost my turn.

The nineteen-year-old group is the most crowded. Fifty-eight potential recruits. The majority of the girls are what the troops call *Starvillian beauties*. Generous bosoms on otherwise ultra-slim figures, not to mention blond hair and slender legs.

The witches determine that three boys are unsullied. They are recruited along with ten girls.

I swallow hard as anguish washes through me.

"Eighteen-year-old group! Step up!" booms the voice of the female general.

We climb the stage and form a line.

The lights blind me. The soldiers must be looking at all of us from their spots below, but I can't shake the feeling that all eyes are on me. The crowd is hidden in the darkness beyond the stage, but I'm aware of their presence. They're whispering, they're shuffling in their seats, they're scratching their heads.

Fourteen eligible candidates. Only one of us will be spared. They've already recruited non-virgins, so no one is safe. I straighten my posture, attempting a look of confidence, although my skin has broken out in goose bumps. Being here is surreal. The moment I've dreaded all along.

"Lila Velez Tcherkassky," calls Landry.

I step forward, and the beam of light falls across my body. Instead of warming me, the light turns my body to ice. I do my best to lift my head and look brave.

One of the witches, a green-haired woman wearing a Sergeant tattoo on her gray-colored face, is looking at me questioningly. "Are you a V-girl?"

I don't answer right away. My fear has evaporated. I find it strange that she avoids using the word *virgin*. I used to hate the term, but I realize now how ridiculous their virginity obsession is, and how foolish I was whenever I took the name as an offense. I was playing by the Starville rules I despise so much. I've put extra weight into the unfair burden that society has placed on me and my virginity.

I hold my head high. "No, I'm not a *virgin*," I answer, putting emphasis on the last word.

Distant sneering reaches my ears. Apparently, Starvillers don't believe me.

The beam of light is still pointing at my body. Both witches touch my arms. The contact burns my skin. I drop my eyes so that they can't see the hate brewing inside me.

They're convinced that I'm being truthful and skip the polygraph test.

"She's not a V-girl and the other candidates are more attractive. Let's put her on hold."

My mind goes numb. I'm staring at my feet when Holly's voice makes me look up.

"I'm not a V-girl."

I thought Holly was keeping herself for a future husband. Is she lying to avoid recruitment? If the polygraph determines that she's lying, they'll punish her and recruit her, anyway. I look at Holly in confusion. Then I bite my lip to suppress a gasp.

The woman in front of the witch is not Holly. Cara Winston is trying to make herself pass for her daughter. She's thirty-five, but training has given her a youthful body. Holly and Cara share the Starvillian beauty features that make them look like twins.

Landry leers at Cara and exchanges looks with the troops below him.

"Holly Marie Winston," Landry orders. "You'll join the Patriot Army as a *G*-class recruit."

I don't have time to worry about Cara. Twelve out of the fourteen eligible people in my group have been recruited, and they seem to be holding their decision on the last candidate, who is being tested with a polygraph.

"Duque Charles Diaz Jurado. Are you a V-man?"

Duque holds up his colostomy bag. "I'm not sure."

At the sight of the waste inside the stoma, the witches, who had been staring at Duque with greedy eyes, wrinkle their noses.

His doom could mean my freedom until next year. I hold my breath. My muscles feel like jelly. I still hate the traitor who hurt Azzy, but I wish things were different. I wish the soldiers would spare us both.

Long moments pass. The troops can't decide who they prefer.

Everyone has their eyes on Duque and me. I'm sure people notice that I'm shivering. I ignore them and look around. Am I waiting for a miracle? For an angel to fall from the sky and stop the ceremony, send the soldiers to hell, and liberate the victims? Am I waiting for Aleksey to appear?

Duque's voice surprises us all. "I pledge my alliance to the army of the Patriot States of America."

A collective gasp echoes throughout the gym. I turn to glance at Rey, who looks as shocked as everyone else. The troop explodes with murmurs. Is Duque's petition allowed? This is an unprecedented act in a recruitment ceremony.

Landry frowns and projects a hologram of the protocol sections with his j-device. He seems to search for anything that would prevent enlistment in cases like this.

I close my eyes, not daring to hope.

Please allow it. Please don't recruit me.

Landry looks at me, and for a moment, I'm afraid he's about to recruit me.

After minutes of consultation with the troops, Landry makes his decision.

"Duque Charles Diaz Jurado, you'll join the Patriot forces as a recruit. Your rank will be recruit class *G*, like all the non-enlisters."

As much as I despise him, as much as I don't want to be recruited, I feel sorry for Duque. I don't see how he'll survive the cruel life of a vassal when he hasn't yet recovered from his injuries.

Before taking his place among the other recruits, Duque leans in to whisper in my ear, "Does this redeem part of my offense?"

He doesn't wait for my answer. He walks backstage, holding his head high and his colostomy bag in front of him.

I have no answer for him. I'm speechless. Did he volunteer because of what he did? Or is this another suicide attempt?

The troops allow us non-recruits to descend the stage and take a seat in the front rows. I'm faking calmness, but I'm a mess inside. In theory, we've been spared from lives as sex slaves. They won't take me as a recruit, but the danger isn't over.

Now comes the worst.

Familiar voice

A CHUBBY ACCORD COP steps forward and addresses the camera.

"I certify that everything was done according to the constitution of the Patriot States of America."

Teams of troops around me break their formations. Their eyes can't hide their excitement.

"Turn down your cameras," orders Landry.

Until this point, the crowd has responded with a muffled noise. Now, the audience gets eerily silent. Everyone knows what will happen next.

A group of soldiers places a dozen recruits on the bench stones while other soldiers keep the recruits' arms immobilized. The monsters have taken off the part of their armor that covers their pelvises. The light falls on the bench stones that will hold the true horror of the recruitment ceremony.

The multiple sexual assaults begin.

My mind is fighting to remain conscious. My muscles are tense, and my breathing becomes ragged. For a few seconds, I can't look away. Just like that time when I lost my mom, I'm unable to close my eyes. I want to scream at them to stop, but I'm frozen. Nobody dares to talk, move, or even cringe. We don't want to draw attention to the fact that our faces are contorting in disgust, in impotence. That could get us recruited.

When I force myself to look away, I can't find a place to lay my eyes where I don't encounter the gruesome sight of trios of soldiers attacking recruits. I can't cover my ears either. The recruits' ear-piercing screams make me realize that they didn't take any pills and therefore they feel the full force of the attacks. I can smell the blood, thick in my lungs. I fight to keep my head up as my mind reels with desperate thoughts.

Don't hurt them. It must hurt so much. Stop.

Above the diabolic symphony of screams, the voice of a soldier reaches me. "My turn."

Immediately, a soldier who was mounting a recruit props himself up on his elbows and relinquishes his position.

Some attackers look so young that, despite their size, they remind me of my mother's assailants. They are enjoying themselves, laughing like they're crazy. Still, I catch sight of some soldiers who don't look comfortable with this show. If they don't like it, why don't they stop it? By not speaking up, they're as responsible as the others. I hate them all equally.

In a moment of infinite terror, a soldier approaches me. It feels as though he'll drag me to a stone, but then he focuses his attention on someone else.

At that moment, a loud wail overpowers the screams of the recruits, startling me. A familiar voice is screaming in rage, pain and disbelief. A soldier is dragging Elena by her long hair to one of the stones.

"*Nooooo*! Luke! Help me!"

The troops laugh as a soldier throws her to the floor. Three other soldiers roughly lift her and place her body on the stone. While a soldier grabs Elena's body by her arms, two more grab her by her ankles and spread her legs.

"Get your hands off of her!" shouts Luke Rivers, making his way to the court. What's he doing? He's going to get himself recruited, and then they'll attack Elena anyway.

The witches, using the strength of their modified genes, drag him to a stone. They punch him over and over and force him to lie flat on his stomach.

Abruptly, the doors of the gym open.

The light of the sun prevents us from making out the appearance of the new arrival. All we know is that a red-caped figure stands on the threshold.

CHAPTER 54

Sacrifice

MY CHIN DROPS TO the floor when I recognize him.

The lanky cop scans the scene, and his eyes narrow. I can sense Tristan's desperation to do something, but what can a single decent cop do against hundreds of soldiers?

He marches into the gym. "I'm Colonel Tristan Froh, from the 25th Accord Unit. According to the protocol, the ceremony should have ended twenty minutes ago."

How is he here? I remember seeing pictures of Aleksey and his Unit boarding a military hovercraft. I look around. If Tristan is here, perhaps my Aleksey is, too. Then it hits me. I was so upset that I didn't notice whether or not Tristan was in those pictures.

The soldiers not engaged in abusing recruits look at Tristan derisively. They seem to find this interruption funny. Sergeant Landry hasn't even bothered to spare a look at the new arrival.

Tristan's eyes rest on the Accord Unit. He won't gain support there.

The young colonel walks directly toward the witches who are about to attack Elena and Luke. I shuffle on my seat nervously. As he forces the witch holding Elena to release her, Tristan seems to be forcing a confidence he doesn't really feel.

"Section seventeen of the twenty-first amendment, *civilians in the process of acquiring Patriot citizenship are not eligible for recruitment.* Let these two people go."

The soldiers burst into a fit of cold, demonic laughter. Looking at the debauchery around us, Tristan's statement sounds naïve.

To my surprise, the soldiers let the siblings go. "As you wish, Colonel."

Luke and Elena dash for their seats, where the Rivers family and servants welcome them with open arms. I look at Elena. Tears fill her eyes, and her face is contorted in terror as if she is screaming, but no sound comes from it. Luke pulls her into his arms and cradles her.

Rocco approaches Tristan and yells, "The 25th Accord Unit was banished from Patriot Territory. Return to your country."

Landry finds this information interesting. "So the cop is an illegal immigrant?"

Tristan moves his earring-device, and a hologram of an official-looking document appears.

"I have written permission from General Maximillian Kei to stay in the country to—"

Abruptly, one of the soldiers grabs Tristan from behind and forcefully tears his earring-device, breaking Tristan's skin. The cop's scream of pain makes even the monsters attacking girls on the stones turn their heads.

Landry steps on Tristan's j-device. "We haven't seen any document," he claims in a sarcastic tone.

I put my hand in my mouth to suppress a cry of horror when they shove Tristan against a stone. The witches call dibs. I've never seen them attack cops. The Accord Unit is protected by UNNO. These soldiers are making a statement: *nobody, not even UNNO, can interfere with us.*

My mind reaches its limit and shuts down. I go numb. My eyes are open, but I see only darkness. A small part of my brain registers Tristan's screams, but the rest is a high-pitched sound. I feel nothing. I'm replacing reality with delusion like Olmo does. In my imaginary world, I attend university. Aleksey picks me up after school every day to ride in his Humvee. Olmo is cured, and everyone I care about is safe and sound.

By the time I return from my delusion, Tristan is drenched in his own blood and is inert. I can't wrap my head around the injustice of it.

He's the only Accord cop brave enough to oppose the soldiers, and his bravery has been punished. My face reddens, my fists clench, and I welcome the fury that replaces the fear.

Tristan's sacrifice is the end of the ceremony. Landry mobilizes the troops and the recruits. They march their way through the doors. The attackers carry their unconscious victims while Tristan's body is carried away by the Accord Unit.

I used to doubt Tristan would do the right thing during the ceremony; now the memory of my distrust slaps me hard. *Please survive this, Tristan.*

Rocco and the local soldiers order us to stay in the gym until the 36th Battalion has left the building.

I watch the contingent become smaller as soldiers leave the gym. The sound of helicopters departing is all over town. I suppress a fit of hysterics. Tristan. Cara. All those recruits and enlistees.

I try–and fail—to find relief in the thought that the worst has happened. I find strength thinking about my family. *Olmo, Azzy. I'll see you soon. We're safe from recruitment.*

But the side of me that is always mulling over pessimistic thoughts brings me back to reality.

For now.

I shiver as a mist covers the glade. I get up and smooth my dress before putting on my cloak.

"It won't work," says Divine as she dismounts Joey's semi-naked body and collapses on the grass. They hold on to each other as though that could solve all the world's problems.

Lately, the couple's inability to reach orgasms has ruined their mood for exhibitionist sex. The events of the past few days have thrown all the Comanches into varying levels of depression. Luckily, the new additions to our ranks, Azzy and Elena, have added spark to our decaying numbers. Unfortunately for TCR, Azzy will soon leave. She'll go with Olmo and Dad to New Norfolk.

TCR members have been hacking Patriot sites, searching for information on Duque, Cara, and Tristan's whereabouts ... or evidence of their deaths. Although the Comanches barely knew Tristan, his attack has struck a chord, not only in Starville but all over the world. Patriots took things too far, and this time there'll be repercussions.

Later, because Joey's leg is still recovering, Divine and I become human crutches as we make our way to town.

We're passing a clutch of trees when I see Rey perched on a branch, holding our old gadget. Divine and Joey are unfazed, but I blush. My voyeurism isn't something I want to share with him.

"How long have you been there?"

Rey jumps to the ground in a graceful movement. "A while."

"Did you know that I—that we—"

He shrugs. "I don't know what you're talking about. I came here to hack the wireless. I hope all the international pressure will force them to liberate the recruits."

I bite my lip. I don't want to remind him that although he has condemned the attack on Tristan, Maximillian Kei must spoil his soldiers. Kei would rather face international scorn than lose the troops' support. It's the support that has made him more powerful than the Patriot president. Tristan's attackers are in prison waiting for a trial, but the other monsters won't ever face charges. The law says that they can take recruits in any way they want.

Duque and Cara won't ever come back. I wish Rey could accept that, but I won't ruin his hopes.

"They'll survive," I say, holding his hand.

Soon, Divine and Joey walk on their own through Genesis Street, as if trying to give us the privacy we don't need. On the eve of recruitment, Rey agreed to be just my friend. But I can tell by his glances that he can't forget what happened. Lines are getting blurred between us, but who cares? I won't live in Starville much longer.

Despite the cold mist covering the town, there are more Starvillers on the streets than usual. We turn on Judges Street and have a hard time advancing through the crowd.

I stop dead in my tracks. Did I just see a flash of red?

My mind must be playing tricks on me. I haven't forgotten the massive span of his shoulders or the regal set of his face. As thoughts spin in my head, I fixate on one constant.

Aleksey Fürst is here.

CHAPTER 55

His one and only

ALEKSEY HAS CAUGHT SIGHT of me, and the pure happiness on his face nearly takes my breath away. He takes a step toward me, but then his gaze fixes on my hand, which is entwined with Rey's. Aleksey freezes mid-stride and glances back at me.

I open my mouth to speak, but no sound emerges. The hurt in his expression sends my emotions into a tailspin. I let go of Rey's hand.

A small part of me is aware that Rey is next to me, perhaps glaring at the cop, but Aleksey doesn't spare him a glance. He has eyes for only me. I can do nothing but stare at the gigantic cop longingly as every fiber of my body screams at me, *run to him*. It's as though we're in our own private bubble, and everyone else has disappeared.

My foot takes a hesitant step toward him. I crave his arms around me so badly that it hurts. But I'm afraid of what would happen to him if he were found fraternizing with a Nat.

After a long pause, he closes the distance between us. His blue eyes smolder. "I need to talk to you. Alone."

I nod. "Please go home, Rey." My mind is too hazy to notice when, or if, Rey leaves.

For a long moment, Aleksey and I stare at each other in silence, ignoring the crowd passing by us. His eyes seem to reflect the same yearning and pain that I feel. It's the yearning to throw ourselves into each other's arms and the pain of not being able to do so without risking our lives.

After a while, his fists clench and his face hardens. "Tell me you're not with him," he says harshly.

I blink. How can he move from one mood to another so easily? He left town without saying goodbye, and now that he's back, he can't even ask me how I've been?

I turn around, making my way toward the river. He follows me.

Once we're almost at the glade, he lifts me so that I'm standing on a large stone and our heights almost match. The contact of his strong hands on my arms burns my skin.

"Lila," he says in a taut voice.

"I'm not with him."

Aleksey exhales. His body relaxes a bit, but something else is nagging him. "He said you love him; is it true?"

Not like I love you. Not even a fraction of how much I love you. I shake my head. I'm not ready to say that now. "Not like he thinks I do."

My answer doesn't seem to be what he was expecting. Did he expect I'd say that I don't love Rey at all? I can't say that, but I can do something else.

Totally surprising him, I wrap my arms around his waist and snuggle my head against his body.

"I missed you," I whisper.

Inhaling deeply, he slides his hands in my hair before his arms constrict around me in a tight embrace. Long moments pass before I find my voice.

"You … abandoned me."

"Tristan was supposed to tell you I'd be back."

I look up at him. "Have you seen him? How is he?"

"He's recovering in an Accord hospital." His tone is full of suppressed anger. "I'll make them pay for what they did."

It sounds as though his work at UNNO, Tristan's recovery, and his revenge plans won't let him stay. Fearing that a new goodbye is in the works, I press my forehead against his chest. I want to be as close to him as possible for the limited time we have together.

"I shouldn't be here, Lila. I left a mess behind me, but I needed to see you."

My heart thuds violently against my ribs when his hands slide to the small of my back. "Are you in trouble?" I ask nervously.

He shakes his head. "Patriots never banished us. They sent us away temporarily because they know my unit is too zealous to play along with their crimes. I didn't want to leave, but I was sure recruitment had been canceled. If we hadn't gone, they would have banished us."

His muscular arms tighten their grip on me. "Tristan got special permission to stay in the country and remain in New Norfolk. He was going to contact you, but they moved the recruitment date, and he got back in the nick of time."

The back of his hand grazes my face. "Lila, I never abandoned you. I did everything in my power to covertly protect you. I bribed some Patriot leaders so that they wouldn't recruit you. Tristan and Sergeant Wong stayed behind so that they could keep an eye on you. Even from Europe, I ordered Tristan to secretly film everything to make UNNO acknowledge recruitment for what it is: institutionalized rape."

I shake my head sadly. I would have made different choices that night before recruitment if I'd had any kind of assurance that I wouldn't be recruited.

To embrace him more tightly doesn't seem possible, but I press my chest against the muscles of his stomach with all my strength. I become overly aware of how close our bodies are. The perfect lines of his chest, the heat that emanates from his body, and his masculine scent overcome my senses. A warm, pleasant sensation spreads through me. We're so tightly squeezed against each other that I notice how my closeness physically affects him. But just when the atmosphere is charging with static and sexual promise, a tortured look crosses his face.

"I saw the recording of the ceremony. You said that you aren't a virgin anymore."

I look down and remain quiet for a long time.

Aleksey takes my chin and tips my head back, forcing me to see him. The intensity of his eyes and the delicious feeling of his fingers on my skin don't allow me to think straight. "There's war ..." I swallow hard. "And recruitment ... All is fair in war. I had to do what I could to feel safe, and I won't let anyone judge me, because—"

He looks away, scowling. "I don't judge you."

Whenever Aleksey is around, contradictory thoughts overcome me. I don't want him to judge me, but I don't want him to be indifferent, either.

I can't hide the hurt in my voice. "You don't care whether I slept with him or—"

"I DON'T CARE?" *Bam*! My back slams against the nearby tree trunk. He lifts my wrists above my head and leans in.

His breath is caressing my ears, making my body shudder. "Don't you ever say that again! I'm burning with a feeling that I have never felt before. It's killing me." He presses his pelvis against mine. It feels as though he's trying to claim me. "I hate that he was your first. I can't think of you two without feeling violent. I hate the circumstances that kept me from being with you that night. I hate him."

His lips find the pulse point at my neck. He sucks and nibbles at it, making a tingling sensation spread throughout my body. "If you hadn't told me that hurting him was hurting you, I'd kill him. The jealousy is so bad at this moment that I can't breathe." His lips slide to my jaw, then down to the hollow of my throat. "The only thing that keeps me from snapping is knowing that when you're with me, you'll feel the difference."

"What difference?" I ask breathlessly.

His low, raspy voice in my ear tickles me. "I'm better in bed. I'm going to make him disappear from your mind."

I stare at him in awe.

"Besides …" His lips tease mine before retreating. "Unlike Diaz, for me there has only been, and will always be, only one woman: You."

I inhale sharply. One more time, he's telling me that he loves me in his own way.

"As for you," Aleksey nibbles my lower lip. "It's just a matter of time, Lila. One day you will love only me."

His hot mouth collides with mine in a consuming, passionate kiss. Fire runs through my blood and searing desire surges through me.

While his right hand undoes the buttons of my dress down to my stomach, his left hand keeps a strong hold on my wrists. "He may have been your first," he says, trailing feather-like kisses from my shoulder to my collarbone and down to the edge of my bra. "But I'll be your last."

Aleksey carries me to the flowerbed. He gently lays me down on the soft cushion that the flowers provide. He then covers my body with his. He tilts my head so that I'm looking into his eyes.

"I'll make love to you until you forget his name and even your own," he says huskily. "The only name you'll be able to scream will be mine."

He buries his face in the crook of my neck, nibbling softly. The way his weight presses against me without crushing me stirs pangs of desire. Aleksey speaks against the side of my neck. "It's not only about making you mine. I want to be yours." His heated words caress my skin. "I'm yours already."

Butterflies flutter in my stomach. He's mine?

I hear a giggle and turn my head. Divine and Joey walk toward us. Flustered, I sit up and button my dress.

"Wow. That was hot! Now I know what you two get from watching us," says Divine.

Joey eyes us knowingly. "We've come for a second try. Never meant to interrupt you."

Aleksey isn't embarrassed at all. Ignoring the newcomers, he gets up skillfully and helps me to my feet. His face looks cool and possessed as he puts on his red cape.

Leaning close, he whispers in my ear, "Let's go to a quieter place."

Chapter 56

The life of a man, no matter how humble,
no matter how powerful
can be condensed to a single moment.
The moment he has found the woman he will love for life.
General Fürst's journal

Sweet surrender

"TAKE OFF YOUR BOOTS," he orders as he steps out of his. He grabs my hand and leads me through the spacious room. Most of the far wall and vast portions of the ceiling are made of a sturdy kind of glass. My eyes open wide as I try to take in all the beauty of the rocky beaches, the tall cliffs, and the purple sky that hovers over a turquoise ocean. I've never seen the sea before, except in books, but Aleksey is a man of his word. He told me once that he would show me the sea, and here we are in a cottage for the staff who work at a UNNO refueling point.

A shiver runs down my spine when his hand touches the small of my back. Aleksey leads me to French doors that open onto a narrow balcony. It's perched several feet above waves that break on the rocks below us. I inhale deeply, taking in the crisp, salty scent of the ocean.

Solid, muscular arms pull me into a tight embrace. "You're my prisoner here, and this time I won't let you leave until we've made love to the point of exhaustion." He looks at me mischievously. "You have nowhere to escape unless you want to fall straight into the sea."

I bite my thumb, feeling my insides squirming. Falling is exactly how I feel. As we watch the sun drowning in the horizon, my stomach drops as though I'm about to plunge into the ocean below me. The moment of our long-awaited sexual encounter is finally here.

He sweeps me up in his arms and carries me back to the room. In the corner, there's a plush Oriental rug in front of a fireplace. In another corner, there's a red divan covered in gold and black cushions.

When I first entered the cottage, the breathtaking sight of the ocean distracted me, but now I'm very aware of the canopied, soldier-sized bed that stands proudly in the center of the room. Its ornate curtains give the impression of luxury.

Aleksey sets me on my feet next to the fireplace. With lithe yet rough movements, he takes off his armor and crosses the room to hang it in a small mirrored wardrobe. God! He looks breathtakingly beautiful wearing only black trousers. They hang loosely on his V line. When he crouches to skillfully start the fire, I can't take my eyes off the strong muscles of his back. The sight of his naked torso sends needy pinpricks of desire across my spine.

As I glance sideways at the bed, a mix of apprehension and excitement constricts my stomach. The unspoken promise of what we will do there hangs in the air, making my legs tremble.

I'm totally wide-eyed, tense, and rooted to the spot when he catches me staring at him.

Looking at me intently, he approaches me with slow, sleek steps. When he notices my mood, he kisses me tenderly. "Why are you nervous?"

Because we're about to explore uncharted territory, and a part of me fears the unknown. Besides, I'm worried about my sexual performance. I'm sure I'll be clumsy in that bed. And because I want to know how long he'll stay, but I'm afraid to ask. To top it all off, I know that I have to tell him that I love him before he leaves me again, but I don't dare. I settle for the easiest answer. "Because there are things I've been keeping from you."

It seems he was expecting this answer. He shoots me my favorite coy smile. "Like the fact that you are still a virgin?"

Shock paralyzes me. I open and close my mouth several times, but I'm speechless.

How …? Is he a psychic?

The night before recruitment, I decided I wouldn't force myself to have sex at the last minute, just when Rey's hardened penis was frantically searching for the opening in the bridal sheet. But it was too late for him to regain control. He came on the sheet and was embarrassed about it. My body, which had been tense and shivering, became extremely relaxed when I realized he wouldn't try again. We were never intimate. The bridal sheet and our clothes always formed a barrier between us, so his erection never touched a square inch of my skin.

Aleksey waits for me to speak, but I explode in a fit of hysterical laughter. I can't embarrass Rey by explaining his misfortune to his nemesis, but I can laugh at my stupidity. I need to release the tension.

The hysterics turn into a nervous giggle. All traces of humor disappear, and I look away, blushing.

"Yes. I'm ... still a ... v—virgin."

A deep breath escapes from him, and he gently cups my face. It's as though he had been holding his breath for my answer.

"How did you know?"

"I didn't. It was a hunch. You have just confirmed it."

"But you—"

"I saw the video of the ceremony. Now that I'm not consumed by jealousy, I've remembered. They didn't use the polygraph to interrogate you."

"But—"

"The soldiers are medieval. It's impossible to know whether or not a girl is a virgin by touching her arms." Piercing me with his blue eyes, he places his strong hands delicately on my hips. The contact is so intimate that I have to remember how to breathe. His deep voice sounds confident. "But I have this theory that when a young girl is initiated into the joys of sex, she acquires a newfound confidence in every step she takes. The rhythm of her hips when she walks is different. And I've noticed that the shape of them changes, too."

A pang of unreasonable jealousy stirs in me. He says he's never been with an inexperienced girl, but he's a sexually experienced man who knows women's bodies well. It kills me that he knows so much about sexuality and that he didn't learn with me. My insecurities are the reason for my stupid attempt at lying. I meant to pretend that I'd had some first-hand experience until I gained enough confidence in my sexual abilities. Or until I was sure that he would love me in spite of everything.

"When we were climbing down the cliff stairs to get here, I paid attention to your hips." He digs his fingers in their round flesh and pulls me close, making our pelvises touch. "The shape of them, the way you move them. I didn't see any difference in how you walk."

His voice turns into a raspy, sensual whisper that tickles my earlobe.

"But after our bodies finally become one, you'll walk in a different way." He inhales against my neck and the base of my throat. "Because the power of my passion will have made an impression on your whole body."

We're dangerously close now. As usual, a heated, sexual energy sizzles between us. The way his erection is pressing against my body tells me he's feeling it, too.

My body tenses when he slowly unbuttons my dress. "You'll feel different, too," he says in a sensual purr. "You'll become self-assured once you learn to enjoy sexual pleasure. With me."

My dress falls to the floor and pools at my feet. He turns my body and pulls my hair aside to leave the nape of my neck uncovered. Hot desire washes over my body when he blows on it softly before covering the area with soft kisses.

"I want to strip your heart … your soul … your mind. And—" he sucks my neck gently. "Your body."

He scoops me up and lays me gently on the plush rug. The contact of the soft material and my skin feels pleasant, but nothing compared to the sight of him standing above me, eyes raking up and down my body. At first I squirm shyly under his penetrating gaze. I feel self-conscious and aware of my body's imperfections. But his eyes scream at me, *you're beautiful. I want you.* That not only calms my nerves, it makes my body writhe in anticipation.

Aleksey unhurriedly puts a knee down on the rug and lithely crawls over my body until he's hovering over me. "You can always stop me by saying no," he murmurs while nibbling my earlobe.

His hands slide under me, forcing my back to arch as he moves to take off my bra. He uses his weight to pin me to the rug. The sensation of bare skin against bare skin feels incredibly warm and pleasant. I grind my body against his, enjoying the friction.

Hot, eager lips slide from my jaw to my collarbone and down between my breasts, sucking the tender skin in their path. Hovering over my breasts, he stops to look at me. I writhe in anticipation. What is he going to do to me?

Aleksey skims his nose and mouth around my breasts, his heated breath caressing my sensitive skin. He blows softly on one nipple before putting it inside his warm mouth. At first he sucks gently, making me tingle all over. When his mouth pressures my nipple with long, profound, almost savage sucking movements, the feeling is unbearable. I whimper, squirming in pleasure under him.

His mouth travels south until it reaches my ankles. Then it slides up my leg slowly until he's nibbling my inner thigh.

Aleksey's muscular arm reaches behind my back to lift my hips into the air. He keeps my body arched as his lips repeat the sensual trajectory up and down my other leg. Aleksey lifts my leg and puts it on his shoulder to better accommodate his head. I love his strength and the way he's using it to move my body. Alternating nibbles and laps of his warm tongue on my inner thighs, he is slowly getting close to the apex of my thighs.

"*Hmm.*" He kisses the sides of my hips. "What do we have here? Did you wrap yourself as a gift for me, Lila?" he says, tearing teasingly at the tie of my underwear. "I love your … garments."

I pant. "I made them myself for you and—" He softly inserts two of his fingers in my mouth. After the initial surprise, I suck them eagerly.

His now-moist, deft fingers caress my already-wet folds. The satisfied noise coming from the back of his throat tells me he's pleased.

"Good job."

Aleksey's voice is so full of pride that I know he's talking about the fact that I'm so ready. He knows that he did this to me, and his smiling face shows joyful triumph. In a slow movement, he unties one side of my underwear and kisses the exposed skin of my hip. He takes his time untying the other side with his teeth, nibbling my skin along the way.

I'm completely naked now, and I've never felt more vulnerable.

The next thing I know, he's naked, too, and he's sucking my nipple. Waves of heated pleasure flash across my skin. His lips trail a path down my chest to my stomach, then to my mound of Venus, where he rubs his stubble before sucking the skin gently.

He pulls down his hands to part my folds, leaving my most sensitive area ready and exposed to his tongue. A sudden flush of embarrassment makes me raise my arm to shield my eyes as he takes a good look at my most intimate parts.

Aleksey grasps my arm, pulling it back. "Don't be embarrassed," he murmurs as his tongue laps at my lower lips. "Looking at you—this is surreal. So beautiful."

Sitting on his heels, he effortlessly wraps my legs around his shoulders. I'm hanging upside down from his massive torso like an acrobat. My shoulders and head are resting on the rug and my arms are over my head. With one arm, he keeps my balance on his body. With his finger, he caresses and opens my lips to create easier access for his warm, moist tongue.

He hums into my folds, making pleasure run through my body. His erection sears my skin, making me aware that he's getting satisfaction from driving me crazy with his mouth.

Aleksey kisses the area softly; he flips his tongue and sucks my sensitive lips gently. Relentlessly.

And then his tongue finds my most sensitive spot.

"Ah! A-Aleksey."

Deliberately, he blows. As I writhe violently, my legs stiffen. He alternates his flapping, flaming tongue with hungry lips that devour and press my now-engorged nub.

I cry out. The sensations are more than I can take. My muscles tense, my toes curl. I don't want him to stop, but this is becoming too much. I feel a delicious tension building inside me. I squirm and my insides start to quiver.

Finally, he increases the pressure of his suction on my clit. Pleasure—scorching, sheer, exquisite pleasure—sweeps over me, and I explode. I try to muffle the vocal expressions of my ecstasy by biting my hand, but he takes my wrist.

"Let me hear you," he says as he kisses each of my finger pads gently.

General Fürst is a very generous lover who keeps taking care of me. Many times.

Still sitting on his heels, he scoops me into his massive arms and cradles me. Aleksey kisses me sweetly as I slowly start to descend from heaven.

"You're so relaxed, so deliciously lubricated." He hums as he places feather-like kisses on my shoulders. "It'll be less painful now that you're so ready for me. Do you want me to continue?"

I press my forehead against his muscular chest and nod.

CHAPTER 57

Her one and only

ALEKSEY CARRIES ME ACROSS the room. He gently lays me on the bed, my butt on the edge of it, and kneels on the floor in front of me. I look at his erection nervously. Like the rest of his body, it is large, hard, and rough.

He leans in to kiss me, and I forget that I'm nervous. In a swift move, he puts his hands on my knees, bending them, spreading them gently.

"Look at me."

I obey. The expression on his face is hungry, almost predatory, as he settles between my legs. My breath comes in loud pants.

I gasp when I feel my Aleksey—*my* stoic, older general—slowly rubbing against my folds, coating the tip of his erection in my wetness. I squirm under his torture.

Still keeping my knees spread apart, he bends his body to kiss my mouth. "Even with your extraordinary, wet response, this will hurt. Tell me when it becomes too much."

I feel him at my entrance for what seems like an eternity. I'm enjoying the feel of his erection rubbing against my most sensitive spots.

"Relax. Deep breaths," he commands while gently kissing my face, sensually sliding his hands all over my legs.

I breathe in and out, relaxing my body. Has it been seconds? Minutes?

Then a pinching sensation.

"*Ow, ow, ow!*" My body involuntarily retreats a little.

"Relax," he says through clenched teeth. He seems to be fighting to control his sexual urges.

As he kisses my mouth and then my nipples, I inhale and exhale deeply. Aleksey pushes the first thick inch of himself against my tight virgin walls, spreading me open. Every time I exhale, he inches in a bit more. I whimper at the foreign sensation, opening my eyes wide.

I don't want to admit that I've reached my limit, but he reads it in my body. Aleksey stops moving and concentrates instead on pleasuring the rest of my body while he's half-buried inside me.

We've kissed before, but never at this level of eroticism, passion, and closeness. His lips and hands have never felt as hot on my skin as they do now. He's leaving marks all over my upper body, making me writhe in pleasure. I was already wet, but now I'm dripping. It doesn't seem physically possible, but he's growing inside me with each kiss, with each touch.

Adoring me. Stretching me.

He inches slowly, pausing constantly to give my body time to accommodate him. I take a sharp breath, my eyes clamped shut. My nails dig into his back as Aleksey begins to enter farther into me, the pain ripping through my body as it spreads to engulf his erection. Half-contented, half-pained whimpers escape from me each time he moves.

Aleksey speaks into my neck, his heated breath tingling my skin.

"Don't tense," he orders in his hoarse, deep voice that makes me melt in desire. "Relax, Lila."

He soothes the pain with a lingering kiss, and I open my eyes, feeling myself relaxing. I glance at our reflection in the mirror. I love the sight of him taking away my virginity, his beautiful eyes closed against the side of my neck, my body lying vulnerable under him. As desire spreads through me, I feel myself opening for him. The pain turns into a not-unpleasant discomfort.

When he's finally deep inside, Aleksey lifts his head. He glances up and down at me, sliding his hands through my hair and looking into my eyes. His pupils dilate. There's a mix of triumph and tenderness in his eyes. "You look gorgeous sprawled underneath me." His breathing is ragged. "Breathless … that look of awe and tenderness on your beautiful face." His voice is raspy, and his eyes seem to be memorizing my face. "Your beautiful green eyes wide open, full of fire, while I'm buried deep inside you."

We stay like that for a long time, looking into each other's eyes. Despite the discomfort, I have never felt so close to him, and I feel my love for him growing. Similar feelings seem to burn inside him. The way he's looking at me now blends adoration, love, and lust all in one. I wouldn't change this moment for anything. Aleksey hasn't ever looked more gorgeous than he is now, when it's obvious that he's fighting his need to start moving to make this a less painful experience for me.

He leans in to kiss me. His hands roam sensually over my body before he returns to my knees to open me even wider. As his kiss gains intensity, my excitement builds and my body wiggles in pleasure. And he hasn't even started to move yet! Can I have another orgasm just from this?

When he feels that I'm ready, Aleksey pulls back slowly, making us both relish the agonizing, exquisite friction. He thrusts forward again, and I scream my lungs out. The pain is back, and I can't decide if this is more pleasure or agony. All I know is that I don't want him to stop.

A feral growl rises from deep in his throat as he eases back one more time. He groans and slowly thrusts again. And again. Each time, he catches a slow, sensual rhythm. Each time is less uncomfortable and more delicious.

"Oh, Lila. You feel … *hmm*," he says through gritted teeth. It seems as if he's using every ounce of his self-control to not speed up.

I look at him in awe and then take a look at the mirror. My breasts are jiggling up and down in response to his thrusts. The sight of his taut, muscular butt tightening and flexing as he moves in and out of me makes the pressure in my core build. His hands leave my knees to grasp my head and kiss me.

It's all too much. The feeling of fullness, the searing heat of our bodies connecting as if we were matching pieces of a puzzle. The notion that even though he's taking it slow with me, he's still rough enough to make me feel like he's claiming me as his.

The exquisite sensations keep building. In a desperate attempt to hold on to something, my nails dig into his bulky biceps. I'm soaring to a high place, and I'm about to fall.

My overheated body tightens and then releases in waves of sheer, unadulterated pleasure. The feeling is so intense that I arch my back before I collapse on the mattress.

Aleksey kisses me deeply, muffling my whimpers. He rests his head next to mine. Against the skin of my neck, his lips murmur how good I'm making him feel. How amazing I am. Beads of sweat cover his ruggedly handsome face.

I want to give pleasure to this man I love so much. Kegel exercises. His size, my tightness. I start to clench. To caress, to press.

He groans in pleasure and surprise. "Lila!"

The walls are closing in on him now in a firmer manner. I feel him shuddering. He finds his release, calling my name, emptying himself inside me. Aleksey's hulky body collapses over mine, and his sounds of pleasure are music to my ears.

The fire has long extinguished; the moon shines through the translucent ceiling, casting a strange glow on our glistening skin. The soft murmur of the ocean harmonizes with our ragged breaths. He stays inside me for a while, breathing harshly against the side of my neck. I feel his smile against my skin.

"Even in sex, you're defiant. I love that, Lila. I love you."

I gasp. He falls asleep, still inside me. I never imagined I'd hear those words like this, with an older military man buried inside me, both of us naked in our post-coital bliss. It isn't exactly romantic, but because it's *my* Aleksey, it's … perfect.

Later, when he finally pulls out, it hurts, both physically and emotionally. I miss the warm connection between our bodies already. He kisses me and pulls me against his chest.

The whole experience was incredible, like nothing I've ever experienced before. I feel gloriously spent and grateful. In every touch, in every sound, I felt his love spilling over my body, mind, and soul. Even after he leaves, I'll always remember him as the man who made this moment so special. I adore him, and I know I would do anything to please this man who taught my body how to feel alive.

Up to this point, we had shared bits of human touch, but there's a connection in the sexual touch that we couldn't have gotten any other way. There are feelings that we can express better through our skin. Through our bodies.

I look at the moon above me and keep smiling until the ocean's song lulls me to sleep.

CHAPTER 58

Hope and love

THE WARMTH OF A BEAM of sunlight on my naked back wakes me up. I try to rise, but strong arms cage me in, keeping me prisoner.

"Are you going to run away, sweet girl?" Aleksey mumbles, still sleepy. "Now that you took what you wanted?"

I giggle. "I could ask the same. You dishonored me. I've surrendered, and, traditionally, it's your turn to bolt and never appear again. Is this the last I'll see of you, Prince Aleksey?"

"Don't delude yourself. I have wanted you since the day I met you," he whispers, smelling my hair. "You make the most delicious sex noises—whimpers and, at times, little mewls. You drive me crazy. I won't ever have enough of you."

I snuggle against his chest contentedly and take a look at the breathtaking sight of the ocean as the sun shines off its surface. His fingers travel lazily up and down my spine. We stay like that for a while. When I look up, the beauty of the ocean pales in comparison to the magnificence of those blue eyes full of love for me.

"How do you feel?" he asks huskily.

My cheeks burn. "It'll sound corny."

"Tell me anyway."

"Reborn and grateful."

"Reborn?"

"As if my life has just started now."

I take a look at the sea, not sure how to put my feelings into words.

"Everything looks new. Don't laugh, but ... the sky seems to have brighter colors, and the sunlight seems to have a different shine. I feel as though I understand what life is about for the first time." I sigh loudly. "It's an illusion, of course. I'm not any wiser, and the sun is just the same. The difference is that you make me feel happy and grateful to be alive."

He grins with a boyish charm. Who is this smiling guy, and where's my serious, brooding Aleksey?

"Then I must be corny, too. I feel exactly the same way."

I wiggle uncomfortably. Hearing those words wakes bittersweet emotions. It's heaven to hear how he feels, but saying goodbye to him will crush me now.

It's time to ask what I've been dreading all along. "How long until you leave?"

"A week."

I cringe, and my chest hurts. I wasn't expecting it to be so soon.

"There are doubts about my neutrality, and I've been assigned to the management of New Norfolk Military Academy."

New Norfolk Island is on the other side of the country and is presently regulated by UNNO. It'll remain a neutral territory until the war ends and the Patriots and Nationalists have agreed how to divide territories. That's where my family is heading for Olmo's treatment. Perhaps my family will see Aleksey from time to time. It'll be a relief to know that he'll still be a part of my life, even if it's from afar. It's heartbreaking to be the one who'll stay.

He loves me, so it's only natural that talking about our final goodbye brings back his usual scowl. But when he speaks, I realize his mind is somewhere else.

"I might as well quit. I'm not neutral anymore," he says, his bulky muscles tensing. "I hate recruitment as much as you do. We UNNO officers aren't supposed to interfere with the sovereignty of Americans." He glares at the ocean as though the blue waves were responsible for the recruitment. "But I hate what Nat and Patriot troops do, what they have done to you. To us."

"They didn't violate your mother, too, did they?"

His face hardens, and I regret my lack of tact.

"Not while I was with her."

I don't know what to say. It's he who breaks the silence.

"Lila, you think recruitment is the worst thing that could happen to you, but there's another form of abuse that people rarely talk about."

I look at him questioningly.

"Forced marriage. That's what happened to my mother."

I stare at him in shock. Noticing my expression, he cradles me in his arms.

"My mother was an illegal German immigrant. My father was a wealthy American merchant with a military past who sold guns to the army. As punishment for staying in the country illegally, my father recruited her as a vassal at a time when the country wasn't yet divided and recruitment wasn't legal."

As he tells his story, I notice that his accent fades. At times, it disappears. Who would have thought that he was half-American?

"He was obsessed with her and took her as his wife. He'd had a rough, violent life and didn't know how to express his passion without hurting her. His possessiveness was his way of demonstrating his love, but it was a cruel, twisted way for her."

"I'm—" He sighs. "A child of rape." When he says this, my heart sinks. "She wasn't submissive and never returned his love, so my father, hurt and determined to get over her, traded her to another master, not knowing that she was pregnant. When I was born, she escaped to Germany, taking me with her."

I open my mouth to ask a question, but then think better of it.

"My father had other wives and had fathered other children, so it took a while before he realized that she was gone." Aleksey shakes his head sadly. "But when he found out about me, he crossed continents to bring me back."

Without releasing me from his embrace, he sits up and speaks in a toneless voice.

"He killed my stepfather, Otto Fürst, and—"

"Oh, no!"

Aleksey shakes his head. "I wouldn't feel sorry for Otto. He was another advocate of marital rape. Besides, he hit my mother and me. When I turned nine, I was taller and stronger than Otto was. I defended my mother and beat the hell out of him. Otto made a deal with me. He would leave my mother alone if I endured his beatings." His fist clenches. "I accepted. Little did I know that the weasel had made a similar treaty with my mother. Otto kept hitting us both in secret, and we kept accepting it because we thought we were protecting the other."

I kiss his chest. These memories hurt him, and I wish that I could make him feel better. His hulky body shudders at the contact, and his arms tighten around me.

We stay like that for a while, listening to each other's hearts.

We go for a walk on a rocky beach. As he promised, I'm walking in a different way, mostly because I'm deliciously sore. His arm is around my shoulder, and his long hair flies with the wind. I can't help it—I ogle him. He looks so human and attractive now that he's talking about his past.

"When my father appeared in my life, I welcomed him as a savior. As the hero who was so much on my side that he had killed my enemy. He manipulated me into thinking that my mother would be better without me. I left her. She was pregnant at the time, and my father kept sending her money. But as soon as my brother was born, she disappeared. If they're alive, I'm sure they're hiding from him.

"My father loved military life, and I learned to love it, too. At twelve, I was already a cadet. He wanted me to become a general for the Patriot armies. But I knew of the cruelty of Patriots in Nationalist cities and vice versa. I decided to stay out of the conflict and join the German training camp for the Accord Units."

I notice that when he talks about his father, his eyes fill with an emotion I can't define.

"Do you love him?" I ask.

"We fight like hell, but—" He stops and looks thoughtful for a moment. "*Mmm*, this is the first time I've admitted this."

"Why?"

He shrugs. "He may have been cruel to others, but he was kind to all of his children. If I needed him, he would leave anything and run to my side." His gaze becomes intense, and he grazes my cheek with his fingers. "Sometimes you love someone you shouldn't."

His blue eyes scan the horizon. "But I'm not about to justify marital rape just because I can't bring myself to hate my father. I'll never forgive him and yet … it's complicated."

"Complicated how?"

He looks at me fixedly and pulls me closer. "Since I met you, I've been thinking a lot about hate—" He smiles at my puzzled expression. "And love."

"And what's your conclusion?"

He looks at the sea, then at me. For a moment, it seems as though he won't answer. Then he speaks in a modulated voice. "Love is a wild, complex feeling that can't be tamed using the whip of what is right and what is not."

I sigh. What he's said is true. Especially for both of us. I jump to keep a wave from touching my boots. "Yes, sometimes, you can't bring yourself to hate someone," I say. It's incredible the way my feelings have changed since I met Aleksey. I used to fear that he was going to force himself on me, and there were many moments when I hated him. I couldn't trust him even when he had proven himself, and look at us now.

He puts his hand around one of my hips, interrupting my musings. "You're sore, aren't you?"

I blush.

"I told you. You won't walk again like you used to, Lila."

He pulls me into his sturdy arms. The waves are soaking our boots, but I don't care anymore.

"I'm reborn, too," he says. "I've had sex so many times, but I had never made love. This was a first for me, Lila, and I can't believe how much I was missing."

This is the moment when I should tell him that I love him, but my voice fails me. I bury my head in his chest, hoping my words will return soon.

"I was so intoxicated with you last night, Lila. I'm not even sure I wasn't dreaming. Did I tell you that I love you?"

I look up at him, smiling. I nod.

"You love me, don't you, Lila?"

"Yes, I love you." And just as I say it, I feel as though an oppression that was constricting my chest has left my body, allowing me to breathe freely.

His elation is evident, and suddenly my feet are not touching the ground.

"*Whoa*! Put me down," I protest playfully. He ignores me. "We can't be together, so let's not get overly enthusiastic."

He sets me down and leans in to kiss me. "Why not?"

I stare at him in disbelief. He knows why.

"You can't fraternize with the enemy or both of us will be executed."

"Lila, you're the reason I fought my way back to Starville. I came for you, to take you away and start a new life with you."

I shake my head. He must be joking. "You can't."

"Aside from the obvious fact that you have led a very difficult life, why don't you allow yourself to have hope?"

"I prefer to expect the worst. I'm always prepared for bad things so that they don't catch me by surprise. If you were to stay with me, you'd get pissed off at me all the time because I'm not an easy person to love."

He looks at me as though I'm crazy. "Neither am I. But I don't understand. Falling in love with you is the simplest thing I've ever done. I fought against love so many times and lost." His eyes look at me with infinite tenderness. "Why do you think you aren't easy to love?"

"I'm a natural-born pessimist, and as much as I try to become stronger and act maturely, I—" I sigh loudly. "I'm a woman. I'm not the weak, simplistic, flawless creature the world expects me to be. I have more endurance than what society believes I have. I'm multidimensional. I'm imperfect. I make mistakes all the time, and I'll make even more as life challenges me. And I don't want to be afraid to make mistakes. First of all, because I'll learn from them, but more importantly because they're what make me human. You would have to be incredibly patient if you were to be with me."

"Imperfect? Not for me. You're multidimensional, human. Everything you mentioned makes me love you more. You forgot to mention the most important part of yourself: You're a fighter. My fighter." Gently, he lays me down on the sand and covers my body with his. "*Meine mutige Kämpferin,* I'll be with you for as long as you want me."

I look up at him and tuck one of his long, blond strands behind his ear. "No, you won't. Everything is against us. Your commission in New Norfolk, the law, recruitment."

Aleksey kisses me deeply, lingeringly. I forget what I was going to say.

He pulls away and looks at me intently. "You don't have to worry about recruitment anymore."

His kiss has left me breathless and has turned my mind into a mushy mess. I look at him in confusion.

"There's a way, Lila. A way that wouldn't have been possible if Tristan hadn't been so valiant and filmed everything. Maximillian Kei has been forced to change the recruitment laws."

The way his hands roam all over my body is distracting. I look at him. "Kei wouldn't abolish recruitment."

Aleksey kisses the hollow of my throat and talks between kisses. "He … will. Not now … but … it'll … happen. In the meantime, the new laws will be the key to your freedom."

A moan escapes my lips. "*Ah!* I don't understand."

He smiles wickedly against my collarbone. "Lila Velez Tcherkassky, you'll join my unit as an *L*-class recruit. L for love."

Epilogue

If, as we see nightfall, we become capable of accepting love,
let's celebrate an alliance with our unbroken illusions.
Who ever knew we would say goodbye to oblivion?
Who ever knew we would accept hope?

General Fürst's journal

THE FEEL OF GENTLE kisses on my shoulder blades wakes me up. He rolls our naked bodies until he's on top. Expertly, he sucks and bites the tender flesh of my neck as his hands explore my body.

Waking up next to Aleksey's hulking body in his New Norfolk room is such a joy. Now that familiarity has set in, I have discovered all of the men inside Aleksey's body: the expert lover, the dominant alpha, the honorable soldier, the poet, the child inside the twenty-five-year-old man. It's through the way he feverishly possesses my body that I catch glimpses of his bestial side. But the Aleksey I enjoy the most is the happy man.

"Can I put my pinky finger in your belly button?" he whispers in my ear.

"*Hmm.*" I'm too intoxicated by the ecstatic sensations his lips have brought to my naked skin to pay attention.

Until I feel it.

"*Ah*! That's not my navel."

"That's not my pinky finger, either," he says mischievously.

Aleksey's tone makes me explode into a fit of laughter, but soon I'm not laughing anymore. The movement brings delicious vibrations that resonate all over my body.

He thrusts deliberately, delicately, deliciously. But my body asks him to speed up, and soon his gentle thrusts turn into merciless pounding. I turn to the mirror and take a look at the naked girl under Aleksey's body. She doesn't resemble a scared doe like she once did. There's confidence in the way I'm receiving his sexual frenzy. Knowing that I'm the one who drives crazy such a powerful, commanding, strong man like him is empowering.

My new confidence comes from the fact that I've finally learned to trust myself completely. As a consequence, I've learned to trust him— with my feelings, with my safety, and with my body. I trust him so much that I'm eager to try C.N. with him. Soon.

After I descend from the heaven of my release, I look up at him in wonder. I marvel at the beauty of the man who is coming undone inside me. There's a remarkable difference between his current enraptured face and the sad expression he had when I first met him. To the rest of the world, he is still an uncompromising, serious man, but in private, he shares with me his playful, fun side. He's happy to the point of giddiness, and his elation is contagious.

When he reaches his climax, his body collapses over mine. Still inside me, he buries his head in the crook of my neck and doesn't move. I love the feeling of his warm breathing on my neck, the way our bodies connect, the violent thud of his heart against his chest. Both of us are enjoying the glorious, euphoric feeling of being in love for the first time in our lives. The best part of walking the path of reciprocated love with him is knowing that I play a huge role in bringing about his blissful mood. I rescued him from his loneliness. And Aleksey seems to be equally satisfied whenever he acknowledges the huge part he plays in boosting my own happiness.

The fact that he recruited me only adds to the blessings I'm enjoying now.

Accord cops are subject to Patriot laws as long as they are in American territory. The new modifications to the recruitment laws—due to recent nasty incidents during recruitment ceremonies, including the assault on Tristan—created a new opportunity for the cops to aid civilians. The Accord Unit recruits them. Because I'm registered in a place where recruitment is legal, General Fürst's unit has recruited me. It wasn't easy. Aleksey paid a team of lawyers to find loopholes in the new laws. Finally, he got the official permission from Maximillian Kei to recruit me. As soon as he got Kei's formal consent, he brought me to New Norfolk, where my family was already living.

Officially, I'm a cadet at New Norfolk's Military Academy, a training center for future Accord cops. I had to pass extensive physical tests, and UNNO officials tested my neutrality with a polygraph. As soon as I complete the two-year training program, I'll join the Accord Unit. Hopefully, by then, recruitment will be a nightmare of the past. But even if that doesn't happen, I'll do my best to help Aleksey build the kind of Accord Unit of which he's always dreamt: one that protects people from recruitment.

This room in the spacious place where UNNO assigned him is an exact replica of the one where I lost my virginity. This room is home now.

Aleksey's gorgeous, naked figure rises from the bed. I can't stop staring at his fantastic rear as he crosses the room. What kind of alchemy brought a man like him into my life? He's beautiful inside and out, and he's rescued me in more ways than one.

"Are we going anywhere?" I ask, mostly because I hope he says no and we can have another round of morning sex.

"Yes, we're going to visit your family."

"Yes!" I shout delightedly, forgetting my lascivious intentions; we'll have all night for those. I'm dying to see the twins. I've bought candies for them and Poncho.

Aleksey secured a medical job for my dad in the Accord hospital. Dad couldn't be happier. He had been dying to practice medicine again. The pay is modest, but he can cover the rent on a small apartment near the hospital. The hospital has staff members who specialize in the kind of fibrosis from which Olmo suffers.

My brother's condition has improved, and he has been gaining weight. Azzy pokes fun at him all the time because he eats almost as much as Aleksey does. Yet she's eating a lot and attaining a healthier weight as well. I don't think the hospital staff has ever met someone like Azalea. Her sassy sense of humor scandalizes the nurses, but her remarkable ability to discuss Olmo's condition and treatments in advanced medical terms has gained the admiration of the medical staff.

After kissing me, Aleksey leaves the lavish room. I wait the customary ten minutes before departing myself. Others shouldn't see us together.

On Sunday through Thursday nights, I sleep with the other cadets in the Accord barracks. On Friday and Saturday nights, plus weekday afternoons, I'm assigned to the service of General Fürst.

To the outside world, I'm supposed to be his assistant. We're not allowed to have a relationship, let alone get married. It doesn't matter. I'm his woman. He's my man. When the war ends, we'll find a way to get married. For now, being together like this is almost as though we're living together. Even during weekdays, there are times when we're supposed to be engaging in office work with his other assistants, but he just hands me a note that says: *Let's go to a quieter place.* Then he takes me to any hidden nook he can find—a closet or a vacant office—to kiss insatiably. Sometimes we take things further.

Next July, for my nineteenth birthday, Aleksey will take a leave of absence—his first one since he joined the military. He has promised to show me the world.

Not everything is perfect in my new life. From time to time, I still have flashbacks. And my sister is having a difficult time after what Duque did to her. Azzy's having nightmares, but she keeps her pain to herself and shows her snarky, cynical side all the time.

Tristan's wounds have required three surgeries, and whenever I think about him, survivor's guilt gnaws at my conscience. Our happiness came at a high cost to him. But whenever I visit him at the hospital he asks jokingly about my relationship with his cousin. Tristan, like Azalea, is determined to survive. He won't lose himself because what happened to him. Hope seems to have become the key to his recovery.

Saying goodbye to Rey was easy and liberating for both of us. We were never meant to be more than friends, and now we can keep loving the people we were meant to love. Still, at times, I worry about him and the rest of the Diazes. Is Duque still alive? How are the Diazes coping? And what about the Comanches? Will they survive the war long enough for me to see them again?

I make my way confidently through the clean New Norfolk streets. The round, metallic-looking buildings seem to reach the dome above us. On a solitary overpass, a Humvee catches up with me. Just like on our first date, he barely stops the vehicle to let me in. Once inside, I muss his hair.

"You took your time, my *Kämpferin*," he says, kissing my hand.

Love isn't the solution to everything. But by accepting love and fighting for it, I've found a reason to let myself hope. One day we'll make this war stop.

By the time that happens, I hope I'll still be a V-girl.

V for Velez.

V for valiant.

V for voyeur.

But not V for virgin.

Acknowledgements

This book wouldn't have been possible without a huge group of friends, family, and fellow bookaholics.

Erin Plaice: If Aleksey and Lila have found their happy ending, it is in great part thanks to your sincere enthusiasm. You're a fantastic book adviser and I cannot thank you enough.

My extraordinary group of Betas: Ash from Wonderland's Reader, Bibliophilic Madness, Maria Kaye, Ana Rodriguez from Bookworm221 in Tumblr, Danielle Werner, and Karine Green. You're great! I might not have taken your advice all the time, but I always valued your opinions.

Aly Gillen and Caro: You are so well-read and so passionate about literature that I felt incredibly smug whenever you praised my ideas. Thank you for the direction you helped me to take.

Thanks to the New Adult book club members, especially Bobbi, Derna, Karina, Natalie, Micheala, Nicola, Lori, and Laura. To the people who voted for their favorite cover, I wish I could mention each of you by name.

Tonya Blust and Books are my fandom: Thanks for turning my book into something readable and free of typos.

Thanks to all the bloggers who revealed the cover and signed up for blitz and tours.

Demelza Watts, thank you for your wonderful portrait of General Fürst and his red cape.

Mr. Eduardo Carrasco from Quilapayun: Thank you for giving me permission to translate "La Paloma" lyrics. Whenever I hear your song, I feel the need to inject hope in my dystopian worlds.

Rachel from *The Rest Is Still Unwritten* and Belinda from *Literaria*: You might not have realized it, but you were my first reviewers. Your reviews helped me to stay focused on my writing when I was about to drop the towel.

My dear family: You have given me the determination to pursue my dreams. I love you all for being there for me when I was full of uncertainty and doubts.

Last but not least: Thanks to all the soldiers who have protected our country from the brutal reality of war by risking—and at times losing— your lives. God bless you.

Discussion questions

- If you were in Lila's position, what might you do differently to attain the same goal?

- How might the current laws affect how society sees consensual sex, rape victims, and rapists? Which laws, specifically, can alter this perception? Or, perhaps, the perception of sex in general? Consider laws of consent and marital rape, and how these crimes are persecuted.

- As of 2015, current American laws give more prison time for minor drug violations than for rape. In The V-Girl, this reality is exaggerated: specific drugs are for soldiers, and rape is legal. Do the consequences of certain actions create a taboo, or do these consequences have no effect on how "normal" something might be perceived as being? How might society shun an unacceptable behavior if consequences are not established?

- How might an "us vs. them" mentality, such as Patriots vs. Nats, help or hinder a political state? How might this mentality currently shape our government? Consider bipartisan systems in your argument.

- In The V-Girl, soldiers are scientifically modified to become stronger, faster killing machines. In the early 2000s, the US Government bought thousands of pills, called Modafinil, to help US soldiers stay awake up to 90 hours at a time during times of war. At what point, if any, do you consider it unethical to modify the natural human state for combat advantage?

- If giving a simple drug to someone to improve their ability to protect people made them more aggressive toward all people, and not just enemies, at what point would this become an unacceptable side effect? How could something like this be regulated?

- Lila shows many symptoms of undiagnosed PTSD due to her mother's attack: panic attacks, nightmares, phobias, avoidance of certain triggers, signs of depression, high alertness, severe emotional distress from reminders, and then some. How does Lila cope with this emotional disorder? Do her coping mechanisms help or hinder her ultimate goal of having consensual sex?

- During the recruitment ceremony, only Tristan stands up to the injustices of the soldiers. Is there a way he could have enough power or influence to halt the ceremony? How could one, or many, prevent the soldiers from attacking the civilians? What would encourage the police, the Accords, to stand up against the soldiers?

- Despite the fact that rape is legal in recruitment, the soldiers still alter the perception of the ceremony by hiding the attacks afterward. Do you think that Starville is an isolated incident? What might happen to the soldiers if footage of the attacks was leaked? To the citizens of the city?

- In many cultures, including Starville's, virginity is a sign of a woman's purity, and anything that might jeopardize this purity affects the woman's overall value as a person. Why might this not apply to men? Are there traits that men possess that directly affect their value as people in Starville? What about in other societies?

- "Ergi" is a term the Vikings used to refer to the submissive man in a gay relationship. Using this word to describe a person in public would lead to banishment or immediate death. This term applied to both willing and unwilling participants in a sexual encounter. Do you think that the world's view of men on the receiving end of sex has changed? Why or why not?

- Consider Tristan and Duque in The V-Girl. Why are their experiences so shameful, as opposed to their attackers' actions?

- When, if ever, is it considered shameful for a man to have consensual sex? For a woman?

- As of 2014, the United States National Crime Victimization Survey found that the actual percentage of men raped by their domestic partner is as high as 38%. Are you surprised? Do you think that this number is accurate? Why or why not?

- Why is it difficult for a man to come forward as a victim of rape? Is it more or less difficult for a man to come forward if he was raped by a woman versus by a man? Why or why not?

- Only 68% of rapes are estimated to be reported to the police. What might prevent a person from coming forward for justice? What if the victim was a man, raped by a woman? How might we work to create a safer environment for victims?

- Consider that only 2% of convicted rapists actually see jail time. How might an "innocent until proven guilty" justice system, like that in the USA, improve these rates?

- Of one in three sexual assaults, the rapist is under the influence of alcohol or drugs. In The V-Girl, ex-soldiers and Accord cops are often seen in taverns or drinking publicly; they are also seen as potential threats. Why do you think these statistics were recorded together? How might one behavior affect or encourage the other?

Statistics taken by RAINN.org

About the author

Mya Robarts is a bookaholic who regrets nothing. She aspired to be a contemporary dance choreographer when she discovered a pull for expressing her choreography ideas in written form.

Robarts is obsessed with books that present damaged characters, swoon-worthy guys, controversial topics and happy endings.

Newsletter
https://tinyletter.com/myarobarts
Twitter
https://twitter.com/MyaRobarts
Tumblr
http://myarobarts.tumblr.com/
Facebook
https://www.facebook.com/MyaRobartsBooks